Accused: About 200

C _____ About 50

_____ , 75

D0622458

Date of trial	Page		
			692
Tried June 2 –	204-209	June	① Bridget Bishop June 10, 1692
June 30	209-212	July 19, 1692	
		②	Sarah Good
		③	Rebecca Nurse
		④	Susannah Martin
		⑤	Elizabeth Howe
		⑥	Sarah Wildes
Aug 5	212-218	Aug 19, 1692	
		⑦	Rev George Burroughs
[Elizabeth		⑧	John Procter
Procter delayed		⑨	John Willard
2° pregnancy		⑩	George Jacobs, Sr
		⑪	Martha Carrier
Sept 9	219-220	Sept 22	
		⑫ Sept 22	Martha Corey
		⑬ Sept 22	Mary Easty
		⑭ Sept 22	Alice Parker
		⑮ Sept 22	Ann Pudeator
			Dorcas Hoar
	Escaped	———	Mary Bradbury
Sept 17	219-220	⑯ Sept 22	Margaret Scott
		⑰ Sept 22	Wilmot Redd
		⑱ Sept 22	Mary Parker
	delayed 2° pregnancy		Abigail Faulkner
			Rebecca Eames
			Mary Lacey
	Died in prison in Dec	———	Ann Foster
			Abigail Hobbs
		⑲ Sept 22	Samuel Wardwell
Sept 19	P.220	⑳	Giles Corey Pressed to death

THE
DEVIL
DISCOVERED

THE DEVIL DISCOVERED

SALEM WITCHCRAFT 1692

Enders A. Robinson

HIPPOCRENE BOOKS
New York

For information, address:
HIPPOCRENE BOOKS, INC.
171 Madison Avenue
New York, NY 10016

Library of Congress Cataloging-in-Publication Data
Robinson, Enders, A.
  The devil discovered: Salem witchcraft 1692 /
Enders A. Robinson
   p.   cm
  Includes bibliographic references and index.
1. Witchcraft - Massachusetts - Salem - History. 2. Trials
- (Witchcraft) - Massachusetts - Salem. 3. New England -
History - Colonial period, ca 1600-1775. 4. Demonology -
History. I. Robinson, Enders A. II. Title: The Devil Dis-
covered: Salem Witchcraft 1692

ISBN 0-87052-009-1

Jacket design: Elizabeth Brewster Rocchia

Printed in the United States of America

In memory of

Samuel and Sarah Wardwell

Love virtue, she alone is free,
She can teach ye how to climb
Higher than the sphery chime;
Or if virtue feeble were,
Heaven itself would stoop to her.

John Milton, "Comus," 1634

TABLE OF CONTENTS

PREFACE

In the fall of 1941 a wooden house on the beach in Marshfield, Massachusetts caught fire. The summer houses in this seaside community stood closely together; they were built with wooden shingle roofs and clapboard siding; and they were surrounded by high, tinder-dry beach grass. Virtually all the houses were vacant. A gale wind blew out of the northeast. The force of the wind quickly blew sparks to the neighboring houses. A wildfire soon raged between the ocean on one side, and tidal marshes and a creek on the other side. Within an hour, the fire had engulfed five hundred houses in a chain reaction. Finally a shift in the wind limited its spread and it burned itself out. Bricks and stones were all that remained; everything else had been consumed by the flames.

This was a firestorm. Conditions were ripe for such a catastrophe: bone dry weather; high northeast winds blowing toward the lightly built wooden houses; an isolated area with, presumably, no one at hand to sound the alarm. Under more auspicious circumstances, only one or a few houses would have burned down. It was not the first firestorm in Massachusetts, nor will it be the last. Ignited by a single spark, the fire was ruled an accident.

Saved by the wind shift was the Bourne House, built in 1660 by Marshfield's first Pilgrim settler, and owned at the time of the fire by my family. In its attic lay piles of scrapbooks, folders, and boxes overflowing with old records and letters. Much of this material, handed down from generation to generation, had been collected by my father, Edward Arthur Robinson.

Born in Missouri in 1872, the son of a mathematics professor, my father settled in Massachusetts as a young man, drawn there to work for his uncle Simon Willard Wardwell, Jr., an inventor.

My father soon grew curious about his Wardwell and Barker relatives, and began to collect everything they could give him about family history. His aunt, Hanna Wardwell, who lived in Marblehead close to the Salem line, owned a fine collection of old prints, books, and family memorabilia. In the 1920s, when she moved to California, she left behind most of her things, and eventually my father stored them with his own papers in our house in Marshfield. Also piled there were records of my mother's family, the Goodales, who were early settlers of Salem Village. Our attic became so full that only narrow passages were left.

Over the last few years I finally cleaned out the entire house. From the attics alone, I filled twenty-six large boxes with old papers of all sorts. Two years ago I searched through many of them, hunting for some family real estate deeds. Instead, I found family documents going back many generations. Gradually I realized that I had discovered accounts of our family's experiences during the Salem witch hunt of 1692. My curiosity piqued, I undertook a general study of primary and secondary sources, keeping an eye out for clues which tied the family papers to published accounts.

For the events of the Salem witch hunt, which took place three hundred years ago, no fully satisfactory explanation has ever been given and, indeed, it is my feeling that there can never be a complete resolution. This is the grimmest of stories, and one which my father believed plunged the family into ignominy, and was better forgotten. Certainly it does not fit comfortably into this day and age, jarring as it does our modern sensibilities and straining credulity as well. But the three-hundred-year interval bears observance and presents an especially apt time to pull together my family's information and place it in context with surrounding events and established scholarship.

What unfolds is a tragedy. It is the story of innocent people caught in a web of intrigue from which they could not extricate themselves. Samuel Wardwell was hanged for witchcraft in Salem on September 22, 1692. His wife, Sarah Wardwell, was condemned to death the following January, but was saved by a last minute reprieve. Samuel and Sarah were my great great great great great great grandparents.

In 1916, in the preface to the fifth edition of his book, *Witchcraft in Salem Village in 1692*, Winfield S. Nevins wrote, "The later generation of readers will find it difficult to believe that no longer ago than 1892 an attempt to secure commemoration of the noble martyrdom of these witchcraft victims was frowned upon. Fear was expressed that opprobrium might be cast on descendants of witch prosecutors. Some thought it better to allow the whole wonderful story of that period to be forgotten, fearing that it might prove a bit unpleasant."

The Salem witch hunt of 1692 was a firestorm of the fiercest sort. Instead of houses, the reputations and lives of people were destroyed. In each previous New England witch hunt, the fire had burned itself out after affecting only one or two families. In the case of the Salem tragedy, scores of families were left in despair and some in utter ruin. The fire was sparked by a unique and fatal convergence of religious, social, political, and economic forces. But why, once ignited, did it rage so wildly, gaining intensity as it claimed more lives? And what served to extinguish the flames? Like the firestorm in Marshfield, was it an accident, or could it, perhaps, have been arson?

This book offers answers to these questions. By combining the Wardwell, Barker, and Goodale records with published source materials, it is possible to reconstruct many of the family groupings of the accused witches and wizards. When this new material is integrated with existing information, much of the dynamics of the Salem witchcraft delusion is illuminated.

The first part of the book (Chapters 1 to 14) gives the entire chain of events in chronological sequence. It explores the motives and relationships of those who fanned the flames of the witch hunt. It examines the people accused of witchcraft and reveals why they found themselves in the path of the fire.

The second part (Chapter 15) provides a closer look at the lives of each of the first seventy-five people accused as witches or wizards. It analyzes their places within their extended families and the community as it describes their examinations and trials.

This part sheds further light on why these individuals were targeted.

The Salem witch hunt has been investigated and chronicled relentlessly. Explanations for its occurrence abound: adolescent hysteria; Puritan fanaticism gone berserk; the French and Indian War; the myriad stresses of an isolated, rigid, insular community at odds with nature and itself. Each theory provides a valuable though partial explanation. Taken together, however, they remain strangely incomplete.

At the core of this tragedy lies a darker explanation, which forms the subject of this book. The Salem witch hunt was driven by conspiracies of envious men intent on destroying their enemies. Their maneuvers were sanctioned by the old guard of Puritan leaders acting in tacit collusion. These groups fueled what had been a smoldering brushfire, and exploded it into a deadly conflagration. Two hundred people were arrested for witchcraft, of whom twenty were executed and eight died in prison. The evidence used against the accused witches was based upon testimony about specters invisible to all except the bewitched. In contrast, the evidence offered in this book is real.

Enders A. Robinson
Lincoln, Massachusetts, 1991

ACKNOWLEDGEMENTS

I am especially indebted to Helen M. Bowdoin for many substantative contributions to this book. Painstakingly going over the manuscript, she offered many useful insights. Her help with revisions proved invaluable.

I want to thank my cousin Marjorie Wardwell Otten for her enthusiastic support of this project over the years and for her many contributions of genealogical and historical material. Grateful acknowledgment is given to Robert Dean Clark of the Society of Exploration Geophysicists; Alison C. D'Amario and Tina Jordan of the Salem Witch Museum; Anne Farnam, director of the Essex Institute in Salem; Alice Bowdoin Goodfellow of Washington College; Professor David D. Hall of Harvard University; Martha Hamilton, former director of the North Andover Historical Society; Michael Hays, assistant vice-president of Prentice Hall Inc.; Gratia Mahony, president of the Andover Historical Society; Professor Daniel Marder of the University of Tulsa; Rufus Perkins; Barbara Thibault, director of education of the Andover Historical Society, and Richard B. Trask of the Danvers Archival Center.

I want to express my sincere thanks to Tanjam Narasimhan of Hippocrene Books for her excellent work in editing and for providing valuable historical insight in the final preparation of the book.

CALENDAR 1692

		JANUARY				
S	M	T	W	T	F	S
					1	2
3	4	5	6	7	8	9
10	11	12	13	14	15	16
17	18	19	20	21	22	23
24	25	26	27	28	29	30
31						

		FEBRUARY				
S	M	T	W	T	F	S
	1	2	3	4	5	6
7	8	9	10	11	12	13
14	15	16	17	18	19	20
21	22	23	24	25	26	27
28	29					

		MARCH				
		1	2	3	4	5
6	7	8	9	10	11	12
13	14	15	16	17	18	19
20	21	22	23	24	25	26
27	28	29	30	31		

		APRIL				
					1	2
3	4	5	6	7	8	9
10	11	12	13	14	15	16
17	18	19	20	21	22	23
24	25	26	27	28	29	30

		MAY				
1	2	3	4	5	6	7
8	9	10	11	12	13	14
15	16	17	18	19	20	21
22	23	24	25	26	27	28
29	30	31				

		JUNE				
			1	2	3	4
5	6	7	8	9	10	11
12	13	14	15	16	17	18
19	20	21	22	23	24	25
26	27	28	29	30		

		JULY				
					1	2
3	4	5	6	7	8	9
10	11	12	13	14	15	16
17	18	19	20	21	22	23
24	25	26	27	28	29	30
31						

		AUGUST				
	1	2	3	4	5	6
7	8	9	10	11	12	13
14	15	16	17	18	19	20
21	22	23	24	25	26	27
28	29	30	31			

CALENDAR 1692

SEPTEMBER

S	M	T	W	T	F	S
				1	2	3
4	5	6	7	8	9	10
11	12	13	14	15	16	17
18	19	20	21	22	23	24
25	26	27	28	29	30	

OCTOBER

S	M	T	W	T	F	S
						1
2	3	4	5	6	7	8
9	10	11	12	13	14	15
16	17	18	19	20	21	22
23	24	25	26	27	28	29
30	31					

NOVEMBER

S	M	T	W	T	F	S
	1	2	3	4	5	
6	7	8	9	10	11	12
13	14	15	16	17	18	19
20	21	22	23	24	25	26
27	28	29	30			

DECEMBER

S	M	T	W	T	F	S
				1	2	3
4	5	6	7	8	9	10
11	12	13	14	15	16	17
18	19	20	21	22	23	24
25	26	27	28	29	30	31

CALENDAR 1693

JANUARY

S	M	T	W	T	F	S
1	2	3	4	5	6	7
8	9	10	11	12	13	14
15	16	17	18	19	20	21
22	23	24	25	26	27	28
29	30	31				

FEBRUARY

S	M	T	W	T	F	S
			1	2	3	4
5	6	7	8	9	10	11
12	13	14	15	16	17	18
19	20	21	22	23	24	25
26	27	28				

MARCH

S	M	T	W	T	F	S
			1	2	3	4
5	6	7	8	9	10	11
12	13	14	15	16	17	18
19	20	21	22	23	24	25
26	27	28	29	30	31	

APRIL

S	M	T	W	T	F	S
						1
2	3	4	5	6	7	8
9	10	11	12	13	14	15
16	17	18	19	20	21	22
23	24	25	26	27	28	29
30						

CHAPTER 1

THIS WONDERFUL AFFLICTION

In his diary Cotton Mather described Salem witchcraft. "The Devils, after a most preternatural manner, by the dreadful judgment of heaven, took a bodily possession of many people in Salem, and the adjacent places; and the houses of the poor people began to be filled with the horrid cries of persons tormented by evil spirits. There seemed to be an execrable witchcraft in the foundation of *this wonderful affliction.* Many persons, of divers characters, were accused, apprehended, prosecuted, upon the visions of the afflicted."[1]

From time immemorial, witchcraft has been linked with charms and magical power, whether for good or evil. In cultures the world over, magicians and sorcerers have attempted to manipulate man and nature. Often alarmingly adept, these practitioners came to be associated with an elaborate array of superstitions and fears. As a result many societies found it necessary to regulate magical practices. Roman legislation distinguished between good and bad magic, and prescribed punishment only for the bad. Accounts of witchcraft during the first thirteen centuries after Christ describe witchcraft as sorcery. Early medieval ecclesiastical records refer to witches as magical practitioners.

In the late middle ages a new understanding of witchcraft became dominant as the Christian concept of a devil was superimposed on folk beliefs about sorcery. In this formulation the supernatural capabilities of a witch were believed to issue

---

1   Cotton Mather, *Diary*, 1:150.

1

from a voluntary pact with the Devil. Soon people were seeing the Devil in everything; fables about demons were accepted as truth. Demonology and witchcraft became one in the same. Witchcraft was made a capital crime.

By 1587 George Gifford defined a witch as "one that works by the Devil, or by some devilish curious art, either hurting or healing, revealing things secret or foretelling things to come, which the Devil has devised to entangle and snare men's souls unto damnation." In 1599 Martin Del Rio defined witchcraft as "an art which, by the power of a contract entered into with the Devil, some wonders are wrought which pass the common understanding of man."

In 1671 Edward Phillips, the nephew of John Milton, described witchcraft as "a certain evil art, whereby with the assistance of the Devil, or evil spirits, some wonders may be wrought which exceed the common understanding of men." In 1689 Cotton Mather wrote, "Witchcraft is the doing of strange, and for the most part ill, things by the help of evil spirits, covenanting with the woeful children of men."[2]

The Devil was the major spirit of evil, the ruler of Hell, and the foe of God. On the grounds that a witch was obeying the orders of the Devil, the witch was seen as an opponent of God. Because the Church was placed on Earth to do God's work, it immediately followed that a witch was an enemy of the Church, a heretic. Because heresy threatened the power structure of society, the prosecution of witches could be justified. Both religious and secular authorities regarded witchcraft as a clear manifestation of the power of the Devil, and were willing to use the sternest measures to eradicate it.

The infamous European witch hunts took place for a period of about two centuries, roughly from 1450 to 1650. A preoccupation with heresy lay at the foundation of these campaigns, which represent one of the strangest phenomena in the history of Western culture. Claiming victims from every European country,

---

2   Cotton Mather, *Discourse*, 96.

the witch hunts were especially remarkable in that they coincided with the European Renaissance. During this period the common people were asserting their independence from old forms of feudalism. Educated men were developing the sciences of physics, chemistry, mathematics, and astronomy. Printers were mass-producing books and pamphlets on all subjects, including philosophy, rhetoric, theology, science and mathematics, agriculture, and architecture.

Ironically, it was often the most educated men who lent their support to the witch craze. The French philosopher Jean Bodin, famous bishops and lawyers, and kings such as James I of England were foremost in this group. Henry More, Ralph Cudworth, Joseph Glanville, Sir Thomas Browne, Richard Baxter, and many other of England's wise men were believers.[3] Although this may seem strange to the modern reader, reflect that the greatest irrational purges of all time have taken place in our own century. Today the term "witch hunt" is in common usage, to be found almost daily in the media.

Records indicate that the persecution of witches was less violent in England than in Scotland and on the Continent. From Germany and France, there are stories of mass executions of literally hundreds of witches at a time. Witches in England were almost always hanged, not burned, because witchcraft was regarded more as a secular offense than a religious heresy. Less severe penalties, such as the pillory, were often used. In England, for the hundred-odd years from 1566 to 1685, the number of persons hanged for witchcraft is estimated to be less than one-thousand.[4] (Because so few original documents are extant, this upper limit is in question and may be smaller.) The execution of ten witches in Lancashire in 1612 was regarded as a sensational event. The largest execution in England was of nineteen witches at Chelmsford in 1645.

Generally speaking, the only tortures used in England were bread and water diets, trussing of the limbs, and enforced

---

3   Trevor-Roper, 168.
4   Robbins, 164

wakefulness. They did not make use of the brutalities of squassation, strappado, thumbscrews, and Spanish boots used on the Continent, unless the alleged witchcraft was also considered to be treason.

The well-chronicled witch hunts of the past have a common structure, as exemplified by the story of Urbain Grandier in France. A popular priest, he excited the envy of some monks who conspired to instigate certain nuns to play the part of afflicted persons.[5] The conspiracy was sanctioned by Cardinal Richelieu and his colleagues on grounds of personal dislike. The possessions and convulsions of the afflicted were charged to the witchcraft of Grandier. "The nuns struck their chests and backs with their heads, as if they had their necks broken. They twisted their arms at the joints. They uttered cries so horrible and loud that nothing like it was ever heard before. They made use of expressions so indecent as to shame the most debauched of men, while their acts would have astonished the inmates of the lowest brothel in the country," wrote Des Niau.[6] Grandier was tried, condemned, tortured, and burned alive on August 18, 1634, fifty-eight years before the Salem witch hunt. Grandier's death may be attributed to imposture, pure and simple, carried out by a conspiracy of envious men, and upheld with the collusion of the government.

The classification of a person as a witch is based on imaginary phenomena created in the minds of the accusers. The accusers make reference to the invisible world of the Devil. From this vantage point, they proceed to accuse their victims of crimes, citing unsubstantiated claims based upon this illusory world. Witchcraft trials take place in kangaroo courts, a mockery of justice.

Witch hunts are instances of a deep intolerance that has surfaced repeatedly over the centuries. The belief that witches

---

5   Robbins, 313.
6   Robbins, 317.

were the agents of Satan inspired the accusers in the European witchcraft epidemics of the sixteenth and seventeenth centuries. At the time of a witch hunt there were always a few brave people who denounced the cruel and patently absurd accusations. But the majority, some fearful for their own safety, resigned themselves to a situation over which they had little or no control.

By the year 1650 the witch-hunting craze in Europe was largely at an end. Instead of superstition and magic, people were turning to explanations of natural phenomena based on scientific experimentation. The settlers in New England participated in this intellectual awakening. They accepted science as an ally, believing that scientific truth could not clash with revealed truth. Ships from Boston and Salem visited many ports, and returned with storehouses of knowledge, both written and oral. Ministers and others sent to England for the latest works by philosophers and scientists.

One of the earliest New England scientists was John Winthrop, Jr. Widely traveled, he had been a student at Trinity College, Dublin. He returned with the first astronomical telescope ever brought to America. Winthrop's observations of American fauna and flora were published in the *Philosophical Transactions of the Royal Society* in 1670.[7] He carried on researches in chemistry and metallurgy, with a view towards establishing mines and industries. The breadth of Winthrop's interests is shown by his correspondence not only with English scientists, but with Continental ones as well.

Thomas Brattle, a New England merchant, was a mathematician and an amateur astronomer. He made observations of Halley's comet, of eclipses of the sun and moon, and of variations of the magnetic needle. His contributions won the attention of Sir Isaac Newton.

In 1690 when the first colonial newspaper, *Publick Occurrences*, was published in Boston, the New England colonies had the highest rate of literacy in the world. Schooling was mandatory for children. To the New England Puritans, reading

---

7   5: 1137-1153.

was essentially a sacred form of mental liberation. Learning how to read and becoming religious were perceived as nearly the same thing. Literacy was at the heart of their cultural politics, and it represented the freedom that they proclaimed for themselves. Harvard College, established in 1636, just six years after the founding of Boston, immediately became the training ground for future civic, as well as religious, leaders.

Not only was learning respected, but also practical technology was well advanced. The population of New England engaged in every type of skilled trade. There were weavers, spinners, potters, joiners, housewrights, wheelwrights, brickmakers and masons, blacksmiths, coopers, painters, tailors, cordwainers, glovers, tanners, millers, maltsters, skinners, sawyers, tray-makers, and dishturners. These trades, in conjunction with agricultural employments, made New England self-sufficient. The settlers of New England came from among Britain's most industrious and intelligent stock. Far from being backward, the colonial people were on the cutting edge of a new world of opportunity.

The Salem witch hunt of 1692 seems totally incongruous. For good reason, no other witch hunt has attracted so much attention. It is remarkable both for the large number of people accused, and because of the late date at which it took place. It is remarkable because it happened among educated people in the midst of the scientific revolution. It is remarkable because it was primarily directed, not at the poor and destitute, but at mothers, wives, and daughters in the upper echelons of society, at rich widows and respectable matrons, at army officers and sea captains, at wealthy merchants and large landholders, and at ministers and church members. Salem is the last of the classic witch hunts.

While sorcery was considered significant in the Salem witch trials, far greater importance was laid upon devil worship. The chief accusation at Salem was that the defendant had made a covenant with the Devil. The person became a witch as soon as the compact was finalized. The fear expressed by the clergy is articulated in this contemporary account by the Rev. John Hale:

"The witches design was to destroy Salem Village, and to begin at the minister's house, and to destroy the Church of God, and to set up Satan's kingdom." The supposed existence of a compact with the Devil was an essential element in establishing a person's guilt. The indictment of Samuel Wardwell, age forty-nine, states that he, "with the evil spirit, the Devil, a covenant did make, wherein he promised to honor, worship and believe the Devil."

The compact was sealed when the person put a mark in the Devil's book. The Devil would then baptize the new witch. Usually the conversion occurred when the person was in a depressed state, which made the Devil's temptations difficult or impossible to resist.

For example, Mary Toothaker, age forty-seven, confessed, "Last May I was greatly depressed, and I was troubled with fear about the the Indians. I used often to dream of fighting with them. I have often prayed but felt that I was the worse for praying. I had thoughts I was rather the worse for my baptism. The Devil appeared to me in the shape of a tawny man and promised to keep me from the Indians. The Devil brought something which looked like a piece of birch bark. I made a mark with my finger by rubbing off the white scurf. He promised, if I would serve him, I should be safe from the Indians. It was the fear of the Indians that put me upon it."[8]

Mary Lacey, Jr., age eighteen, said, "The Devil appeared to me in the shape of a horse. I was in bed and the Devil came to me and bid me obey him and I should want for nothing, and he would not bring me out. The Devil put such thoughts in my mind as not to obey my parents."

The supposed baptism could take place in various ways. In Samuel Wardwell's case "he was baptized by the Black Man at Shawsheen River alone, and was dipped all over, and believes he

---

8   While Mary Toothaker and her nine-year-old daughter were in prison for witchcraft in 1692, the Indians burned her house and barn. Three years later the Indians killed Mary and carried away her daughter, who was never seen again.

renounced his former baptism." The Black Man refers to the Devil.

The Devil appeared to the alleged witches in various forms. Ann Foster, age seventy-two, confessed, "The Devil appeared to me in the shape of a bird several times. Such a bird as I never saw the likes of before. He came white and vanished away black. The bird sat upon a table. It had two legs and great eyes."

Mary Bridges, Jr., age thirteen, said, "A yellow bird appeared to me out of doors and bid me serve him. He promised me money and fine clothes. I promised to serve him. But he gave me neither money nor fine clothes. I thought when he appeared, it was the Devil. The next time I saw such a shape, it was a black bird." Mary's half-sister Sarah Bridges said, "The Devil came, sometimes like a bird, sometimes like a bear, sometimes like a man, but most frequently like a man."

The Salem trials shared much in common with both English and Continental ones. The legend of witches flying on the kind of poles used for broom handles was accepted as fact at the Salem trials. Anne Foster of Andover testified, "I and Martha Carrier did both ride on a stick or pole when we went to the witch meeting at Salem Village. The stick broke as we were carried in the air above the tops of the trees, and we fell. But I did hang fast about the neck of Goody Carrier and we were presently at the village. I was then much hurt of my leg. I heard some of the witches say that there were three hundred and five in the whole country, and that they would ruin that place, the Village."

Richard Carrier of Andover confessed, "I can not tell how long it is since I rode to Salem Village. I was there twice and rode with Mary Lacey. The Devil carried us. Sometimes he was in the shape of a horse, sometimes in the shape of a man. The first time he was a horse, the second time a man. When he was a horse, our pole lay across the horse. When he was a man, our pole was on his shoulder. When we went to Ballard's he was a man. He was in the shape of a Black Man who had a high crowned hat."

Of all the aspects of witchcraft the witch meeting, or *sabbat*, has attracted the most attention. The witch meeting combined the old legends of sorcery and the new ideas of heresy, with its blasphemous parodies of the sacraments, licentious drinking, and a conspiracy to set up the kingdom of Satan. Puritan Massachusetts was neither a monarchy nor a republic, but a theocracy. Witchcraft was considered treason against God, which in turn meant that it was treason against the state. The clergy promoted the notion that a witch meeting threatened the very fabric of society.

Elizabeth Johnson, Jr., age twenty-two, testified, "There were about six score that I saw at the witch meeting at the Village. They had bread and wine at the witch sacrament. They filled the wine out into cups to drink. They agreed that it was time to afflict folks and to pull down the kingdom of Christ and to set up the Devil's kingdom."

Mary Toothaker said, "I was twice at Salem Village witch meeting. They did talk of 305 witches in the country. Their discourse was about the pulling down the Kingdom of Christ and setting up the Kingdom of Satan. I heard the beating of a drum at the Village meeting and think I also heard the sound of a trumpet."

Mary Bridges, Jr., age thirteen, was tired of the long-drawn out church services and yearned for the fun forbidden to Puritan teenagers. "I rode to the Salem Village meeting upon a pole," she said. "The black man carried the pole over the tops of the trees. I admit I was at the witch meeting at Chandlers at Andover last week. I thought there were nearly a hundred at it. My shape was there. I did not know that my mother was a witch, but I knew my sisters Susannah and Sarah were witches. They drank beer at the witch meeting. It stood there in pots and they drew it out of a barrel." Mary's half-sister Sarah Bridges admitted, "I have sometimes ridden upon a pole. I was at the witch meeting at Chandlers Garrison at Andover. I thought there were 200 witches there. They ate bread and drank wine."

A witch was a living person, for example, a neighbor who, to all outward appearances, might seem quite harmless. A witch could be either male or female, although the word *wizard* was often used for a male witch. The chief instrument of the witch was its own *specter*. The *specter* was the phantom or spirit of the witch. Other equivalent words used for specter were *apparition*, *appearance*, and *shape*. Being Satanic, a specter was considered a detestable device. The crimes were usually performed not by the witch itself, but by its specter. The witch could send its specter abroad to do great mischief while absenting itself from the scene of the crime; or, if present, even practicing kindness to its victims.

The word *ghost* was generally reserved for a phantom or spirit of a dead person, often someone the witch had killed by its specter. The ghost, clothed in a white sheet, the winding sheet that was used to wrap the dead person's body for burial, would appear crying out for revenge against the witch.

The witch could also be aided by one or more familiars or imps, given to a witch by the Devil. A *familiar, familiar spirit*,[9] or *imp* is a low-ranking demon. The familiar was typically viewed as appearing in the shape of a small animal, such as a bird or snake. The little creature was in constant attendance on the witch, who was responsible for its care. The faithful familiar is to be distinguished from occasional visitations of the Devil disguised as an animal.

Witches' marks, extra nipples on a witch, are considered proof of witchcraft. Most extant descriptions, however, show that such protuberances were natural, caused by some physical formation like a mole or birthmark. The judges in seventeenth-century England and New England ruled that these nipples were used to nourish the witch's familiars. Cotton Mather wrote about "imps sucking persons." Therefore witch marks were *prima facie* evidence of witchcraft. At the Salem witch trials the search for these marks was used as a test for discovering witches.

In examining alleged witch Bridget Bishop, "a jury of women found a preternatural teat upon her body, but upon a second search, within three or four hours, there was no such thing to be

---

9   "And Saul had put away those that had familiar spirits, and the wizards, out of the land." (1 Sam. 28.)

seen."[10] At her witchcraft examination, Elizabeth Johnson, Jr. of Andover was asked where her familiar sucked her. She showed one of her knuckles of her finger and said that was one place. It looked red. She said, "I have two more places where they suck me." Women were ordered to search them out and they found two little red specks. "That is all there is to be seen. They are plain to see when they are newly sucked," said Elizabeth. One of the places was located behind her arm.

On April 20, 1692, Abigail Hobbs, a young woman of twenty-two, imprisoned for witchcraft in Salem, confessed that "the Devil in the shape of a man came to her and would have her afflict Ann Putnam [Jr.], Mercy Lewis, and Abigail Williams, and brought their images with him in wood, and gave thorns, and bid her prick them into those images, which she did accordingly into each of them, and then the Devil told her they were afflicted, which accordingly they were, and they cried out they were hurt by Abigail Hobbs." The three girls mentioned here, together with Mary Walcott, Elizabeth Hubbard, and Elizabeth Parris, have gone down in history as the inner circle of afflicted girls at Salem Village.

The Devil made it possible for the alleged witches to afflict people. The witches engaged in various torments from simply squeezing or pinching an article of clothing to sticking pins into puppets made for that purpose. Mary Bridges, Jr. said, "I afflicted people by sticking pins into things and clothes, while thinking of hurting them. The dead taught me this way of afflicting."

Ann Foster confessed, "Goody Carrier came to me and would have me bewitch two children of Andrew Allen's. I had two puppets made, and stuck pins in them to bewitch the children. One of the children died, and the other became very sick. I tied a knot in a rag and threw it into the fire to hurt a woman at Salem Village, and she was hurt. I hurt the rest by squeezing puppets and so almost choked them."

---

10   Cotton Mather, *Wonders,* 137.

Elizabeth Johnson, Jr. said, "I afflicted Sarah Phelps by puppets. I brought out three puppets. Two of them were made of rags or stripes of cloth. The other was made of a birch rhine. One puppet had four pieces or strips of cloth wrapped one upon another. It was to afflict four persons with. There was thread in the middle under the rags. I afflicted by pinching that puppet. A second puppet had two such pieces of rags rolled up together and three pins stuck into it. I afflicted Ben Abbot's and James Frye's two children and Abraham Foster's children with that puppet and the other. I afflicted Ann Putnam, Jr. with a spear." When asked whether the spear was iron or wood, she said, "Either of them would do."

Mary Lacey, Sr. confessed, "I take a rag, cloth or any such thing, and roll it up together, and imagine it to represent such and such a person. Then whatever I do to that rag or cloth so rolled up, the person represented thereby will be in like manner afflicted."

Because of the magnitude of their crimes, witches were commonly called *malefici* or evil-doers. The clergy preached that a witch could agitate the elements and disturb the minds of people. They claimed that a witch, without administering poison or doing any other physical act, could inflict harm and even kill.

When Rebecca Nurse was examined, the magistrate said to her, "When this witchcraft came upon the stage there was no suspicion of Tituba. She professed much love to that child Betty Parris, but it was her apparition that did the mischief, and why should not you also be guilty, for your apparition does hurt also."

Ann Putnam, Sr., an afflicted woman of age thirty, expressed her fear of the alleged witch Rebecca Nurse as follows: "On the first day of June 1692 the apparition of Rebecca Nurse did fall upon me and almost choked me. She told me that now she was come out of prison, and now she would afflict me all this day long and would kill me if she could. She told me she had killed Benjamin Houlton and John Fuller and Rebecca Shepard. She also told me that she and her sister Cloyce had killed young John Putnam's child. Immediately there did appear to me six children in winding sheets which called me aunt, which did most grievously frighten me. They told me that they were my sister Baker's children of Boston and that Goody Nurse and Mistress Cary of Charlestown and an old deaf woman at Boston had murdered them, and charged me to go and tell these things to the magistrates or else they would tear me to pieces, for their blood did cry for vengeance. Also there appeared to me my own sister Bayley and three of her children in winding sheets and told me that Goody Nurse had murdered them."

As seen from the above testimony, the afflicted person had a powerful weapon. This was a gift known as *spectral sight.* Spectral sight was the alleged ability to peer into the invisible spiritual world of the Devil. In this way the afflicted person could see the specters of the offending witches. This enabled the afflicted person to name the witches so that the accusers could file complaints against them, so that the magistrates could imprison them, so that the grand jury could indict them, so that the trial jury could find them guilty, so that the executioner could hang them. The court, as a matter of policy, admitted as evidence any spectral information provided by the afflicted. From spectral evidence, there was no escape. In the Salem tragedy spectral evidence was used to imprison nearly two hundred people, and to execute twenty of them.

Cotton Mather, the most active and influential clergyman in the witch hunt, fervently preached that witches must be hunted down. He claimed that witches, having signed the Devil's book, were agents of the Devil in his plot to destroy the Church. He preached that the witches were aiding the Devil, both in person and with specters, by tormenting the afflicted. He said that their purpose was to compel the afflicted to sign the book and become witches themselves. In his mind, those accused as witches were the persecutors, while the afflicted were suffering martyrs.

Because of his extensive writings in support of the doctrine, there can be no question that Cotton Mather believed in witchcraft. Nor is there any question that he believed in spectral evidence. A question does arise, however, regarding how much credence he gave to this evidence in prosecutions. From his writings it seems plain that, while he supported the admission of spectral evidence, he did not believe in convicting persons on that alone. He felt that further corroboration was needed. A personal confession was the best evidence of witchcraft.

In the Salem tragedy about fifty persons accused as witches confessed to their guilt. Some of the clergy regarded such a confession as a valuable document that revealed the innermost secrets of nature. From the confessions, Cotton Mather hoped to lay bare the invisible world of the Devil. A major element of a confession was the admission that the accused wrote his or her name in the "Devil's book." Although witchcraft confessions are nothing more than intellectual fantasies, they do represent valuable historical documents. Not only do they tell us about witchcraft beliefs in 1692, but they also provide information about the personal lives of the people involved.

Witchcraft was a crime in 1692. The mechanics of apprehending criminals in 1692 were much the same as those in use today. In order to understand the legal process, it is useful to outline the steps taken to arrest and convict an alleged witch. Three main groups, the *afflicted*, the *accusers*, and the *accused*, are to be distinguished.

A witch could hurt someone either by using its own body or by its specter, but usually did so with its specter. An *afflicted person* was one hurt by a witch. With spectral sight, the afflicted person could see the specter. The afflicted would then "cry out" upon the witch, thereby making the witch's identity known to all.

The person so identified became an *accused person*. Although the afflicted person was the original accuser, the term *accuser*, as used here, is reserved for persons who accused in a legal sense. In this more technical usage, an accuser, or *complainant*, was the person who filed the legal document known as a *complaint*. The complaint document would charge the accused person with hurting the afflicted person by witchcraft. Note that the terms accuser is used in this book to refer to the person who initiated legal action by filing the complaint.

In the late 1930s with funding from the Works Project Administration (the WPA), a team of clerical workers searched old court records in Massachusetts for all the extant Salem witchcraft documents, and transcribed them by typewriter. The original typescript was deposited in 1938 with the Essex County Clerk of Courts, and the carbon copy went to the Essex Institute in Salem. In 1977, the DeCapo Press published in three volumes the entire WPA collection under the title *The Salem Witchcraft Papers*.[11] Universally abbreviated *SWP*, this work is the basic reference used in the present book to identify the complainants.

After the filing of the complaint document, a magistrate would issue an *arrest warrant* for the accused. A constable or marshal would use this warrant to arrest the accused person. The accused person would be brought before the magistrates for a preliminary *examination*. Witnesses would be called to give testimony. The magistrates would then decide whether to release the accused person, or to commit her or him to prison to await trial. While in prison an accused person might be examined again, and more witnesses called. Some witnesses might give written *depositions* that could be used later.

Next the case went to a *grand jury*. The grand jury could either clear or indict the accused person.[12] If there were an indictment, the case would go to court, where guilt or innocence would be determined by *trial by jury*. If the verdict were guilty, the justices would give the sentence. Because witchcraft was a capital offense, the sentence was always death by hanging. In glaring contrast to our current system of jurisprudence, the accused person was never allowed representation by a lawyer or other counsel for the examinations, the grand jury inquest, or the trial.

---

11   Boyer and Nissenbaum, eds.

12   Few of the indictments were for the crime of afflicting certain girls at times and places described on the arrest warrants. Instead most were for the crime of afflicting the girls, not always the same ones, in the court room at the time of the preliminary examinations. The reason was that there were many people present to witness such courtroom antics.

To swell the tide of testimony against the accused in the examinations, the inquests, and the trials, many people were brought in as witnesses for the prosecution. Called by legal summons documents, some testified freely while others had to be induced to speak. Although some witnesses made accusations, they are quite distinct from the accusers, the complainants. The accusers who instituted the legal complaints were the driving force of the prosecutions; the witnesses who were called to confirm the legal accusations were subordinate. This distinction is important.

The courtroom examinations in 1692 followed an all too predictable pattern. The circle of afflicted girls were brought into the room. When the accused person glanced at them, they instantly succumbed to their afflictions, "fits" in which they writhed on the floor in "strange agonies and grievous torments." Captain John Alden,[13] a sea captain who was accused, described the girls as "those wenches who played their juggling tricks, falling down, crying out, and staring in people's faces." However when the accused person touched an arm or another part of their bodies, they immediately revived and came to themselves. The cure ostensibly occurred because the disabling "fluid" flowed out of their bodies and back into the witch.

The afflicted girls swore that their fits were caused by the accused person. They swore that they had seen a specter come out of the accused person's body and physically attack them, causing them great pain and torment. This testimony became the decisive evidence used by the court to establish that the accused person was a witch. Such spectral evidence was used until the last phase of the witch hunt. If the accused had made a confession, it also was presented in court. For further evidence, witnesses were brought in to present malicious gossip against the accused; this slander constituted *personal evidence*.

---

13   Captain John Alden was the son of John and Priscilla Alden, the Plymouth Colony pilgrims made famous by Longfellow's poem, "The Courtship of Miles Standish."

At the turn of the twentieth century, Winfield Nevins wrote, "The examining magistrates, the judges and other officials were misguided in their sense of duty, unjust to the accused, and unnecessarily severe with the prisoners. The accused were treated, from the moment some babbling child uttered a suspicious word against them, to the burial of their bodies after execution, with a harshness a little short of brutality, and with far more severity than any evidence would indicate that persons accused of other crimes in those days were treated. Their rights, even as the rights of accused persons were understood in 1692, were not protected."

How can the actions of the afflicted girls be accounted for? What explanation can be offered for the fits in which they related the most marvelous tales? The afflicted girls often testified to events that happened before they were born, and described places to which they had never been. They talked about supernatural events and said they saw the ghosts of the dead.

Certainly the afflicted girls, as well as some of the adults called to testify, exhibited hysterical outbursts during the examinations. But the hysteria of the inner circle of afflicted girls was generally well controlled. With remarkable precision, they could turn their outbursts on and off at will. These bewitched young girls were able to charm their audiences. One might say they were more bewitching than bewitched.

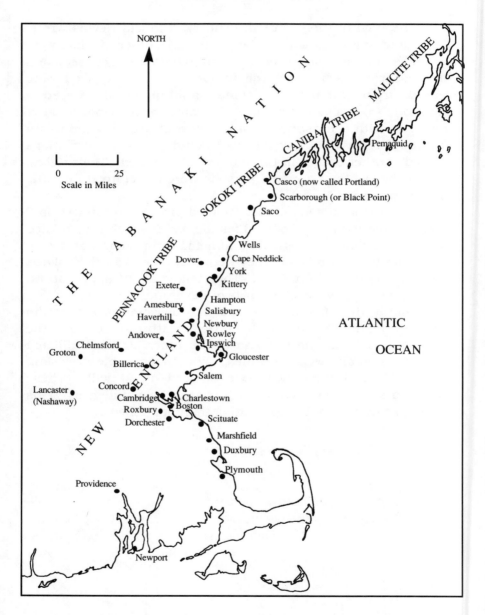

Map 1. Frontier between New England and the Abanaki Nation in 1692.

CHAPTER 2

WILLIAM STOUGHTON

In the decades of the 1620s and 1630s Massachusetts was settled as a Puritan commonwealth. Thousands of people, dissatisfied with conditions in England, flocked to the New England shore. The controlling minority of these immigrants were Puritans, who came because they were unable to express their religious sentiments in England. But the majority simply sought to escape the rigidity of the English class system and to build better lives for themselves in the New World. Virtually all were hard-working members of the emerging middle class. A new class system emerged, one in which priority of settlement and accumulated wealth played the greatest roles.

The Puritans held to the premise that everyone was a sinner. They believed that a regenerate (*born again*) person could become a *visible saint* by entering into a *covenant of grace*, a legal compact with God. They also believed that an entire nation could enter into such a covenant. The two covenants, personal and public, though branches of the same, were treated as distinct entities. Saints could dwell alone without a pledged society; a society could achieve this honor even though most of its citizens were not gracious. The doctrine of a national covenant allowed the rulers of New England to believe that they were the chosen people of God, even as the people of Israel in the Old Testament.

The government of Massachusetts, a theocracy, was based on the charter of the Massachusetts Bay Company. The charter was the very foundation of their Bible state. Upon it was based the right to government by God's elect, the right to exclude *error*, and the right to the established Congregational church.[14]

The Puritan, or Congregational, church, was comprised of individual, self-governing groups called congregations. The church in Salem was the first congregation in America. The members of each congregation elected their own minister; there were no bishops or other authorities to govern over them.

The only way to become a *church member* was to be elected by the members of a congregation. Anyone desiring admission had to first satisfy the minister and the elders that he or she was qualified, and then answer searching questions by the members on the floor of the meeting house. The church members were the visible saints of the Puritans. Only a select few were found worthy enough to attain this status. Significantly these were generally drawn from the middle and upper classes of Puritan society. Poor people, the large majority in New England, had little chance of ever becoming church members.

By limiting church membership to visible saints, the Puritan Church pretended to such excellence as the world had not witnessed since the time of Christ and the Apostles. Might this mean that other citizens had the right to worship in the church of their choice? Hardly! The Congregational church was the only legal church in New England, and by law all citizens were required to attend. Everyone, including children, was supposed to go to Sunday services, one in the morning and another in the afternoon, and a Thursday afternoon service as well. Each service was two or three hours long. However, in 1692 the seating capacity of all the churches in Boston would accommodate only about one-third of the population. Clearly, many in New England never entered a church, at least not on a regular basis.

The essence of the *congregational way* was the autonomous church, founded on the covenant of grace and limited to a few visible saints. This structure deliberately excluded most

---

14   "There shall not be found among you any one that uses divination, or an enchanter, or a witch, or a charmer, or a consulter with familiar spirits, or a wizard, or a necromancer." Deut., 18:10-11.

townspeople, who had both to submit to the rule of the *righteous few*, and to pay taxes for its support.   Presbyterians in Britain denounced the Puritan covenant as an artificial notion, predicting civil war in any society that dared to unchurch the majority.   Soon the debate was joined by Calvinists in Europe, who were alarmed at what appeared as the most sinister tendency of the Congregational church, *perfectionism.* Calvinists accepted regeneration as a genuine experience, but would not allow any person, even the most devout minister, to say to another, "You are infallibly elected."

Only male congregational members, the so-called freemen, were allowed to vote in political elections.   The clergy, through their influence on church membership, were thus able to keep a tight control on the elected government.   During the first great exodus to New England in the 1630's about 20 percent of the population were church members; by 1692 less than 4 percent of the much greater population held this status.[15] All others were disenfranchised; they could neither vote nor serve in other official capacities, such as jurors.

The freemen elected the governor.   They also chose the magistrates who were the assistants to the governor.   The assistants directed the general affairs of the land and dispensed justice to the people.   In effect, the assistants made up both the upper legislative body and the highest judicial body of government. Also elected by the freemen were the deputies, who comprised the lower legislative body, and the justices of the peace, who settled minor cases.

The decade of the 1640s brought civil war to England, the royalists defending the crown against the Puritan roundheads. The Puritans resorted to a witch hunt to flush out perceived enemies, the heretics.[16] Since only those records favorable to the

---

15   In 1692, there were less than 4,000 church members, about equally divided
       between men and women, in a population close to 100,000.
16   Robbins, 249.

official side were preserved, the truth about the victims of this English witch hunt can only be imagined today.

After a series of bloody battles, the Puritan forces under Oliver Cromwell were victorious, and King Charles I was beheaded. The Puritans, holding the upper hand in England, proceeded to purify church buildings by destroying everything in them, the art of centuries past, leaving only bare walls and rubble. Without the religious motivation to leave England, the migration of Puritans to New England came to a standstill.

In the 1650s, England was subjected to rule of the austere Puritan Commonwealth. In the face of such strictures, many people, including some Puritans, longed for the good old days under the crown. Still, the intellectual contribution of many Puritans, notably the magnificent poet John Milton, deserve emphasis. The fruits of their principles, in the following generation, are seen in the political views of their scholar, John Locke. The Declaration of Independence is based on his writings. We are indebted today to the vision and courage of those Puritans who established many of the freedoms we take for granted. The leading New England Puritans were not among this group.

In 1660, the people of England had their way. The Puritan government fell, and the monarchy was restored. Charles II, son of the beheaded king, was placed on the throne; this event is called the *Restoration.* At this point, many of the most repressive English Puritans who had served under Cromwell fled to New England, the last bastion of Puritan safety. On the same tide were some returning New Englanders, who had lived in England during Puritan rule. Among them were the Rev. William Stoughton and the Rev. Increase Mather. (William Stoughton was the chief justice for the witchcraft trials in 1692.)

William Stoughton had been educated for the ministry at Harvard, graduating in the class of 1650. He then accepted the ministry of a church in England. While in England, he studied for, and received, his Master's degree at Oxford. Following his return to Massachusetts in 1660, he gave up the ministry in favor of politics. Before entering government service, he had preached in company with Increase Mather. Stoughton first became a magistrate, an assistant to the governor, in 1671. Stoughton leaned heavily on his religious training for guidance in determining guilt or innocence. A vigorous prosecutor, he was narrow and dogmatic in applying the most rigid Puritan doctrines. He never married.

The Restoration was the severest of setbacks for the Puritan orthodoxy. Charles II sent a letter in June 1662 expressing his desire that Congregational church membership would no longer be required for voting privileges, and that all landholders would be allowed to vote for civil and military officials. Yet New England officialdom turned a blind eye to the king's letter and carried on as before.

Economically, New England merchants had no cause for complaint, as the British exclusion of Dutch, French, and Spanish traders opened golden opportunities. Europe was entering an age of enlightenment, and new immigrants brought with them the seeds of change. Further, the majority of New Englanders eagerly hoped for freedom of religion, which would give the franchise to all citizens, making the elective process democratic.

Following the Restoration, the most important social development in New England was the emergence of a merchant class. This wealthy group found itself frequently clashing with the Puritan government. By the early 1680s, pressures from the increasingly diverse and restless population were seriously undermining the inflexible system imposed by the Puritan leaders, whose vulnerability was sensed by their opponents in England. The official downfall of the Puritan government of New England came in 1684 when Charles II annulled the charter of the Massachusetts Bay Company.

When the news reached Boston, the adherents of the old Puritan order were outraged. They well knew that the king's decree annulling the charter made the existing government in Massachusetts illegal. Undeterred, the Puritan rulers in Boston simply ignored the decree and continued to exercise power as before. The usual slowness of British administrators to take action provided leeway for the Puritans' defiance.

King Charles II died in 1685, and was succeeded by his brother King James II, a Roman Catholic and no friend of Puritanism. Finally, in May 1686, the elected governor of Massachusetts, Simon Bradstreet, was displaced and a temporary council appointed by the king began to rule Massachusetts. It was presided over by Joseph Dudley, and William Stoughton was deputy president, but most of the other Puritan leaders were excluded. The temporary council was composed almost exclusively of rich Massachusetts merchants. Relishing their newly found power, they went about satisfying their political desires. Free from the limitations of an elected legislature, they proceeded to enjoy a feast of executive privilege.

Sir Edmond Andros, the royal governor newly appointed by the king, arrived in Boston on December 19, 1686. At once he took over control from Dudley and Stoughton. Both, however, quickly accepted seats in his council. The council was expanded to include representatives from all the New England colonies, and later from New York. There still was no elected legislature. Andros' new government, the Dominion of New England, eventually extended from Maine to the Delaware River. It no longer embodied the interests of Massachusetts merchants alone, and in fact ruled against them on several important measures.

The Puritan faction of Massachusetts, now almost completely excluded from the direction of public affairs, began stirring up popular support against Andros' rule. More important, they found convenient new allies in most of the very merchants who previously had been their outspoken opponents. The Puritans' animosity against Andros turned to genuine hatred when he established an Anglican church, King's Chapel, in Boston.

In England royal authorities started the process of writing an entirely new charter for New England, a terrifying prospect for the old guard Puritans. A royal charter would forever put an end to their Puritan Commonwealth; their exclusive place in the world as the covenanted people of God would be lost. For the New

England Puritans, these were unhappy times. Made of stern stuff, they were not about to give in.

In May 1688, the Rev. Increase Mather, the senior minister of the Second Church (Old North Church) in Boston, was sent to England, instructed by his cohorts to use his powers of negotiation to make the proposed royal charter as much like the old charter as possible. Upon arriving he found that the heart of the monarch was steeped in despotism, and not at all inclined to favor liberty in the colonies. However, in November 1688, King James II was forced to abdicate in a coup known as England's *Glorious Revolution.*

William of Orange, a Dutch stadholder, and his wife Mary, Protestant daughter of James II, succeeded to the throne of Great Britain as joint sovereigns. King William III and Queen Mary were to protect the Protestant religion in Britain. In March 1689, word of the Glorious Revolution reached Boston. The Puritans leaders, using the popular support that they had garnered, took their own action. On the morning of April 18, 1689 they revolted, and imprisoned Andros, the representative of the deposed king.

Regaining control of the government, the Puritans set up a provisional government, and ruled under the laws of the old charter. They dismissed Andros' council and happily re-instituted the Board of Assistants in its place. They brought back the respected, but now aged, Simon Bradstreet to serve as elected governor, largely as a figure head. The most striking effect of the "tyranny" of Andros was the disintegration of the party of moderate Puritans, and the emergence of a powerful group of conservative Puritans. This *old guard* was made up of hard-liners who had long defended the traditional Puritan ideals. The provisional government was in their hands. Because William Stoughton had served on the council under Andros, he had lost the confidence of the old guard, and they excluded him from the Board of Assistants. For the first time in his political life, Stoughton found himself in a precarious position.

Two new names were included in the Board of Assistants, Jonathan Corwin and Peter Sergeant. These men had not previously been high office-holders in the colony. Corwin was from Salem, and Sergeant from Boston; both were staunch members of the old guard. (Both of them were justices in the witchcraft trials of 1692.)

After their overthrow of Andros' government, the New England Puritans faced grave uncertainties about the permanence of their usurped rule. King William, although a Protestant, soon let it be known that he was not happy with their act of defiance. In fact, plain for all to see, their provisional government was nothing but an outlaw government.

At home, King William had his own troubles. His accession to the throne of Great Britain had started a war with France. Then in 1690 he met the former King James II in battle in Northern Ireland, the last military action in history in which two kings participated as combatants. The English war with France soon spread to America, where it was known as King William's War.

By the end of 1689, the French and the Indians had reduced American occupation of northern New England to a narrow coastal strip in New Hampshire and southern Maine. The front can be traced by a line beginning at the seaport town of Casco, Maine,[17] seventy-five miles northeast of Salem; running southwesterly along the Maine coast to York, Maine; from there inland to Exeter, New Hampshire; and then southwesterly to Andover, Groton, and Lancaster in Massachusetts. During 1690, the French kept the Indians supplied from Canada and encouraged them in further attacks on the northern settlements. In retaliation, in September and October 1690, New England ventured a military expedition to take Quebec, which ended in disaster. It was led by Sir William Phipps, a native of Maine. Phipps had been knighted for discovering and taking possession of the wealth of a sunken Spanish galleon for the English crown. By the end of 1690, all the remaining settlements in Maine had

---

17   Casco is the old name for the town later called Falmouth and now the city of Portland, Maine. In 1689, the population of Casco was about 600 persons.

been destroyed by the Indians, except for three towns, Wells, York, and Kittery, in the extreme southwest corner of the province.

In their wartime plans, the Puritan old guard discounted the advice of the field commanders. In March 1690, in Andover, Captain John Osgood and Lieutenant John Barker resisted the reorganization of the Upper Regiment, the regiment of militia in northwestern Essex county. (John Osgood's wife, Mary, was arrested for witchcraft on September 8, 1692. John Barker's daughter, Mary Barker, and his brother, William Barker, were arrested for witchcraft on August 29, 1692, and three days later William's son, William Barker, Jr., was arrested.)[18]

The frontier towns in Massachusetts, under intermittent attack by the Indians, were hesitant to risk sending their able-bodied men as far away as Canada to fight a war. When towns balked at having their young men impressed for military duty, the Puritan rulers regarded their discontent as insubordination. After the surrender of Casco, Maine to the Indians on May 20, 1690, Major Bartholomew Gedney, went on a recruiting mission and found farmers from Salem Village reluctant to depart for the northeast. (Bartholomew Gedney was one of the justices in the witchcraft trials of 1692.) In July 1690 the Rev. John Emerson of Gloucester implored Major General Wait Still Winthrop to release members of the town's militia company which had been impressed into the army. (Wait Still Winthrop was one of the justices in the witchcraft trials of 1692.)

The war impoverished New England. In 1691 the French reorganized the Indians in New Hampshire and Maine, who renewed their attacks. The onslaught engendered fear throughout New England. As the frontier in Maine and New Hampshire was driven back by Indian raids, a steady stream of refugees and orphans fled south on the dirt tracks to Massachusetts.

---

18   John Barker and William Barker are the writer's great, great, great, great, great, great, great-uncles.

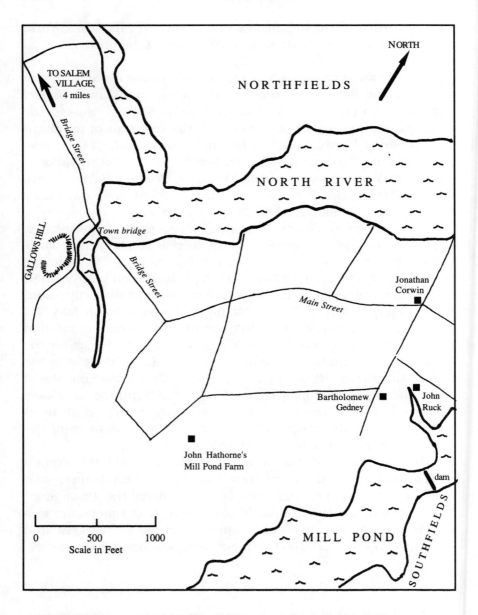

Map 2. Western sector of Salem Town in 1692 showing some houses.

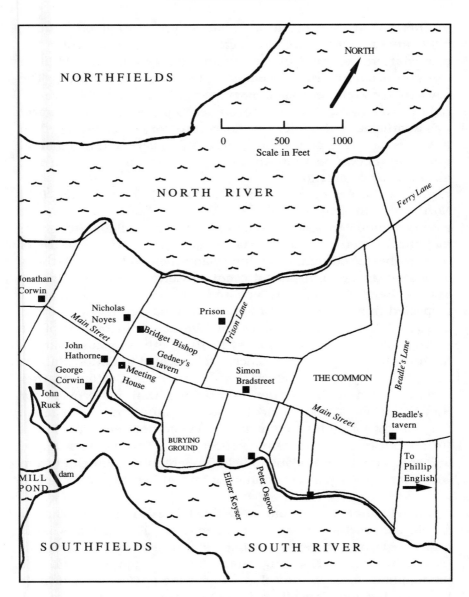

Map 3. Central sector of Salem Town in 1692 showing some houses.

Increase Mather, meanwhile, had stayed in England, waiting his chances. When attention again was directed to writing the new charter, he found himself unable to prevail. King William was an uncompromising defender of the Church of England. The new charter would include freedom of religion, and would give the right to vote to all citizens with property. Although the prospect was anathema to the Puritan leaders, ordinary citizens looked on it with favor. This group, led by wealthy traders and merchants, welcomed liberation from authoritarian Puritan rule, even if it meant a royal governor.

While the senior minister of Boston's Second Church (Old North) was in England, his son, the Rev. Cotton Mather, the assistant minister, served as acting minister. William Stoughton had always been close to the Mather family. As representative of the Dorchester church, Stoughton had attended Cotton Mather's ordination in 1685, a pivotal event in Cotton's life. Stoughton always liked Cotton Mather, and, in turn, Cotton Mather respected him. Their close friendship would never waver. Now, in 1691, William Stoughton, finding himself on the outside of the Puritan old guard, yet in full sympathy with its goals, made a fateful move to regain admittance. He appealed to Cotton Mather, his junior by many years. In response, Cotton Mather recommended to his father in England that he provide for Stoughton as "a real friend to New England, willing to make amendment for all his miscarriages," whom he desired his father "to restore to the favor of his country."[19]   The Mathers, father and son, were both anxious to help Stoughton, a staunch Puritan who shared their particular philosophy and beliefs.

At Whitehall in England on October 7, 1691 the new charter for Massachusetts Bay was declared in force. The ministers of the crown regarded Increase Mather as the head of the clergy of Massachusetts. Knowing that the ecclesiastical was the predominant force in the colony, they were anxious to conciliate him. To this end, they allowed him to nominate the governor, the

---

19   Hutchinson, 1: 365.

Council, and all the officers appointed under the new charter. He chose them, of course, from among his friends.

Increase Mather nominated Sir William Phipps as the new royal governor. Phipps was a good Congregationalist, and an admirer and follower of Increase Mather. However, he was not one of the old-guard Puritans. Why did Mather pick him instead of Stoughton? Phipps was a military man, well-regarded in England. The French were menacing, and King William wanted a military commander to govern New England. Had Mather not suggested Phipps, then the king might well have chosen an English military officer to be the royal governor. This, in Mather's view, would have been a calamity. As a result, he contented himself by choosing William Stoughton as the lieutenant governor. The crown accepted all of Increase Mather's recommendations.

The functions of the former Board of Assistants would be taken over by the Council of the new charter. Mather's recommendations insured that the members of the new Council were essentially the same as on the provincial board. Jonathan Corwin and Peter Sergeant were included. Thus, the old-guard Puritans would remain in control.

At the time of his appointment, October 1691, Sir William Phipps had been in England for a while. The new governor was to carry the royal charter with him over the ocean to New England, and begin his rule. As it happened, that process took half a year; Phipps was not to arrive in Boston until May 1692.

Increase Mather returned on the same ship. Back home again, he found himself in a dominant position. All the members of the executive branch of the new government were indebted to him for their nomination, including the governor and the lieutenant governor. To the Mathers, father and son, this was a family triumph.

In his diary, under the date of April 1692, Cotton Mather wrote, "The time for favor was now come! The set time was come! I am now to receive an answer of so many prayers. All the Councilors of the Province are of my own father's nomination and my father-in-law, with several related unto me, and several brethren of my own church, are among them. The Governor of the Province is not *my enemy*, but one whom I baptized, namely, Sir William Phipps, one of my own flock, and one of my dearest friends."[20]

William Stoughton found himself beholden to Cotton Mather, whose recommendation had made possible his re-emergence to political power. It cannot be doubted that the coincidence of Stoughton's passions, prejudices, and policy with those of the Mathers provided a decisive and driving force in what was to follow in the fateful year of 1692. In that year the Mathers were in the flush of their political influence.

In 1692, Salem had three magistrates, John Hathorne, Jonathan Corwin, and Bartholomew Gedney. In their office as magistrates, it was their responsibility to try legal cases, criminal and civil, that came before them and to pass sentence. (All three were justices in the witchcraft trials of 1692. In their capacities as magistrates, John Hathorne and Jonathan Corwin carried out most of the preliminary examinations of the accused witches at the time of arrest.)

John Hathorne was fifty-one years old in 1692, his rank and his steadfastness of purpose making him an influential force in Massachusetts politics. John was born in 1641 in Salem Village, the son of Major William Hathorne, the most powerful magistrate in Salem.[21] When John reached the age of twenty-one, his father gave him a small portion of Mill Pond Farm on the outskirts of Salem Town. Although the family homestead and extensive land holdings were in Salem Village, John received none of it. His

---

20   The Rev. Cotton Mather baptized the forty-year-old Phipps on March 23, 1690, and received him into membership in the Second Church (Old North) in Boston.

21   Major William Hathorne was born in England in 1607 and died in Salem Town in 1681, age 74. He had eight children: a daughter, name unknown; Sarah, born 1635; Eleazer, born 1637 and died in 1680; Nathaniel, born in 1639 and died a young man; John, born 1641; Ann, born 1643; William, Jr., born 1645 and died in 1678; Elizabeth Hathorne, born 1649.

father divided the Salem Village property into two equal parts and conveyed it to his younger daughters as marriage portions. The sisters were wedded to brothers, Ann to Joseph Porter and Elizabeth to Israel Porter. For the father to give the family estate to his daughters instead of his sons, with the result that the land left the Hathorne family and went to the Porter family, was an unusual departure from accepted social traditions.

John Hathorne had three brothers; all three died mysterious deaths. The middle brother, Nathaniel Hathorne, died as a young man in his twenties. The youngest brother, Captain William Hathorne, Jr., died at age thirty-three. The oldest brother, Eleazer, who had married a sister of Jonathan Corwin, died at age forty-three. In January 1680, Eleazer had bade his wife and three children farewell and set out in his sloop for Wells, Maine. A fortnight later, a special messenger brought a letter to Jonathan Corwin. Dated January 31, 1680, it began, "Mr. Eleazer Hathorne died this afternoon at two o'clock." It then explained that the sloop had been loaded with lumber as Mr. Hathorne directed, and had been accurately inventoried, but that Mr. Corwin might expect a slight shortage, as a few boards of pine had been taken from the cargo for Mr. Hathorne's coffin. The missing boards were accounted for, but Eleazer's death was not.

Major William Hathorne thanked God that one of his sons, John, had been spared to fight on in his stead for his Puritan principles. "Before the old man's inner eye still gleamed the vision of the Divine State upon earth, but often in his daydreams he saw this Promised Land attacked by an army of demons and imps led by the Devil."[22] The next year, 1681, the old man, Major William Hathorne, died, never resigned to the loss of his three sons.

In 1683, John Hathorne was elected to represent Salem as a deputy (a member of the lower legislative chamber), and the next year, as a magistrate, an assistant to the governor (a member of the upper legislative chamber). In the art of punishing the guilty, John Hathorne was a worthy successor to his father, who had

---

22   Loggins, 87.

held the position before him. John fought with vigor for the principles of Major William Hathorne.

John would go to extraordinary lengths to safeguard his property. When the king dissolved the old Massachusetts Bay charter, landowners became fearful that the title of their lands might revert to the king. As a cautionary measure, they went about fabricating sham deeds to show that they had legally purchased their lands from the Indians. In 1686 John Hathorne was instrumental in forcing several Indians to give up title to all the land in Salem for a pittance. Wording the bogus deed as pretentiously as possible, John Hathorne by this act admitted that the Salem earth had once belonged to the "children of the Devil," the American Indians.

Even as a young man of twenty-five, John had entered into land speculation in Maine. He had bought from an Indian known as Robin Hood, a tract of land consisting of about nine thousand acres in the part of Maine that was to become Lincoln County. That tract embodied hopes and dreams of great riches to John Hathorne.[23] The loss of Maine to the French and the Indians in 1690 in King William's War dashed these hopes. John Hathorne, however, through his shipping trade, took quick advantage of opportunities for war profiteering. He purchased, for two hundred fifty pounds sterling, a prize ship towed into Salem harbor by the ship *Pelican*. While John Hathorne was enlarging his personal fortune, thousands of others in New England were made nearly destitute by the war.

In the troubled years leading up to 1692, Hathorne stood happily in the ranks of the Puritan old guard. He upheld the most rigid Puritan standards. Fearing democratic rule, he opposed any form of religious freedom. He disapproved of the use of the

---

23   John Hathorne's great great grandson Nathaniel Hawthorne immortalized the elusive promise of this tract of land in Maine in his novel *The House of the Seven Gables*. It was this famous Hawthorne who added the w to the traditional spelling of the family name; whichever way it is spelled, it is pronounced the same.

Anglican *Book of Common Prayer*, and he supported the death penalty for religious heresy.

In early 1692, on hearing rumors of the new charter, John Hathorne was of the opinion that the Rev. Increase Mather had failed in his task. Hathorne became apprehensive about the security of his position under a newly appointed royal governor. But his greatest fear was the provision in the new charter that gave universal suffrage. If membership in the church were no longer a qualification for voting, his stern punishments might no longer be appreciated. The year 1692 was a pivotal juncture in his life.

Magistrate Jonathan Corwin was also fifty-one years old in 1692. The Corwin family was one of the most prominent and affluent in Salem. Corwin's father had settled in Salem in 1638 and had accumulated a fortune, serving in the upper levels of the colony's government. Through fortuitous marriages, the Corwins were allied with the most notable families of Massachusetts. Jonathan Corwin waited until he was thirty-five and then, in 1676, married Elizabeth (Sheafe) Gibbs, thirty-one, a widow who had inherited a great fortune.[24]

During 1692, John Hathorne earned a reputation as the most ardent of witch hunters. In the same year Jonathan Corwin's mother-in-law, Margaret Thatcher,[25] was repeatedly cried out upon as a witch.

In October 1692, William Stoughton, serving as chief justice for the Salem witchcraft trials, wrote a thank you letter to the

---

24 Elizabeth (Sheafe) Gibbs' deceased husband was Robert Gibbs (1636-1673).

25 The maiden name of Margaret Thatcher (1625-1694) was Margaret Webb. Her first husband was Jacob Sheafe, by whom she had Elizabeth, and her second husband was Rev. Thomas Thatcher, who died in 1687. Margaret's first husband died in 1659 leaving the largest estate ever probated in the colony to date. Her father, Henry Webb, died the next year, again leaving the largest estate ever probated in the colony to date. Within a year, Margaret's net worth, in today's equivalent, increased to more than eight million dollars.

Rev. Cotton Mather. "Considering the place that I hold in the Court of Oyer and Terminer, still laboring and proceeding in the trial of persons accused and *convicted for witchcraft*, I express my obligation and thankfulness to you. Such is your design, your enmity to Satan, your compassion, such your instruction and counsel, your care of truth, that all good men will greatly rejoice that the spirit of the Lord has thus enabled you to lift up a standard against the infernal enemy, that has been coming in like a flood upon us." At that point many accused witches were in jail awaiting trail. Despite her being called a witch, Corwin's enormously rich mother-in-law, of course, was not among them. Why did Stoughton praise Cotton Mather so profusely for his design and instruction?

CHAPTER 3

COTTON MATHER

The year 1692 had opened as a particularly troubling one in New England. The winter was cruel;[26] taxes were intolerable; pirates were attacking commerce; smallpox was rife. The French were actively supporting the Indians on a bloody warpath.

The armies of the French and the Indians represented a lethal threat to the people of New England. King William's War had been going on for three and a half years. Morale was low, tension high, in the wake of periodic massacres by the Indians. While the heaviest fighting occurred in New Hampshire and Maine, raids had repeatedly been made on the northern towns of Essex County in Massachusetts, Andover, Billerica, and Haverhill, in particular. New England towns were hard pressed to support the war with their tax money and their young men.

On January 25, 1692 one hundred fifty Abanaki Indians attacked "wretchedly secure" York, Maine, fifty miles northeast of Salem. Most of the houses were burned, and the minister and seventy-five other men, women, and children were killed. About one hundred were marched off into captivity. The Rev. George Burroughs, the minister at neighboring Wells, Maine, supplied the authorities in Boston with a description: "Pillars of smoke, the raging of the merciless flames, the insults of the heathen enemy, shouting, hooting, hacking [the bodies], and dragging

---

26   The year 1692, at the center point of the "little ice age," was one of the coldest years in the history of civilization.

away 80 others."[27] (George Burroughs was arrested for witchcraft on May 4, 1692 and hanged on August 10, 1692.)

Captain John Floyd of Romney Marsh (now Chelsea), Massachusetts, in command of a militia company which included Salem men, found the town of York in ruins. On January 27, 1692 he wrote to his superiors, "The 25 of this instant, I, having been informed that York was destroyed, made the greatest haste that I could with my Company for their relief, if there were any left, which I did hardly suspect."[28]

Captain John Alden of Boston was given the assignment of redeeming the York captives from the Indians. His instructions read, "It will be necessary that you represent unto them their baseness, treacheries and barbarities practiced in this war, having always declined a fair pitch battle, acting instead like bears and wolves."[29] The Puritans regarded the Indian style of fighting as diabolic; today it is called guerrilla warfare.

Captain John Alden had previously negotiated a truce with the Indians, but unscrupulous traders and land speculators operating from Massachusetts soon violated its conditions, thereby inciting the Indians.[30] Now that the Indians were

---

27   Petition from Wells, January 27, 1692 (*Massachusetts Archives*, 37:259).

28   *Massachusetts Archives*, 37:257; 37:318.

29   Instructions to Captain John Alden, February 5, 1692 (*Massachusetts Archives*, 37:305).

30   Major Richard Waldron of Dover, New Hampshire during King Philip's War had issued "general warrants" to seize every native known to be a "man slayer." Vicious Puritan traders for years used this authority to kidnap Indians and transport them to the West Indies as slaves. Their vessels would lurk in concealed inlets about the harbors of Maine with a view to this traffic. They knew that their business stirred up the Indians, but what was the peace of a few small farmers and fishermen compared to the profits of the slave trade? There were a considerable number of slaves throughout New England, and in Salem and Boston black slaves were bought and sold. Captain John Alden, a long-time trader on the Maine coast, spurned those engaged in these Indian kidnappings, as did the French Huguenots and traders of other backgrounds who had made their home there.

answering in kind, the same unprincipled men, unwilling to admit their guilt, shifted the blame to Captain Alden for his efforts to reach a peaceful compromise. (Captain John Floyd and Captain John Alden were arrested for witchcraft on May 28, 1692.)

The new royal charter represented a grave threat to the Puritan rulers who saw that their provisional government was nearing its end. Now, for the first time, they would be faced with a situation where the common rabble could vote in political elections. Their Puritan church would no longer hold exclusive control over the lives of the people.

As if these external threats were not enough, the Rev. Cotton Mather found an internal threat, the threat of witchcraft. To understand why the Puritan leaders considered witchcraft such a danger in 1692, it is very instructive to study the lives and characters of the Mathers, father Increase and son Cotton.

Some historians laud the New England Puritans as begetters of the highest American virtues, while others revile them as the source of the deepest American woes. Some cherish them as the symbol of spotless devotion to religious truth; others spurn them as the epitome of icy self-righteousness. In American folklore, the Puritans always seem to fall at one extreme or the other: splendid morality or niggardly repression, religious insight or blind bigotry, political freedom or savage persecution.

Confronted with a myriad of apparent contradictions, writers seldom place a Puritan in the middle ground of history. In all accounts, however, Increase Mather fares better than his more brilliant son. The father usually is placed on the positive side, whereas the son almost invariably is placed on the negative side. Cotton Mather is seen as the one who, through his writings and sermons, triggered the witch hunt of 1692. His father is often credited with using his influence to bring the witch hunt to an end. Their positions in history are chiefly associated with their participation in this tragic story, but at opposite extremes.

The heritage of the Mathers placed them squarely in the elite of Puritan society. Increase Mather (1639-1723) was the son of

Richard Mather. Richard (1596-1669) came to America in 1635 and was the minister of the Dorchester church, near Boston. The most revered of the New England Puritans was John Cotton (1585-1652). He emigrated to America in 1633 and was the minister of the First Church in Boston. The Rev. John Cotton and the Rev. Richard Mather were two Moses-like figures among the American Puritans.

Even in youth, Increase Mather demonstrated that he would equal or outshine the eminence of his father Richard. Increase graduated from Harvard in 1656. He preached his first sermon on his eighteenth birthday, and then went to Trinity College in Dublin, Ireland to obtain a Master's degree. He became the minister of the Second Church (Old North Church) in Boston. In 1662, he married the Rev. John Cotton's daughter Maria Cotton.

On February 12, 1663 the couple's first child Cotton Mather was born. Bearing the distinguished names of both *Cotton* and *Mather*, the boy may have felt destined for greatness. By 1674 he had mastered the entrance requirements for Harvard College and was accepted. Entering at the age of eleven and a half, he is the youngest student ever admitted to the college to this day. The normal time spent on the undergraduate degree was three years. When Cotton attended, the total enrollment at Harvard was never more than twenty students; in his own class there were only four. The ages of most of the students ranged from about fifteen to eighteen. As an eleven-year-old boy with a stutter, Cotton was discouraged when some of the students threatened him. After only a month at college he returned home for the rest of the freshman year, studying with his father and on his own.

Early in 1674 his father, Increase Mather, predicted that God would strike New England by the sword. The summer of 1675 fulfilled the prophecy; King Philip's War erupted, a war waged by Indians to drive the white men into the sea.[31] The Indian leader

---

31   In 1675 the native population of New England was about 20,000, having declined from nearly 100,000 in the year 1600, largely due to the white man's diseases. The white population of New England was over 80,000 by 1675. The Indians had already lost an undeclared economic war, and were

was King Philip; his Indian name was Metacom. King Phillip was the son of Massasoit, the Indian chief who had befriended the Pilgrims, making possible their first thanksgiving. The Indians said that "they had been the first in doing good to the English, and the English the first in doing wrong. When the English first came, their King's father [Massasoit] was as a great man, and the English as a little child. He constrained the other Indians from wronging the English and gave them corn, and showed them how to plant, and let them have a hundred times more land than now the King [Philip] has for his own people."[32]

The first attack was made by the Wampanoag Indians against Plymouth Colony in June 1675. As the Indians swept northward into Massachusetts, all the settlements went on the alert, no man leaving his house without a gun. Each settlement had several garrison houses where the populace would assemble for protection, often staying for weeks at a time while under siege.[33]

A combined colonial force was organized to prevent the powerful Narragansett Indians of Rhode Island from joining the other New England tribes. The army met the Indians near

---

suffering continual degradation and loss of territory. King Philip's War, from 1675 to 1676, represented the final attempt of the Indians to retain their hold in Southern New England; they lost decisively. Philip's army had some 3,000 warriors, about 2,500 of whom were either killed or sold into slavery. Because about that many more women and children were killed, nearly one-fourth of the Indian population of New England was destroyed in the war.

32   Easton, 10.

33   The American soldiers also took scalps, and were sometimes paid bounties for them by the government. The bounty was equivalent to several thousand dollars today. In major encounters, the Americans indiscriminately killed old men, women, and children. In reporting the interrogation of an Indian woman, Captain Samuel Mosely added, "The aforesaid Indian was ordered to be torn to pieces by dogs, and she was dealt with all." Captive Indians who were not hanged were sold into miserable slavery in the West Indies. Unable to cope as slaves, many of them were killed trying to escape.

Kingston, Rhode Island in December 1675. In what came to be known as the Great Swamp Fight, the Indians' fort was demolished. The Narragansetts fled northward and, joining with other Indians, attacked settlements throughout New England. Of the ninety settlements in New England, fifty-two were attacked and thirteen completely destroyed. The white population was decimated; literally one man out of every ten was killed by the Indians, and like numbers of women and children. In proportion to the population, King Philip's War was the bloodiest war in American history.

The fighting came within twenty miles of Boston. Cotton heard his father's many prayers to God for victory, and believed them efficacious. Increase set apart a special day to beseech God to kill the Indian leader, King Philip, by a stroke of providence. In less than a week the deed was accomplished. On August 12, 1676 King Philip was shot. "This Agag was now cut into quarters, which were then hanged up, while his head was carried in triumph to Plymouth, where it arrived on the very day that the church there was keeping a solemn thanksgiving to God. God sent them the head of a *leviathan* for a *thanksgiving-feast*," wrote Cotton Mather.[34] King Philip, like his father Massasoit before him, provided the Pilgrims with a reason for a thanksgiving celebration, his head instead of corn.

Despite their defeat in King Philip's War, the Indians continued to fight the white man, mostly with guerrilla tactics, in northern New England for nearly another one hundred years.

At age thirteen, Cotton saw the fulfillment of another of his father's prophecies, that Boston would be punished by a judgment of fire. On the morning of November 27, 1676 his family's house burned down along with forty-five others and the Old North Church. After the fire the Mathers lived temporarily with John Richards, a prominent member of the Second Church (Old North

---

34   In its so-called mercy, the General Court shipped King Philip's nine-year-old son to Bermuda where he was sold as a slave. This was done against the advice of some ministers who advocated death.

Church).[35] (John Richards was one of the witchcraft justices in 1692.)

Cotton Mather graduated from Harvard in 1678 at age fifteen. Still suffering from a speech impediment, he at first believed himself unfit for the ministry and studied medicine. In the seventeenth century, medical practitioners were divided into physicians and surgeons. The surgeons were usually barbers. They performed amputations and phlebotomy (the drawing of blood), as well as extracting teeth. Their sign is used by barbers to this day, a red pole wound with a narrow white bandage.

Physicians of that day had little knowledge of the body or mind. Their training was in certain customary remedies. They had no understanding of the reason behind administering such remedies, nor of what quantities should be used. Among the herbs employed were crude tobacco leaves, fivefinger, brambles, strawberry roots, powdered sumac, powdered elecampane roots, wormwood, wild carrot seeds, sweet fennel seeds, raisins, maiden hair, liverwort, elder buds, knotgrass, shepherd's pouch, pollipod, borrage, buglose root, rosemary, primrose, cowslips, violets, and peony seeds. Other common ingredients were red lead, lead ore, wax, oven-dried horses' livers, and the fillings of a dead man's skull. The most revolting substances, best left unmentioned, comprised many of the remedies. Physicians freely prescribed the medicines, whether or not they knew the physiological effects on the patient.

The following cure for a distracted woman is a specimen of the remedies used in that period. "Take milk of a nurse that gives suck to a male child. Also take a he cat and cut off one of his ears or a piece of it. Let it bleed into the milk and then let the sick woman drink it. Do this three times."

On August 22, 1680 Cotton Mather was invited to preach a sermon at the Dorchester church, and six months later he was made assistant in his father's church, the rebuilt Second Church (Old North Church). Five years later, he was ordained the

---

35 John Richards had become a magistrate, an assistant to the governor, in 1680.

assistant minister in the church. Apparently there were no more thoughts about violets, horses' livers, and other physic (the old word for medicine).

The Puritans clergy portrayed vivid pictures of the supernatural. They preached that any variation from the known routine of nature, however small or great, was a divine sign. Comets, for example, were supernatural manifestations set in the sky to mark some special event, such as famine, war, or pestilence. "A great and blazing comet" preceded the wheat blight of 1665 in Massachusetts. The comet of 1680 gave Increase Mather inspiration for a sermon entitled "Heaven's Alarm to the World." When John Cotton died, a comet appeared in the heavens as testimony "that God had removed a bright star, a burning and a shining light out of the Heaven of his church here."

In 1681 a group of eminent New England clergymen, after long discussions about the dangers to religion from the growth of rationalism, decided to combat the unwelcome trend with proofs of the supernatural. They set themselves the task of gathering and publishing every instance they could find of "divine judgments, tempests, floods, earthquakes, thunders as are unusual, strange apparitions, or whatever else shall happen that is prodigious, witchcrafts, diabolical possessions, remarkable judgments on noted sinners, eminent deliverances, and answers to prayer."[36]

In 1684 Increase Mather completed his part of the project and published it under the title *An Essay for the Recording of Illustrious Providences.*[37] In his book he relates how certain holy men were preserved at sea, when all others on the ship were lost. He regarded meteorites as missiles hurled from Heaven. He assigned to the sphere of the supernatural every manifestation of nature which could not be explained. He writes, "There is also that which is very mysterious and beyond human capacity to comprehend, in thunder and lightning." He calls lightning

---

36   From the preface of Increase Mather, *Providences.*
37   The running title was *Remarkable Providences.*

"Heaven's arrow" and gives numerous instances in which men were smitten with the fire of God. Not until the next century would his countryman Benjamin Franklin give the scientific explanation of lightning.

On the dark side, Increase Mather promulgated the belief that the world was governed by magic and witchcraft. To him, any ill happenings were caused by the powers of the air, the Devil. A thunderstorm was the work of malignant spirits; persons in league with the Devil sank ships, ruined crops, and caused death and sickness.

In his book, Increase Mather includes essays on: "A remarkable relation about Ann Cole of Hartford." "Several witches of the colony." "Of the possessed maid at Groton." "An account of the house at Newbury lately troubled with a demon." "And of one in Portsmouth lately disquieted by evil spirits." "A woman at Berwick molested with apparitions, and sometimes tormented by invisible agents."

The essay on Anne Cole says that in the year 1662 she "was taken with very strange fits, wherein her tongue was improved by a demon." Various measures were tried, but "after the suspected witches were either executed or fled, Ann Cole was restored to health."

Increase Mather's account of the possessed maid at Groton is fundamental to any study of New England witchcraft. The event took place in 1671; the girl was Elizabeth Knapp, age sixteen. Mather's essay says, "Elizabeth Knapp was taken after a very strange manner, with violent agitations of her body. A demon began manifestly to speak in her. The things uttered by the Devil were chiefly railings and revilings of Mr. [Samuel] Willard, pastor to the church in Groton. She cried out in her fits that [the specter of] a woman, one of her neighbors, appeared to her, and was the cause of her affliction. The person thus accused did visit the poor wretch, and prayed earnestly with and for the possessed creature, after which she confessed that Satan had deluded her, making her believe evil of her good neighbor without any cause.

Nor did she after that complain of any apparition from such an one."[38]

The essay on the house at Newbury says that on December 8, 1679, "there were five great stones thrown in while the man's wife was making the bed, the bedstead was lifted up from the floor, and a cat was hurled at her, a long staff danced up and down in the chimney." Such things went on for months, but "all the while the Devil did not appear in any visible shape." In their attempts to catch the Devil, sometimes "they would think they had hold of the hand that scratched them, but it would give them the slip."

His work was an immediate success, widely read in front of the fireplace, at work in the fields, over mugs in the tavern. People started to speak with awe of the magicians, witches, and imps which this eminent author held before them. At one extreme, some historians say that this book planted the seed which sprouted into the rankest harvest of witchcraft in the history of New England.[39] At the opposite extreme, other historians lament that its significance as one of the first

---

38   In 1671, through prayer and understanding, the Rev. Willard convinced Elizabeth Knapp that her affliction was not due to the witchcraft of her neighbor. This realization not only made her well, but made her love her neighbor. In 1692, the Rev. Willard's approach, however, was decisively rejected by the authorities; they chose to take every accusation, however absurd, of the sanctioned afflicted girls as gospel. The Rev. Willard was an opponent of the Salem witch hunt. In a letter of October 8, 1692 his friend Thomas Brattle wrote, "I cannot but admire that these [sanctioned] afflicted persons should be so much countenanced and encouraged in their accusations. I often think of the Groton woman [Elizabeth Knapp] that was afflicted. There was as much ground to countenance the Groton woman, and imprison on her accusations, as there is now to countenance these afflicted persons, and to imprison on their accusations. It is worthy of our deepest consideration, that in the conclusion, after multitudes have been imprisoned, and many have been put to death, these afflicted persons should admit that all was a mere fancy, as the Groton woman did."

39   Wertenbaker, 269.

scientific writings in America is, for the most part, neglected.[40] Increase Mather describes one notable "experiment" that was used on "suspected persons." Its purpose was to determine "whether the stories of witches not being able to sink under water were true. Accordingly a man and woman had their hands and feet tied, and so were cast into the water, and they both apparently swam after the manner of a buoy, part under, part above the water. Whether this experiment were lawful, or rather superstitious and magical, we shall συν θεω inquire afterward."[41]

The son of Increase Mather now deserves attention. Of all the Puritans, Cotton Mather is most often singled out as the epitome of their way of life. His lifetime, from 1663 to 1728, represents that period midway between the arrival of the first American settlers and the American Revolution. The object of meager praise and violent blame, Cotton Mather has not fared well in history. His few defenders have concentrated on his religious forms and literary abilities rather than his personality. Most historians hasten to disclaim any favorable interest in him, and have been almost eager to defame him. Yet he remains the best known of the American Puritans.[42]

Modern readers know Cotton Mather most intimately through his profuse writings. In his diary he bared his soul,

---

40 Murdock, *Increase Mather*, 167.

41 The Greek words συν θεω mean "with God," i.e., God willing. Unfortunately for Increase Mather, but fortunately for them, "the suspected persons took flight, not having been seen in that part of the world since."

42 Cotton Mather understood Hebrew, Greek, Latin, Spanish, and Iroquois, and wrote in them all. From his diary, it appears that in one year he kept sixty fasts, and twenty vigils, and published fourteen books, besides discharging the duties of his pastoral office. His publications amount in number to 382. His style abounds with puns and strange conceits, and he makes a great display of learning. So precious did he consider his time that, to prevent long visits, he placed the admonition "BE SHORT" over his study door.

undertaking to set down how God dealt with him. By putting his thoughts, acts, and spiritual experiences into words, he hoped to unravel the mystery of his fate. His diary became a testimonial to his unremitting quest for personal holiness. Of all of New England's Puritan writers, Cotton Mather appears as the most morbidly introspective. His visions gave rise to intolerable tensions for which he sought relief. The traumatic experience of looking into the pit of Hell, which was the favorite Puritan vista, seemed almost to turn his mind into a chamber of horrors.

Cotton Mather was a man tortured by his Puritanical fears and fantasies. He felt that the cosmos revolved around himself. The theme of his diary is a titanic struggle for his soul between God and Satan. God was fighting so that Cotton Mather could further His work on earth, whereas Satan was fighting to prevent it. The Deity's chief concern in the universe was Cotton Mather, his doings, the state of his soul, and his personal welfare. Repeatedly, Cotton Mather's diary affirms that God wished him well, that mercies for him were being stored up in Heaven pending his arrival, and that everything he did had Heaven's wholehearted approval.

Cotton Mather not only walked with God, but also, on occasion, talked with God. His diary was an expression of his duty to keep a record, for the benefit of posterity, of his "sweet conversation" and "extraordinary intimate communion" with God. In one entry, God told him, "Go into your great chamber and I will speak with you." Doing as directed, he had the gratification of receiving "unutterable communications from the Holy Ghost." In a 1705 entry, on a truly memorable day, he "conversed with each of the three Persons in the Eternal Godhead." Yet curiously, in all the revelations given to Cotton Mather, none offered anything new. No one who was granted the astonishing privilege of looking into Heaven and Hell emerged with a more stereotypical description of those places.

Cotton Mather's war with the Powers of Darkness took the form of an all-out effort to preserve and strengthen the old ways of his ideal Puritanism against what he saw as the corroding effects of worldliness and mercantile prosperity. When he wrestled with the Devil, he complained that a "carnal, giddy, rising generation" cheered loudly whenever Satan seemed on the point of pinning him down. Through his books and sermons he hoped to make people "serious and powerful, and afraid of sin."

The Puritan preachers in New England developed a type of sermon known as a *jeremiad*, with a recognizable literary style. The name comes from the Old Testament Book of Jeremiah; a typical verse is 9:4, "Take ye heed everyone of his neighbor, And trust ye not in any brother." The preachers claimed the "tyranny" of Andros was a punishment for the people's breach of the religious covenant. To sustain their appeal, the clergy needed a succession of evils. But the usual troubles, such as Indian wars, party squabbles, decay of trade, and smallpox, had begun to lose their effect.

The jeremiad labored under the continual need to pile up horrible tales of woe resulting from sin. Cotton Mather, the most expert of its practitioners, was driven to uncover fresh material. In 1689 he preached about the weakened position of European Protestants, and called upon New England to assist them through prayer and by renouncing sin.

Searching for more and more effective means to lash the conscience of New England, Cotton Mather seized on a fear lying ripe for exploitation, witchcraft. Witchcraft was an internal threat of the most insidious sort; a witch could be your neighbor, even your brother or sister, husband or wife. Cotton Mather started preaching, "Satan is marshaling his forces for a final decision." In sermon and pamphlet, he warned that the Prince of Darkness was preparing to exterminate New England. The Devil would return the country to his own children, the Indians, he said. The whole colony began to listen.

So that no one should miss the point, Cotton Mather constantly enlarged upon the sinister threats of witchcraft during the three years (1689-1692) of the existence of the provisional government. He preached that all our sins have been "at least implicit witchcrafts." Cotton Mather feared that New England would become possessed with the Devil. Through his popular writings Cotton Mather had directly influenced the general public. The ruling Board of Assistants, dominated by the old guard, gladly supported his point of view.

His close friend on the Board was Samuel Sewall. Samuel Sewall's father had settled in New England earlier, but had then returned to England, where Samuel was born in 1652. With the Restoration, the whole family fled to New England in 1661. Samuel Sewall graduated from Harvard College in 1671. He became a magistrate, an assistant to the governor, in 1684. In 1692 he was living in Boston, where he had gained a reputation for fairness. Samuel Sewall admired Cotton Mather and often went to hear his sermons. Frequently they dined together and they carried on an active correspondence. (Samuel Sewall was one of the justices in the witchcraft trials of 1692.)

In 1688 in England, Sir Isaac Newton wrote *Principia Matematica*, in which he gave the "System of the World." His book has governed the scientific understanding of the visible universe ever since. In the same year in New England, Cotton Mather wrote *Memorable Providences Relating to Witchcraft and Possessions*. This book, published the next year, was Cotton Mather's first attempt to give a scientific account of the invisible world of the Devil. The book is based on his first-hand observation; he uses as data the experiences of the Goodwin children in the summer and fall of 1688. In Latin, he wrote, "Haec ipse miserrima vidi," or "these things these wretched eyes beheld."

The family of Boston mason John Goodwin was well regarded, and his children had been religiously educated. The eldest, Martha Goodwin, thirteen years old, was a plain girl with long, straight black hair. A pretty young Irish woman with a fair complexion worked as laundress for the Goodwin family. Martha, taking a dislike to her, accused her of stealing some of the family linen. The young woman's mother, Mary Glover, better known as Goody Glover or the Widow Glover, came to her daughter's defense.[43]   Goody Glover spoke harshly, perhaps profanely, to Martha.   After the encounter, Martha fell into an agitated state, described by Cotton Mather as "odd fits that carried in them something diabolical."   One of her sisters and two of her brothers, following her example, also fell into fits.

Cotton Mather learned of this episode soon after his father left for England in May 1688.   He visited the children, and became the most active and forward of any minister in the Goodwin case.   When it appeared, his book *Memorable Providences* gave the case credibility.   Few learned persons expressed any doubt about the "facts" presented in the book, readily accepting the preternatural agency of witchcraft as the cause of the children's afflictions.   Mr. Richard Baxter, an eminent English cleric, in a preface to an edition published in London in 1691, says, "The evidence is so convincing that he must be a very obdurate Sadducee who will not believe."[44]

In the spirit of the times, Cotton Mather wrote his book in the guise of a scientific report.   He describes the "afflictions" of the children as follows.   "Sometimes they were deaf, sometimes dumb, sometimes blind, and often all this at once.   Their tongues would be drawn down their throats, and then pulled out upon their chins to a prodigious length.   Their mouths were forced open to such a wideness that their jaws went out of joint, and anon clap together again, with a force like that of a spring-lock, and the like would happen to their shoulder blades and their elbows, and hand wrists, and several of their joints.   They would lie in a benumbed

---

43   The titles *Mr.* and *Mrs.* were reserved for men and woman of rank, with *Mrs.* used for either married or single women as the title *Miss* did not exist at that time.   The common titles for a married man and woman were *Goodman* and *Goodwife*.   *Goody* was used as a familiar form of the title *Goodwife*.

44   Cotton Mather (*Discourse*, 99) wrote, "Since there are Witches, we are to suppose that there are Devils too.   It was the heresy of the ancient *Sadducees* in Act. 23:8. *The Sadducees do say, That there is neither Angel nor Spirit.*   And there are multitudes of Sadducees yet in our day; fools that say, *Seeing is believing;* and will believe nothing but what they see."

condition and be drawn together like those who are tied neck and heels, and presently be stretched out, yea, drawn backwards to such an extent that it was feared the very skin of their bellies would have cracked. They would make most piteous outcries that they were cut with knives, and struck with blows that they could not bear." All their afflictions were during the day; they slept comfortably at night.

The Puritan ministers of Boston and Charlestown kept a day of fasting and prayer at the troubled house. Afterwards the youngest child had no more fits. Had not magistrate William Stoughton interposed, the matter might have ended there. Goody Glover, described by Cotton Mather as "a scandalous Irish woman," was arrested, brought to trial, and sentenced to death for witchcraft. Most scandalous of all, the underlying reason for her condemnation was that she was a Roman Catholic. Gallows were erected on Boston Common.

On the day of the hanging, November 16, 1688, the Goodwin children were present in the front row. Cotton Mather, his Bible in hand, said prayers for them, making frequent references to God and Christ. Goody Glover was brought forth. Because of the heavy chain on her legs, the gait of the witch on the way to her execution was difficult and stumbling. The hangman, eager to do his office, tightened the chain clapped about her body as he pulled her along, inflicting excruciating pain. Cotton Mather whispered to Martha that the witch was being pulled to the fire of Hell. The noose of the stiff rope was put around Goody Glover's neck. As she died, she was choked until she was black in the face. When she was cut down, Martha could see the gashing red marks left on her neck.

Goody Glover had declared that the afflicted children would not be relieved by her death because others had a hand in their affliction. According to Cotton Mather, "the three children continued in their furnace as before, and it grew rather seven times hotter than it was." Cotton Mather took Martha Goodwin as a guest into his household. He wrote, "I took her home chiefly that I might be a critical eye-witness of things that would enable me to confute the sadducism of this debauched age." For a few days she behaved normally, but on November 20, 1688 she cried, "Ah, they have found me out," and immediately fell into her fits.

Martha complained that Glover's chain was upon her leg, and, trying to walk, her gait exactly matched that of the chained witch before she died. An invisible chain would be clapped about Martha's body, and she cried out in pain and fear as the specters tightened it around her. Rushing to her aid, Cotton Mather valiantly tried to knock the invisible chain off her as it began to be fastened. He writes, "But ordinarily, when it was on, she would be pulled off her seat with such violence towards the fire, that it was as much as one or two of us could do to keep her out. And if we stamped on the hearth, just between her and the fire, she screamed out, 'That by jarring the chain, we hurt her.' I may add that the specters put an unseen rope, with a cruel noose, about her neck, whereby she was choked until she was black in the face; and though it was got off before it had killed her, yet there were the red marks of it, and of a finger and thumb near it, remaining to be seen for some while afterwards."

He gave her his Bible, the one he had taken to Boston Common, to read some scriptures, but "she said that she sooner die than read them." Yet she had read the same scriptures in the Anglican *Book of Common Prayer*.[45] She could read whole pages of a Roman Catholic book, but always skipped over the names of God and Christ. What more proof of witchcraft could there be?

Combining agility of body and quickness of mind, children are capable of extraordinary behavior. Were the "afflictions" of the Goodwin children the manifestations of witchcraft, or were they fraud, pure and simple? Cotton Mather considered this question. In the scientific spirit of the times, he decided to carry out some experiments. One experiment involved his upstairs study. He knew that the Devil would not dare enter his study, a

---

45   *The Book of Common Prayer* was authorized by the Church of England, and banned by the Puritans. The Church of England is also known as the Anglican church. After the American Revolution, the American branch was named the Episcopal church.

place of God. He had observed that whenever Martha was brought up to his study, she became well. When her fits came upon her downstairs, only with extreme difficulty could she be dragged upstairs. He wrote, "The demons would pull her out of the people's hands, and make her heavier than perhaps three of herself. With incredible toil (though she kept screaming, 'They say I must not go in!') she was pulled in. She then could stand on her feet, and, with an altered note, say 'I am well.' To satisfy some strangers, the experiment was repeated divers times, with the same success."

After Cotton Mather finished his book, the Goodwin children became well and lived normal lives. One might conclude that his account serves as evidence of his own inattention and strong prejudice. But three centuries later, can such a simple judgment be made? Cotton Mather concluded that his experiments showed that the afflictions of the Goodwin children could only be explained by witchcraft. In the Puritan teaching, supernatural intervention was made to appear as a commonplace event. Behind the witchcraft accusation against Goody Glover lay an element of superstition, even terror. To the Puritan clergy of seventeenth-century America, the Devil was every bit as real as God.

Read by thousands of people in both New England and England, Cotton Mather's book met with much acclaim. Together with his numerous sermons and pamphlets, this book represented a major effort to instill in the minds of the people a belief in the reality of witchcraft and a fear of witches. Although witchcraft was an element in the general belief of the times, it took his aggressive and inflammatory arguments to persuade key authorities that witchcraft was the major enemy of New England. With unbounded faith in his own power, Cotton Mather saw himself as divinely appointed to lead in the salvation of New England by driving out the Devil.

To Cotton Mather, New England was a former realm of the Devil, and the Indians inhabitants were Satanic agents. In this fair land, God had enabled the visible saints to gain a foothold, but now the Devil had opened a counter-attack. The present Indian war was only the outward manifestation of the assault;

there were also witches who would tear down New England from within. As the young and vigorous acting pastor of the Second Church (Old North Church) in Boston, Cotton Mather skillfully and cunningly had laid the groundwork for the witchcraft delusion which erupted in February 1692.

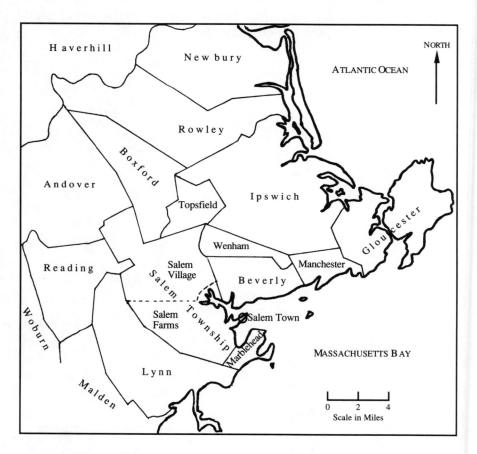

Map 4. Salem Village and surrounding towns in 1692.

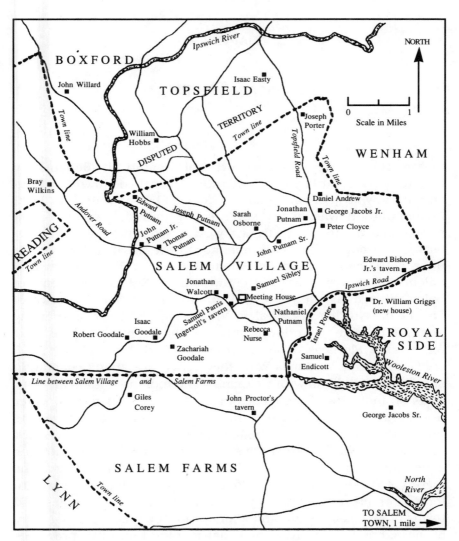

Map 5. Salem Village showing roads and some houses. The disputed territory was in the part of Topsfield south of the Ipswich River and north of the indicated town line with Salem Village

CHAPTER 4

THOMAS PUTNAM

Salem Town, fifteen miles north of Boston, is delightfully situated on a great bay of the Atlantic Ocean. The town itself lies on a narrow strip of land, almost encircled by sea water. In 1692 its population was about seventeen hundred. A vast forest stretched away to the north and west, broken here and there by farms. A group of farms five mile northwest of Salem Town made up a settlement known as Salem Village.[46] Salem Town and Salem Village were parts of the township of Salem. Northeast of Salem Village lay the town of Wenham. North was the town of Topsfield. Northwest of Salem Village was Andover, a sparsely populated town. Andover was on the frontier of the vast American wilderness. The Indians controlled this wilderness.

During King William's War, the French in Canada constantly supplied the Indians with weapons. The Indians would carry out raids on individual farmhouses in the frontier settlements. After first killing or taking captive the occupants, they plundered the house, then burned it and the barns with their contents, livestock included. With their captives they would fall back into the sanctuary of the deep forests. The settlers were completely at the mercy of these hostile incursions, which they had no power to foresee or prevent. The continual harrying of the villages and towns of New Hampshire and Maine, with the ever recurring story of massacre and captivity, was fast turning these two provinces back into wilderness, which is what the Indians wanted. Every attempt to reach and destroy the Indians proved worse than

---

46   Salem Village is now the town of Danvers, Massachusetts.

futile. New England was losing ten lives for each Indian killed. By the end of 1690, most of New Hampshire and Maine had been depopulated, and an increasing number of Indian raids were leaving their mark in Massachusetts.

A seventeenth-century family reached far beyond a nuclear family of parents and children; recognized kinship extended into a network of direct and indirect relationships. Although each family included a multitude of relatives, the obligations to minor relationships were felt only slightly less than those to immediate ones. A brother-in-law would be called "brother" and treated as such. A spouse's parents would be addressed as one's own parents. People connected only by remote ties of marriage were included as if they were blood relations. The extended family was the fundamental unit in the structure of New England society.

The death of a spouse and the remarriage of the remaining partner further increased the web of relationships. The surviving partner gained a whole new set of relations by the new marriage. Yet the partner did not lose the relations of the spouse who died. The surviving partner still addressed the first spouse's kin as his own, and still treated them with the same deference. Such extensive family ties held the fabric of society together.

With few exceptions, divorces did not take place. Spouses, however, often died young. From time to time smallpox and other epidemics occurred. Women died in childbirth and men died in battle and accidents. The greatest toll came from the Indian wars.

With life so tenuous, second and third marriages were common, and many orphaned children had to be placed. The repeat marriages, in theory, could create a bewildering series of relationships. In practice, this usually was not the case because people picked partners from their own restricted social class. Often a widowed person married a brother, sister, or cousin of the deceased partner. Orphans were usually placed with relatives.

The well-defined class system tended to keep specific extended families together as groups with cohesive bonds, while separate from extended families of other classes. The membership of an extended family could cross town borders, but still remain distinct from other extended family groups. An understanding of Salem witchcraft may be gained by looking at individuals not as separate units, but as part of an extended family. In so doing, many disparate individuals become joined together and consistent patterns appear. This approach often provides the key to why certain people were accused of witchcraft.

A valuable clue, of course, is the maiden name as well as previous married names of a woman. In this book names are exhibited in a chronological sequence. For example, Sarah Good's full name is Sarah (Solart) Poole Good, which shows that her maiden name was *Solart*, that her previous married name was *Poole*, and that her current married name is *Good*. The maiden name is always in parentheses. If the maiden name is unknown, the notation (mnu) is used.

In 1692 the people involved knew that certain families were being attacked in the witch hunt. During the three hundred years since that time, much of this interpersonal knowledge has been lost. Court records, as well as most of the other documents that have been preserved, treat each individual as a separate legal entity, thereby concealing underlying family structures. For this reason, historical accounts of Salem witchcraft largely have dealt with events in a chronological sequence. These studies can be usefully augmented by an examination of the cross section of family structures. When integrated, the chronological and the cross-sectional approaches help clarify many of the complex inter-relationships which fueled the witch hunt.

In the years following 1660, Salem Town entered an era of economic expansion as mercantile and trading ventures grew. The rising prosperity did not benefit all segments of the population equally. The wealth was centered; the merchants were clearly dominant.

Salem Village was not an independent town, but came under the jurisdiction of the township of Salem. By 1690 only some farmers in Salem Village, those with close merchant ties, continued to exercise any sustained influence in town politics. Many of the village farmers resented the political authority of the strong mercantile group in Salem Town. To the farmers, this domination made their difficulties more acute than anything experienced by farmers in neighboring towns independent of Salem.

The early settlers who arrived in the great Puritan migration to New England in the 1630s and 1640s had found ample land. European diseases had wiped out the local Indians. The settlers took possession of the soil; they had large families, and many of their children lived to adulthood. But, unlike the rich soil in England, New England farmland was poor. Good farmland in New England became scarcer much more rapidly than would be expected, in view of the total land area available. The western and northern expansion of New England was limited by the presence of hostile Indians. Finding adequate farmland for second-generation children was a major concern. With the arrival of more and more immigrants, the paucity of land became a serious problem.

The borders of Salem Village were not well defined in the early land grants. As a result, some of the villagers engaged in sharp boundary disputes with the neighboring towns of Wenham, Topsfield, and Andover in the late 1670s and the 1680s.

For example, as early as 1639, the General Court granted land on the Ipswich River to the township of Salem. This land formed the northern part of the original bounds for Salem Village. However, four years later the Court granted the same land to Ipswich. When Ipswich was divided to create the town of Topsfield, the greater part of the land in question was included in the new town's limits. No heed was paid to the Salem Village farmers who found themselves, without their consent, permanently bereft of the benefits that had been promised them. Tensions grew, and the farmers of Salem Village in October 1686 empowered a committee to defend their claims against the claims of Topsfield.

Typical of the prevalent animosities was the one between the Putnam family of Salem Village and the Towne, Howe, Easty, Hobbs, and Wildes families of Topsfield. John Putnam, Sr. had settled on land in the disputed territory between Salem Village and Topsfield.   One day Jacob Towne and John Howe came in defiance of John Putnam, Sr. and cut down a tree in front of his face.   As there were two against one, Putnam had to swallow the insult.   Shortly thereafter, John Putnam, Sr. returned with an adequate force of sons and nephews and they proceeded to fell some trees.   The sound of the axes reached the ears of the Topsfield men, and Isaac Easty, Sr. and his son John Easty, and John Towne and his son Joseph Towne, Jr. undertook to stop to them.   When Putnam was warned against cutting the timber, he said contemptuously, "I will keep cutting and carrying away." The Topsfield men asked him, "What, by violence?"   Putnam answered, "Aye, by violence."   Outnumbered, the Topsfield men withdrew.   Such scenes were repeated on the disputed ground for a whole generation, right up to 1692.

(These Topsfield men would feel the sting of witchcraft accusations in 1692.   Jacob Towne and John Towne were brothers; two of their three sisters, Rebecca (Towne) Nurse and Mary (Towne) Easty were hanged, and the third sister, Sarah (Towne) Cloyce, was imprisoned, for witchcraft.   The hanged Mary (Towne) Easty was the wife of Isaac Easty, Sr.   John Howe's sister-in-law, Elizabeth (Jackson) Howe, was also hanged for witchcraft in that year.)

Because of conflicting pressures the people of Salem Village grew apart, gradually dividing in two opposing factions.   One faction benefitted from its mercantile connections with Salem Town.   These people tended to live on the east side of Salem Village, the section adjacent to the town.   This faction was led by the Porter family.   In 1692 the leader of the Porter family was Israel Porter, age forty-eight.

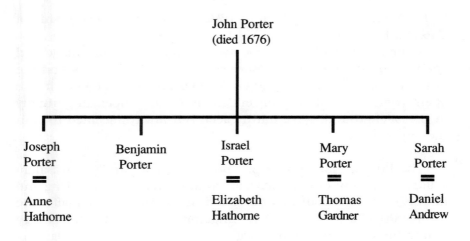

In New England each township was governed by a group of elected *selectmen*. Their term lasted for only one year, so each year an election was held. A large township such as Salem had five or six selectmen. Most would come from Salem Town, but one, or sometimes two, would come from Salem Village. Israel Porter was elected nine times as a selectman in the thirteen years, 1680 to 1692. Three of the four years when he was not a selectman, one or both of his brothers-in-law, Daniel Andrew or Thomas Gardner, were elected to that office. Because the selectmen ran Salem Village as well as Salem Town, the Porters were the most powerful family in Salem Village.

The other faction in Salem Village did not identify with Salem Town. These people mostly lived on the more remote, western side. They were exclusively farmers and they favored the old ways of Puritanism. Except in a couple of cases, no one from this group was ever elected as selectman of Salem Town. Because they had no political power in Salem Town, they worked for the independence of Salem Village. Once free of Salem Town, they hoped to gain more control of their own lives. They had been the driving force to found the Salem Village church in order to be free of the one in Salem Town. This faction in Salem Village was led by the Putnam family, which in 1692 was under the leadership of Thomas Putnam.

From about 1680 on, these two factions in Salem Village had been in continual conflict. More specifically, the Porters and the Putnams were at constant odds. The Putnams worked out in the open, trying to achieve their ends; the Porters, operating quietly in the background, were hardly seen but always seemed to gain the upper hand.

The Putnam family was one of the original families in Salem Village. The founding father was John Putnam, born in England in 1580. When about fifty years old, he sailed with his wife, the former Priscilla Gould, to New England. A man of great energy and industry, he acquired a large estate. He died in 1662, leaving three sons, Thomas Putnam, born in 1615, Nathaniel Putnam, in 1619, and John Putnam, in 1625. In regard to this family, this book does not refer to the original John, but to his sons as its three heads.

Thomas Putnam, the eldest, (designated as patriarch Thomas Putnam), inherited a double share of his father's lands. Patriarch Thomas Putnam had received a good education. He was the first clerk of Salem Village, and prominent in military, ecclesiastical, and municipal affairs. He attained the rank of lieutenant in the militia, and was a constable. In the seventeenth century the office of constable represented a distinguished elected position, carrying with it high authority, covering the whole executive branch of local government. Patriarch Thomas Putnam died in 1686, age seventy.

Nathaniel Putnam married Elizabeth, daughter of Richard Hutchinson.[47] Nathaniel was a deputy in the Massachusetts legislature, and was constantly involved with the interests of the community. He had great business ability, possessing energy and

---

47 Nathaniel Putnam died July 23, 1700, leaving a large family and a substantial estate. Calvin Coolidge, the thirtieth president of the United States, was a direct descendant of Nathaniel Putnam.

management skill. His wife died in 1688, leaving him a widower at the time of the witchcraft epidemic.

John Putnam (designated John Putnam, Sr.) was as energetic as his brother Nathaniel. He married Rebecca Prince, stepdaughter of John Gedney, Sr. John was often elected a deputy in the legislature, and accumulated a large amount of land. He attained the rank of captain in the militia.[48]

By 1692 patriarch Thomas Putnam was dead; his two brothers were alive. Nathaniel Putnam was seventy-three, and John Putnam, Sr. was sixty-three. Although these two brothers were still active, the real energy of the Putnam family lay in the younger generation.

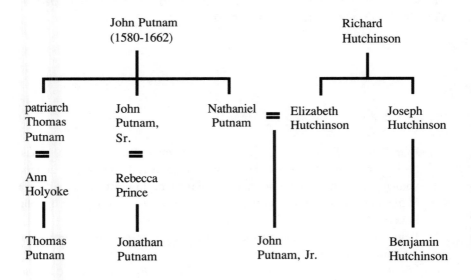

John Putnam, Sr.'s eldest son, Jonathan Putnam, was serving as one of the two constables in Salem Village in 1692. Nathaniel Putnam's son John Putnam, Jr. was the other constable in 1692,

---

48   Captain John Putnam, Sr. died in 1710.

so the Putnam family at least held the local administration of Salem Village under its control.[49]

Nathaniel Putnam's wife, Elizabeth, had a brother, Joseph Hutchinson. Joseph's youngest son, Benjamin Hutchinson,[50] was raised by Nathaniel Ingersoll, the Salem Village innkeeper.

Patriarch Thomas Putnam (1615-1686) married Ann Holyoke, daughter of Edward Holyoke, in 1643, when he was twenty-eight. They had eight children between 1645 and 1662. Only two were boys, Thomas Putnam (born 1653) and Edward Putnam (born 1654).[51] In 1692 Thomas Putnam, age thirty-nine, was a sergeant in the militia and the clerk of the parish. He was the leader of the Putnam family. Edward Putnam, age thirty-eight in 1692, was deacon of the church.[52]

---

49   John Putnam, Jr. was not the son of John Putnam, Sr. In colonial times, if two people had the same name, then the older was designated *Sr.* and the younger, *Jr.* The two did not have to be related. In most cases they were father and son, but in this case John Putnam, Jr. was the nephew of John Putnam, Sr.

50   Benjamin Hutchinson and his father, Joseph Hutchinson, were members of the fringe group of the conspiracy.

51   We always refer to the father as *patriarch Thomas Putnam* (because he was dead by the time of our story, 1692), and the son as simply *Thomas Putnam*.

52   Edward Putnam was deacon for a period of forty years, finally resigning as a result of advancing age. In 1733, as he was entering on his eightieth year, he gave this account of his family. "From the three brothers proceeded twelve males. From these twelve males, forty males, and from these forty males, eighty-two males. There were none of the name of Putnam in New England but those from this family."

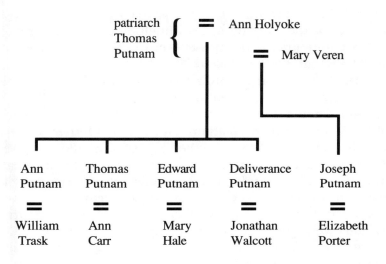

In 1665 patriarch Thomas Putnam lost his wife, Ann. As a rich widower, he married Mary Veren the next year. The widow of a successful Salem ship captain, Mary was part of the social group of wealthy Salem merchants, and she did not identify in any way with the simple farmers of Salem Village who were the friends and backers of her new husband. In 1669, when he was fifty-four, the patriarch Thomas Putnam had a boy by Mary, his third son and their only child. This boy, Joseph Putnam, would turn out to be the bane of his two older half-brothers, especially the eldest, Thomas.

In 1678, at the age of twenty-five, Thomas Putnam married Ann Carr, daughter of George Carr, one of the richest men in Salisbury. George Carr owned four hundred acres of farm land; he ran a shipworks; and he operated a ferry on the Merrimack River. He died in 1682, four years after Thomas Putnam's marriage to his daughter. At his death, George Carr left an estate worth more than one thousand pounds sterling. Roughly, one pound sterling then was equivalent to one thousand dollars now, so his estate was worth more than one million dollars in today's currency.

The widow and two sons of George Carr firmly held the family enterprises in their control. Thomas Putnam filed a protest in court in 1682. He charged that the widow Carr and her two sons were cheating the Carr daughters (including his wife Ann), and their husbands (including himself), out of their fair share. This protest failed, and failed miserably.

In 1682, ten years before the witch hunt, the patriarch Thomas Putnam was the wealthiest person in Salem Village. His eldest son, Thomas Putnam, looked forward to the time when he would hold this exalted position. However his father broke with established custom. When he died in 1686, he did not give the bulk of his estate to his eldest son. Instead he bequeathed virtually all of his estate to his second wife, Mary, and their young son, Joseph Putnam, then sixteen years old. Thomas Putnam, together with the other children by the first marriage, essentially were cut out. Convinced they had been cheated, they were enraged. Thomas Putnam, his younger full-brother, Edward Putnam, and their brothers-in-law, Jonathan Walcott and William Trask, tried to break the will in court. The four declared that they had been wronged, and the source of the wrong was their hated step-mother, Mary Putnam.[53] Their challenge was soundly defeated. Thus Thomas Putnam had suffered two crushing defeats in his attempt to gain his rightful property. The first defeat had come on his wife's side from his mother-in-law, the widow Carr. The second defeat came on his father's side from his step-mother, the widow Mary Putnam.

The pride of Thomas Putnam suffered a still worse blow in 1687. An unusual clause in his father's will had specified that Joseph Putnam should come into his inheritance at the age of eighteen, rather than at the usual age of twenty-one. On his eighteenth birthday, September 14, 1687, half-brother Joseph Putnam became one of the richest men in Salem Village, his

---

53 After his step-mother, Mary (Veren) Putnam, died in 1695, Thomas Putnam tried to break her will. His case was based on the testimony of a good friend, Dr. William Griggs, the only physician in Salem Village, who declared that she had not been of sound and disposing mind at the time the will was drawn up. Despite this testimony, Thomas Putnam lost the case. (Essex Probate, Docket 23077.)

wealth now substantially greater than that of both his half-brothers, Thomas Putnam and Edward Putnam.   Thomas Putnam's anger was without bounds because, by all rights, it was he, as eldest son, who should have inherited his father's wealth, not Joseph.   His hatred was further aggravated by a provision in the will which appointed Israel Porter as an overseer of the estate. This appointment of the chief Putnam rival as an overseer resulted from the influence of the despised second wife, now widowed, Mary Putnam.   Always close to the Porters, she had completely identified herself and her son, Joseph Putnam, with them and their causes.   She now looked forward to marrying her son into the Porter family.

Joseph Putnam thrived on his meteoric rise to power in Salem Village.   In 1690 he capped his success, at age twenty, by marrying Elizabeth Porter, the sixteen-year-old daughter of Israel Porter.   The Porter family, in the intervening years, had surpassed the Putnam family in both wealth and prestige.   This marriage now further widened the gap.   It brought a substantial amount of the wealth that had belonged to patriarch Thomas Putnam into the control of the Porters.   Joseph Putnam was seen as a turncoat by the Putnam clan.   The whole Putnam family began to despise him, regarding him as a traitor.

Joseph Putnam's social and economic rise was paralleled by an increase in his political power.   The old days when the Putnam family dominated the political life of Salem Village were coming to an end.   True political power was no longer centered in Salem Village, but had shifted to Salem Town.   It was here that the Porter family held sway.   The rise of the Joseph Putnam tipped the scale decisively to Porter dominance.   The Putnam family saw Joseph Putnam as working against their best interests, and placed him firmly on the side of their enemies.

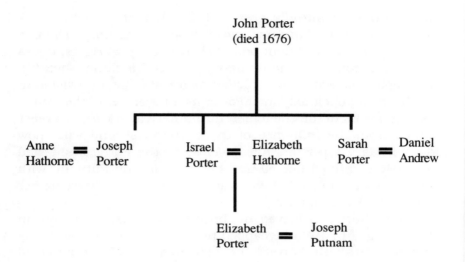

By 1692 Joseph Putnam, only twenty-three, was the wealthiest Putnam by far, and the second richest man in Salem Village. The richest was his uncle-by-marriage Joseph Porter, while the fourth richest was another uncle-by-marriage Daniel Andrew. Joseph Putnam's mother-in-law was Elizabeth (Hathorne) Porter and his aunt-in-law was Anne (Hathorne) Porter. Elizabeth and Anne were the sisters of John Hathorne, magistrate of Salem. Their father, Major William Hathorne, now dead, had willed his extensive land holdings in Salem Village to Elizabeth and Anne. Their brother John Hathorne had been born on this estate. The land which he so valued was now Porter property. John Hathorne had been excluded from his family heritage.

Ten years previously, patriarch Thomas Putnam had been the wealthiest person in Salem Village by a wide margin. Now, in 1692, his successor, eldest son Thomas Putnam, ranked only sixteenth among the one hundred five householders. It rankled Thomas Putnam that he had been cheated out of two fair inheritances, one on his wife's side and the other on his father's side, by two iron-fisted widows. From these two successive breaches of trust, he must have felt deeply humiliated, even dishonored.   In magistrate John Hathorne, Thomas Putnam recognized a potential ally.

The Putnam family was on good terms with magistrates John Hathorne and Jonathan Corwin.   When the General Court convened on May 12, 1686, John Hathorne represented Salem as an assistant to the governor, and John Putnam Sr. as deputy. When the General Court convened on February 3, 1691 Jonathan Corwin represented Salem as an assistant, and John Ruck and Nathaniel Putnam as deputies. At the sitting of the General Court on September 6, 1691, John Hathorne and Jonathan Corwin were present as assistants, and John Putnam Sr. and Manasseh Marston as deputies.

The eldest daughter of Thomas Putnam and his wife, Ann, was also named Ann, born in 1680. In 1692 father Thomas was thirty-nine, wife Ann was thirty-one, and daughter Ann was twelve. Since both mother and daughter were named Ann, we will adopt the custom common to the period and refer to the mother as Ann Putnam, Sr. and her daughter as Ann Putnam, Jr. Daughter Ann was intelligent and well educated. She signed her name in a beautiful hand.   She was precocious, with a quickness of wit equal, as it proved, to almost any emergency.

Throughout New England there were many young people who lost their homes.   Epidemics, accidents, and frontier wars had taken the lives of one or both parents. Life was a bit easier for an orphaned boy because there were always openings for apprentices and manual laborers.   It was more difficult for a girl who was made homeless. Usually she was placed with another family as a servant. It is surprising and significant that, even if the girl was related to her new family, she was still expected to act as a servant. Whether her condition and status would ever change for the better was dubious. Because her father's estate was usually considerably diminished or destroyed, little would remain for her dowry. Few men were interested in a woman without a dowry, so her marriage prospects and her long-term material well-being were especially bleak.

In 1692 a young woman was living with the Thomas Putnam family in Salem Village as a servant. She was Mercy Lewis, an orphan aged seventeen, originally from Casco, Maine. When the Indians killed her parents in 1689 in Casco, the Rev. George Burroughs, the minister in that town, took her into his family. Because of the constant threat of more Indian raids, Mercy was placed in the household of William Bradford in Salem, and finally in the household of Thomas Putnam in Salem Village, as a servant. In a peculiar sense this was a step upward for her, because her own family had been much less well-to-do than the Putnams.

Thomas Putnam's brother-in-law was Jonathan Walcott, whose house stood close to the Salem Village parsonage. A wheelwright by trade, Jonathan had made the wheels for the guns for the fort at Winter Island, near Salem, in 1673. Jonathan Walcott had married, in 1664, his first wife, Mary Sibley, who died in 1683. Jonathan took as his second wife, in 1685, Deliverance Putnam, Thomas Putnam's sister.

Mary Walcott, born in 1675, was Jonathan's daughter by his first marriage.[54] The children of Thomas Putnam often played at the house of their aunt, Deliverance Walcott. In 1692, the precocious Ann Putnam, Jr., although only twelve, spent much time with Mary Walcott, who was seventeen.

The village innkeeper, Nathaniel Ingersoll, a close friend of Thomas Putnam, was the uncle of Jonathan Walcott. Ingersoll's house and tavern also stood close to the Salem Village parsonage. In 1692 Nathaniel Ingersoll was fifty-nine years old. His inn was destined to become the center of activities of the Salem Village witch hunt. An active participant in the witchcraft prosecutions, he always stood ready to provide decisive evidence against the accused.

---

54   Jonathan Walcott's daughter Mary was the fifth of six children by his first wife, Mary. In 1692, he had four children by his second wife, Deliverance, the youngest William being born March 27, 1692.

In 1644, when Nathaniel Ingersoll was only about eleven years old, his father had died. The young orphan went to work on Governor Endicott's Orchard Farm in Salem Village. This farm was regarded as a good school of instruction for boys intending to make agriculture their pursuit in life. Young John Putnam, Sr. was there for the same purpose, and a lifelong friendship developed.

When nineteen, Nathaniel Ingersoll took up residence at his own farm, which he had inherited from his father. Soon after, he married Hannah Collins. Their property lay on the road from Salem to Andover, and by the roadside he built an inn. Its great room served as a tavern, licensed to sell beer and cider. For nearly seventy years, his doors were open for hospitality. Here Increase and Cotton Mather, and all manner of magistrates and ministers, were entertained.

Ingersoll's was the only tavern in the center of Salem Village, and in that endeavor Nathaniel Ingersoll made much money. Like their European cousins, the New England settlers liked to drink, and the selling of spirits was a lucrative business. For this reason the granting of a tavern license became a gauge of status in seventeenth-century New England, reserved for the elite. When village affairs were to be transacted, Ingersoll's inn was usually designated for the meeting. Before Salem Village had a meetinghouse, the people met for worship in his great room. Even after the meetinghouse was built, church-goers still would adjourn to his tavern for a friendly drink and a something to eat.

Nathaniel Ingersoll became both a deacon in the church and a lieutenant in the militia. From the first, he commanded the confidence and respect of men. He often acted as an umpire to settle differences. It was his lot to become involved in innumerable controversies, and to act decisively in some of them.

In a military sense, too, his inn was the headquarters of the village. On his land, a couple of hundred feet from the inn, stood the block-house where watch was kept against Indian attacks. There a sentinel was posted day and night, under his supervision.

The Ingersolls had only one child, a daughter named Sarah. They induced their neighbor, Joseph Hutchinson, who had

several sons, to give one to them for adoption. Benjamin
Hutchinson, born in 1668, was an infant when he was adopted,
and the Ingersolls brought him up as their own child. He lived
with them until 1689 when he married, and moved into a house
nearby. In 1692, in addition to farming, Benjamin Hutchinson
helped take care of the inn. The Ingersoll daughter, Sarah, never
married and worked serving food and drink in the tavern. In this
capacity, she overheard certain things in 1692 which otherwise
would have been lost to the record.

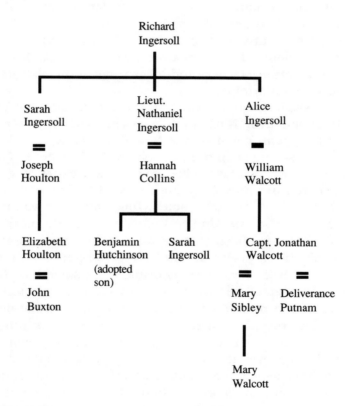

As seen on the chart, Nathaniel Ingersoll was the uncle of
Jonathan Walcott, and the great uncle of Mary Walcott. Jonathan
Walcott's marriage to his second wife, Deliverance Putnam,

linked the Ingersoll and Walcott family group to the Putnam family.

Joseph Houlton was Nathaniel Ingersoll's brother-in-law, and John Buxton was Houlton's son-in-law.

Other friends of Thomas Putnam deserve mention. One was Elizer Keyser of Salem Town, tanner, who was age forty-five in 1692. He was the first cousin of Thomas Putnam.[55] Another was Ezekiel Cheever, a church member of Salem Village, who was age thirty-seven in 1692. He was the son of Ezekiel Cheever, Sr., the famous school teacher of early New England.[56]

The military was an essential feature of colonial life. Survival demanded that the people be in a state of universal and thorough readiness to protect themselves from Indian hostilities. Authority was early obtained from the Massachusetts legislature to form a foot company in Salem Village. Men of every description, in fact, almost any man who could carry a musket, belonged to it. Its officers were elected, and were usually from the upper echelons of village society. Every title of rank, from corporal to captain, once obtained was used with pride ever after.

---

55   Elizer Keyser was the son of Elizabeth (Holyoke) and George Keyser. Elizabeth was the sister of Ann (Holyoke) Putnam, the mother of Thomas Putnam.

56   Ezekiel Cheever, Sr. also had a son, Samuel Cheever, by his first wife. Samuel Cheever graduated from Harvard College in 1659, a classmate of Samuel Willard. In 1692 Samuel Cheever was the minister at Marblehead and Samuel Willard, the minister of the Third Church (Old South) in Boston. The first wife of Ezekiel Cheever, Sr. died about 1650, and he married Ellen Lothrop in 1652. They had several children, including Thomas Cheever and Ezekiel Cheever, Jr. (referred to as simply Ezekiel Cheever without the Jr. in the text). Thomas Cheever graduated from Harvard College in 1677, one year after Thomas Brattle and one year before Cotton Mather. Ezekiel Cheever, Jr., born about 1655, inherited the Lothrop estate in Salem Village, where he resided. He sold his house in Salem Town to the Rev. Nicholas Noyes (Harvard class of 1667) in 1684. The Rev. Noyes lived in that house during the witchcraft period.

In 1692 Jonathan Walcott was the captain of the Salem Village company. He was also one of the deacons of the parish, so he was known as either Captain, or Deacon Walcott. Nathaniel Ingersoll, the other deacon, was the lieutenant. He served with that commission until late in life, and was always known as either Lieutenant, or Deacon Ingersoll. Thomas Putnam, the clerk of the parish and one of the sergeants, was always known by this rank. This company of militia had frequent drills. Their field was on the land of Nathaniel Ingersoll. The village company was almost as highly regarded as the village church. At the close of a parade, it was a common practice for the captain to give notices of parish meetings.

This chapter concludes with a chart identifying the relationships of the twelve male members of Thomas Putnam's extended family who are integral to this story. The eight most important are shown in plain type; the four ancillary members, in italic type. Not included in this grouping is the outsider Joseph Putnam, the rich young half-brother of Thomas and legatee to the estate which Thomas had trusted he would inherit himself.

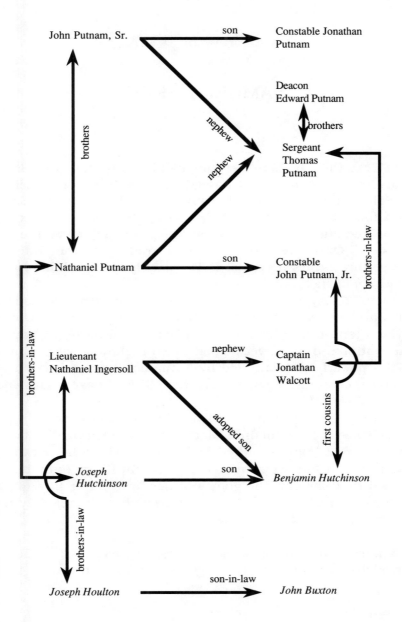

CHAPTER 5

SAMUEL PARRIS

In 1672, although there were about fifty households in Salem Village, only eleven or twelve residents qualified as members of the Salem church, the visible saints.[57] In the same year Salem Town authorized a church in Salem Village, but not a full-fledged, covenanted one. The Rev. James Bayley was appointed the first minister. Only twenty-two, he had graduated from Harvard College three years previously. The parish voted to build him a house, but did not do so.

In 1672, Bayley married Mary Carr of Salisbury, the sister of Ann Carr, who would marry Thomas Putnam in 1678. During Bayley's tenure in Salem Village, discord and bickering caused him continual trouble, yet he performed faithful service. But by 1679 a powerful minority led by Nathaniel Putnam had turned against the young minister, and the following year he resigned and left Salem Village.

Bayley went to Connecticut in 1682 where his wife died in 1688. Three of their children, Mary, John, and Sarah, died before her. In 1692 Bayley moved to Roxbury, where he became a physician. In the witch hunt of 1692, Ann (Carr) Putnam, Sr. claimed that she saw the ghosts of her "own sister Bayley and three of her children in winding sheets" who told her they had been murdered by Rebecca Nurse.

The second minister of Salem Village was the Rev. George Burroughs, born in Virginia. He graduated from Harvard in 1670,

---

57   Perley, *History of Salem*, 2: 443.

the class following the Rev. Bayley's.   He married, and was
admitted into the Roxbury church on April 12, 1674, where he had
a child baptized.   Unhappy, perhaps, with the precepts of
Puritanism, Burroughs gravitated to Casco, Maine, in the
summer of 1674.   Maine had been settled under an English royal
grant separate from Massachusetts, and the original immigrants
were not Puritans.

Burroughs was the third minister ever to settle in Casco.   The
first two, the Rev. Richard Gibson and the Rev. Robert Jordan, had
been Anglican.   The Rev. Gibson had come from England in 1637,
and preached for five or six years before he returned.   The Rev.
Jordan had come in 1640 at age twenty-eight and died in Casco in
1679 at age sixty-eight.   With the help of the Rev. Jordan,
Burroughs commenced his ministry there in 1674, although no
Puritan church was then gathered.   Burroughs' outlook was
somewhat ecumenical, and he wished to serve the spiritual needs
of all the residents, not just the small Puritan minority.   He lived
on the Neck, the prime location, where the town granted him two
hundred acres.

The next year, 1675, King Philip's War broke out, and after the
slaughter of several families, many of the inhabitants fled south
for refuge.[58]   One of the reasons given for the outbreak was a
general complaint among the tribes that the English would not
sell them ammunition, which they needed for their hunting.
With so many of the inhabitants gone from Casco, the number of
victims falling to the hatchet and scalping knife was
considerably reduced.   However, in the summer of 1676 the war
was renewed in earnest; many of the remaining settlers were
killed; and all the houses were completely destroyed.   A fortunate
few were able to escape, some to Bang's Island, which lies at the

---

58   The greatest number of refugees fled to Salem, where on January 11, 1676,
     it was voted, "These persons, being driven from their habitations by the
     barbarous heathen, are admitted as inhabitants into the town."

mouth of the harbor. From this place, the Rev. Burroughs wrote to the garrison at Black Point for help.[59]

Surviving this harrowing experience, Burroughs and his family returned to Massachusetts. They settled in Salisbury, where he was preaching in 1680. He started giving sermons in Salem Village in November of that year, and in early 1681, at age twenty-nine, George Burroughs was chosen as minister of the Salem Village church. In February 1681 the parish voted to build a parsonage which was completed later that year. In the meantime, John Putnam, Sr. had allowed the Rev. George Burroughs to live in his house, a period of about nine months. The Rev. Burroughs' relationship with the Putnam family deteriorated rapidly. Burroughs' wife died in September 1681, but he had received little of his salary, and had not even enough money to pay her funeral expenses. Burroughs had to borrow money from John Putnam, Sr. to pay for the funeral wine.

By early 1683, largely due to the influence of the Putnam family, the minister's salary still was not being paid in full. In March 1683, Burroughs resigned from his position at Salem Village and returned to Casco, Maine. That frontier town was being rebuilt, and he again became its minister.

In the preceding year, John Putnam, Sr. as the chairman of a committee of village people had agreed that the village owed Burroughs thirty-three pounds sterling in back salary (equivalent to about thirty-three thousand dollars today). Moreover Putnam had deliberately and formally agreed that the

---

59 A letter written from Saco asking help from the governor in Boston states, "On the 11 of this instant we heard of many killed of our neighbors in Casco, and on the 12 instant Mr. Josslin sent me a brief letter written by Mr. Burroughs, the minister. He gives an account of 32 killed and carried away by the Indians. Himself [Burroughs] escaped to an island, but I hope Black Point men have fetched him off by this time, 10 men, 6 women, and 16 children. The Lord in mercy fit us for death, and direct the hearts and hands to do what is most needful in such a time of distress as this. Brian Pendleton. Winter Harbor, at night, the 13 of August 1676."

six-odd pounds sterling that Burroughs owed him should come out of the thirty-three pounds sterling when paid.

In May 1683 Burroughs visited Salem Village to meet with the people for an accounting whereby he would be paid enough of his back salary so that he could settle debts. While the meeting was in progress, he was arrested by a marshal on the complaint of John Putnam, Sr. for debt. Burroughs answered that "he had no goods to show, and he was now reckoning with the inhabitants, for we do not yet know who is in debt, but there was his body." Burroughs was taken away as a prisoner.

The purpose of Putnam's complaint was to intimidate Burroughs. As soon as written records were produced, Putnam was forced to withdraw the case. Burroughs, an honest man, then returned home to Casco, and never pressed for the amount that the village owed him.

The story of the Rev. George Burroughs continues in the next chapter.

The third minister of Salem Village, the Rev. Deodat Lawson, was engaged the next year, 1684. Lawson had come to America from England about ten years previously. Because the Salem Village church was not a full-fledged church, neither the Rev. James Bayley nor the Rev. George Burroughs had been ordained.[60] The Putnam family was pressing to make the village church a covenanted church. This would require the ordination of the minister. Joseph Porter and his brother-in-law Daniel Andrew opposed the ordination of the Rev. Lawson, and a strong anti-ordination group was formed. The Rev. Lawson, like his two predecessors, decided to make a timely exit from Salem Village. At the expiration of his contract in 1688, he left. The old factions lived on with increasing bitterness.

The fourth minister, the Rev. Samuel Parris, born in 1653 in England, was the son of Thomas Parris, a London cloth

---

60 At the hanging of the Rev. Burroughs in 1692, the Rev. Cotton Mather told the crowd that Burroughs was still not a properly ordained minister.

merchant. The family emigrated to Barbados, and was able to send Samuel to Harvard. In 1673, when Samuel was twenty, his father died, leaving him a twenty-acre section of a cotton plantation in Barbados. Not doing well at Harvard, Samuel left without graduating and returned to run the plantation. Unsuccessful once more, he moved to Boston in 1681. There, in 1682, he purchased a wharf and warehouse. Failing again in this business venture, Samuel Parris turned to the ministry, and in 1688 became the minister in Salem Village. He was ordained on November 19, 1689, the day the church was organized as a covenanted body.[61] Of the twenty-seven members, all were Putnams or Putnam friends, except for Peter Cloyce. However, all the households of Salem Village, about one hundred, were taxed for the minister's pay and the other church expenses.

From the first, Samuel Parris was interested in money. Before accepting the position, he had insisted that "when money shall be more plentiful, the money paid to me shall be increased." After serving one year as minister, Samuel Parris wanted more. The village allowed him the use of the minister's house and land. That was not enough. He wanted to own the property outright and made his most outrageous demand. He insisted that the village deed this property to himself and his heirs forever. By obtaining the support of the Putnam family, his demand was met on October 10, 1689. This action rent the community in two. About half the people in Salem Village formed a vocal anti-Parris group; the other half were pro-Parris.

---

61   The seventeen male members of the newly covenanted Salem Village church were Samuel Parris, Pastor; Nathaniel Putnam; John Putnam, Sr.; Bray Wilkins, age 79; Joshua Rea; Nathaniel Ingersoll; Peter Cloyce; Thomas Putnam; John Putnam, Jr.; Jonathan Putnam; Benjamin Putnam; Ezekiel Cheever; Henry Wilkins; Benjamin Wilkins; William Way; Peter Prescott. The ten female members were Elizabeth, wife to Samuel Parris; Rebecca, wife to John Putnam, Sr.; Anna, wife to Bray Wilkins; Sarah, wife to Joshua Rea; Hannah, wife to John Putnam, Jr.; Sarah, wife to Benjamin Putnam; Sarah Putnam; Deliverance Walcott; Persis, wife to William Way; Mary, wife to Samuel Abbie.

The Putnams led the pro-Parris faction of the west side, only the traitor Joseph Putnam demurring; the Porters led the anti-Parris faction of the east side. This division of the community was exacerbated by existing economic and social tensions.

By 1691 the anti-Parris group had begun to withhold their ministry payments. The Rev. Parris was driven to desperate lengths to extract his salary. His urgent appeals and political maneuverings eventually turned into bitter law suits. Not one to mince words, Parris denounced his opponents as "knaves and cheaters." Displaying once more the ingrained behavior previously exhibited in his commercial activities, he fought with increasing ruthlessness against the anti-Parris group. His setbacks over the years apparently had produced a set of obsessions which now reached their ultimate manifestation. He was beset by paranoia, shaped in part by his pattern of failure in trade and commerce. The source of his injustices, according to Parris, was a conscious collaboration between his opponents and the powers of Satan. He ranted about "a lamentable harmony between wicked men and devils in their opposition of God's kingdom and interests." The wrongdoers had become "haunted with an evil and wicked spirit" and had gone for advice "to the Devil, to a witch." By the summer of 1691 the division of Salem Village into two warring camps over this issue was complete.

The anti-Parris forces, under the leadership of the Porters, attacked. An entirely new Village Committee was elected in October 1691 from this faction. The new members included Joseph Putnam (the twenty-two-year-old traitor to the Putnam cause), his newly acquired kinsmen Joseph Porter and Daniel Andrew, and two other men of similar anti-Parris views. This committee forcibly opposed the Rev. Samuel Parris and repudiated the policies of the previous, Putnam-controlled group. Joseph Putnam called the crucial meetings in late 1691. At these meetings it was voted to investigate the fraudulent conveyance of the parsonage to Samuel Parris in 1689. Joseph Putnam worked effectively behind the scenes. Together with his father-in-law, Israel Porter, he successfully opposed the Rev. Parris. Recently elected as a selectman, Joseph Putnam was now positioned to influence the larger politics of Salem Town.

The pro-Parris forces under the leadership of the Putnams readied their counterattack. On February 14, 1692 Parris lamented "the present low condition of the church in the midst of its enemies," predicting ominously that "shortly the case will be for otherwise." Influenced by the teachings of Cotton Mather, Samuel Parris had hit upon a lethal method to bring down his enemies.[62]

Cotton Mather, as noted earlier, had meticulously described the bewitchment of Boston's Goodwin children in 1688 in a best-selling book. In 1692 some Salem Village girls went into "fits," antics remarkably similar to those of the possessed Goodwin children. With all their gyrations and screechings, it indeed seemed that the Salem Village girls were in pain. Salem Village's two leading professionals, its minister, the Rev. Samuel Parris, and its physician, Dr. William Griggs, carefully studied the afflictions of the girls. They concluded that their agony was caused by witchcraft.

But how could the witches causing these terrible hurts be exposed? The Rev. Parris and Dr. Griggs soon came up with the solution; they let it be known that the girls were crying out upon the witches who were tormenting them. Concerned people came and listened to the girls. They heard them name certain women who were neighbors. Sometimes a name was brought up indirectly; other times a direct accusation of witchcraft was made. With this information, the parents and guardians of the girls took action. They accused three women of witchcraft and had them arrested. The accused women were examined by the magistrates and then imprisoned. According to the experience of previous witchcraft cases in New England, this solution should have ended the witch scare, and life should have returned to

---

62   Samuel Parris' wife, Elizabeth Parris, died in Salem Village in 1696. Soon afterwards he was dismissed as minister and he left Salem Village for good. Parris married again, and had four children by his second wife Dorothy, who died in Sudbury in 1719. Parris died there in 1720, age 67.

normal. But this was not the case in Salem Village. The girls' afflictions did not stop. In fact the number of afflicted people grew, and they cried out upon more and more people. The accused were hunted down and arrested.

The church in Salem Town had two ministers in 1692, the senior minister, John Higginson, Sr., and the assistant minister, Nicholas Noyes. In that year, the Rev. John Higginson, Sr. was a venerable elder statesman of the Puritan faith.[63] In 1629, at age thirteen, he had come to Salem with his parents in the early Puritan migration. His father, the Rev. Francis Higginson, became the first minister of the Salem church. Because Harvard had not yet been founded, Francis was unable to give his son John a college education. Undaunted, John moved to Connecticut in 1641, married the daughter of a minister, and bore sole charge of a church there. In 1660 John was made minister at Salem. In 1692 he was seventy-six and had preached for fifty-five years, the last thirty-two in Salem. His daughter, Ann, age twenty-nine, was married to William Dolliver of Gloucester.

The Rev. Nicholas Noyes was born in 1647 in Newbury. He graduated from Harvard in 1667, and preached for thirteen years in Connecticut. Well-respected, he was unanimously called to become the assistant minister in Salem in 1683, a prestigious position. He was extremely fat and never married.[64] Referring to the celibacy of the Rev. Nicholas Noyes, as well as William Stoughton and two other prominent men, a local poet wrote,

> Though Rome blaspheme the marriage bed
> And vows of single life has bred,

---

63   Rev. John Higginson Sr., born 1616, married Sarah Whitfield, daughter of Rev. Henry Whitfield of Guilford, Conn. They had seven children, including eldest child John Higginson Jr., born in 1646, (who was a justice of the peace in Salem in 1692), and daughter Ann, born 1663. After the death of his wife in 1675, John Higginson, Sr. married widow Mary (Blackman) Atwater. He died in office in 1708, age 92.

64   Nicholas Noyes died in Salem on December 13, 1717.

Chaste Parker,[65] Stoughton, Brinsmade,[66] Noyes
Show us the odds 'twixt force and choice
These undefiled contracted here
Are gone to heaven and married there.

The younger minister, Nicholas Noyes, Harvard educated, described by Cotton Mather as "my excellent friend," was one of the foremost proponents of the witch hunt in 1692. The older minister, John Higginson, Sr., less highly educated, urged moderation. On Monday, June 6, 1692, Higginson's daughter, Ann Dolliver, was visiting him at his home. The constable came to the door with a warrant, arrested Ann for witchcraft, and took her away to prison.

---

65   Thomas Parker was the minister at Newbury. He died in 1677 in his eighty-second year. According to Cotton Mather, "after he had lived all his days a single man, he went unto the apocalyptical virgins."

66   William Brinsmade was the minister at Marlborough, who, according to Cotton Mather, "went away from Harvard College without any degree at all," adding, "Yet this *disaster* hindered not his serviceableness in the churches of the faithful."

CHAPTER 6

GEORGE BURROUGHS

"Glad should I have been, if I had never known the name of this man, or never had the occasion to mention so much as the first letters of his name. But the government requiring some account of his trial, it becomes me with all obedience to submit unto the order. This G. B. was indicted for witchcraft. He was accused as being as head actor at some of their hellish rendezvous, and one who had the promise of being a *King in Satan's kingdom*. He was accused for extraordinary lifting, and such feats of strength as could not be done without a diabolical assistance."[67] This account of George Burroughs was written by Cotton Mather in 1692. A far different account, however, has since come to light.

George Burroughs, born in 1651, graduated at the top of his class from Harvard in 1670, and was the college's first outstanding athlete. In 1673, he married his first wife Hannah in Roxbury, and soon moved to Maine to become the first minister in the frontier town of Casco. He was living there at the beginning of King Philip's War in 1675. Because of this war, George Burroughs' fate would be inextricably bound with that of the Hathornes, a leading family of the Puritan old guard. Yet, because of his Virginia heritage, he was destined to remain an outsider.

Captain William Hathorne, Jr. was the younger brother of John Hathorne, the magistrate of the witch hunt. With no signs of his brother's talent for business and administration, the young William turned his energy to the military, seeking his fortune in

---

67   Cotton Mather, *Wonders*, 120.

King Philip's War.[68] As lieutenant in the Salem company under Captain Joseph Gardner,[69] he had distinguished himself in the campaign against the Narragansett Indians in Rhode Island. When the captain was killed in battle in December 1675, his lieutenant took command. Only thirty years old, William, Jr. was at once promoted to the rank of captain. Of all the young Salem officers who fought in the war, he was the most dashing and the most ruthless. Following the Rhode Island campaign, he returned to Salem in the summer of 1676 to train recruits. At this time, he married Sarah Ruck.[70]

In August 1676, right after his marriage, Captain Hathorne was ordered to march with his company to the northeast to seek out and kill all hostile Indians. When his company arrived in Dover, New Hampshire, in September, they found hundreds of friendly Indians gathered there, trading and enjoying themselves. These were local tribes with whom Major Richard Waldron, the military commander at Dover, had signed a peace treaty.

Together, Captain Hathorne and Major Waldron devised a plan. They proposed a sham fight after the English fashion as part of the festivities. The two sides, white men and Indians, were drawn up for the mock battle, which the trusting Indians entered into with great spirit. Meanwhile, Hathorne ordered his men quietly to surround them. The Indians opened the fight by firing the first volley. Once their guns were discharged, the Salem troops rushed in and seized the Indians without the loss of a single man. They took four hundred Indians captive. Their treachery flouted all accepted rules of warfare.

Waldron, an old hand at selling Indian captives as slaves, welcomed this alliance with the son of Major William Hathorne,

---

68 *New England Historical and Genealogical Register*, 42:363-368. Church, 161-163.

69 In March 1675, John Hathorne, at age 34, married Ruth Gardner. The bride was only 14. Captain Joseph Gardner was her uncle and guardian.

70 Sarah Ruck was born August 12, 1656, the daughter of Hannah (Spooner) and John Ruck of Salem Town.

the most powerful magistrate in Salem, in contriving such a large-scale kidnapping. By arrangement, two sloops, now being used as slavers, were waiting in the deep water anchorage in the inlet, and more than two hundred of the Indian captives, the strongest, were chained in the holds, body against body. The first landing was at Boston, where about ten of the captives were hanged; the slavers then plied their way to Bermuda where the rest were sold. Since a slave at that time was worth about ten thousand dollars in today's currency, this venture netted Captain Hathorne and Major Waldron, after expenses and other payoffs, close to a million dollars, in addition to the praise they received for serving their country so well. "The *stunningest wound* of all given to Indians was, when by a contrivance [of Captain Hathorne], nearly four hundred of them were, on September 6, 1676, surprised at the house of Major Waldron, whereof one-half were sold for slaves," raved the Rev. Cotton Mather in his history of King Philip's War.

After loading the captives into the slavers, Captain William Hathorne, Jr. immediately pushed eastward with his forces into Maine. There, during October and November 1676, he searched for more Indians to crush by stealth or battle. Although his efforts were largely fruitless, he established himself as a daredevil leader. At year's end, his troops were demobilized, and he returned to his bride in Salem, a rich and successful man. But their happiness did not last.

Two years later, at the end of 1678, Captain William Hathorne, Jr. died a painful and mysterious death at age thirty-three. His ill-found wealth, left to his widow, soon disappeared. His death struck a major blow to the Hathorne family, leaving them suspicious and frightened about its cause. An old Indian wound might best have been blamed, but witchcraft presented a more tempting explanation. The Indians were the Devil's children, and the Prince of the Air could take revenge through the agency of a witch. The fate of the proud Hathorne family would depend on the dead Captain's brother, John Hathorne.[71]

The town of Casco, Maine suffered heavily from the Indians during King Philip's War in 1675, and was completely destroyed by 1676. The Burroughs family managed to escape and settled in Salisbury, Massachusetts. In 1680 the ministry in Salem Village was vacant. Burroughs preached there in November 1680, and in early 1681 was chosen as minister. In September of that year his wife, Hannah, died. Burroughs was a strong man of unusual vitality. Although not tall, he was dark and handsome, and athletic, highly educated, and intelligent as well. He attracted the attention of young Sarah Hathorne, the widow of Captain William Hathorne, Jr., and the two were married in 1682. The dead captain's brother, John Hathorne, whose stern Puritanical father had died the preceding year in April, disapproved of their marriage.[72] Very likely, John looked askance at Burroughs'

---

71   William Hathorne Jr. left his childless wife, Sarah (Ruck) Hathorne, an estate valued at five hundred pounds sterling (equivalent to a half-million dollars today), a considerable amount at that time. Among the inventory was an item for five pounds sterling still due from the country for military service, a small amount compared to the rest of the fortune. Yet, in a petition to the General Court the widow, Sarah (Ruck) Hathorne, stated. "My husband, being deceased, has left me in a mean condition, being indebted to several persons, and not in a capacity to make payment, without receiving my late husband's arrears from the country." The petition was granted. (Loggins, 84. *Massachusetts Archives*, 69:237.)

72   John's father, Major William Hathorne, who died at age seventy-four, left an estate of seven hundred fifty pounds sterling. The whereabouts of the inheritance of the five hundred pounds sterling of the Rev. Burroughs' new wife, Sarah (Ruck) Hathorne, is unknown. After his marriage to Sarah, the Rev. Burroughs was not even able to discharge a small "debt for two gallons of Canary wine, and cloth, &c., bought of Mr. Gedney [the Salem innkeeper and the father of magistrate Bartholomew Gedney] on John Putnam, Sr.'s account, for the funeral of Mrs. [Hannah] Burroughs." Furthermore, because his salary was largely not being paid, Burroughs had

Virginia background, regarding him as an interloper unworthy of his sister-in-law.   Their marriage also displeased Sarah's own family, the Rucks, who were powerful Puritan businessmen in Salem Town and good friends of the Hathornes.

In 1683, Burroughs, with his new wife, Sarah, left the ministry in Salem Village, and returned to his former ministry in Casco, Maine.   Since no other Harvard graduate had been willing to accept the rigors and dangers of such a remote frontier outpost, the position had remained unfilled during his absence.

The first record of his return is in June 1683, when he relinquished 170 of the 200 acres which had been granted to him prior to the war.   The town offered to give him 100 acres "farther off," in compensation.   The town records contain Burroughs' reply, "As for the land taken away, he freely gave it to us, not desiring any land anywhere else, nor anything else in consideration."   Compare the generosity of the Rev. Burroughs with the greed of the Rev. Samuel Parris!

Burroughs' fine gesture paints his character in a thoroughly selfless and virtuous light.   Nothing has been found during the whole course of his ministry or personal life to suggest differently.   The substantial coastal acreage that he gave to the town was situated on the Neck, the prime location in the fast-growing settlement.   Meanwhile speculators like Bartholomew Gedney, an inhabitant of Salem, were making fortunes on Casco real estate.[73]

In 1686 a small company of French Huguenots, Protestant victims of the French king's revocation of the Edict of Nantes in 1685, settled on the Neck.   One was Peter Bowdoin (originally Pierre Baudouin) who in 1688, bought from George Burroughs

---

to continue borrowing money during the period he and Sarah lived in Salem Village.

73   Bartholomew Gedney was never himself an inhabitant of Casco or any other place in Maine. He owned a shipyard in Salem Town, and became a Salem magistrate as well as a major in the militia. He was one of the witchcraft judges who sentenced the Rev. Burroughs to death in 1692.

twenty-three acres extending across the Neck, making them next-door neighbors. In ministering not only to Puritans, but to all people, the Rev. Burroughs displayed a rare tolerance for those of differing social and religious precepts, an attitude not appreciated by some of the habitually rigid clergy living in the comfort and safety of Boston.

Quite unawares, the people of Dover, New Hampshire were walking a narrow path between life and death. Major Richard Waldron, long established as the town's leading citizen, was the owner of a sawmill and gristmill. By 1689, Waldron was seventy-five years old, still vigorous and hearty.

In April 1689, the Indians renewed their hostilities at Saco, Maine, a town about twenty miles south of Casco. In June, they surprised Dover, New Hampshire. Not a single sentinel stood guard over the doomed village. The Indians had not forgotten the treachery of Major Richard Waldron and Captain William Hathorne, Jr. in 1676. Now, thirteen years later, Indian warriors rushed into Major Waldron's house, hatchets in hand. Turning to reach for his pistols, Waldron was struck down by a hatchet blow on the back of his head. Badly wounded, he was dragged into the great room and put upon the chair where he had often served as judge. "Who shall judge the Indians now?" they asked the dying man. They tore his shirt from him, and each took his turn slashing him, saying "See, I cross out my account!" After killing or taking captive the rest of the household, they plundered and burned the house, along with many others in that unfortunate town.

In the course of the summer of 1689, the Indians were joined by the French. In August, the fort at Pemaquid, Maine fell. This success of the French and the Indians threw the Maine settlers into a panic. They hurriedly abandoned all of the settlements to the north and east of Casco, and that town, now an outpost, became the rallying point for the fugitives. For defense there was Fort Loyal, a picketed enclosure on the Neck built on a low bluff by the seaside, three thousand feet east of Burroughs' house. The fort had a few light guns to command the approach by land as well as by water. The meetinghouse, also on the same seafront, was a thousand feet east of the fort. In addition to the fort, there were four garrison houses in the town, which served as refuge points in case of attack.

The daring enemy now hovered about each last remaining settlement in New Hampshire and Maine, killing, scalping, and burning on every side. Soldiers, sent into the forests to hunt down the assassins, found no Indians, and returned empty handed.

The Massachusetts authorities, responding to cries for help from all quarters, in August 1689 sent a regiment of seven companies. Major Jeremiah Swayne of Reading was in command. Relief came not a moment too soon, for Indians were now attacking every settlement along the coast, from Berwick to Casco.

One of the seven companies was led by Captain Simon Willard of Salem Town; another company was led by Captain William Bassett of Lynn. (Captain Simon Willard's nephew, John Willard, was accused and hanged for witchcraft on August 19, 1692. Captain Bassett's wife and several others of his family were accused and arrested for witchcraft in 1692. Mary (Swayne) Marshall, the sister of the regimental commander, Major Swayne, accused several people of witchcraft in 1692, possibly acting as a front for her brother.)

A second expedition, acting in concert with Swayne's, but designed to take the war to the devastated region beyond Casco, was sent under the command of Major Benjamin Church, an experienced veteran of King Philip's War. This force came to the relief of Casco, arriving there by ship on September 20, 1689. A bitter fight ensued; the battle was gallantly, desperately fought. Casco was saved, the inhabitants coming in for a full share of credit for the victory. Church, never generous in giving war credit to others, singled out the Rev. Burroughs for his gallantry. In his dispatch from Casco, dated September 22, 1689, Major Church wrote, "As for the minister of this place, I am well satisfied with him, he being present with us yesterday in the fight."

The enemy retreated into their forests, and the war quieted down for the remainder of the year 1689. But the townspeople of Casco justly feared that vengeance would be visited on them in the coming spring, 1690. Conferring with Major Church, they told him that they wanted to abandon the settlement. Major Church, however, persuaded them to remain, assuring them that, if the government provided the means, "he certainly would come with his volunteers and [friendly] Indians to their relief."

Back in Boston in the winter of 1689-1690, Major Church labored hard to keep his promise. He advised the ruling party of Casco's exposed situation, "at every opportunity entreating those gentlemen in behalf of the poor people of Casco, informing them of the necessity of taking care of them, either by sending relief early in the spring, or suffer them to draw off, otherwise they certainly would be destroyed."[74] Their answer was, "They could do nothing until Sir Edmund was gone." The Puritan old guard, having overthrown Sir Edmund Andros, the royal governor of the deposed King James II, were preparing to send him as a prisoner to England. Sir Edmund finally left Boston for England on February 10, 1690.

In February 1690, Captain Simon Willard, stationed in Casco, was ordered to pursue the Indians to their headquarters in the forest. The order was given despite the knowledge that Willard previously had written to Boston stating that his men needed supplies, and that the soldiers' parents were anxious because their sons had not been returned as promised. Captain Willard, an experienced officer from Salem, was the son of Major Simon Willard, the commander-in-chief during King Philip's War. The ineptitude, indifference and intransigence of the government in

---

74 Maine, settled by non-Puritans, became a refuge for Massachusetts families fleeing from Puritan rule. Faced with the Indian menace, the Maine towns one by one acquiesced to Massachusetts rule in the mid-seventeenth century on the promise that Massachusetts would defend them in time of need. Now, when the time arrived, Massachusetts exhibited no compunction to defend these people, many of them considered heretics and outcasts.

Boston to the fate of so many people soon would become apparent to all; a calamity exposing their fatal misjudgment lay ahead.

For the Rev. Richard Martin, the minister in Wells, Maine, the terrors of Indian ferocity were overwhelming. Work in the fields was curtailed by the continual fear of Indian raids; the only places where people felt safe were the garrison houses. But the garrisons already were packed with refugees from the town and the ruined villages along the coastline. Under these precarious conditions, Martin resigned, leaving Wells without a minister.

Burroughs had preached in Wells, Maine as early as 1688. He was well-known in Maine's coastal settlements, Casco, Scarborough, Saco, and Wells, for serving both the physical and spiritual needs of the people. Soon after the outbreak of King William's War, he was the only minister hanging on in Maine, except for the Rev. Shubael Dummer in York.

The wife of George Burroughs, the former Sarah (Ruck) Hathorne, was horrified to hear of Major Richard Waldron's grisly death in the Indian attack on Dover in June 1689. Sarah always had dreaded that the treachery perpetuated by Major Waldron and her dead husband, Captain William Hathorne, Jr., was neither forgiven nor forgotten by the Indians. Now, in the bitter winter of 1689–1690, she was frightened to stay in Casco, the furthest outpost in Maine, which was anticipating an Indian attack come spring. Others were leaving Casco; understandably she longed to return to Salem, the seat of her influential family, and to the protection they provided. Her husband, now attending to the spiritual needs of the settlers spread along the coastline from Casco south to Wells, decided to remove his family to Wells, considered secure. But before her husband could give her this promised security, Sarah died. Her body was placed on a ship for a final journey down the coast of Maine into her home port of Salem.

Burroughs, with his seven children, moved permanently to Wells in the early spring of 1690, filling the vacant position as the town's new minister. Undaunted, he continued his ministry along the whole of the desolate coast. To the pioneering settlers of Maine, Burroughs had become the man of the hour. His vitality, courage, and leadership fitted him for any emergency. He was perceived by his parishioners as fearless, and he instilled a degree of his own hope and courage into them, enabling them to live through their dark time. Accounts reveal that their respect for him reached close to veneration. It was in Wells that Burroughs married his third wife, Mary.[75]

Though only a poor village, Casco was one of the strategic points to be held if a foothold was to be retained in Maine. Casco had received several warnings of an impending attack to come sometime in the spring of 1690. Thirty Indian canoes had been sighted in the bay, besides several fires on the shore. Nonetheless, Casco received no help from the authorities in Boston. Captain Simon Willard, in command of the Salem company at Casco, wrote on April 9, 1690 to Boston, giving an account of their danger. His plea was of no avail.

Six weeks later, the assault came. The Indians, led by French officers, attacked Fort Loyal at Casco on May 16, 1690. The French had seen to it that these Indians were among the most formidable marauders ever to set foot on the New England war-path; the position of the settlers was hopeless. When the fort hoisted the white flag, they surrendered to Portneuf and the other French officers, stipulating that men, women, and children, well or wounded, be allowed to depart unharmed. The French officers swore "by the ever living God" to fulfill these conditions to the letter. But the French commander refused to honor his pledge. Instead of finding the promised protection, the survivors were abandoned to the fury of the Indians, who wreaked their vengeance unchecked. The victims, including women, children, and wounded, were scalped and then hacked to pieces. The houses were plundered and set on fire, leaving Casco untenanted, except

---

75   Because of the destruction of records during the Indian wars, the maiden name of Burroughs' third wife is unknown.

by the unburied bodies on the ground. Casco once again had been completely destroyed; the date was May 18, 1690.

Soon after the bloodshed, four English vessels hove into view, bringing reinforcements. Seeing no flag flying, they understood that they had come too late, and stood off to sea again.

On May 20, 1690, the terror-stricken inhabitants of Wells sent by express the following letter to Major Charles Frost, the commander-in-chief of the army in Maine. "The Indians and French have taken taken Casco fort and, to be feared, all the people are killed and taken. We are in a very shattered condition, some are for removing and some are for staying. We must have more assistance."

Two days later, the inhabitants of Wells dispatched a letter to the Council in Boston with this earnest appeal for help. "Our sad condition puts us on your charity. The enemy is very near us. Saco is this day on fire. If we have not immediate help, we are a lost people."

The few who escaped the slaughter at Casco fled south. All the garrisons from Casco south to Wells withdrew in a panic to Wells, where they were ordered to make a stand. This abandonment of the fortifications left the Indians free to overrun the New Hampshire border. Inhabitants of Fox Point in Newington were slaughtered. Captain John Floyd and his men pursued the Indians, forcing them to leave behind some of their captives and booty. Newmarket and Exeter were assaulted. The companies of Captain Wiswall and Captain Floyd fought bitterly with the Indians at Wheelwright's Pond in Lee. Captain Wiswall, his lieutenant, sergeant, and twelve of his men were killed. Captain Floyd kept up the fight, before being driven off the field. The victorious Indians moved westward leaving bloody tracks of destruction behind them. This was June 1690. (Captain Floyd was arrested for witchcraft on May 28, 1692.)

These were dark days for Wells. The citizens understood all too well that at any time they could be the victims of captivity or the most terrible murders. But led by the unwavering resolve and faith of their minister, they would not lose heart.

Raids by small parties of Indians on northern New England farmhouses continued during the rest of 1690 and into 1691. In June 1691 a large force of Indians, over two hundred, attacked Wells, expecting an easy conquest. The assault, however, was bravely repulsed and the Indians withdrew, swearing revenge. Foiled in this attempt, the enraged Indians fell upon the little fishing hamlet at Cape Neddick, five miles south along the coast. There they killed nine men loading a vessel, set the buildings on fire killing the women and children, and disappeared as suddenly as they had come.

The principal garrison at Wells, that of Joseph Storer, was a large establishment, fit to accommodate a great number of persons as a temporary refuge. Its sturdy block house was surrounded by a high palisade; on the outside, small cabins were erected by various families, close enough for them to rush inside when warned of danger. The garrisons, sometimes called forts, were so well built that the Indians seldom succeeded in their attacks on them.

On July 21, 1691, George Burroughs sent the following dispatch from Wells to Boston. "We being at the front, remotely situated, for strength weak, and the enemy beating upon us, we are fair for ruin, and humbly conceive your honors are sensible of it. The enemy killed and drove away upward of one hundred head of cattle, besides sheep and horses; some of our corn is already lost, and more in great hazard. We therefore, distressed, make our humble address to your honors for men, with provisions and ammunition." The requested supplies never came; the cowardly and uncaring, safe and snug in Boston, felt no compunction to assist the settlers in their struggle for survival.

Once again, on September 28, 1691, with the embattled garrisons surrounded by Indians, Burroughs appealed to the Council in Boston. A young man, venturing forth less than a hundred feet outside the garrison to fetch some firewood, had been captured by the stealthy Indians. Burroughs writes, "Whereas it has pleased God, to let loose the heathen upon us, keeping us in close garrison, and daily lying in wait to take any that go forth, whereby we are brought very low, not all the corn is judged enough to keep the inhabitants themselves one half year. We therefore humbly request your honors to continue soldiers among us to remain with us for winter. We had a youth, seventeen years of age, last Saturday carried away, who went (not above gunshot) from Lieut. Storer's garrison to fetch a little wood in his arms. We have desired our loving friends, Captain John Littlefield and Ensign John Hill, to present this to your honors." The remarkable tenacity and bravery of Burroughs in this real war stands in stark contrast to Cotton Mather's sorry behavior in his imagined war against the witches!

Roving scalping parties continued to kill settlers in nearby New Hampshire towns during the remainder of the year 1691. At the same time the Indians were preparing for a more aggressive campaign against the remaining garrisons in Maine.

In January 1692 the town of York, just south of Wells, was laid waste. Those who reached the garrisons were saved; those who did not, met a horrible death, or a more cruel captivity. The minister in York, the Rev. Shubuel Drummer, was killed at his own door, while trying to mount his horse. His clothes were stripped from his body. His wife and son, the only survivors in his large family, were carried into captivity, where she soon died. Cotton Mather, from eye-witness accounts, wrote that one of the "bloody tygers" was seen strutting about among the captives wearing the clothing of the murdered minister.

Wells, still with its minister and encouraged by his fighting spirit, staunchly persevered, despite being "destitute of clothing" for the winter's cold. Because of Burroughs' foresight in keeping the inhabitants away from their farms and within the garrisons, the town had been spared up to this point. But spring was approaching and the people knew that a large force might attack the garrisons momentarily.

The government in Boston utterly failed in its responsibility to assist the lonely outposts of Maine in this crisis. The appalling apathy of the Massachusetts authorities towards the fate of the great number of people pent up in the garrison houses was a betrayal, and one which verged on the criminal.

On May 2, 1692, for a brief moment, the people of Wells thought that the aid they had so long hoped and prayed for finally had arrived. On that day Field Marshal John Partridge rode into Storer's garrison with a few men. But instead of carrying good news of reinforcements, Partridge carried an arrest warrant. To the astonishment of his parishioners and comrades, the Rev. George Burroughs, the garrison's bastion of strength, a true minister of God, was arrested for witchcraft; the afflicted girls of Salem Village were claiming that "he was above a witch, for he was a conjurer." At the precise point when he was most needed, Burroughs was taken captive and carried from Wells to Salem prison to stand trial for his life.

Only four weeks later, in June 1692, the inevitable Indian attack did come. And when it came, the settlers stood ready. Fortified by the spirit, perseverance, and skills learned from their minister, they were able to survive the onslaught.

Two months later, on August 10, 1692, the Rev. George Burroughs, age forty-one, was hanged in Salem. Like his fellow minister at York, his clothes were also stripped from his dead body, this time by white men, and lots were cast for them. The Rev. Cotton Mather watched on horseback, silent witness to this inhumanity.

The province of Maine had lost its last minister. George Burroughs had fought gallantly beside the soldiers, when all but one other minister in Maine had deserted their parishioners for the safety of Boston. Despite constant danger, he had ridden to the remnants of the coastal villages to minister to the people. He had offered courage to the dispirited and frightened soldiers, carrying supplies and fighting alongside them. In the stricken towns, he had comforted the wounded and buried the dead. Time and again, he had risked his life for all in need. Yet he died neither in battle nor in service to his people. On a barren Salem hilltop, George Burroughs was killed at the whim of a covert group

of envious men who had the audacity to claim that they did God's
will.

Wrote Cotton Mather, "Faltering, faulty, unconstant, and
contrary answers are counted as some unlucky symptoms of guilt,
in all crimes, especially in witchcrafts. Now there was never a
prisoner more eminent for them, than G. B. His tergiversations,
contradictions, and falsehoods were very sensible. He now goes to
evince it, *That there neither are nor ever were witches.* The jury
brought him in guilty, but when he came to die, he utterly denied
the fact, whereof he had been thus convicted."[76]

---

76   Cotton Mather, *Wonders*, 128-129.

CHAPTER 7

COLLUSION AND CONSPIRACY

Social and political conditions courted disaster in Salem Village. Friction between two rival factions, exacerbated by the inflammatory rhetoric of Parris, sparked a witch hunt. Yet the normal checks and balances in the New England community should have limited its growth and brought it to a speedy end. In the case of Salem witchcraft, quite the opposite happened. The witch hunt spread easily and rapidly. The entire system of New England justice under law seemed to collapse.

Many reasons have been advanced to explain why the Salem witch hunt was transformed from a brushfire into a firestorm. Was the Salem witch hunt a product of mass hysteria, and was it fueled by growing numbers of accusations of neighbor against neighbor? Did it spread like a fire out of control, indiscriminately burning all in its path, rich and poor alike? Or was the firestorm ignited by a small group of men? Did one tightly-knit conspiracy provide the accusations? Did they keep the flames blazing fiercely for the express purpose of bringing down their enemies, and the enemies of their superiors? Was the witch hunt as methodical as a controlled burn?

The New England Puritans carefully preserved official documents. In the case of the Salem witch hunt, however, some documents were soon lost or destroyed. Still, for an event that took place three hundred years ago, a relatively large number survive. So although there are gaps in the record, a remarkably detailed story can be pieced together. Comparable legal records for the European witch hunts, on the other hand, have all but disappeared.

In the Salem witch hunt, much has been blamed on the hysteria of the general public. But hysteria alone does not generate arrest warrants. An accuser must file an official written document, the complaint, with the magistrates in order for them to make out an arrest warrant.

The written complaint consisted of three parts. The first listed the people accused as witches. The second listed the accusers, that is, the names of the adults who were making the complaint. The third consisted of the children who claimed affliction.

The complaints are legal documents which place the names of the accusers on record. A complaint represents the point when an accuser took the legal step necessary to have someone arrested as a witch. This is the place where the all-inclusive general public is replaced by specific individuals, those people who saw to it that a particular person was arrested as a witch. At this pivotal legal juncture the accusers could no longer remain concealed but had to expose themselves.

On the basis of the complaint, the authorities issued an arrest warrant. Following a person's arrest, he or she would be examined by the magistrates. With a single exception, every person who was examined in the Salem tragedy was committed to prison.

Most of the legal complaints drawn up in 1692 are extant today, the names of the accusers boldly standing forth. If the accusers represented a random sample of the general public, then it can be concluded that the witch hunt was caused by mass hysteria. However, if the accusers were members of a small interlocked group, then it can be concluded that this group formed a conspiracy. The question of whether the witch hunt was driven by mass hysteria or by conspiracy can be answered by simply tabulating all the legal complaints filed with the official documents.

Many of the complaint documents appear among the legal records preserved in the *Salem Witchcraft Papers*. In cases when a complaint is not extant, its contents in a large measure can be reconstructed from extant arrest warrants and other official documents in the *Salem Witchcraft Papers*. In this way it is possible to put together a series of thirty legal complaints that were filed from February 29, 1692, the beginning of the witch hunt, to July 1, 1692. This period represents the first half of the Salem witchcraft delusion, and is known as the Salem Village witch hunt. Accusing seventy-four people, these complaints include everyone known to have been imprisoned for witchcraft in eastern New England during this period, except for the infant child of Sarah Good and for nine people about whom very little is known by any account. (These nine are treated in the end of the last chapter.) The following numbered table lists the complaints in chronological order. Reference will be made to this table throughout the rest of the book.

COMPLAINT TABLE©

Date	Accused	Accusers	Afflicted
No. 1 Feb. 29	Sarah Good Sarah Osborne Tituba	Thomas Putnam Edward Putnam Joseph Hutchinson Thomas Preston	Elizabeth Parris Abigail Williams Ann Putnam, Jr. Elizabeth Hubbard
No. 2 Mar. 19	Martha Corey	Edward Putnam Henry Kenny	Abigail Williams Ann Putnam, Sr. Ann Putnam, Jr. Mercy Lewis Elizabeth Hubbard
No. 3 Mar. 23	Rebecca Nurse	Edward Putnam Jonathan Putnam	Abigail Williams Ann Putnam, Jr.
No. 4 Mar. 23	Dorcas Good	Edward Putnam Jonathan Putnam	Ann Putnam, Jr. Mary Walcott Mercy Lewis

No. 5 Mar. 29	Rachel Clinton	Complaint (filed at Ipswich) not extant	Not extant
No. 6 Apr. 4	Sarah Cloyce Elizabeth Proctor	Jonathan Walcott Nathaniel Ingersoll	Abigail Williams John Indian Mary Walcott Ann Putnam, Jr. Mercy Lewis
No. 7 Apr. 11	John Proctor	No formal complaint. Arrested at his wife's examination (above).	Same as for his wife
No. 8 Apr. 18	Giles Corey Bridget Bishop Abigail Hobbs Mary Warren	John Putnam, Jr. Ezekiel Cheever	Abigail Williams Ann Putnam, Jr. Mary Walcott Mercy Lewis Elizabeth Hubbard
No. 9 Apr. 21	William Hobbs Deliverance Hobbs Nehemiah Abbot, Jr. Mary Easty Sarah Wildes Edward Bishop, Jr. Sarah Bishop Mary Black Mary English	Thomas Putnam John Buxton	Ann Putnam, Jr. Mary Walcott Mercy Lewis
No. 10 Apr. 30	Philip English Lydia Dustin Susannah Martin Dorcas Hoar Sarah Morrell George Burroughs	Thomas Putnam Jonathan Walcott	Abigail Williams Ann Putnam, Jr. Mary Walcott Mercy Lewis Elizabeth Hubbard Susannah Sheldon
No. 11 May 7	Sarah Dustin	Thomas Putnam John Putnam, Jr.	Abigail Williams Ann Putnam, Jr. Mary Walcott Mercy Lewis

No. 12 May 8	Bethia Carter Bethia Carter, Jr. Ann Sears	Thomas Putnam John Putnam, Jr.	Ann Putnam, Jr. Mary Walcott Mercy Lewis
No. 13 May 10	George Jacobs, Sr. Margaret Jacobs	Thomas Putnam John Putnam, Jr.	Abigail Williams Ann Putnam, Jr. Mary Walcott Mercy Lewis Elizabeth Hubbard Sarah Churchill
No. 14 May 10	John Willard	Benjamin Wilkins, Sr. Thomas Fuller, Jr.	Bray Wilkins Daniel Wilkins
No. 15 May 12	Alice Parker Ann Pudeator	Complaint not extant	Mary Warren Parker's indictment carries the names of Ann Putnam, Jr. Elizabeth Hubbard Mary Warren. Pudeator's indictment carries the names of Ann Putnam, Jr. Sarah Churchill Mary Warren.
No. 16 c. May 13	Abigail Somes	Complaint not extant	Mary Warren Somes' indictment carries the names of Mary Walcott, Elizabeth Hubbard, Mary Warren.
No. 17 May 14	Daniel Andrew George Jacobs, Jr. Rebecca Jacobs Sarah Buckley Mary Whittredge Elizabeth Hart Thomas Farrar Elizabeth Colson	Thomas Putnam Nathaniel Ingersoll	Ann Putnam, Jr. Mary Walcott Mercy Lewis Abigail Williams

No. 18 May 15	Mehitabel Downing	Complaint and arrest warrant not extant.	Mary Warren
No. 19 May 18	Roger Toothaker	Complaint not extant	Ann Putnam, Jr. Mary Walcott Elizabeth Hubbard
No. 20 May 21	Sarah Proctor Sarah Bassett Susannah Roots	Thomas Putnam John Putnam, Jr.	Ann Putnam, Jr. Mary Walcott Mercy Lewis Abigail Williams
No. 21 May 23	Benjamin Proctor Mary De Rich Sarah Pease	Nathaniel Ingersoll Thomas Rayment	Abigail Williams Elizabeth Hubbard
No. 22 May 28	Elizabeth Cary	Thomas Putnam Benjamin Hutchinson	Mary Walcott Mercy Lewis Abigail Williams
No. 23 May 28	John Alden John Floyd Elizabeth Fosdick Wilmot Redd Sarah Rice William Proctor Elizabeth Howe Arthur Abbot Martha Carrier Mary Toothaker Margaret Toothaker	Jonathan Walcott Joseph Houlton	Ann Putnam, Jr. Mary Walcott Mercy Lewis Abigail Williams
No. 24 May 30	Elizabeth Paine Elizabeth Fosdick	Nathaniel Putnam Joseph Whipple	Mercy Lewis Mary Warren
No. 25 Jun. 2	Elizabeth Paine Elizabeth Fosdick	Peter Tufts	Tufts' slave
No. 26 Jun. 4	Mary Ireson	Edward Putnam Thomas Rayment	Abigail Williams Ann Putnam, Jr. Mary Walcott Mary Warren Susannah Sheldon Elizabeth Booth

No. 27 Jun. 3	Job Tookey	Complaint and arrest warrant not extant	Ann Putnam, Jr. Mary Walcott Elizabeth Hubbard Mary Warren Susannah Sheldon Elizabeth Booth Sarah Bibber
No. 28 Jun. 5	Ann Dolliver	Complaint not extant	Mary Warren Susannah Sheldon
No. 29 Jun. 28	Mary Bradbury	Complaint and arrest warrant not extant.	Ann Putnam, Jr. Mary Walcott
No. 30 Jul. 1	Margaret Hawkes Candy	Thomas Putnam John Putnam, Jr.	Ann Putnam, Jr. Mary Walcott Mary Warren

They are the faction. O conspiracy,
Sham'st thou to show thy dangerous brow by night,
When evils are most free? O, then, by day
Where wilt thou find a cavern dark enough
To mask thy monstrous visage? Seek none, conspiracy!
Hide it in smiles and affability.
For if thou put thy native semblance on,
Not Erebus itself were dim enough
To hide thee from prevention.[77]

Even a cursory study of the preceding table reveals a hard core of accusers belonging to the extended family of Thomas Putnam. Besides Thomas Putnam there were his brother Edward Putnam, his brother-in-law Jonathan Walcott, his uncle-in-law Nathaniel Ingersoll, his uncles John Putnam, Sr. and Nathaniel Putnam, and his first cousins Jonathan Putnam and John Putnam, Jr. These men formed the Putnam contingent of a conspiracy.

---

77   Shakespeare, *Julius Caesar*, act 2, sc. 1. Native semblance means true form. Erebus refers to the gloomy and dark space under the Earth, the underworld. From prevention means from discovery.

Thomas Putnam exerted complete control over the actions of the two afflicted girls living in his household, his eldest daughter, Ann Putnam, Jr., age twelve, and his servant Mercy Lewis, age seventeen.

Jonathan Walcott had similar authority over another of the afflicted girls, his daughter Mary Walcott, age seventeen. Mary's natural mother was dead, and her step-mother was Thomas Putnam's sister, Deliverance (Putnam) Walcott. Mary's great uncle was Nathaniel Ingersoll.

The afflicted girls also include Elizabeth Parris, age nine, and Abigail Williams, age eleven. Elizabeth, called Betty, was the daughter of the Rev. Samuel Parris; Abigail, called Nabby, was his niece who also lived in his household. The Rev. Samuel Parris, a strict disciplinarian, would not have allowed their participation without his tacit approval.

The name of Elizabeth Hubbard, age seventeen, also appears among the afflicted girls. She was the great niece of the wife of Dr. William Griggs. Working as a servant in his household Elizabeth, by necessity, took her cues from him.

Whenever we see the names of either Elizabeth Parris or Abigail Williams on a complaint, we know that the Rev. Parris was involved. Whenever we see the name Elizabeth Hubbard, we know that Dr. Griggs was involved. These men never would have permitted such exploitation otherwise. It follows that Parris and Griggs were also members of the conspiracy, making up the professional contingent.

Why, then, did the Rev. Samuel Parris and Dr. William Griggs not sign their names on the complaints? As minister and doctor, they occupied the two highest professional positions in the community, guarding the spiritual and physical health of those entrusted to them. To become involved with the actual legal mechanics of a witch hunt would have been unseemly. Yet one is tempted to say that they signed the complaints with invisible ink.

In other ways, Parris was most conspicuous. In the guise of doing his duty, he willingly acted as a witness against many of those accused. Also he acted as scribe in taking down many of the examinations and writing them up for the official record.

The Putnam contingent of the conspiracy handled all the legal documents. One or more members of this contingent signed the complaints for seventy-one of the seventy-four people imprisoned in the Salem Village witch hunt. The three exceptions were accused witches Rachel Clinton, John Proctor (who was arrested with neither a formal complaint nor an arrest warrant), and John Willard.

Below the conspiracy there was a fringe group, all of whom were members of the extended family of Thomas Putnam. These four, Joseph Hutchinson, Benjamin Hutchinson, Joseph Houlton and John Buxton, played various roles in the witch hunt, but were not full-fledged members of the conspiracy. They were allowed to put their names on some of the complaints in addition to the names of the main conspirators. For a few complaints, some trusted friends were also allowed to participate. The conspiracy and its fringe group are shown in Figure 1.

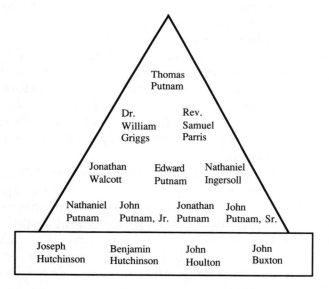

Figure 1. The conspiracy of ten with the fringe group of four at the base. Except for Dr. Griggs and the Rev. Parris, all were members of the extended family of Sergeant Thomas Putnam.

The first four girls afflicted in the witch hunt were Elizabeth Parris and Abigail Williams from the Rev. Parris' household, Ann Putnam, Jr., the daughter of Sergeant Thomas Putnam, and Elizabeth Hubbard, servant in Dr. Griggs' household. These four were joined by Mercy Lewis, servant in Sergeant Putnam's household, and Mary Walcott, the daughter of Captain Jonathan Walcott. These six girls, from the households of the four main conspirators, comprised a select group which may be called the inner circle of the afflicted. Although there were many other young girls in the families of the conspirators, none ever appeared in any witchcraft proceeding. The inner circle is shown in Figure 2.

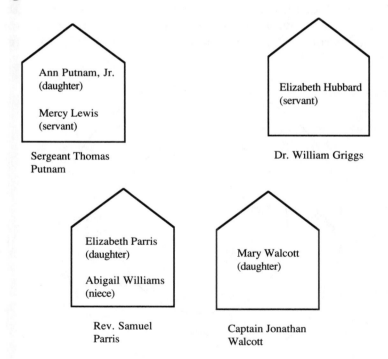

Figure 2. A depiction of the four households in which the inner circle of afflicted girls lived.

Soon others joined the ranks of the afflicted at Salem Village. One was John Indian, a slave belonging to the Rev. Parris. Four other young women require special mention. The first is Mary Warren, age twenty, a servant in the house of John Proctor. The second is Sarah Churchill, also age twenty, a servant in the house of George Jacobs, Jr. The third is Susannah Sheldon, age eighteen, who lived with her widowed mother Rebecca Sheldon. The fourth is Elizabeth Booth, age eighteen, who lived with her parents. These four, proving themselves useful to the conspiracy, made up the outer circle of the afflicted, and were recruited to work hand-in-hand with the inner circle.

The remainder of the afflicted in Salem Village consisted of several young women, and also a few older women, married and single, as well as a boy or two. These were kept at arm's length by the conspiracy, who relegated them to a few minor and insignificant roles. The circle of afflicted girls of Salem Village is shown in Figure 3.

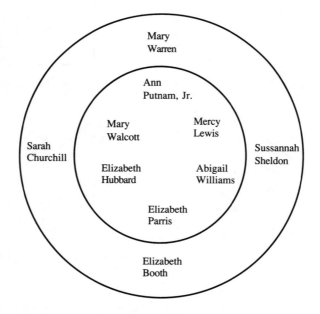

Figure 3. Inner circle and outer circle of the afflicted.

The entries of the Complaint Table can be highlighted to clarify the work of the conspiracy. Whenever the name of one or more conspirators appears in an entry, the word *Conspiracy* is entered in its place. In a similar manner the words *Fringe group*, *Inner circle* and *Outer circle* are entered.

For example in the first complaint the names Thomas Putnam and Edward Putnam are replaced by Conspiracy. The name Joseph Hutchinson is replaced by Fringe group. The names Elizabeth Parris, Abigail Williams, Ann Putnam, Jr., and Elizabeth Hubbard are replaced by Inner circle. If this scheme is followed for each entry, the following table is obtained.

ANNOTATED COMPLAINT TABLE©

Date	Accused	Accusers	Afflicted
No. 1 Feb. 29	Sarah Good Sarah Osborne Tituba	Conspiracy Fringe group Thomas Preston	Inner circle
No. 2 Mar. 19	Martha Corey	Conspiracy Fringe group Henry Kenny	Inner circle
No. 3 Mar. 23	Rebecca Nurse	Conspiracy	Inner circle
No. 4 Mar. 23	Dorcas Good	Conspiracy	Inner circle
No. 5 Mar. 29	Rachel Clinton	Independent of Salem Village	
No. 6 Apr. 4	Sarah Cloyce Elizabeth Proctor	Conspiracy	Inner circle John Indian
No. 7 Apr. 11	John Proctor	Conspiracy	Inner circle John Indian

No. 8 Apr. 18	Giles Corey Bridget Bishop Abigail Hobbs Mary Warren	Conspiracy Ezekiel Cheever	Inner circle
No. 9 Apr. 21	William Hobbs Deliverance Hobbs Nehemiah Abbot, Jr. Mary Easty Sarah Wildes Edward Bishop, Jr. Sarah Bishop Mary Black Mary English	Conspiracy Fringe group	Inner circle
No. 10 Apr. 30	Philip English Lydia Dustin Susannah Martin Dorcas Hoar Sarah Morrell George Burroughs	Conspiracy	Inner circle Outer circle
No. 11 May 7	Sarah Dustin	Conspiracy	Inner circle
No. 12 May 8	Bethia Carter Bethia Carter, Jr. Ann Sears	Conspiracy	Inner circle
No. 13 May 10	George Jacobs, Sr. Margaret Jacobs	Conspiracy	Inner circle Outer circle
No. 14 May 10	John Willard	Benjamin Wilkins, Sr. Thomas Fuller, Jr.	Bray Wilkins Daniel Wilkins
No. 15 May 12	Alice Parker Ann Pudeator	Conspiracy	Inner circle Outer circle
No. 16 c. May 13	Abigail Somes	Conspiracy	Inner circle Outer circle

No. 17 May 14	Daniel Andrew George Jacobs, Jr. Rebecca Jacobs Sarah Buckley Mary Whittredge Elizabeth Hart Thomas Farrar Elizabeth Colson	Conspiracy	Inner Circle
No. 18 May 15	Mehitabel Downing	Conspiracy	Outer circle
No. 19 May 18	Roger Toothaker	Conspiracy	Inner circle
No. 20 May 21	Sarah Proctor Sarah Bassett Susannah Roots	Conspiracy	Inner circle
No. 21 May 23	Benjamin Proctor Mary De Rich Sarah Pease	Conspiracy Thomas Rayment	Inner circle
No. 22 May 28	Elizabeth Cary	Conspiracy Fringe group	Inner circle
No. 23 May 28	John Alden John Floyd Elizabeth Fosdick Wilmot Redd Sarah Rice William Proctor Elizabeth Howe Arthur Abbot Martha Carrier Mary Toothaker Margaret Toothaker	Conspiracy	Inner circle
No. 24 May 30	Elizabeth Paine Elizabeth Fosdick	Conspiracy Joseph Whipple	Inner circle Outer circle
No. 25 Jun. 2	Elizabeth Paine Elizabeth Fosdick	Peter Tufts	Tufts' slave

No. 26 Jun. 4	Mary Ireson	Conspiracy Thomas Rayment	Inner circle Outer circle
No. 27 Jun. 3	Job Tookey	Conspiracy	Inner circle Outer circle Sarah Bibber
No. 28 Jun. 5	Ann Dolliver	Conspiracy	Inner circle Outer circle
No. 29 Jun. 28	Mary Bradbury	Conspiracy	Inner circle Outer circle
No. 30 Jul. 1	Margaret Hawkes Candy	Conspiracy	Inner circle Outer circle

In the above table, it is seen that out of thirty complaints only three were not originated by the conspiracy. Complaint No. 5 accusing Rachel Clinton is a special case involving the town of Ipswich. Complaint No. 14 accusing John Willard was filed by the Wilkins family with the complete approval and cooperation of the conspiracy, who allowed the inner circle to act as seers as well as afflicted persons. Complaint No. 25 accusing Elizabeth Paine and Elizabeth Fosdick is especially interesting. This complaint, duplicating Complaint No. 24 filed by the conspiracy, was filed by Peter Tufts, whose daughter-in-law was Maria (Cotton) Tufts. Because she was the first cousin of the Rev. Cotton Mather, this complaint links him to the conspiracy.

The Rev. Samuel Parris, age thirty-nine in 1692, was a founding member of the conspiracy and a prime conspirator. He lived in the Salem Village parsonage with his wife Elizabeth, age forty-four, their daughter Elizabeth Parris, called Betty, age nine, and his niece Abigail Williams, age eleven. Also he owned two slaves, Tituba and her husband, John Indian. The names of Betty and Abigail appeared on the first complaint, filed on February 29, 1692. It states that Betty and Abigail were afflicted by Sarah Good, Sarah Osborne, and Tituba. The complaint was filed by Thomas Putnam, his brother Edward Putnam, Joseph Houlton and Thomas Preston. Parris' name does not appear. Thomas

Preston, in putting his name on this complaint, had been duped by the conspiracy. The son-in-law of Rebecca Nurse, he quickly realized his folly and withdrew his support for the witchcraft proceedings.

Betty was an active participant in the courtroom until early April, when the Rev. Parris withdrew her from further participation and sent her to live in Salem Town with the family of Stephen Sewall. The youngest of the afflicted girls, Betty was beginning to show preliminary symptoms of a mental breakdown. At his wife's insistence, he drew the line at the health of their daughter. His niece Abigail Williams was made of sterner stuff. After Betty left the circle, Abigail Williams and Ann Putnam, Jr. continued as the most active of the group. They were now also the youngest.

In all, Abigail alleged she was afflicted by forty-four persons. She testified against many in court. Even Joseph Hutchinson, a member of the fringe group of the conspiracy, was upset by the outrageous lies of Abigail Williams. In a deposition he tried to discredit Abigail's veracity. Because Abigail was the niece of the Rev. Parris, Hutchinson's deposition did little good.

Dr. William Griggs was another founding member of the conspiracy. Dr. Griggs and the Rev. Parris were often brought together by their professional interests. In those days the approaches of physician and cleric in dealing with sickness were similar, converging somewhere between the occult and faith healing. The physical (sickness) and the spiritual (sin) were regarded as parts of the same whole. As already seen, Cotton Mather himself had studied medicine before entering the clergy.

Originally from Boston, Dr. Griggs was the first physician to practice in Salem Village. In 1692, he was about seventy-seven years old and his wife, whose maiden name was Rachel Hubbard, was sixty-four years old. The Hubbard family was distinguished, whereas Griggs came from modest beginnings. Not particularly successful, he paid a tax of only sixteen shillings in Salem Village in 1690. In 1692 Dr. Griggs was not reluctant to see some of the Salem Village midwives arrested for witchcraft, since they had been dispensing medicine which was generally regarded as more beneficial than his own.   For example, testimony against Elizabeth Proctor, an accused witch, claimed that she was responsible for the death of a man because Dr. Griggs had not been sent for "to give him physic."

Elizabeth Hubbard, the great niece of Dr. Griggs' wife, was living with the old couple and working as their servant. Elizabeth was a good friend of Mary Walcott; both seventeen, they spent much time together. Dr. Griggs' house was only about one-half of a mile from Jonathan Walcott's house.   However, on February 16, 1692, close to the start of the witch hunt, Dr. Griggs bought a better house, situated close to the Beverly line, nearly three miles from the Walcott house. Elizabeth still visited the Walcott house, but now she often spent the night. Ann Putnam, Jr. and Mercy Lewis lived at Thomas Putnam's house, over a mile from the Walcott house. Ann managed to visit the Walcott house regularly to see her aunt and play with the children. Mercy Lewis often went with Ann; Mercy was the same age as Elizabeth Hubbard and Mary Walcott. Ann, only twelve, was friends with Abigail Williams, age eleven, who lived in the Rev. Parris' parsonage, the nearest house to the Walcott house, just a few hundred feet away. Also at the parsonage was little Elizabeth Parris, age nine. These six girls, the two Elizabeths, Mary, Ann, Mercy, and Abigail, made up the inner circle.

If as a physician, Dr. Griggs refrained from filing any legal complaints, we see his hand in the actions of his servant, Elizabeth Hubbard.[78] Elizabeth Hubbard maintained a spiteful and malicious role throughout the witchcraft scare.   In a deposition, Clement Coldum stated that on May 29, 1692 "I asked

---

78   At the examination of Elizabeth Proctor on April 11, 1692, "Benjamin
      Gould gave in his testimony that he had seen Goodman Corey and his wife,
      Proctor and his wife, Goody Cloyce, Goody Nurse, and Goody Griggs in
      his chamber last night. Elizabeth Hubbard was in a trance during the
      whole examination." Of course, Goodwife Griggs, being the wife of a
      conspirator, was exempt from any possibility of being charged.

her if she was not afraid of the Devil? She answered me no, she could discourse with the Devil as well as with me." Coldum was ready to testify under oath as to his testimony. James Kettle was also willing to testify against Elizabeth and stated the "the last of May, having some discourse with Elizabeth Hubbard, I found her to speak several untruths." The records show that she was afflicted by seventeen persons, and she testified against many.

On February 10, 1693, when the witchcraft craze was coming to an end, Dr. Griggs, "being aged and infirm," conveyed his newly purchased house to his son, Jacob Griggs of Beverly. When Dr. Griggs died in 1698, his library consisted of "nine physic books," worth 30 shillings, and "bibles & other books," worth 15 shillings. His medical equipment included a case of lances, two razors, a saw, and seven instruments for chirurgeon [surgeon]. His wife survived him, living to be ninety.

Sergeant Thomas Putnam, age thirty-nine, a founding member of the conspiracy, acted as ringleader. Much can be learned by looking at events from the perspective of this man, the chief filer of the legal complaints that led to the arrest of alleged witches. Repeatedly he claimed that his eldest daughter, Ann Putnam, Jr., and his servant Mercy Lewis were afflicted and tormented by a multitude of witches. He demanded justice.

His wife Ann Putnam, Sr.[79], age thirty, entered into this macabre play-act as an afflicted person on a number of occasions. In fact she was in court almost as often as her daughter and her servant, all of them acting out the afflictions of witchcraft. Together, the three were responsible for the spectral evidence leading to many imprisonments, some of which resulted in death.

---

79   Ann Putnam, Sr. was born on June 15, 1661 in Salisbury, the daughter of George Carr. In 1678 she married Thomas Putnam, born on March 12, 1653 in Salem Village. At the time of the outbreak of the Salem witchcraft in February 1692, Ann Putnam, Sr. had six children ranging from Ann, Jr., age 12, to Timothy, age ten months, and she was pregnant with Abigail.

Mother Ann and daughter Ann were a particularly formidable pair of actors. People from miles around trooped into the courtroom to watch their performances under bewitchment. They regarded their afflictions as a matter of life and death. During the course of the witch hunt, Ann Putnam, Jr. alleged that she was afflicted by a total of sixty-two persons. She testified against many people in court, and gave a number of affidavits.

In 1692 Mercy Lewis was a well-educated young woman. She was born in 1675, the daughter of Philip Lewis of Casco, Maine. The town was destroyed by the Indians in 1676. For the duration of the war, no white person ventured within this desolate locality, but after the conclusion of peace in November 1678, resettlement slowly took place. The Lewis family settled on Hogg Island as tenants of Edward Tyng. Tyng's main residence was on the Neck, the most desirable location in Casco, and the center of the present-day city of Portland. His closest neighbor was the minister, the Rev. George Burroughs.

When Mercy Lewis' parents were both killed by the Indians in 1689, she was taken into the house of the Rev. Burroughs. In 1690, as the only minister for all the towns between Casco and Wells, Maine, he took up residency in Wells. Because of the danger of repeated Indian attacks in Maine, Mercy was placed in the home of William and Rachel Bradford. Mercy lived a part of a year with them, during which they did "judge in the matter of conscience of speaking the truth and untruth, she would stand stiffly [original document torn]." She was finally placed as a servant in the home of Sergeant Thomas Putnam in Salem Village. According to the records she was afflicted by fifty-one persons. She testified against scores of people in court, and gave many affidavits against the accused witches. In her deposition against George Burroughs, she stated, "I saw the apparition of George Burroughs, whom I very well knew. He brought to me a new fashioned book, and told me I might write in that book, for that was a book that was in his study when I lived with them. But I told him, I did not believe him, for I had often been in his study, but I never saw that book there. But he told me that he had several books in his study which I never saw in his study, and he could raise the Devil."[80]

Although Sergeant Thomas Putnam operated mostly in the background, he did step out in the open to file legal complaints; indeed, he filed more than anyone else. In addition, he testified in a great number of cases, including those of Sarah Buckley, the Rev. George Burroughs, Martha Carrier, Giles and Martha Corey, Mary Easty, Sarah Cloyce, Thomas Farrar, Sr., Dorcas Hoar, George Jacobs, Sr., Susannah Martin, Rebecca Nurse, Elizabeth and John Proctor, Sarah Proctor, Tituba, and John Willard. Of these people, ten were executed, and two condemned to death but reprieved at the final moment.

Sergeant Thomas Putnam's brother, Deacon Edward Putnam, age thirty-eight in 1692, was a member of the conspiracy and his closest ally in carrying out the witch hunt.

Another member, Captain Jonathan Walcott, was the father of Mary Walcott by his first wife. At the time of the witch hunt, he was fifty-two, and married to his second wife, Deliverance, the sister of Thomas and Edward Putnam. Not only did Captain Walcott encourage his daughter Mary Walcott to act out the role of an afflicted girl, but he testified with great effectiveness against many accused witches himself.

Records show that Mary Walcott alleged that she was afflicted by fifty-nine persons. She gave many affidavits and frequently testified in court against people. Mary Walcott and Ann Putnam, Jr. were taken to Andover on June 11, 1692, to initiate a witch hunt in that area. Again, on July 26, the two girls visited that town to spur on the Andover witch hunt.

Thomas and Edward Putnam's sister Ann had been married to William Trask. Both she and William had died by 1692. Still,

---

80 On May 14, 1691 Priscilla Lewis, Mercy's older sister, married Henry
    Kenny, Jr. His father, Henry Kenny, was a signer of the complaint against
    Martha Corey and a witness against Rebecca Nurse.

the Trask family helped the Putnams in the witch hunt. John Trask appeared as a witness against Sarah Bishop, the wife of Edward Bishop, Jr.

Sergeant Thomas Putnam's two uncles John Putnam, Sr. and Nathaniel Putnam were eager to help. They were members of the conspiracy, but were not as active as the younger Putnams.

John Putnam Sr., had married Rebecca Prince, step-daughter of John Gedney, Sr., the wealthy owner of the Ship Tavern in Salem Town.[81] In 1692 John Putnam, Sr. believed that his nephews, the two Prince boys, were being cheated out of their inheritance by Sarah Osborne. To destroy Sarah Osborne, John Putnam, Sr. saw to it that she was one of the first three witches accused. Sarah Osborne died in prison a couple of months later. John Putnam, Sr. also took his revenge on the Rev. George Burroughs by testifying against him in the witchcraft trials.

John Putnam, Sr.'s son, Constable Jonathan Putnam, was also a member. He and his first cousin, Edward Putnam, signed the complaint that put Rebecca Nurse behind bars, as well as the complaint that put four-year-old Dorcas Good into chains.

The other uncle, Nathaniel Putnam, signed the complaint against Elizabeth Paine and Elizabeth Fosdick. His son, Constable John Putnam, Jr., also a member of the conspiracy, signed several complaints and testified against many.

Lieutenant Nathaniel Ingersoll, the innkeeper, was the final member of the conspiracy. He was the uncle of Captain Jonathan Walcott. Lieutenant Ingersoll worked closely with Sergeant Thomas Putnam and Captain Walcott to keep the flames burning. With a wary eye toward maintaining goodwill so as not to impair

---

81   John Gedney, Sr., who died in 1688, was the father of John Gedney, Jr., who died in 1684, and Bartholomew Gedney, one of the witchcraft justices. After John Gedney, Jr. died, his widow moved into the house of John Gedney, Sr. and kept the tavern. Shortly thereafter, John Louder, one of the servants in the house, saw a "black thing" to which he testified in 1692 as evidence against Bridget Bishop. After John Gedney, Sr.'s death in 1688, his son's widow continued to keep the tavern, which in 1692 was known as the "Widow Gedney's."

the profits of his tavern, Ingersoll signed only a few complaints. However, when called as witness he gladly testified against those accused. It was no coincidence that two of his competitors in Salem Village, tavern-owners John Proctor and Edward Bishop, Jr. were both arrested for witchcraft, and that Proctor paid with his life.

Except for the departure of Elizabeth Parris, the inner circle of afflicted girls remained unchanged throughout the witch hunt. Of the six girls, only three, Elizabeth Parris, Ann Putnam, Jr., and Mary Walcott, were living in their parents' homes. The other three, having lost one or both parents, had been placed in the conspirators' households, and, except for Abigail Williams, were servants.

Since none of the four girls in the outer circle of afflicted lived in the households of conspirators, they required careful control at all times.

The daughter of George and Elizabeth Booth of Salem Village, Elizabeth Booth, age eighteen, was a member of the outer circle, participating in examinations, inquests, and trials. Not a favorite of the conspiracy, her name was only chosen for use on a couple of complaints. It appears on the warrant for the arrest of John Alden, Jr. (Alden, the sea captain and trader who worked his ship along the Maine coast, had engaged in the fur trade with Indian friends before King William's War.) Elizabeth's actions as an afflicted girl were supported by her mother and younger sister, Alice, age fourteen. On October 11, 1692, nineteen days after the executions on September 22, Elizabeth Booth married Jonathan Pease, age twenty-three, and started a family of her own. Her afflictions were over; of the witches whose apparitions had hurt her, John Proctor and Wilmot Redd had been hanged, Giles Corey pressed to death, and the pregnant Elizabeth Proctor was in prison, sentenced to death, but under reprieve until the child was born.

Susannah Sheldon, age eighteen, another member of the outer circle, suffered from a deep and abiding fear of the Indians. Her parents, Rebecca (Scadlock) and William Sheldon had resided in Saco, Maine, but were driven out by the Indians in 1676 during King Philip's War. Susannah, only a baby at the time, barely escaped death as the family fled the slaughter which ensued. Taking up residence in Salem, the family returned to Saco as soon as it was safe. With the outbreak of King William's War, the Indians again destroyed their farm. The family escaped death, but this time Susannah's father was badly wounded in trying to protect her. The family then moved to Salem Village.

Susannah's older brother, Godfrey, age twenty-four, encountered the Indians in Maine on July 3, 1690 in the service of his country. Surprised in an ambush, some of the soldiers panicked and tried to flee. Godfrey was last seen alive being pursued into the forest by a stout Indian, brightly daubed in war-paint, a gun in one hand and a hatchet in the other. Godfrey's hacked body was later found without its scalp.

Susannah's father, crippled by his wounds, fell and cut his knee. He died two weeks later, on December 2, 1691, less than three months before the witchcraft outbreak. Susannah stayed on in Salem Village with her widowed mother and remaining siblings. Having lost everything to the Indians, they were almost destitute. Cotton Mather and other divines were constantly railing that witches and Indians both were agents of the Devil. The records show that Susannah was afflicted by eleven alleged witches, and bore witness against them in examinations, inquests, and trials.

Mary Warren, age twenty, who proved to be the most faithful and dependable member of the outer circle, was an orphan. At the outset of the witch hunt she was a servant in the household of John Proctor of Salem Farms, a part of Salem township just south of Salem Village. Both John Proctor and his wife were imprisoned on April 11, 1692. On April 18, one week later, Mary herself was accused and imprisoned. The complaint was filed by

Ezekiel Cheever and John Putnam, Jr. for afflicting the inner circle girls.

Parris' description of Mary Warren's examination on April 19 is dramatic. At the end he notes "that not one of the sufferers was afflicted during her examination after once she began to confess, though they were tormented before." She was imprisoned at Salem, where she was examined and accused her master, John Proctor, and his wife Elizabeth, as well as Giles Corey.

Mary Warren displeased the conspirators when she wanted to tell the truth. Imprisoned witches Mary Easty, Edward Bishop, Jr. and his wife, Sarah, gave the following deposition which states how Mary Warren discredited the afflicted girls. "About three weeks ago today, when we were in Salem Jail, we heard Mary Warren several times say that the magistrates might as well examine Keyser's daughter, who has been distracted many years, and take notice of what she said as well as any of the afflicted persons. Mary Warren said when I was afflicted I thought I saw the apparitions of a hundred persons. She said her head was distempered; that she could not tell what she said. And Mary told us that when she was well again, she could not say that she saw any of [the] apparitions at the time aforesaid."

Early in June, however, Mary Warren was released and allowed to continue her active participation in the afflicted group. Altogether she claimed to have been afflicted by fourteen persons.

Sarah Churchill, age twenty, was the second most dependable member of the outer circle. She came from a family in Saco, Maine with considerable property and a heritage of English gentry. After her parents had been killed by the Indians, she was reduced to the position of servant in the household of George Jacobs, Sr. of Salem. Soon after the outbreak of the witch hunt, she became one of the afflicted. Jacobs called the afflicted girls "bitch witches" and was otherwise very disrespectful of her. Sarah was often in court as part of the afflicted group. She was also a witness against her master.

George Jacobs, Sr. was imprisoned on May 10, as was his granddaughter, Margaret Jacobs.   Shortly thereafter, Sarah Churchill herself was accused and imprisoned.   Her name appeared on the list of those in Salem Prison, along with Mary Warren.   Sarah Churchill had angered the conspiracy because she, too, wanted to tell the truth. Sarah Ingersoll, who worked in the tavern, gave this deposition.   "Sarah Churchill after her examination came to me crying.   She said she had lied in saying that she set her hand to the Devil's book.   She lied because they threatened her and told her they would put her into the dungeon, along with the Rev. Burroughs.   She said she had undone herself in belying herself and others.   She said also that if she told Mr. Noyes [assistant minister at Salem] but once that she had set her hand to the book, he would believe her, but, if she told the truth and said that she had not set her hand to the book a hundred times, he would not believe her."   Sarah Ingersoll was the daughter of conspirator Nathaniel Ingersoll.

On June 1 Sarah Churchill testified that her master, George Jacobs, Sr., as well as Ann Pudeator and Bridget Bishop, made her a witch.   Sarah's imprisonment was of short duration, as she was in court again on July 2 to testify against Ann Pudeator.

Mary Warren and Sarah Churchill were the only two afflicted girls to be imprisoned, albeit briefly.   Both were taken shortly after their masters had been incarcerated. The extant depositions show that the two were distressed with the roles they were playing in the witch hunt, and wanted to tell the truth.   But naturally, being terrified in prison, they preferred to return to their acting. Each twenty-years old, they were older than all the rest of the afflicted in the circle, and as servants and orphans they stood alone in a dangerous world.

John Indian, husband of Tituba, was used in court as an afflicted person.   He could reliably demonstrate how grievously he was tormented by whomever was under examination.   No doubt he was convinced that he would stand a better chance of survival among the afflicted than among the accused, and sensibly, he played his part well. It is most probable that others who joined the ranks of the afflicted from time to time acted from the same pragmatic standpoint. None, however, gained admittance to the favored circles, inner or outer, of the Salem Village afflicted.

When it was formed in February 1692, the nascent conspiracy never could have guessed the extremes to which they would be allowed to go. Its members suspected that vindictive people in Salem Village and neighboring communities would support their cause of rooting out certain undesirable people as witches. They trusted that the powerful personage, John Hathorne, who gave original encouragement would continue in his support. What they could not foresee, however, was that the highest level of government, the ruling, old-guard Puritans, would not only act in collusion to support their cause of destroying the "enemies of the church," but would give them a free hand in determining who those enemies were.

It did not take long for the conspiracy to find this out; the crucial day was April 11, 1692. On that day two witches, Sarah Cloyce and Elizabeth Proctor, were examined in the large meetinghouse in Salem Town.[82] The aged and ill governor, Simon Bradstreet, now only a figurehead, did not attend. But members of the ruling old guard did: Thomas Danforth (the deputy governor), Isaac Addington of Boston (the secretary of the province), Major Samuel Appleton of Ipswich, James Russell of Charlestown, Capt. Samuel Sewall of Boston, Jonathan Corwin, and, of course, John Hathorne, the last five being assistants to the

---

82   William Rayment, age 26, testifying for Elizabeth Proctor, said that when he was at Ingersoll's tavern on March 28, 1692 an afflicted girl cried out, "There is Goody Proctor. There is Goody Proctor. I'll see her hang!" When Goodwife Ingersoll sharply reproved the afflicted girls, Rayment said that "they seemed to make a joke of it." The accused, whenever possible, tried to present evidence showing the imposture of the afflicted girls, but it did no good.

governor.[83] The examinations were officially described as taking place "at a council held at Salem." These Council members concurred in the methods used by the conspiracy, thereby stamping the witch hunt with their seal of approval.[84] William Stoughton was the only one of this core of high ranking men who was not present at the meeting. The overwhelming evidence of the complicity of the ruling old guard was born out in all events which followed.

Figure 4. The pyramidal structure of the witch hunt.

In the Salem Village witch hunt, a hierarchical structure exists. The pyramid has the sponsors at the top, made up of several clergy in collusion with the old-guard Puritan rulers.

---

83   Appleton, Russell, Corwin, and Hathorne were related by marriage. Corwin and Hathorne had conducted all the previous examinations at Salem Village.

84   "Mr. Samuel Parris was desired by the honorable Thomas Danforth, deputy governor, and the council, to take in writing the examinations. Upon hearing, and seeing what was then seen, together with the charge of the afflicted persons," the accused Sarah Cloyce and Elizabeth Proctor, and well as John Proctor, "were, by the advice of council, all committed."

They sanctioned the agents, consisting of the accusers and the afflicted circle of girls. Under them are the people who suffered, predominantly women, accused as witches. At the base is the mass of the populace who either were not affected directly, or were brought in on special occasions to provide malicious gossip about their accused neighbors. This structure is explained in the following table.

THE HIERARCHY OF THE WITCH HUNT

THE SPONSORS	
The Clergy	A small number of Puritan ministers intent on retaining tight control of their congregations through intimidation. The threat of witches was a contrivance to hold onto their power.
Old guard Puritans	Key members of the upper legislative body (board of assistants or council) acting in collusion. Accustomed to ruling with an iron hand, and fearing the general franchise granted by the new charter, they sought to keep the population under their control at all costs.
THE AGENTS	
The Accusers	A conspiracy of envious and vengeful men who saw in the real or imagined sicknesses of their children the means to bring down their enemies.
The Afflicted	Children caught up in the hysteria sanctioned and supervised by the accusers.
The Victims	
The Accused	Women, and some men, who were members of families that attracted the wrath of the old guard or the envy of the accusers.
THE POPULACE	
The Unaffected	The remaining population who watched, acquiescent, until they saw that anyone was fair game.

Salem is hardly the first instance when witchcraft accusations were used by political rulers to further their aims. One hundred years before these events, Shakespeare wrote *King Richard III.* In the play, the throne of England is vacant following the death of King Edward IV. Edward's wife, now his widow, wants her son to succeed to the throne. Richard uses any means, including murder, to prevent this and to gain the throne for himself. To silence the claims of Edward's widow, Richard accuses her of witchcraft.

> I pray you all, tell me what they deserve
> That do conspire my death with devilish plots
> Of damned witchcraft, and that have prevailed
> Upon my body with their hellish charms?
> Look how I am bewitched; behold my arm
> Is like a blasted sapling, withered up:
> And this is Edward's wife, that monstrous witch,
> Consorted with that harlot strumpet Shore,
> That by their witchcraft thus have marked me.[85]

To Shakespeare, witchcraft accusations were impostures, simple but lethal, used by connivers and fanatics in desperate and brutal attempts to seize and hold positions of power.

---

85   Shakespeare, *King Richard III*, act 3, sc. 4.

CHAPTER 8

SUPERSTITION'S SWAY

The winter of 1691-1692, was unusually cold and bitter, the ponds frozen thick with ice, the landscape wrapped deep in snow. The widely scattered farms of Salem Village lay desolate and vulnerable. The meetinghouse, symbol of New England theocracy, stood out proudly, dominating the tavern, the parsonage, and the small group of houses which formed the village center. The watch house, constructed early in King William's War, sat close at hand. Fearful of an Indian attack, the village posted sentinels, night and day.

The meetinghouse, like those throughout New England, served as both church building and town hall. All large meetings, either religious or political, were held in this unheated building. As the days grew shorter, the meetinghouse grew damper and icier with each succeeding week. Gladly did the villagers flock from that gloomy building into Lieutenant Ingersoll's tavern, warmed by the glowing embers in its large fireplaces. The comfortable tavern served as the community center; on Sundays people would thaw out there before the afternoon service and warm up before the ride or walk home. Either the meeting house or the tavern could serve as courthouse, depending on the size of the audience. During those long winter evenings as people gathered in the tavern over mugs of hot cider and buttered rum, the talk swung anxiously between the minister's sermon, Indian raids, and Satan's design on New England. Cotton Mather had exhorted his readers to "tell mankind that there are Devils and Witches, and that New England has had examples of their existence and operation, and that not only the wigwams of Indians, where the pagan Powaws [medicine men] often raise their masters [devils], in the shapes of bears and snakes and fires, but the houses of Christians have undergone the annoyance of evil spirits."[86]

Less exposed than their neighbors in Haverhill, Andover, and Billerica, the Salem Village farmers still needed to stay on constant alert in case of attack by an Indian raiding party. This was the fourth year of King William's War, and the Indians were still hard at their horrible work of killing and plundering. Continued news of massacres at isolated farmhouses had set the entire town on edge.

Now, however, a change had occurred in the treatment of prisoners. Previously, the Indians took few captives, most of whom led miserable existences before their untimely deaths. A doomed captive first would be handed over to the squaws, who would seize him by the hair, hands, and feet like so many furies, before passing him on to the warriors. But now the Indians could march the captives to Canada, where the French would pay good money for them. The French would then ransom them to the English, or use them in exchange for French prisoners. This gentler procedure meant that the Indians took fewer scalps but more prisoners.

Cotton Mather wrote, "On September 28, 1691, seven persons were murdered and captivated at Berwick: and on the day following thrice seven of Sandy Beach; on October 23, 1691, one Goodridge and his wife were murdered at Rowley, and his children captivated; and the day following the like fate befell a family at Haverhill. But the winter must not pass over without a storm of blood! The Popish Indians did on January 25, 1692, set upon the town of York. The inhabitants found their houses to be invested with horrid savages, who immediately killed many of those unprovided inhabitants and more they took prisoners."

On that cold and snowy morning a large force of Indians took the entire settlement of York, Maine by surprise. Their stealthy footfalls deadened by the fresh snow, the Indians burst open the

---

86   Cotton Mather, 1689, in Burr, 99.

doors with their hatchets, killing and scalping. The houses were ransacked and then set on fire. After killing about seventy-five persons, the Indians seemed to tire of the blood shed by their weapons. They marched off toward Canada with about one hundred captives, some still in their nightclothes, leaving behind the few people who had managed to take refuge in the garrisons. Some of these survivors trod their way back the fifty miles to Salem, bringing eye-witness accounts of the fates of relatives and friends.

"Truly the dark places of New England, where the Indians had their unapproachable kennels, were habitations of cruelty, and no words can sufficiently describe the cruelty undergone by our captives in those habitations. The cold, and hunger, and weariness, and mockings, and scourgings, would ever deserve the name of cruelty; but there was to this also added unto the rest, that they must ever now and then have their friend made a 'sacrifice of Devils' before their eyes," wrote Cotton Mather.

James Key, a child of five years, "lamented with tears the want of his parents" to his Indian captor. "This monster striped him stark naked, and scourged him so that he was all over bloody and swollen, with taunts remembering him of his parents. The child had a sore eye; his master with the thumb of his right hand forced the ball of the eye quite out. About nine or ten days later, the child being tired and faint, sat him down to rest, at which this horrid fellow being provoked, he buried the blade of his hatchet into the brains of the child, and then chopped the breathless body to pieces before the rest of the company. ...

"Mehitabel Goodwin, a captive, had with her a child about five months old. Her Indian master, lest he should be retarded in his travel, snatched the babe out of its mother's arms, and before her face knocked out its brains, and stripped it of the few rags it had hitherto enjoyed, and ordered her to wash the bloody clothes. Returning from this melancholy task, she found the infant hanging by the neck in a forked bough of a tree. ...

"Mary Plaisted was made captive about three weeks after her delivery of a male child. At night the cold ground in the open air was her lodging. She must now travel through woods and rocks, and over mountains, and frost and snow, until she could stir no further. Sitting down to rest, her diabolical master took the child from her, and carried it unto a river, where stripping it of the few rags it had, he took it by the heels, and against a tree dashed out its brains, and then flung it into the river. ...

"A maid about fifteen or sixteen years of age burst into tears, telling her Indian master that she could go no further. Whereupon he cut off her head, and scalping it, he ran about laughing and bragging what an act he had done, showing the scalp unto the rest. ...

"When the children cried, the manner of the Indians was to dash out their brains against a tree. And very often when the Indians were near the water, they took the small children, and held them under water till they had nearly drowned them. And the Indians in their frolics would whip and beat the small children. This was Indian captivity!"[87]

These atrocities against captive children were nearly outdone by the gratuitous torture of the dumb farm animals on the raided farms. When Cotton Mather called the Indians "agents of the Devil," everyone knew what he meant.

In February 1692, in the kitchen of the Salem Village parsonage six girls clustered around Tituba, Parris' woman slave. Betty Parris, Abigail Williams, and Ann Putnam, Jr., were pre-teenagers; the other three, Elizabeth Hubbard, Mary Walcott, and Mercy Lewis, were teenagers, each seventeen years old. Cooped up by the endless procession of dreary winter days, and tensed from the news of the massacre at York, their impressionable and vivid imaginations were enchanted by Tituba's chatter of the voodoo in her native Barbados. Intrigued and excited, the girls pored over an improvised crystal ball, trying to foretell their futures. Asking "what trade their sweethearts should be of" they saw a frightful image, "a specter in likeness of a coffin."

---

87   Cotton Mather, *Magnalia,* book 7, 597-600.

The girls were both enthralled and frightened by talk overheard from their elders about the Devil's plot to destroy their homes through his agents, the Indians and witches. First, frail and sensitive Betty Parris, and then Ann Putnam, Jr. and Abigail Williams, began acting in strange and unusual manners. The three would creep into holes, and under chairs and stools. They contorted themselves into odd postures and made strange gestures. They uttered foolish and ridiculous speech of which neither they nor anyone else could make sense. At first it seemed like a game, but soon it became clear that it was something more. The three young girls were sometimes dumb, as if choked. They complained of pains, like those from pins being thrust into their bodies. Alarmed, the Rev. Parris observed that their "singular distempers" or "fits" were much like those of the Goodwin children recently described by Cotton Mather in his book on witchcraft. Dr. William Griggs offered no physical reason for their "afflictions." Instead he said, "They are under the evil hand." This meant that they were bewitched, and Sergeant Thomas Putnam, the father of Ann, so understood it. Witchcraft was a legal crime of the vilest sort.

Thomas Putnam promptly paid a visit to John Hathorne. This was quite in order because John Hathorne, as magistrate and an assistant to the governor, represented the highest legal authority in Salem township. In his capacity as magistrate, John Hathorne, like his father before him, spent his life listening to every squabble, major and minor, that a town full of contentious people could provide. Time and again John Hathorne had to deal with difficult people, like Sarah Good, brought before his court on charges of debt and other failures to live up to the strict Puritanical code. Might such flaunting of the Puritan ethic result from the practice of witchcraft? Whatever the case, John Hathorne was as much convinced of the need and duty to root out witchcraft as Cotton Mather himself. Hathorne, a native of Salem Village and a long-standing friend of the Putnam family, assured Sergeant Thomas Putnam that he would provide the legal means necessary to bring the witches to justice. The conspiracy was born.

First Elizabeth Hubbard, and then her two teenage friends, Mercy Lewis and Mary Walcott, became afflicted, joining the ranks of the three younger girls. The inner circle of the afflicted was now complete. The fathers or guardians of these six girls were the Rev. Samuel Parris, Dr. William Griggs, Sergeant Thomas Putnam, and Captain Jonathan Walcott.

Here were four of Salem Village's most prominent citizens: the minister, the physician, and two important political and military leaders. Each held a vested interest in witchcraft. The Rev. Parris recognized in it a powerful weapon with which to defeat his enemies, those who questioned his demands in Salem Village. With his opponents eliminated, Parris knew that his tenure in the ministry would be secure. Dr. Griggs practiced his own brand of folk magic in conjunction with his medical treatments, and now glimpsed a golden opportunity to do away with the midwives and other rivals, such as Dr. Roger Toothaker, who competed successfully with him in medical practice. Sergeant Putnam and Captain Walcott, natural leaders, found in witchcraft a means to achieve political power denied them by conventional means. Specifically, Thomas Putnam saw a way to retaliate against those with whom the Putnam family had long-standing and often justifiable grudges. The Putnams could regain land which the Topsfield men had claimed as their own. In fact, by means of a witch hunt, the Putnams might gain total political control of Salem Village. At the close of February 1692 the conspiracy was born and the witch hunt began.

The conspirators had many perceived enemies whom they could accuse of being witches. At the outset they chose four. Two of the four were regarded as weak and eccentric, Sarah Good and Sarah Osborne. These women were chosen as the first victims because they lacked family or community support. The other two, in contrast, were strong women of high standing, Martha Corey and Rebecca Nurse. They had widespread support and both were church members. Their rank can be appreciated from the fact that only about a dozen women in Salem Village held the status of church membership, and less than twenty men.[88] If the conspiracy could bring down two church members, it might bring down anyone.

The naming of the witches was the most delicate feature of the witch hunt, requiring as much credibility and conviction as possible. According to traditional beliefs, witches used their specters to afflict people, and only the afflicted had the spectral sight needed to see these specters. This meant that the names had to come from the mouths of the afflicted children themselves. In order to carry out their deceit, the conspirators resorted to manipulation and stealth. The afflicted girls were never taken into their confidence. Instead, by subtle means, the men indicated to the girls the names of the witches. The afflicted girls, readily picking up on these cues, cried out upon the designated witches in their fits. Yet, no one in the community was ready to act on these disclosures, since those named as witches were family, friends, and neighbors. Had nothing further been done, the witch hunt would have ended then and there. But the conspirators stepped in and filed the legal complaints required for the issue of arrest warrants.

Parris offered Tituba, his Indian slave, to set off the witch hunt. He claimed that Tituba had taught his daughter Betty and her cousin Abigail the art of necromancy.[89] In the kitchen of his parsonage, she had instructed the girls in the use of the black magic which she had learned in the West Indies. Parris' plan was to implicate her as a witch and then, by using threats, force her to name more witches. Intimidated by Parris' relentless abuse, Tituba gave the evidence needed to launch the witch hunt.[90] She

---

88 Perley, *History of Salem*, 2: 445.

89 In her examination on March 2, 1692 Tituba said, "I would not hurt Betty. I loved Betty."

90 Much later Tituba said that the Rev. Parris beat her and abused her to make her confess. She said that everything in her confession, and her accusations of Sarah Good and Sarah Osborne, as well as of other women later, were

claimed that there were four witches at large in Salem Village. When asked, "Tell us true, how many women come when you ride abroad?" Tituba answered, "Four of them, these two, Good and Osborne, and those two strangers. I ride upon a stick, or pole, and Good and Osborne behind me."

In one of his more skillful maneuvers, Parris dropped some suggestions about witch-finding to Mary Sibley, sister-in-law of fellow conspirator Jonathan Walcott.[91] Mary then told Tituba and her husband, John Indian, about a way to "find out witches." Following Mary's instructions, John Indian made a cake from rye meal and the children's urine, baked it in the ashes, and fed it to the dog. As soon as the dog gulped down the cake, the afflicted girls went into their fits, appearing convulsed and distorted.

Now the afflicted girls could see the specters of the witches who were tormenting them. They cried out upon Tituba; they said that she appeared to them as a specter, pinching, pricking and tormenting them. They also cried out upon the two designated women, Sarah Good and Sarah Osborne. The accusations of these two women had first come from Tituba.

Sarah Good, age thirty-eight, was poor, friendless, and disliked by many because of her persistent begging, her landless husband, William Good, being unable to earn a sufficient living as

---

the result of his abuse. Tituba had the strength to bear the abominable mistreatment and survive.

91   Samuel and Mary Sibley were near neighbors of the Rev. Parris. Within a week or two, people were saying that Mary Sibley herself ought to be charged with witchcraft because "diabolical means were used by the making of a cake." To counteract any such suspicions, Parris announced that he met with Mary on March 25, and "discoursed said sister in my study about her grand error, and said sister Sibley assented to the same with tears and sorrowful confession." With his characteristic boldness, Parris had managed to put the lid on this embarrassing situation.

a day laborer.[92] Sarah Osborne, age fifty and bed-ridden, was not poor. In fact, she was picked because she seemed about to prevail in a legal case against the Putnam family, a dispute over the inheritance of the Prince boys. The townspeople wanted to get this little witchcraft scare behind them. Many believed the charges of witchcraft, and hoped that these accusations would end the afflictions. But to the conspiracy these were just test cases required to start their witch hunt.

On February 29, 1692 the conspiracy took the necessary legal action. They filed a complaint [No. 1] against Sarah Good, Sarah Osborne, and Tituba for afflicting girls of the inner circle. The legal system was set in motion. On the basis of this complaint, the Salem magistrates, John Hathorne and Jonathan Corwin, issued warrants for the arrest of the three accused women. On March 1, 1692, the two magistrates in their impressive magisterial clothing and attended by marshals and constables, rode on horseback the five-mile journey from Salem Town to Salem Village. The marshals and constables, bearing long staffs, wore the bright red coats that were the official dress of men charged with the enforcement of law. Hathorne was an exacting and zealous judge known for his harsh penalties.

The magistrates examined the three women in Ingersoll's tavern, using its main room as the court room. First Sarah Good and Sarah Osborne were examined, then Tituba. Tituba claimed that she had been taught how to find out a witch in her own country, Barbados. At first she denied being a witch herself. She was stripped and her body was searched. The marks of the Devil were found upon her body. She then readily confessed that the Devil urged her to sign his book, and told her to work mischief on the children. All three women were committed to prison.

---

92   Samuel Abbey and his wife Mary testified, "William Good and his wife Sarah Good being destitute, we out of charity let them live in our house for some time. Sarah Good was so spiteful and maliciously bent that we were forced, for quietness sake, to turn her and her husband out of the house. Ever since, she has behaved herself very crossly and maliciously, calling our children vile names and has threatened them often."

In the Boston prison, the three women were put in irons; each was chained to a stout oak post so she could not take a single step in the cell. The teeth of the iron were to leave cruel marks on their arms and legs. Sarah Osborne fell seriously ill and died in prison on May 10, 1692. The jailers unlocked her fetters, and scooped a shallow grave for her in the prison yard. No stone was placed at her burial place; her empty chains in the dark cell served as her only marker. The slave Tituba was kept in jail, being brought out from time to time to give testimony to implicate others as witches. More than a year later, at the end of the witch hunt, Parris callously refused to pay the prison fees necessary for her release, so she was sold in slavery to a new owner in Virginia. The new-born baby that Sarah Good took into prison with her soon died, and Sarah died that summer on the gallows. Three witches and an infant were imprisoned, and all but one died.

The threat of witches in league with the Devil to defeat God's work in New England tied in neatly with the apocalyptic vision of the Rev. Cotton Mather. It also furthered the designs of magistrate John Hathorne.

On March 11, 1692, Parris invited neighboring ministers, the Rev. John Hale of Beverly and the Rev. Nicholas Noyes of Salem, to join him for prayer and observe the afflictions. At first, unused to an audience, the afflicted girls were silent, but before long they began to act and speak strangely. They went into their fits, twisting their limbs, then becoming very stiff. Abruptly the fits would cease. Parris held private fasts at his house.[93] Soon fasts were being held by others in Salem Village, and then by people in neighboring parishes. Word traveled fast; it became impossible to stop talk of the sinister disease.

When Tituba's examination ended on March 2, 1692, Sergeant Thomas Putnam knew that the conspiracy had to make a few quick strikes in order to maintain momentum. No time could be

---

93   The purpose of a fast was that, "We may escape the judgment of the Lord, not for the merit of our own fasting, which is none, but for the mercy of God." Lewis Bayley, *The Practice of Piety*, London 1631 (27th ed. 516)

lost at this critical stage. Giddy with their initial success, the conspiracy decided to act boldly. Their own girls, the inner circle, had won the sympathy of nearly the whole village. A few choice words and the mention of a couple of names were all that was required to set the girls off again.

Some of the girls may well have believed that the names they blurted out came by accident, the gift of spectral sight by which they could see the specters of the witches afflicting them. Others may have guessed that it came by design, the plan of their elders who planted the names of supposed witches into their impressionable minds. Whether accident or design, the results were the same.

Of the four designated victims, Sarah Good and Sarah Osborne had been detected; two remained to be identified. The afflicted girls performed on cue. When asked, "Who afflicts you?" they knew what exactly which names would please their elders. Soon after the arrests of Tituba, Sarah Good, and Sarah Osborne, the inner circle began accusing Martha Corey and Rebecca Nurse.

Martha Corey and her husband, Giles Corey, lived in Salem Farms, a part of Salem township east of Salem Town, and south of Salem Village.[94] Members of the anti-Parris group, the Coreys always sided with the Porters against the Putnams. Martha Corey was a respected member of the Salem congregation and a tireless attendant of church meeting in Salem Village. From the beginning Martha Corey was one of the few who did not believe that the girls suffered from witchcraft. Indeed she scoffed at the idea of demoniac possession. She had tried to restrain her husband from going to Salem Village to watch the examinations of the first three accused. Giles, eighty years old, was still a powerful man. When words failed to dissuade him, Martha took the saddle from his horse and hid it. But still he went.

Ann Putnam, Jr. in her fits saw and named Martha Corey as a witch. Because Martha Corey was a church member, her

---

94   Salem Farms today is the town of Peabody; Salem Town is the center of the city of Salem.

accusation had to be handled with kid gloves. More evidence was needed before a complaint could be filed. Accordingly, on March 12, 1692 Deacon Edward Putnam and his friend Ezekiel Cheever, a tailor, asked Ann Putnam, Jr. to take a good look at Martha's specter and tell them what she was wearing. Information about Martha's clothes had been indirectly mentioned to Ann previously. However, Ann was cautious. She shook her head and said, "I am blind now. I cannot see." Ann explained that this spell had been cast by Martha, to protect herself.

Next, the two men went to Martha's house. As hoped, they found her alone in the kitchen. Without witnesses, any account of what transpired would be her word against theirs. Talk traveled fast in Salem Village, and Martha knew full well that she had been named by the girls. She said, "I know what you have come for. You are come to talk to me about being a witch." Her visitors would later turn this as evidence against her. In order to ensnare her, they tried to give the impression of fairness. They said they had come to talk things over, and casually mentioned that Ann Putnam, Jr. was afflicted.

From local gossip, Martha had heard that the afflicted girls could describe the clothes that the witches wore. She had changed her clothes as a defense. She asked the two men, "Did Ann tell you what clothes I have on?" They realized that Martha easily might have outwitted them. Saved by the prescience of Ann, they replied, "She did not, for she told us that you came and blinded her." In reporting this in their deposition they remarked, "Martha showed us a pretty trick."

Failing in their indirect approach, they turned accusatory. They told Martha that Ann had cried out upon her. Sternly they pointed out the dishonor of a church member being proved a witch. Their attempts to break her down came to nothing. Martha quietly answered, "I do not think that they [the three in prison] are witches. If they were, we could not blame the Devil for making witches of them, for they were idle slothful persons and minded nothing that was good. But you have no reason to think so of me, for I have made a profession of Christ and have rejoiced to go and hear the word of God."

"Woman, outward profession of faith cannot save you!" they retorted. And they were right. Martha incorrectly believed that her religion could shield her from this political attack on her life. After much talk the visitors left; they had enough to use against her.

One week later, on Saturday March 19, 1692, the legal act was made. The conspiracy filed their second complaint [No. 2]. It was against Martha Corey for afflicting Elizabeth Hubbard, Mercy Lewis, Abigail Williams, Ann Putnam, Jr., and also her mother, Ann Putnam, Sr.

Timing was crucial. The conspiracy filed the complaint against Martha Corey on a Saturday, knowing that she would be arrested on Monday morning. She therefore would be able to attend Sunday church services, presenting an ideal opportunity for the accusers. The afflicted would display their suffering from her witchcraft in church. To make things look legitimate they needed a supposedly disinterested observer. For this purpose the Rev. Deodat Lawson was invited to Salem Village on that Saturday, March 19, 1692. On Sunday, he would preach the services with Martha Corey present.

As minister at Salem Village from 1684 to 1688, Lawson had been close to the Putnam family. The Porter family, on the other hand, had made his life so uncomfortable that he had decided to give up his position in Salem Village. Here was a friend, ready to go along with almost any bizarre plot that the conspiracy could hatch.

The plan was for the girls to act out their parts in church and implicate Martha Corey once and for all in acts of witchcraft. In this way, Martha's credibility as a church member, her only defense, would be destroyed. The stage was carefully set by Thomas Putnam and the Rev. Samuel Parris, whose niece Abigail Williams would take the leading role.

Lawson reached Salem Village in the early afternoon, and stayed at Ingersoll's inn, where he began his investigations. Mary Walcott came in and spoke to him, but she "suddenly was bitten, so that she cried out of her wrist." Lawson examined her wrist by candlelight. He "saw apparently the marks of teeth, both upper and lower set, on each side of her wrist."[95]

Later that evening he visited the parsonage. Upon his arrival, Abigail Williams had a "grievous fit." Running through the house she screamed, "Whish! Whish!" flapping her arms in an attempt to fly. Now a specter entered the room. Of course none but Abigail could see it, but everyone looked to where her eyes were focused. The child called the specter by name. It was the specter of Rebecca Nurse. Abigail said to the Rev. Lawson, "Do you not see her? Why, there she stands!" When the specter offered Abigail a book to sign, she yelled, "I won't! I won't! Oh, I won't! I am sure it is none of God's book! It is the Devil's book for all I know!" After that she ran into the huge fireplace, came out with firebrands, and hurled them about the house. Then she dashed back in and tried to climb up the chimney. Abigail's sterling act was an instant success. The Rev. Lawson came down firmly on the side of Parris and the other conspirators. He was never brought into the conspiracy because there was no need. A firm believer in witchcraft, he was their easy pawn.

The next day, Sunday March 20, 1692, the Rev. Lawson led both church meetings at Salem Village, the morning and afternoon services. The afflicted were in their places in the meetinghouse, stage-players ready for their act. Martha Corey was there too. During morning public worship (there was also a morning private worship, for church members only), the afflicted had "sore fits." These fits interrupted the Rev. Lawson's first prayer at key points. After the psalm was sung, Abigail Williams called to the Rev. Lawson, "Now stand up and name your text." After it was read, she said, "It is a long text." At the beginning of sermon Mrs. Pope, who was an afflicted woman, said to him, "Now there is enough of that."

During the afternoon service Abigail Williams, upon the Rev. Lawson's referring to his doctrine, burst out, "I know no doctrine you had. If you did name one I have forgotten it." At sermon time,

---

95   Lawson, *A Brief and True Narrative*, 152-154.

with Martha Corey again present, Abigail Williams cried, "Look where Goodwife Corey sits on the beam suckling her yellow bird between her fingers." Then Ann Putnam, Jr. called out, "There is a yellow bird sitting on the Rev. Lawson's hat, as it hangs on the pin in the pulpit." At that point others in the congregation restrained Ann from speaking so loudly. It was more fitting that Abigail Williams, the niece of the minister, take the lead in church. But all these ridiculous remarks, so absurdly out of place, were not only tolerated but tacitly encouraged. The act succeeded; the witchcraft of Martha Corey was established.

On the following day, Monday March 21, 1692, Martha Corey was arrested and examined before the magistrates. Now, instead of serving as a church, the Salem Village meeting house was serving as a courthouse.[96] Spectators thronged to see the novelty. The Rev. Nicholas Noyes, assistant minister at Salem Town, opened with a prayer. The prisoner was then called in to answer the allegations against her. She asked if she, too, might pray, as her church record was her defense. In answer, magistrate Hathorne said that he did not come to hear her pray, but to examine her.

The ranks of the afflicted had grown. The entire inner circle of six girls was there. Also present were several afflicted adults, "Mrs. Pope, Mrs. Putnam, Goodwife Bibber, and and an ancient woman named Goodale." Bathsheba (Folger) Pope, the wife of Joseph Pope of Salem Village, was at all of the proceedings until early spring. Ann Putnam, Sr. was the wife of Sergeant Thomas Putnam and the mother of the afflicted girl Ann Putnam, Jr. Sarah Bibber, age thirty-six, the wife of John Bibber of Wenham, was a scandal-mongering matron who had been hovering at the

---

96   Today a replica of the Salem Village meetinghouse, a reminder of the days of superstition, stands not at its original location, but on the farm of Rebecca Nurse.

edge of the afflicted group from the first.[97] Margaret Goodale was the second wife of Robert Goodale.[98]

Ann Putnam Sr., who commanded the distinguished title Mrs., occupied a unique and pivotal position throughout the affair. Wife of the conspiracy's ringleader, mother of the most active of the inner circle, afflicted herself, the precise nature of her involvement remains elusive. That her own affliction served to encourage her husband's accusations and her daughter's antics may be granted. But whether her behavior sprang from coercion by a dominating husband, or from a genuine belief in the terror and power of witchcraft (as she had been taught by her father, George Carr), is impossible to say. Then again, perhaps her purpose was synonymous with her husband's, and she was the conspiracy's silent member. In any case, her participation with the afflicted offered the powerful model of a grown-up with which to reinforce not only her own daughter's behavior, but that of the entire inner circle.

---

97   Later, testimony was given to discredit Sarah Bibber; however it did no good. Joseph Fowler testified, "Goodman Bibber and his wife lived at my house and she was a woman who was very idle in her calling and very much given to tattling and tale-bearing, making mischief among her neighbors. Thomas Jacob testified, "Goodwife Bibber, who is now an afflicted person, did for some time live in our house and would often speak, against one and another, those things that were very false. This John Bibber's wife could fall into fits as often as she pleased." John Porter testified, "Goodwife Bibber, sometimes living with us, would have strange fits when crossed, a woman of unruly turbulent spirits, and double-tongued."

98   After this episode, the elderly Margaret (Lazenby) Goodale dropped out of the afflicted ranks. Robert Goodale, was born in England in 1604, came to Salem in 1634, and became a large landowner in Salem Village. By his first wife, Katherine, Robert Goodale had Isaac, born 1633, Zachariah, born 1640, and Jacob, born 1642. Isaac is the six-times great grandfather of the writer's mother, Doris (Goodale) Robinson. Katherine died in 1645, and Robert married Margaret Lazenby in 1647.

As the examination of Martha Corey got underway, the girls acted out their afflictions on the front benches. John Hathorne asked Martha why she hurt them. She answered, "I am an innocent person. I never had to do with witchcraft since I was born. I am a gospel woman!" But the afflicted told her, "Ah! You are a gospel witch!"

Deacon Edward Putnam and Ezekiel Cheever sat in the audience. The reason for their visit to her home on Saturday, March 12, 1692 soon became apparent. Whatever she had said then was now being twisted into evidence against her. Hathorne asked, "How could you tell that the child [Ann Putnam, Jr.] was bid to observe what clothes you wore when some came to speak with you." Before she could get two words out, Cheever interrupted, "Do not begin with a lie." Edward Putnam also said the same thing. Hathorne asked, "Who told you that?" Before Martha could complete her answer, Cheever interrupted, "You speak falsely." And on it went.

Those afflicted, children and adults, vehemently accused Martha Corey of hurting them, at that very moment in the assembly, by biting, pinching, and strangling. And they said that in their fits they saw her likeness coming to them and bringing a book for them to sign. She replied, "I have no book." They said that she had a familiar, a yellow bird, that used to suck between her fingers. She replied, "I have no familiarity with any such thing."

Mr. Hathorne, the magistrate, said, "Give glory to God, and confess." In reply, Martha said, "I cannot confess." Hathorne insisted, "Do you not see how these afflicted do charge you? Tell us who hurts these children." She answered, "They are poor distracted creatures, and no heed should be given to what they say. We must not believe distracted persons." Hathorne rebuked her, "You charge these children with distraction. It is a note of distraction when persons vary in a minute, but these fix upon you. This is not a matter of distraction. It is the judgment of all that are present, that they are bewitched, and only you say they are distracted." Martha, realizing that no defense was possible, asked, "When all are against me, how can I help it?"

Mrs. Pope complained of "grievous torment in her bowels as if they were torn out." She vehemently accused Martha Corey as the instrument, and threw her muff at her, but missed. She then took off her shoe, and hit Martha on the head with it. After this display, the rest of the afflicted swung into action. When Martha made any motion of her body, hands or mouth, the afflicted would cry out. When she bit her lip, they cried out of being bitten. If she grasped one hand with the other, they cried out of being pinched by her, and produced marks. For another motion of her body, they screamed of being pressed. When she leaned to the seat next to her, or if she stirred her feet, they stamped and cried out in pain.

The afflicted agreed that the Black Man was whispering in Martha's ear at that very moment. One of the girls now spotted the yellow bird; in fact, it was sucking Martha between her fingers. Immediately, Hathorne gave the order to get the bird. But the girl who saw it said, "It is too late now, for she has removed a pin, and put it on her head." Upon searching Martha Corey's head, the officials found a pin sticking upright.

Hathorne sternly told Martha, "We have come to be a terror to evil doers!" Martha retorted, "You are all against me, and I cannot help it." Martha was a member of the Salem church. Her minister, the Rev. Nicholas Noyes, known for his bluntness, solemnly spoke, "I believe it is apparent that she practiced witchcraft in the congregation." When Hathorne asked what she had to say to that, she replied simply, "If you will all go hang me, how can I help it?" The magistrates committed Martha Corey to prison to await trial. The crying out of the afflicted abated.

As she was being led out of the courtroom Martha exclaimed, once again, "I am a gospel woman!" Her statement, tragically, was beside the point. The Putnams had shown that they could do away with their enemies, one by one, even church members. The next church member in line was Rebecca Nurse, the last of the original designated victims.

The witch hunt was on in earnest. Tituba and the first two designated witches, Good, and Osborne, were committed in a simple enough way, the conspiracy assuming correctly that they would find no strong defenders.

With Martha Corey it was another story. Her worthiness had been scrupulously tested by the Puritan church, and she had been elected to church membership, a signal honor. The high degree of respectability that she enjoyed should have proven strong enough to ward off any suspicion of witchcraft. But this was not the case. Although a church member, she was now imprisoned for witchcraft. The conspiracy's careful planning had scored an important victory.

Recall that on Saturday evening March 19, 1692, Abigail Williams, in the presence of the Rev. Parris and the Rev. Lawson, was afflicted by the specter of Rebecca Nurse. This could mean only one thing. Rebecca Nurse, seventy-one-year-old matriarch of the Nurse family, was a witch. A couple of days beforehand, gossip of the possible accusation of Rebecca Nurse had been in the wind, and Israel Porter and his wife, Elizabeth, learned of it. Israel Porter was the leader of those who opposed the Putnam family.

Elizabeth Porter's maiden name was Hathorne; she was the sister of magistrate John Hathorne. The Nurse family was a close ally of Israel Porter. He and his wife Elizabeth realized they must warn Rebecca Nurse that the girls were accusing her.

On Saturday March 19, 1692, Israel Porter and his wife left their home on Frost Fish River and rode south on Ipswich Road to Orchard Farm, home of the Endicott family. There they turned northwest and rode to the Nurse farm, where old Francis and Rebecca Nurse, together with their four sons and four daughters, tended three hundred acres.

Rebecca had the well-earned reputation of being what every Puritan mother strove to be. She was a church member, pious, and steeped in scripture. She had reared her children lovingly, with regard to both their spiritual and temporal welfare. Now in old age, Rebecca was hard of hearing and infirm. When the Porters arrived, they found her lying ill upstairs. Rebecca's brother-in-law Peter Cloyce and Israel's brother-in-law Daniel Andrew were already there for the meeting.

Rebecca inquired about the afflicted children. To her, they were poor little girls. She was sorry that she could not be with them in their distress because she had been ill these seven or eight days. She said, "I go to God for them. But I am troubled. Oh, I am troubled at some of their crying out. Some of the persons they have spoken of are, as I believe, as innocent as I." The Porters had no choice but to tell Rebecca what was happening. The girls had cried out on Rebecca. Ann Putnam, Jr. had spoken her name first, but the others had quickly picked it up. Rebecca replied, "Well, if it be so, the will of the Lord be done. As to this thing I am as innocent as the child unborn. But surely, what sin has God found in me, unrepented of, that He could lay such an affliction on me in my old age?" The Porters made a record, witnessed by Daniel Andrew and Peter Cloyce, of their favorable impression. They later presented it in court as testimony for Rebecca. Under usual circumstances, testimony from Israel Porter would have been enough to clear anyone, since he was a powerful member of the community. But highly placed officials sanctioned the witch hunt; his testimony was to go unheeded.

On Wednesday March 23, 1692 the conspiracy filed a complaint [No. 3] against Rebecca Nurse; she was arrested the next morning. For the Puritans, Thursday was Lecture Day. In addition to both morning and afternoon church services on Sundays, the Puritans also set aside Thursday afternoons for services called lectures. Rebecca's examination would be in the morning, before the afternoon church meeting.

During Martha Corey's examination, Rebecca Nurse's name had been mentioned several times. With all the gossip, no one was surprised by her arrest. She was brought for examination before magistrates John Hathorne and Jonathan Corwin in the Salem Village meetinghouse. The Rev. John Hale, minister of Beverly, began with prayer, after which Rebecca Nurse was accused of much the same crimes as Corey.

As a respected elderly woman of good character and a church member, Rebecca was treated with deference. She asserted her own innocence with earnestness, and refused to confess. The afflicted were mostly the same as in the examination of Martha Corey. Ann Putnam, Sr. occupied a conspicuous place as an afflicted person, effectively encouraging her young daughter Ann, Jr. and the other afflicted girls as well.

When he began the examination, magistrate John Hathorne appeared torn. On the one hand, he and Corwin were the first of the high ranking Puritan old guard to sanction the witch hunt, which was still of limited scope at this point. On the other hand, his sister Elizabeth Porter knew nothing of his complicity, and she had urged him to free Rebecca Nurse.

Rebecca made her plea. "I can say before my eternal father that I am innocent, and God will clear my innocence." Hathorne answered, "Here is never a one in the assembly but desires it. But if you be guilty, I pray God discover you."

Deacon Edward Putnam testified that she had tortured his niece Ann Putnam, Jr. in his presence. Rebecca answered, "I am innocent and clear, and I have not been able to get out of doors these eight or nine days. I never afflicted no child, no, never in my life." For once, Hathorne tried to help. He asked, "Are you an innocent person relating to this witchcraft?"

The answer came from the afflicted. One of the girls fell into convulsions, then the others. To the bewilderment of all, they set up "a most hideous screech and noise." Their dreadful sounds were heard at a great distance; the Rev. Lawson, preparing his sermon for the afternoon service, heard them over at the parsonage. Inside the meetinghouse there was near panic. People shrank back in fear from their neighbors, not knowing who was going to be hurt. Above the din rose the voice of Ann Putnam, Sr. As the specter of Rebecca Nurse tormented her, Mrs. Putnam gave the most terrible shrieks of all. She screamed, "Did you not bring the Black Man with you? Did you not bid me tempt God and die? How often have you eaten and drunk to your own damnation?" The afflicted children writhed in their fits, as though they also were tortured by Rebecca's vengeful specter.

By the time the uproar had subsided enough for Hathorne to proceed, his moment of compassion had passed. "What do you say to them?" he asked.

"Oh, Lord help me!" cried poor Rebecca as she held out her hands helplessly. The girls immediately held out theirs. Whatever move Rebecca made, they cleverly mimicked. Before the eyes of everyone, Rebecca was demonstrating her witchcraft. An innocent woman would weep before such a scene, and many women spectators were now weeping. Yet Rebecca did not. All knew that tears were impossible for a witch. Hathorne said, "It is awful to see these agonies, and you, an old professor [of the faith], thus charged with the Devil by the effects if it. Yet you stand with dry eyes, when there are so many wet." Rebecca stoutly answered, "You do not know my heart." Hathorne said, "You would do well if you were guilty to confess. Give glory to God." "Would you have me belie myself?" she asked.

Hathorne now accused her of the most serious charge. Ann Putnam, Sr. wanted Rebecca convicted not of sorcery alone, but also of murder. The ghosts of little children in their winding sheets had appeared to Mrs. Putnam, calling her aunt, telling her that Witch Nurse had killed them. "What think you of this?" Hathorne asked Rebecca. She answered, "I cannot tell what to think. The Devil may appear in my shape." "They accuse you of hurting them, and if you think it is by design, you must look on it as murder," Hathorne replied.

Ann Putnam, Sr. swore that it was murder. But nothing could shake the denial of Rebecca. The meetinghouse had to be made ready for the Rev. Lawson's sermon that afternoon. It was almost noon. Hathorne ordered her imprisoned. Parris had taken the notes of the examination, and, in the peace of his parsonage, began to put them together for the official record.

That afternoon the Rev. Lawson delivered his Lecture Day sermon. In it he said that the very intensity of the diabolic assault reaffirmed New England's special relationship to God. He said, "The covenant people of God, and those that would devote themselves entirely to his service, are the special objects of Salem's rage and fury." In his incendiary oration, he offered this encouragement, "To our honored magistrates, here present this day, to inquire into these things. Do all that in you lies, to check and rebuke Satan."

On March 23, 1692 the conspiracy filed a complaint [No. 4] against Dorcas Good, Sarah Good's pretty little four-year-old daughter. Her specter, it was reported, was running wild in Salem Village, biting the afflicted girls in return for what they had done to her mother. The girls showed marks on their arms from a small set of teeth. They claimed to be in torment whenever the small child cast her eyes in their direction.

Today some people still maintain that witchcraft was really being practiced in Salem Village, and that the accusers were merely doing their duty to rid the countryside of the witches.[99] Return to the evidence as presented in contemporary accounts. The Rev. Lawson, who was on the scene, and was a firm believer in the menace of witchcraft, wrote:

"The magistrates and ministers also did inform me that they apprehended a child of Sarah Good and examined it, being between 4 and 5 years of age. As a matter of fact, they did unanimously affirm, that, when this child did but cast its eye upon the afflicted persons, they were tormented. They held her head, and yet so many as her eye could fix upon were afflicted.[100] They did several times make careful observation of this. The afflicted complained they had often been bitten by this child, and produced the marks of a small set of teeth. Accordingly, this was

---

99 "It should be clear by now that our historians have erred in their assumption that there was no witchcraft practiced at Salem, or if there were it was of little consequence. In Bridget Bishop, Candy, and Mammy Redd we have three people who practiced black magic, and with demonstrable success. In the Hoar family and George Burroughs we have people who established a reputation for black magic and then traded on it, although whether they were actually witches remains uncertain. There are other cases, like those of Sarah Good and Samuel Wardwell, which I have not treated in detail because the evidence is suspicious but not conclusive." Hansen, 86.

100 This is the only place where the minister refers to Dorcas with an animate pronoun.

also committed to Salem Prison. The child looked hale, and well as other children. I saw it at Lieut. Ingersoll's."

To relieve the "grievous afflictions" of the inner circle, Dorcas was cruelly confined in chains in her prison cell. Because her tiny wrists and ankles slipped out of the manacles and fetters, the blacksmith was ordered to make special ones for the child. The Rev. Lawson continues:

"On the 26th of March, Mr. Hathorne, Mr. Corwin, and Mr. Higginson were at the prison-keeper's house, to examine the child.[101] It told them there, it had a little snake that used to suck on the lowest joint of its forefinger; and when they inquired where, pointing to other places, it told them, not there, but there, pointing on the lowest point of forefinger; where they observed a deep red spot, about the bigness of a flea-bite. They asked who gave it that snake, whether it was the great Black Man. It said no, its mother gave it."

Dorcas' mother, Sarah Good, was in Boston prison. After the death of Sarah's infant, Dorcas was moved from Salem to Boston prison. The date was April 21, 1692. One week later, mother and daughter were moved from Boston to Ipswich prison, and on May 25, 1692 they were returned to Boston prison. On Tuesday July 19, 1692 Dorcas' mother was hanged in Salem. Terrorized in chains for the better part of a year, Dorcas Good was finally released on December 10, 1692 on a recognizance bond of fifty pounds sterling, posted by Samuel Ray of Salem, a true Samaritan. Before her release, the fee for making her special manacles and fetters also had to be paid.

The Rev. Lawson had described her as a "hale and well looking girl," when she was put into prison. After the child came out, she would never fully regain her senses. But the magistrates and ministers had protected New England from the witchcraft of a four-year-old.

Young Joseph Putnam, twenty-two years old and later to be the father of General Israel Putnam of Revolutionary War fame,

---

101 John Higginson, Sr. was the elder minister of the Salem church.

quickly recognized the handiwork of the conspiracy. Allied with the powerful Porter family, Joseph let it be known that if the conspiracy took steps to have him arrested, they would do so at their own peril. He kept his guns loaded, and for six months his horses were saddled and ready for instant flight. His half-brother Sergeant Thomas Putnam, leader of the conspiracy, respected the stand-off.

Yet the Porter family failed completely in their attempt to protect Rebecca Nurse. All of the designated witches were to die, four innocent women, remarkable for their fortitude and bravery. Sarah Good, Martha Corey, and Rebecca Nurse were hanged. Sarah Osborne died under miserable conditions in jail.

In the dead of night, the sons of Rebecca Nurse recovered their mother's body from the shallow grave on Gallows Hill and secretly buried her, in dignity, on her own land. In the nineteenth century a commemorative stone was erected on her grave. Standing in a quiet grove in the field beside her house, the marker was inscribed with a verse written especially for it by the poet John Greenleaf Whittier.

Rebecca Nurse
Yarmouth, England 1621
Salem, Mass. 1692

O Christian Martyr who for truth could die
When all around thee owned the hideous lie!
The world redeemed from Superstition's sway
Is breathing freer for thy sake today.

CHAPTER 9

AN ARMY OF DEVILS

"*An Army of Devils* is horribly broke in upon our English settlements, and the houses of good people there are filled with the doleful shrieks of their children and servants, tormented by invisible hands, with tortures altogether preternatural," wrote Cotton Mather.[102]

When Captain Stephen Sewall of Salem, brother of Samuel Sewall, saw what was happening in Salem Village, he believed it to be the work of the Devil. As a friend, Sewall had agreed to look after the Rev. Parris' daughter, nine-year-old Elizabeth Parris. Sewall and his wife observed Betty having "sore fits" at their house on March 25, 1692. The afflictions were especially worrying when Betty reported, "The great Black Man came to me and told me, if I would be ruled by him, I should have whatsoever I want, and go to a Golden City." Mrs. Sewall replied, "It was the Devil, and he was a liar from the beginning. I bid you tell him so, if he comes again." The next time the Devil came to her in her fits, Betty did accordingly. Captain Sewall, in dead earnest, described little Betty's meeting with the Devil to the Rev. Deodat Lawson.

It was a story too good for the Rev. Lawson to pass up. The first writer on the scene in Salem Village, Lawson had the inside track on the afflicted and the accused. He saw that he had the makings of a best seller on witchcraft. Using all the artistic license afforded great authors, Lawson took Captain Sewall's story together with other stories that he had heard in Salem Village

---

102 Cotton Mather, *Wonders*, 14.

and produced in a few weeks a lurid collection for the curious. The result was the first printed account on the afflictions of the possessed girls and the witchcraft examinations. It was entitled *A Brief and True Narrative, of some Remarkable Passages Relating to sundry Persons Afflicted by Witchcraft at Salem Village, Which happened from the Nineteenth of March, to the Fifth of April 1692. Collected by Deodat Lawson, Boston, Printed for Benjamin Harris, and to be sold at his shop, over against the Old Meeting House. 1692.* In a foreword, Benjamin Harris wrote, "We suppose the curious will be entertained with as rare an history as perhaps an age has had, whereof this narrative is but a forerunner."

In his book, which sold at a most gratifying clip, Lawson wrote, "The 31 of March there was a public fast kept at Salem for the afflicted persons. Abigail Williams said that the witches had a mock sacrament at a house in Salem Village, and that they had red bread and red drink." Did Abigail, a girl of only eleven, originate this story? Because she was gifted with spectral sight, her story was implicitly credible. Her account is but the first of a whole series of testimony in which the accused are said to attend the black sabbat, the witches' sabbath. The theme of the establishment of the Devil's church was constantly pounded by Cotton Mather and other Puritan ministers. Abigail often overheard such conversations in the Parris home and at church, and no doubt shaped her story accordingly.

Lawson continued, "The first of April, Mercy Lewis, Thomas Putnam's maid, in her fit said, they did eat red bread like man's flesh, and would have had her eat some, but she would not, but turned away her head, and spit at them, and said, 'I will not eat, I will not drink, it is blood. That is not the bread of life. That is not the water of life. Christ gives the bread of life. I will have none of it!' The first of April also Mercy Lewis saw in her fit a White Man, and was with him in a glorious place, which had no candles nor sun, yet was full of light and brightness; where was a great multitude in white glittering robes, and they sung the song in the fifth of Revelation, the 9th verse,[103] and the 110 Psalm,[104] and the 149 Psalm,[105] and said with herself, 'How long shall I stay here? Let me be along with you.' She was loath to leave this place, and grieved that she could tarry no longer. This White Man has appeared several times to some of them, and given them notice how long it should be before they had another fit, which was sometimes a day, or day and half, or more or less. It has fallen out accordingly."

Lawson then described supernatural occurrences which offered definite proof of witchcraft at Salem Village. The first was the Devil's unsuccessful attempt to turn the afflicted girls into witches. Lawson wrote, "They are in their fits tempted to be witches, and are shown the list of the names of others. They are tortured because they would not yield to subscribe or touch the book, and are promised immediate relief if they would do it."

Next he described the method of curing known as the *laying on of hands*. "The afflicted girls did mutually cure each other, even with a touch of their hand, when strangled and otherwise tortured."[106] He then made clear that the girls were seers. He wrote, "The girls could also foretell when another's fit would come. They would say, 'Look at her! She will have a fit presently!'

---

103 "Thou art worthy to take the book, and to open the seals thereof: for thou wast slain, and have redeemed us to God by thy blood out of every kindred, and tongue, and people, and nation."

104 "He shall judge among the heathen, he shall fill the places with the dead bodies." In this case the heathens, of course, were the Indians, who three years previously had killed Mercy Lewis' parents. Her identification of Indians and witches as the Devil's agents was a product of Puritan teaching.

105 "To execute vengeance upon the heathen."

106 Later the court would bring the accused to touch the afflicted. If the accused were really a witch, then the evil fluid would flow out of the afflicted and back into the witch, temporarily curing the afflicted. In each case that the experiment was tried, the afflicted did experience the cure. In other words, whenever the touch test was used, it supported the charge of witchcraft.

and it happened accordingly. Many can bear witness that heard and saw it."

Now came the most damning accusation of all: spectral evidence of witchcraft. Lawson observed, "When the accused person was present, the afflicted persons saw her likeness [her specter] in other places of the meetinghouse, suckling her familiar, sometimes in one place and posture and sometimes in another." Lawson believed that the testimony of the afflicted girls about seeing specters stood beyond question. He observed that some of the most dependable of the afflicted girls affirmed that they saw the same things out of their fits as they did in them.

The Rev. Lawson discussed the accused witches too. Explaining why so few puppets were found, he wrote, "Natural actions in the witches produced preternatural actions in the afflicted, so the witches are their own image without any puppets of wax or otherwise." On the importance of imprisoning the accused witches, he commented, "Once they are confined, the afflictions of the girls became much less. The confined witches did not appear to them as much, biting or pinching them, etc."

Lawson revealed secrets of the Devil's campaign and the plan of attack. The accused "have a company of about 23 or 24, and they did muster in arms, as it seemed to the afflicted persons." Would this military company of witches be able to defeat the militia company of Salem Village men under the command of Captain Jonathan Walcott? Salem Village was destined to become the very center of the battle. There the Devil and his emissaries were expected to wage a most furious fight.

Lawson's book, appealing to all the fancies, superstitions, and beliefs of its readers, excited tremendous interest. Its effect was to help stir the cauldron of witchcraft frenzy and madness which the conspiracy now was poised to exploit to the fullest extent. The clergy preached that the Devil's plan to destroy Salem Village was but the beginning of a systematic plot which could end in the destruction of New England. The Devil had his agents, the witches, stationed throughout Essex County, if not the whole province.

Darkness, mystery, diabolism, all brooded over this hellish scene. The Devil was abroad in person, giving his sanction and assistance. His sacrament was administered by his followers in that very village, the final stimulant and consolation for the hour of battle. Lawson notes, "The afflicted persons reported that the witches keep days of fast and days of thanksgiving, and sacraments. Satan endeavors to transform himself to an angel of light, and to make his kingdom and administration resemble those of our Lord Jesus Christ. The witches had a fast, and told one of the afflicted girls, she must not eat, because it is fast day. She said she would. They told her they would choke her then, which, when she did eat, was endeavored."

The hour was indeed upon the people of New England. "Satan rages principally amongst the visible subjects of Christ's Kingdom, and makes use (at least in appearance) of some of them to afflict others, that Christ's kingdom may be divided against itself, and so be weakened," continued Lawson.[107] It was the duty of the clergy to arouse the people, promptly, in all their sins and weaknesses, to the terrible strength of the enemy, the near presence of the Devil.

Sunday April 3, 1692 was a sacrament day at Salem Village. On the following day the conspiracy planned to file a complaint against Sarah Cloyce, a church member and one of Rebecca Nurse's two sisters.[108] Now they were going to stage a performance in church to demonstrate to the whole congregation Sarah's damnable witchcraft. Upon entering the meetinghouse,

---

107 These elect or visible saints, the members of the Puritan church, were those whose outward conduct supported their own assertion that they had experienced the influx of God's grace. Generally speaking, they came from the well-to-do class. However, most of the inhabitants of New England were poor, some destitute.

108 The PBS television series "Three Sovereigns for Sarah" tells the story of Sarah Cloyce and her two sisters, Rebecca Nurse and Mary Easty. Daughters of William and Joanna (Blessing) Towne, the three are called the Towne sisters.

Sarah heard the Rev. Samuel Parris name as his text, John 6:70: "Have not I chosen you Twelve, and one of you is a Devil." Because Puritans believed that church members were elected by God, Parris' text implied that a church member had betrayed her election, just as Judas had betrayed Christ's choice. Suspecting mischief, Sarah rose and left the building. The wind shut the door forcibly behind her. Her early departure disappointed the afflicted girls who were ready to put on their show, as they had done for Martha Corey. Later they would use the slamming of the door as evidence against Sarah, claiming that she went out in anger, thus giving them reason to suspect her.

On Monday April 4, 1692, as planned, the conspiracy filed a complaint [No. 6] against Sarah Cloyce, and against Elizabeth Proctor as well. The complainants were tavern-owner Deacon Nathaniel Ingersoll and his nephew Jonathan Walcott. The accused Elizabeth Proctor managed a competing tavern which was run in a more relaxed manner than that of the Deacon and accordingly was more popular. Elizabeth Proctor was also a successful midwife, another reason for her accusation.

The examination of these two women was to be a major production. Various high dignitaries of the province were to be present. To insure they all could attend, the date was set for the examination on the following Monday, April 11, 1692. In anticipation of the growing number of spectators, the examination was held at the much larger meeting house in Salem Town. The deputy governor, the secretary of the province, and five magistrates, as well as several ministers, were present.

Indeed, so many of the magistrates were present that the court took the form of a council (the highest of the colonial tribunals) under the presidency of the deputy governor, Thomas Danforth.[109] The presence of these officials, their lines of questioning, and their verdicts make clear that the highest levels of government and church sanctioned the witch hunt. This

---

109   Boyer and Nissenbaum, eds., *Salem Witchcraft Papers (SWP)*, 661.

examination firmly establishes the complicity of the ruling old guard in the actions of the Salem Village conspiracy.

Sarah Cloyce was examined first; Elizabeth Proctor followed. During the hearings, both women were cried out upon by the afflicted girls and women, with their customary clamors and screechings. Elizabeth's husband John Proctor, come to offer his support, was also cried out upon, and with such a vengeance that he was arrested [No. 7] on the spot.[110] The three were committed to prison.

Samuel Sewall, one of the magistrates, made this entry in his diary, "April 11, 1692. Went to Salem, where, in the Meeting House, the persons accused of witchcraft were examined. Was a very great assembly. 'Twas awful to see how the afflicted persons were agitated. Mr. Noyes prayed at the beginning, and Mr. Higginson concluded." In the margin he wrote, "Vae, vae, vae, witchcraft," Latin for "Woe, woe, woe, witchcraft."

The witch hunt now was spreading to neighboring towns. The next Monday, April 18, 1692, Ezekiel Cheever and Sergeant Thomas Putnam filed a complaint [No. 8] against Mary Warren and Giles Corey, both of Salem Farms, Bridget Bishop of Salem Town, and Abigail Hobbs of Topsfield. The four were examined the next day in Salem Village. (The examination of Mary Warren, a member of the outer circle of afflicted girls, was treated in Chapter 7.)

Martha Corey, previously arrested and examined was the third wife of Giles Corey. In 1692, Giles Corey was eighty years old. Civil and criminal charges had followed him most of his life. In 1660 Corey had bought fifty acres from Robert Goodale, who owned over five hundred acres in Salem Village. In 1675, one of Robert Goodale's sons, Jacob Goodale, age thirty-three, was living

---

110 "And John Proctor of Salem Farms, being personally present, was by Abigail Williams and Ann Putnam, Jr. charged by several acts of witchcraft by him committed on the person of Mrs. Pope and others, who were accordingly afflicted, apparent to all."

and working on Corey's farm. Corey was extremely strong, and in a fit of temper "unreasonably beat Jacob with a stick of about one inch diameter nearly 100 blows in the presence of Elisha Kebee, who told Corey that he would knock him down if he did not forbear." About ten days later, Corey went to the house of Jacob's brother Zachariah Goodale and told him that Jacob had taken a fall. Corey said he was afraid that Jacob had broken his arm, and desired him to take Jacob to Mrs. Mole's, in town. Zachariah went to Corey's house and found Jacob confused, pale, stooping, and unable to walk properly. Zachariah asked Corey if Jacob had any other injury besides to his arm, but Corey would not answer. Corey, a stubborn man, refused to help. Instead his second wife, Mary, helped Zachariah take Jacob to town, where Jacob died a few days later. An inquest was held. The coroner's jury, headed by Dr. Zerubabel Endicott, son of the late governor, said, "The man had been bruised to death, having great bruises with the skin broken, and having clodders of blood about his heart." Corey was brought before the court and fined, "upon suspicion of having abused the body of Jacob Goodale."

Legend has it that the ghost of Jacob Goodale appeared from time to time, crying out about his foul murder.

> Look! Look! It is the ghost of Jacob Goodale
> Whom fifteen years ago this man did murder,
> By stomping on his body! In his shroud
> He comes here to bear witness to this crime.[111]

Jacob Goodale's mother, Katherine, had died in 1645, when he was only three. Two years later, in 1647, Jacob's father, Robert Goodale, married Margaret Lazenby who, as Jacob's step-mother, raised the little boy with loving care. On March 21, 1692, seventeen years after Jacob's death at the hands of Corey, Margaret Goodale, characterized by the Rev. Lawson in his popular book as "an ancient woman, named Goodale," appeared

---

111 Henry Wadsworth Longfellow, "New England Tragedies."

among the afflicted at the examination of Corey's third wife, Martha.

Now, on April 18, 1692, on the complaint of Ezekiel Cheever and Sergeant Thomas Putnam, Giles Corey himself was in custody and under examination. Jacob's brother Zachariah Goodale, some years earlier, had placed his son Joseph Goodale under the guardianship of his good friend Ezekiel Cheever. Ezekiel was not a member of the conspiracy, but maintained a close relationship with the Putnam family.

Giles Corey, obstinate as a mule, spoke slowly. Four weeks earlier, on March 21, 1692, at his wife's examination, he had been tricked by the magistrates into reporting some events concerning her which, in his naivete, he had regarded as unusual. However, he knew full well that his wife had never practiced witchcraft, and that in no way could she be held responsible for the girls' fits. Now he stood in court, and in bewilderment he heard the same false accusations being made against himself. Through their relentless grilling, the magistrates succeeded only in one thing. They aroused the fighting spirit of Giles Corey. In front of him the afflicted girls tumbled about, squalling and crying out that he was a terrible wizard. In just the same manner had they howled and cried out on his wife.

Committed to prison, Giles would reflect on all of this. He would have no more to do with this macabre and preposterous charade. Dogged in his determination, intrepid to the last, nothing was ever to shake his conviction that both he and his wife were innocent of witchcraft. He did not yield to the inconceivable torture used on him, a man of eighty, to put him to his death in September.

Bridget Bishop, the next person examined, had been previously been married to Thomas Oliver. He died in June 1679, and his widow became owner of his valuable house in the center of Salem Town. Envy soon led to witchcraft accusations. Bridget Oliver was charged with witchcraft in February 1680, but was not convicted.[112]   A few years later she married Edward Bishop, sawyer of Salem.   They lived in her house, the former Oliver house, and he "held this estate in the right of his wife Bridget, the widow of Thomas Oliver."[113]

The conspiracy, looking for an easy target in 1692, found her the perfect candidate. Although she had escaped the vicious attack on her life a dozen years earlier, Bridget Bishop now realized that she was a marked woman. She had always lived in Salem Town; she had never been in Salem Village before the day of her examination, April 19, 1692. The Rev. Samuel Parris, a faithful scribe, took down her testimony. The afflicted girls affirmed that she had used her witchcraft to hurt them. Hathorne asked, "What do you say to it?" She answered, "I never saw these persons before, nor I never was in this place before."[114] But the truthful answer of Bridget was overwhelmed by the lies that then were thrown at her.

Mary Walcott claimed that her brother had struck at the specter of Bridget, and Mary herself had seen and heard the coat of the specter tear when it was hit. They searched the coat that Bridget was wearing, and found a tear. This was hard evidence that Bridget was indeed a witch.

---

112 "The Negro of John Ingersoll testified, before the Court of Commissioners, against Bridget Oliver, of Salem, as a witch. Among other things, he deposed that he saw the shape of said Bridget on a beam in the barn, with an egg in its hand, and that while he looked for a rake or pitchfork to strike her shape, it vanished. She was required to give bonds for her appearance before the Court of Assistants, or be imprisoned till their session." (Felt, entry of February 22, 1680.)

113 Upham, 2:253.

114 The husband of Bridget Bishop was Edward Bishop, sawyer, of Salem Town. Upham (1:143) mistakenly identified her husband as the father of Edward Bishop, Jr. of Salem Village, the tavern owner who was accused on April 21, 1692. Following Upham, Starkey (107) incorrectly stated that "the real gossip centered around Bridget's conduct as tavern keeper." Bridget Bishop was neither a tavern keeper nor a resident of Salem Village, but was a respectable matron of Salem Town.

Magistrate Hathorne continued, "They say you bewitched your first husband to death." Bridget answered, "If it please your worship, I know nothing of it." As she spoke, she shook her head. In response the afflicted girls went into fits portraying horrible torture. Asserting her innocence, she rolled her eyes to heaven, and instantly all the possessed girls rolled theirs too. When Hathorne asked if it did not trouble her to see the girls tormented, her reply was an insolent "No!" And as the examination went on, the magistrates found more than ample evidence to commit her to prison. Bridget Bishop was the first witch to be hanged.

The fourth accused person examined that day was Abigail Hobbs, age twenty-two. Whereas Giles Corey and Bridget Bishop had stood up to the authorities, Abigail Hobbs went right along with them. In all probability she believed that her good performance would place her in the elite group of the afflicted, which she longed to join. Her neighbors always had regarded her as a wild young woman, and in fact she was accustomed to shocking the people of Topsfield by her wanderings about the woods at night. Priscilla Chubb, age thirty-one, reported, "Abigail Hobbs told me that she did not care what anybody said to her, for she had seen the Devil, and had made a covenant or bargain with him."

In the disorder of the court, Abigail was in her element. Hathorne inquired, "Do not some creatures suck your body? Where do they come, to what parts, when they come to your body?" Realizing what he wanted, the young woman plunged headlong into a confession. She described in detail an unholy sabbat meeting in Parris' pasture. She then confessed, "I will speak the truth. I have been very wicked. I have seen dogs and many creatures." Hathorne asked, "What dogs do you mean, ordinary dogs?" and her answer was, "I mean the Devil!" Hathorne then asked her, "How often? Many times? What appearance was he in?" She answered, "Like a man. It was at Casco." Hathorne asked, "Where, in the house or in the woods, in the night or in the day?" She answered, "In the woods, in the day, about 3 or 4 years ago."

The afflicted girls shrewdly guessed what was up. They fell silent when the confession began, just as they had done when Tituba first set this precedent. Tituba, after all, had been tutored by Parris. At appropriate times, the girls gave Abigail their active support by nodding their heads. Afterward several of the afflicted girls assured the magistrates that this witch, Abigail Hobbs, was a pitiful creature, and that they were intensely sorry for her. Because their elders regarded her as belonging to the enemy camp, the girls well knew that she would never be accepted as a recruit into their ranks. She was being used only for the purpose at hand, the securing of a confession, the first since Tituba's. Cotton Mather and other clergy needed free confessions as evidence for their theological claims that witchcraft was rampant. The success of this venture gave the authorities the impetus to seek further confessions.

To the magistrates, the witch hunt served to ferret out perceived enemies of the state. To the clergy, the witch hunt was a symbolic fantasy, a pitched battle between an army of Devils and a valiant little band of God's elect. Absurdities and untruths were mere details which bothered neither group. Both magistrates and clergy were united in their determination to do away with those that "have confessed, that they have signed unto a book, which the Devil showed them, and engaged in his Hellish design of bewitching and ruining our land."

Despite Abigail's waywardness and despite the fact that her exuberant confession rang false, the authorities accepted her testimony as fact. When Abigail was interviewed privately in prison on May 12, 1692, she admitted that "she had made two covenants with the Devil, first for two years, and after that for four years, and she confessed herself to have been a witch these six years." She confessed to more abominations, including murder. They asked her, "Were they men, women, or children you killed?" She answered, "They were both boys and girls." They questioned, "Were you angry with them yourself?" "Yes, though I do not know why now," she replied. Then they asked, "Did you know Mr. Burroughs' wife? Did you know of any puppets pricked to kill her?"

Her efforts to please the magistrates were to no avail. There was to be no special treatment shown to this confused young woman. She was a confessing witch and belonged in jail. The authorities locked her up, correctly assuming that they could always count upon her as a witness for the prosecution, right up to the point when they would decide to sentence her to death.

Before the Salem witchcraft delusion came to an end, nearly two hundred people, mostly good and honest women, many from the leading families of Salem, Beverly, Andover, Billerica, and Newbury, were imprisoned. In the first wave of incriminations, the Salem Village witch hunt, the accused typically persisted in their claims of innocence. But great pains were taken to make some of the accused confess. After the initial confession of Tituba, nobody else confessed until Abigail Hobbs did so on April 19, 1692. As time wore on, the magistrates gave subtle indications to the accused that confessing witchcraft might be the only way to obtain mercy. In the second wave of the delusion, the Andover witch hunt, covering the period from July 15, 1692 to the end of the accusations in November 1692, a great many of the accused would confess.

On April 21, 1692, following Abigail Hobbs' moment in court, the conspiracy filed a complaint [No. 9] against nine people, an unprecedented number. They were William Hobbs, his wife Deliverance Hobbs, Nehemiah Abbot, Jr., Mary Easty, Sarah Wildes (all of Topsfield), Edward Bishop, Jr., his wife Sarah Bishop, Mary Black (all of Salem Village), and Mary English of Salem. All nine were accused of afflicting Mercy Lewis, Ann Putnam, Jr., and Mary Walcott.

On the morning of April 22, 1692, the accused were arrested and all but Mary English were taken to Deacon Ingersoll's tavern in Salem Village for examination. Mary English was dealt with separately, and her case is included with that of her husband Philip English in the next chapter.

Edward Bishop, Jr. and his wife, Sarah, stood up for their rights and denied the accusations. He recently had shown the courage to accost John Indian in his fits, and thus had rapidly brought John back to normal. With this success, Bishop sensibly recommended that a similar treatment be tried on the afflicted girls. The authorities were not interested; in fact, Bishop's logic was an irritant. They now had him in custody, and would keep him, along with his wife, from trying any such cure.

Edward Bishop, Jr. owned a tavern on the eastern edge of Salem Village on the Ipswich Road. His tavern was more popular than that of Deacon Ingersoll, a conspirator. The following testimony was given at the examination. Bishop permitted customers to stay until late hours drinking, playing at shovel-board and making a general uproar, whereby "young people were in danger to be corrupted." The Rev. John Hale was afraid that if this did not come to a stop, "Edward Bishop, [Jr.]'s house would have been a house of great profaneness and iniquity."

Not only were these goings-on unpuritanical, but they disturbed the sleep of neighbors, notably the Trasks, relatives of the Putnams. One spring night in May 1690, Christian Trask, the wife of John Trask,[115] burst into the tavern, hurled some of the game pieces into the fire, and reproved Sarah Bishop. But Christian "received no satisfaction from her about it." The next night Christian became distracted with fits like the Salem Village girls. When Christian recovered, she said she had been bewitched by Sarah Bishop. Christian searched the prophecies of the scriptures. At Sunday church service, she again fell into a distracted fit, "manifesting that she was under temptation to kill herself or somebody else." And so she continued until she indeed did die, on June 3, 1690, at age twenty-nine. At a jury of inquest held on June 24, 1690, it was found that she had taken her own life by cutting her windpipe with a small pair of scissors. However, the scissors were so small that after the Rev. John Hale had observed them, he said he judged it impossible for her "to

---

115 John Trask married Christian Woodbury in 1679. They had five children, the last born January 1, 1690.

mangle herself so without some extraordinary work of the Devil
or witchcraft." All this prior history was presented as evidence
against the Bishops. They were committed to prison.

Deliverance and William Hobbs, Abigail's parents, were
members of the Topsfield group whom the Putnams regarded as
enemies. The parents were easy prey, since Deliverance was
known to be subject to much the same fantasies as her daughter.
Everything was set to launch Deliverance into the never-never
land of the Devil. The moment she entered the room, the afflicted
girls set up shriekings and shrillings that unnerved the entire
courtroom. Abigail Williams and Ann Putnam, Jr. cried out,
"There is Goody Hobbs upon the beam. She is not at the bar."
Hathorne asked, "What do you say to this? Though you are at the
bar in person, yet they see your appearance upon the beam."
Deliverance looked up above her at the great wooden beam. She
could only say, "I have done nothing."

Deliverance was cooperative. Beginning her confession, she
made every effort to give the information requested of her.
Willingly she agreed to any statement put to her by Hathorne. She
said, "Last Lord's Day in this Meeting House I saw a great many
birds and cats and dogs, and heard a voice say 'Come away.' " He
asked, "What persons did you see?" She answered, "Goody Wildes
and the shape of Mercy Lewis." But, since Mercy Lewis was one of
the elite inner circle of afflicted girls upon whom the whole witch
hunt depended, this did not sit well with Hathorne. Deliverance
caught herself just in time, quickly adding that Mercy's specter
never hurt her, but "Goody Wildes tore me almost to pieces." She
then said that Goody Wildes had brought her the book. She
rambled on and agreed that every previously accused person was
indeed a witch.

The day before, at Deacon Ingersoll's tavern, the place where
the examination was now being held, Mary Walcott and Abigail
Williams had cried out, "There stands [the specter of] Goody
Hobbs!" Benjamin Hutchinson then had struck at it with his

rapier.[116]   Knowing of this incident, Hathorne asked, "Did you receive any hurt yesterday?" Deliverance answered, "Yes. In my right side, like a prick, and it is very sore, and it was done while I was in a trance."

Deliverance's husband, William Hobbs, in contrast, dug right in and spoke bluntly, "I am as clear of witchcraft as a new born baby."   Hathorne confronted him with the suffering of the afflicted girls, asking, "Can you now deny it?"   He stoutly answered, "I can deny it to my dying day." Hathorne got down to business, demanding, "When were you at any public religious meeting?"   He replied "Not a pretty while!" "Why so?" retorted Hathorne. "Because I was not well. I had a distemper that none knows," answered Hobbs.   Hathorne persisted, "What is the reason you go away when there is any reading of Scripture in your family? If you put away God's ordinances, no wonder the Devil prevails with you."   The Puritan magistrate had plenty of evidence to use against him. Deliverance and William Hobbs were sent to prison.

The Wildes' extended family were part of the Topsfield group despised by the Putnams. Sarah Wildes tried to defend herself as best she could, but the magistrates lost no time with her. She was a witch, as evidenced in Deliverance Hobbs' confession. Sarah was committed to prison.

Mary Black, a slave attached to the household of Nathaniel Putnam, was supposed to follow in Tituba's footsteps and give a lively confession that might implicate many new people. Instead she had the fortitude to feign bewildered incomprehension of what was wanted of her. When they asked, "Do you prick others?" she was answered, "No, I pin my neckcloth." Doing their best to make a bad situation better, the afflicted girls came running up to the magistrates, showing their hands bleeding from her pricks.

---

116 Benjamin Hutchinson, age twenty-four, the adopted son of Nathaniel Ingersoll, ran the tavern.

Mary Black still did not flinch, but no matter. She, too, was led away to prison.

With the seventh prisoner, Nehemiah Abbot, Jr., events took an unprecedented turn. Since he was from Topsfield, the girls had never seen him before. They had to rely on a verbal description they had received, namely that of an old gray man with a wen on his head. By mistake, not the prisoner but his father, Nehemiah Abbot, Sr., age sixty, had been described to girls. When the girls looked at the prisoner, a young "hilly faced" man with strands of hair falling over his eyes, they were completely confused. Scared of punishment if they were at fault, the girls groped for a safe path. Mercy Lewis blurted out, "It is not the man." The other girls were more cautious, examining his scalp in search of the wen which was supposed to identify him. Because there was none, the prisoner, Nehemiah Abbot, Jr., was discharged. Although a failure, the performance succeeded nicely in giving an impression of the painstaking care taken by the girls and the diligence used by the magistrates.

Later in the witch hunt, unofficial charges were made that the magistrates were unfair, habitually imprisoning everyone accused. John Hathorne used this case to refute that claim. In point of fact, Nehemiah Abbot, Jr. was the only person arrested for witchcraft in 1692 who was released after preliminary examination. Everyone else for whom a complaint was filed was imprisoned, including members of Abbot's extended family.

Last examined that day was Mary Easty. At age fifty-eight, she was the middle of the three Towne sisters. Her two sisters, Rebecca Nurse and Sarah Cloyce, were already in prison. Mary carried herself with courage, good sense, and grace. Neither as timid as Rebecca nor as assertive as Sarah, she displayed a quiet dignity which engendered in magistrate John Hathorne a moment of doubt. Realizing that the whole witch hunt could come to an end if the Putnams persisted in picking off eminently respectable people like Mary Easty, Hathorne asked the afflicted girls, "Are you certain this is the woman?" But the question released renewed demoniac energy in the girls. They howled with pain; they quivered and whimpered; they shrieked. Mary Easty turned her head a bit to one side. In response, her specter forcibly twisted the girls' heads into the same position. Their heads were thrust to such an angle that their necks appeared almost broken. Ann Putnam, Jr. shrilled, "Oh, Goody Easty, Goody Easty, you are the woman! You are the woman!" Turning to Mary Easty the magistrates asked what she thought of this. Mary spoke with candor and honesty, "It is an evil spirit. But whether it be witchcraft I do not know." She was imprisoned with the rest.

Hathorne harbored misgivings. Mary's quiet self-possession and her gentle manner made even the jailers speak up for her. Hathorne had estimated correctly that the general populace would tolerate a full-blown witch hunt. Now he foresaw a point at which that toleration could shatter. Hathorne's own sister, Elizabeth Porter, an avid defender of Rebecca Nurse, was turning her attention to Mary Easty. Hathorne realized that he might be treading on the limits of public patience. The objectives of the witch hunt could be achieved without Mary Easty.

Questioning the afflicted girls again, Hathorne sternly asked them one by one, "Are you certain this is the woman?" Facing this imperious magistrate, every girl except Mercy Lewis wavered. On this basis, Hathorne released Mary Easty from prison on May 18. She returned home to Topsfield. While her family and neighbors were overjoyed, the Putnams were furious. The conspirators went to John Hathorne to convince him that the same case could be made for the release of her sisters, and in turn the release of others, such as the imprisoned members of the John Proctor family.

Thomas Putnam presented the following "facts" to Hathorne. His servant Mercy Lewis alone had held out against the release of Mary Easty. As soon as the release took effect, Mercy Lewis was taken violently ill with agonizing paroxysms. She suffered periods in which her jaws were locked. However, there were intervals of respite, during which she prayed, "Dear Lord, receive my soul. Lord, let them not kill me quite." Mercy's incoherent outcries were directed at the witchcraft of Mary Easty. Thomas Putnam confided in Hathorne that, without relief from this witchcraft, Mercy Lewis was sure to die.

Hathorne held out for further evidence to confirm this affliction. Ann Putnam, Jr. and Abigail Williams, the youngest of the afflicted girls and the most reliable, were picked. The two were stationed at Mercy's bedside. With their spectral sight, they were able to make positive identification of the specter of Mary Easty in the act of hurting Mercy Lewis. For confirmation, Mary Walcott was brought in. She saw Mary Easty's specter put chains about Mercy's neck and choke her. Mary Walcott explained why the girls had been uncertain when Hathorne had questioned them before Mary Easty's release. Mary Walcott said that Easty's specter had blinded the spectral eyes of all the girls except Mercy Lewis. The blinded girls, not seeing Easty's specter, supposed her to be innocent. Because Easty was unable to put out Mercy Lewis' spectral sight, she had to kill Mercy.

Thomas Putnam warned Hathorne that, if she were not relieved, Mercy Lewis would not live until morning. John Hathorne relented; he entrenched himself firmly in the camp of the conspirators once more. Turning his back on his sister's pleas, he issued a new arrest warrant for Mary Easty. The constables were dispatched to arrest her and, in the middle of night, they pounded and shouted at her door. She was taken to prison the same hour, and once again put in irons. Immediately Mercy Lewis came out of her fits and slept peacefully. The witch hunt was back on track.

1. John Cotton (1584-1652). Puritan clergyman; "Patriarch of New England;" maternal grandfather of Cotton Mather.

2. Richard Mather (1596-1669). Puritan clergyman; father of Increase Mather.

COTTON MATHER.

3. Increase Mather (1639-1723). Puritan clergyman; president of Harvard from 1685 to 1701; father of Cotton Mather.

4. Cotton Mather (1663-1728). Puritan clergyman and religious zealot who helped to ignite the Salem witch hunt of 1692.

5. John Winthrop (1588-1649). First governor of Massachusetts Bay Colony; grandfather of witchcraft justice Wait Still Winthrop.

6. John Endicott (1589-1665). Governor of Massachusetts; persecutor of the Quakers; father of Dr. Zerubabel Endicott.

7. Simon Bradstreet (1603-1697). Governor of Massachusetts from 1679 to 1686, and from 1689 to 1692.

8. Sir Edmond Andros (1637-1714). Royal governor of New England from 1686 to 1689, appointed by King James II.

9. Sir William Phipps (1651-1695). Royal governor of New England from 1692 to 1694, appointed by King William III. This old print depicts Phipps landing in Boston from England on May 14, 1692 to take up his rule.

10. William Stoughton (1630-1701). Leader of the Puritan old guard; chief justice in the Salem witchcraft trials of 1692; acting governor of Massachusetts from 1694 to 1697.

11. Roger Williams (1603-1683). Minister in Salem in 1631 and 1634; banished from Massachusetts in 1635; founded Rhode Island in 1636. Established and maintained friendly ties with the Indians. An early advocate of democracy and religious tolerance.

12. Trial of George Jacobs, Sr. for witchcraft before the third sitting of the Court of Oyer and Terminer in Salem on August 5, 1692. (Nineteenth century painting by T.H. Matteson; original in the Essex Institute.)

13. House of George Jacobs, Sr. in Salem. Jacobs was executed for witchcraft on August 19, 1692.

14. House of Phillip English in Salem. English and his wife, Mary, were accused and arrested for witchcraft, but managed to escape.

15. House of Cotton Mather in Boston, as it appeared in the nineteenth century.

16. House of Rebecca Nurse as it looks today in Danvers, Massachusetts, formerly called Salem Village. Rebecca Nurse was executed for witchcraft on July 19, 1692. (Photograph by Henry W. Rutkowski. Courtesy of the Danvers Archival Center.)

17. Preliminary examination of an accused witch before magistrate John Hathorne, who, according to Nathaniel Hawthorne, "made himself so conspicuous in the martyrdom of the witches that their blood may fairly be said to have left a stain upon him. So deep a stain, indeed, that his old dry bones, in the Charter Street burial-ground, must still retain it."

18. Nathaniel Hawthorne (1804-1864). American romanticist; great great great grandson of William Hathorne, Sr. (1607-1681), who was "a bitter persecutor, as witness the Quakers;" great great grandson of magistrate John Hathorne (1641-1717), who, "too, inherited the persecuting spirit." Nathaniel Hawthorne wrote, "At all events, I, the present writer, as their representative, hereby take shame upon myself for their sakes, and pray that any curse incurred by them may now and henceforth be removed."

CHAPTER 10

WOE TO THE INHABITANTS

"*Woe to the inhabitants* of the Earth, and of the sea; for the Devil is come down unto you, having great wrath," preached Cotton Mather, picking his text from Revelations, 12:12.

Philip English, a wealthy merchant, was Salem Town's largest shipowner. In March 1692, he had been elected as a selectman. Elected with him was Daniel Andrew, the brother-in-law of Israel Porter. In fact, all the selectmen elected in March had friendly ties to the Porters.

On Saturday April 30, 1692 the conspiracy filed a complaint [No. 10] against Philip English, Lydia Dustin, Susannah Martin, Dorcas Hoar, Sarah Morrell, and the Rev. George Burroughs. All except Philip English were arrested and imprisoned on Monday May 2. The marshal reported "Mr. Philip English not being to be found."

The following Friday May 6, 1692, a second warrant was made out for the arrest of Philip English. But it was not until Monday May 30, 1692 that the merchant gave himself up, about six weeks after the arrest of his wife, on April 21.

The details of what happened to Philip English and his wife, Mary, during these six weeks is given in the following account by Susannah Hathorne. Her father was the son of magistrate John Hathorne and her mother was the daughter of Philip English.

"Substance of Madame Susannah Hathorne's account of her grandfather English, etc. Mr. English was a Jerseyman, came young to America and lived with Mr. W. Hollingsworth whose only child he married. He owned above twenty sail of vessel. His wife had the best education of her times. Wrote with great ease, and has left a specimen of her needlework in her infancy or youth.

"She was cried out upon. The officers, the high sheriff, and deputy with attendants came at eleven at night. When the servant came up, Mr. English imagined it was upon business, not having had the least notion of the suspicions respecting his wife. They were in bed together in the western chamber of their new house, and had a large family of servants.

"The officers came in soon after the servant who so alarmed Mr. English that with difficulty found his clothes. The officers came into the chamber, following the servant, and opening the curtains read the mittimus. She was then ordered to rise but absolutely refused. Her husband continued walking the chamber all night, but the officers contented themselves with a guard upon the house till morning. In the morning they required of her to rise, but she refused to rise before her usual hour. After breakfast with her husband and children, and seeing all the servants, she was conducted to the Cat and Wheel, a public house. Six weeks she was confined to the front chamber, in which she received the visits of her husband three times a day.

"After six weeks her husband was accused, and their friends obtained that they should be sent to Boston till their trial should come on. In Arnold's custody they had bail and liberty of the town, only lodging in the jail. The Revs. Moody and Willard of Boston visited them and invited them to public worship on the day before they were to return to Salem for trial.[117] Their text was, 'When they persecute you in one city, flee ye into another.'[118] After Meeting the ministers visited them at the jail, and asked them whether they took notice of the discourse, and told them

---

117 The Rev. Joshua Moody (1632–1697), Harvard class of 1653, was an evangelical Puritan minister. He refused to admit to the prevailing witchcraft delusion, and performed deeds of mercy. Later, he took refuge from his Boston critics by becoming minister at Portsmouth, New Hampshire. The Rev. Samuel Willard was the pastor of the Third Church (Old South) in Boston.

118 Matt. 10:23.

their danger and urged them to escape since so many had suffered. Mr. English replied, 'God will not permit them to touch me.' Mrs. English said, 'Do you not think the sufferers [the accused] innocent?' The Rev. Moody said, 'Yes!' She then added, 'Why may we not suffer also?" The ministers then told him if he would not carry his wife away they would.

"The gentlemen of the town took care to provide at midnight a conveyance, encouraged by the Governor, jailer, etc., and Mr. and Mrs. English were conveyed away, and the Governor gave letters to Governor Fletcher of New York who came out and received them, and carried them to his house. They remained twelve months in the city. Great advantages were proposed to detain them at New York, but the attachment of the wife to Salem was not lost by all her sufferings, and she urged a return. They were received with joy upon their return [in 1693] and the Town had a thanksgiving on the occasion. [The Rev. Nicholas] Noyes, the prosecutor, dined with him on that day in his own house."[119]

Philip English continued his mercantile career which spanned a total of fifty years until his death in 1736. The accusation against Philip English and his wife, Mary, and the confiscation of his property demonstrate that his enemies included highly placed government officials. Among them were the Corwin family. Sheriff George Corwin was instrumental in taking much property which was never returned to him. Philip English favored the Church of England, and had wanted to use his riches to erect an Anglican church building in Salem. The seizure of his fortune after his arrest would prevent any such possibility from occurring. However, years later Philip English was instrumental in bringing an Anglican Church to Salem, St. Peter's, giving the land on Prison Lane where the church was built.

The Rev. George Burroughs represented tolerance of the kind that prominent magistrates and clergy wanted to suppress.

---

119 Cited in the diary of the Rev. William Bentley of Salem, entry for May 21, 1793.

Burroughs' arrest offers insight into why the witch hunt was sanctioned. Samuel Sewall was a most respected Puritan magistrate. His dealings with Burroughs are helpful in tracing the plot to high levels.

Burroughs graduated in the Harvard class of 1670, a year before Sewall. As noted earlier, Burroughs became minister at Salem Village in 1681, leaving after two years because of political divisions in the parish. From Salem Village he went to Casco, Maine, and from there to Wells, Maine. As a respected clergyman, he stopped to dine with Sewall on November 18, 1685. Five years later, he addressed the Wednesday night meeting of the South Church Society, where Sewall heard him speak on the Beatitudes. On Monday March 14, 1692, Sewall served as his banker, sending him twenty-six pounds cash in exchange for a note written by Burroughs' brother in London.[120]

Only five weeks later, on April 20, 1692, twelve-year-old Ann Putnam, Jr. had a vision, "In the evening I saw the apparition of a minister, and cried out, 'Oh dreadful! What are ministers witches too? Oh dreadful, tell me your name that I may know who you are.' He tortured me and urged me to write in his book, which I refused. Then he told me his name was George Burroughs, and that he was above witch, for he was a conjurer." Ann had been only three years old when Burroughs left his ministry at Salem Village for Maine.

On April 21, 1692, the day after the appearance of Burroughs' specter to Ann Putnam, Jr., her father, Sergeant Thomas Putnam, wrote in a letter to magistrates Hathorne and Corwin, "We thought it our duty to inform your Honors of what we conceive you have not heard, which are high and dreadful, of a wheel within a wheel, at which our ears do tingle. Humbly craving continually your prayers and help in this distressing case, that you may be a terror to evil-doers, we remain to serve you in what we are able." Thomas Putnam's bold signature is affixed to the letter. Under his leadership, the conspiracy was thriving.

---

120 Such a note would correspond to a personal check today.

The complaint of April 30 against George Burroughs and the others was signed by Captain Jonathan Walcott and Sergeant Thomas Putnam of Salem Village. Field Marshal John Partridge was promptly sent to Wells, Maine to arrest Burroughs, and "convey him with all speed to Salem before the magistrates there, to be examined, he being suspected for a confederacy with the Devil."

The savage war with the Indians was raging, and the fears of Field Marshal Partridge and his men, sent to arrest the wizard Burroughs, were increased by the very real danger to which they were exposed on their journey. Wells was completely cut off by land, surrounded by hostile Indians lurking, it seemed, behind every tree. Even by sea, French privateers made the voyage dangerous. Instead of taking the road that led through recently devastated York, Field Marshal Partridge and his men took an obscure, tortuous path through the forests and across the river at Quampegan. On the way back with their prisoner, whom they believed to be in league with the Devil, they feared that at any moment he would turn his powers on them. Upon entering the deep forest, a black cloud shut out the sky, and thunder roared in terrifying crashes. Lightning split a tall pine above their heads, and its fragments fell over them. Yet their prisoner stayed calm throughout the storm. That dark place in the forest, made memorable by this episode, is today called Witchtrott. On May 4, 1692 the men delivered Burroughs to the authorities in Salem.

On May 9, 1692 Burroughs was examined by four magistrates: William Stoughton, John Hathorne, Jonathan Corwin, and Samuel Sewall, key members of the old guard. At first, the examination was held in private, "none of the bewitched being present." Asked when he last partook of the Lord's Supper, he answered that it was so long ago he could not tell. He admitted that none of his children except the eldest was baptized. He denied "that his house at Casco was haunted, yet he admitted there were toads."

When the afflicted girls were brought before him, "many if not all were grievously tortured." As Burroughs glanced around, the "malevolence" of his gaze "knocked down all of the afflicted which stood behind him." When he looked toward Mercy Lewis, who had lived in his household three years before, "she fell into a dreadful and tedious fit." Asked what he thought of these things, Burroughs said, "It is an amazing and humbling Providence, but I understand nothing of it."

The usual fantastic testimony was presented. Susannah Sheldon claimed that the two dead wives of Burroughs had appeared to her in their winding sheets, and confided that he had killed them. Susannah Sheldon and Ann Putnam, Jr. testified that Burroughs "brought the book and would have them write." Sarah Bibber claimed that he had "hurt her, though she had not seen him personally before, as she knew." Mercy Lewis said, "He carried me to an exceeding high mountain and showed me all the Kingdoms of the Earth and told me that he would give them all to me if I would write in his book, and if I would not he would throw me down and break my neck."

Ann Putnam, Jr. testified, "The form of two women appeared to me in winding sheets, and they turned their faces towards [the specter of] Mr. Burroughs and told him that he had been a cruel man to them, and that their blood did cry for vengeance against him. And immediately he vanished away. The two women turned their faces towards me, and looked as pale as a white wall. They told me that they were Mr. Burroughs' two first wives, and that he had murdered them. One [Hannah (mnu)] told me that she was his first wife, and he stabbed her under the left arm and put a piece of sealing wax on the wound. She pulled aside the winding sheet and showed me the place, and also told me that she was in the house [where] Mr. Parris now lives when it was done. The other [Sarah (Ruck) Hathorne] told me that Mr. Burroughs and the wife he has now [Mary (mnu)] killed her in the vessel as she was coming to see her friends, because they would have one another."

Further testimony against Burroughs concerned his feats of strength, considered by the magistrates as one of the "more certain signs" of his witchcraft. Unlike the usual minister who was "too good" to soil his hands, and physically too weak to do any good if so inclined, George Burroughs habitually pitched in and carried the heavy loads of military and other supplies being taken off the ships by canoe. Burroughs had proved a better student at Harvard than Cotton Mather, and was the first of Harvard's great athletes. By working alongside the common man, unheard of in such a rigid class system, Burroughs had instilled spirit and hope among his parishioners living under constant fear of attack. Samuel Webber related that Burroughs "put his fingers into the bung of a barrel of molasses and lifted it up, and carried it round." This was no more than a story, springing from the genuine affection that the soldiers in Maine felt for the Rev. Burroughs. Yet, now this story was being turned into evidence against the man they loved. Captain Simon Willard gave this truthful account. "Mr. Lawrence at Falmouth in Casco Bay was commending Mr. George Burroughs for his strength, for Mr. Burroughs can hold out this gun with one hand, Mr. Burroughs being there. But I saw him not hold it out. The gun was about seven foot barrel. I could not hold it long enough to take sight."

No finer tribute was expressed than this statement which crept into Elizer Keyser's testimony against Burroughs. "Captain Daniel King said he believes that Burroughs is a child of God, a choice child of God, and that God would clear up his innocence." The rest of Keyser's testimony, of course, was a diatribe against Burroughs, or more precisely his specter which, according to Keyser, was "something like jelly, that used to be in the water and quaver with a strange motion, and then quickly disappear."

Why was Keyser's account of a specter like jelly accepted by the magistrates, while Captain King's testimony was pushed aside as worthless? The magistrates regarded the public with a condescension verging on contempt. They believed that the more absurd, improbable, or even impossible something was, the more likely that the populace would accept it, trusting that their leaders would not assert a seeming impossibility unless it were true. Therefore, the very absurdity of spectral testimony made its application possible; a person who otherwise could not be reached could readily be convicted on spectral evidence.

A final example of the spectral evidence used against Burroughs is the deposition of Benjamin Hutchinson. "On the

21st April 1692. Abigail Williams said that there was [the specter of] a little black minister that lived at Casco Bay. He said that he had killed three wives, two for himself and one for Mister Lawson.[121] He said that he could hold out the heaviest gun with one hand, which no man can hold out with both hands. I asked her where this little man stood. She said just where the cart wheel went along. I had a three-pronged iron fork in my hand and I threw it where she said he stood. She presently fell into a little fit. When it was over she said you have torn his coat, for I heard it tear. I asked whereabouts. She said on one side. Then we came into the house of Lieutenant Ingersoll's. I went into the great room and Abigail came in. She said there he stands. I said where, and presently drew my rapier, but he immediately was gone, as she said. Then she said there is a gray cat. Then I said whereabouts does she stand. There, she said. I struck with my rapier. Then she fell in a fit, and when it was over she said, you killed the cat and immediately [the specter of] Sarah Good came and carried it away. This was about 12 o'clock."

On Saturday May 7, 1692, the conspiracy filed a complaint [No. 11] against Sarah Dustin, and on May 8, 1692, one [No. 12] against Bethia Carter, Bethia Carter, Jr., and Ann Sears, all of Woburn. On Tuesday May 10, 1692, the conspiracy filed a complaint [No. 13] against George Jacobs, Sr. and his granddaughter Margaret Jacobs. Included with the list of afflicted girls was Jacob's servant, Sarah Churchill, who testified against him, and thereafter was a member of the outer circle of the afflicted.

John Willard had married into the Wilkins family of Salem Village. His wife, Margaret (Wilkins) Willard, was the daughter of Thomas Wilkins, and the granddaughter of Bray Wilkins, age eighty-one. Constable John Putnam, Jr. tried to employ John Willard to take in some of the accused. Appalled at the idea of

---

121 The Rev. Deodat Lawson succeeded the Rev. Burroughs as minister at Salem Village.

capturing innocent people, Willard refused. On Saturday April 23, 1692, the apparition of John Willard came for the first time to Ann Putnam, Jr. She told the apparition, "I am very sorry to see you so. You were one that helped to tend me, and now you have come to afflict me." But Ann's pleas to the specter did no good. She said that on the April 24, 1692, Sabbath day, "The apparition of John Willard did so grievously afflict me that he forced me to cry out against him before all." On the next day, John Willard visited Sergeant Thomas Putnam's house and denied the allegations. For three or four days Ann was silent before she started in again, saying, "The apparition of my little sister Sarah, who died when she was about six weeks old, is crying out for vengeance against John Willard."

In desperation, Willard went to house of his grandfather-in-law, Bray Wilkins, knowing of his friendship with the Putnams. He asked Bray to pray with him. Bray abruptly put him off, and did not hear from him again. Bray stated, "Whether my not answering his desire did offend him, I cannot tell, but I was jealous afterwards that it did."

On Tuesday May 3, 1692, John Willard asked his uncle-in-law Henry Wilkins (a son of Bray) to go to Boston with him for election week. Henry's son, Daniel Wilkins, age seventeen, and the beau of Mercy Lewis, entreated him not to go with Willard, saying "It would be well if Willard were hanged." This surprised Henry Wilkins, but he went with Willard anyhow. After his father had been gone a few days, Daniel Wilkins became ill.

Bray Wilkins had also gone to Boston, staying at his brother-in-law's house. Many family members met there for dinner with their guest, the Rev. Deodat Lawson. Bray's son Henry Wilkins, and Bray's grandson-in-law John Willard, arrived. Soon after, Bray said, "Willard looked upon me in such a sort as I have never before discerned in anybody." Bray then fell into a strange condition, of which he later said, "I cannot express the misery I was in, for my water was suddenly stopped, and I had no benefit of nature, but was like a man on a rack." He told his wife, "I am afraid that Willard has done me wrong." Bray's pain continued, and finding no relief, his "jealousy" also continued. Mr. Lawson was "amazed, and knew not what to do." However "a woman, accounted skillful, used means." Bray lay there in bed, recuperating.

Meanwhile, in Salem Village Daniel Wilkins' sickness grew worse each day. Dr. William Griggs, one of the conspirators, was called in. Griggs, true to form, "affirmed that his sickness was by some preternatural cause, and would make no application of any physic." Mercy Lewis was there and "affirmed that she saw the apparition of John Willard afflicting Daniel. Quickly after came Ann Putnam, [Jr.], and she saw the same apparition."

On Tuesday May 10, 1692, while Daniel lay sick at home in Salem Village and Bray lay sick in Boston, Bray's son Benjamin Wilkins, Sr. took legal action. Although not a member of the conspiracy he was allowed to file a complaint [No. 14]. It was, of course, against John Willard, charging him with afflicting Bray Wilkins and Daniel Wilkins. This time the girls in the circle were not afflicted, but acted as seers and soothsayers, using their spectral sight to detect witchcraft. A couple of months later they would be called in this capacity to Andover.

A warrant for Willard's arrest and appearance at Beadle's Tavern in Salem on Wednesday May 11, 1692 was issued. On Thursday May 12, Constable John Putnam, Jr., one of the conspirators, reported: "I went to the house of the usual abode of John Willard and made search for him, and in several other houses and places but could not find him, and his relations and friends then gave me account that to their best knowledge he was fled." John Willard made his escape to Lancaster, about forty miles west of Salem, and went into hiding. Lancaster had been founded by Major Simon Willard, commander-in-chief during King Philip's Indian War of 1675-1676. Because of the destruction inflicted on the frontier towns during the conflict, many birth records were lost, but it can be inferred that John Willard was one of the major's grandsons. Major Simon Willard had died in 1676, at the bleakest point in that war, but in 1692, Lancaster was still home to several of his children and grandchildren.[122] Lancaster was the most exposed part of the frontier with the Indians; to flee further would have put John Willard in enemy territory.

Bray Wilkins, still sick, returned to his home in Salem Village. He said that on the evening of May 14, 1692, "some of my friends coming to see me, one of the afflicted persons, Mercy Lewis, came with them, and they asked whether she saw anything. She said, 'Yes. They are looking for John Willard, but there he is on his grandfather's belly.' And at that time I was in grievous pain in the small of my belly." In addition, Mercy Lewis said, "I also see the apparition of John Willard afflicting Daniel Wilkins, and [the apparition of] John Willard tells me he will kill him within two days."

Two days later, on May 16, 1692, as foreseen by Mercy Lewis, Daniel Wilkins died, "bewitched to death." Daniel and Mercy, both seventeen, "were nursed on the self-same hill, fed the same flock, by fountain, shade, and rill. But O the heavy change, now thou art gone, now thou art gone and never must return!"[123]

A second arrest warrant was issued. On Tuesday, May 17, 1692, the marshal wrote to the magistrates John Hathorne and Jonathan Corwin, then at Boston, "This day going to Salem Village by your order, I found all the five persons brought there which we were in pursuit of. We had no sooner secured them in the watch house but Constable John Putnam, Jr. came in with John Willard, having seized him at Nashaway."[124]

---

122 Major Simon Willard (1605-1676), founder of the towns of Concord, Groton, and Lancaster, had three wives, seventeen known children, and nearly one hundred grandchildren. The most famous son was the Rev. Samuel Willard, born in Concord in 1640, who became pastor of the Third Church (Old South) in Boston, and from 1701-1707 was vice president of Harvard. Another son was Captain Simon Willard who was born in Concord in 1649, moved to Salem, and was the commander of a company of Salem soldiers in Maine, 1689-1690.

123 John Milton, "Lycidas."

124 Nashaway, or Nashua, or however it was spelled, is the Indian name for Lancaster, Massachusetts. Two months later, on July 18, 1692, the

Mercy Lewis said she was able to predict the exact time when Willard was captured. Apparently the biblical injunction, "And I will cut off witchcrafts out of thine hand, and thou shalt have no more soothsayers," did not apply to her.[125]   Bray admitted, "I continued so in grievous pain, and my water much stopped, till Willard was in chains, and then as near as I can guess I had considerable ease. But in place of a stoppage, I was vexed with a flowing of water, so that it was hard to keep myself dry."

On Thursday May 12, 1692 the conspiracy filed a complaint [No. 15] against Alice Parker and Ann Pudeator for afflicting Mary Warren. Also they filed a complaint [No. 16] against Abigail Somes for afflicting Mary Warren and others. The accused were imprisoned.

Ann Pudeator was the widow of Jacob Pudeator, the nephew of John Brown, whose son (or grandson) married Mary, the daughter of Philip English. Both Jacob Pudeator and Philip English were from the island of Jersey in the English Channel. Jacob Pudeator had left Ann quite wealthy, and she lived in a spacious house in the best section of Salem Town.

In her examination, Ann Pudeator claimed that the twenty little vessels or pots found in her house were filled with grease for making soap, but the magistrates preferred to believe that they were witch ointments. Samuel Pickworth later testified that, as he was standing one evening near Captain Higginson's house, he saw a woman who he thought was Ann Pudeator. He said, "In a moment of time, she passed by me as swift as if a bird flew by me, and I saw the woman go into Ann Pudeator's house." Predictably, Ann Putnam, Jr. confirmed this witch's flight, testifying, "[The specter of] Ann Pudeator told me that she flew by a man in the night into a house."

Indians destroyed Lancaster and massacred many of its inhabitants, including women and children.

125   Micah 5:12.

On Saturday May 14, 1692, the conspiracy "made a complaint in behalf of their majesties" against eight people [No. 17]. Those accused were Daniel Andrew; George Jacobs, Jr. and his wife, Rebecca Jacobs; Sarah Buckley and her daughter, Mary Whittredge; Elizabeth Hart; Thomas Farrar; and Elizabeth Colson. They accused them "for high suspicion of sundry acts of witchcraft by them done or lately committed on the body of Ann Putnam, Jr., Mercy Lewis, Mary Walcott and Abigail Williams & others whereby much hurt is done to their bodies, therefore craves justice." Daniel Andrew and George Jacobs, Jr. fled, and remained in hiding until the witchcraft delusion was over. The others named on the complaint were imprisoned.

With the accusation of Daniel Andrew the conspiracy struck down the fourth richest man in Salem Village. Andrew was the brother-in-law of Israel Porter. The accusation of the two recently elected selectman, Daniel Andrew and Philip English, marks the brightest blaze of the firestorm. The conspiracy successfully removed both men from their elected offices. A special election was held in July, at the height of the craze. The moderator of the meeting was none other than conspirator Captain John Putnam, Sr. Andrew and English, now tainted men, and three other selectmen were voted out, and five new men were chosen in their places.

CHAPTER 11

SIR WILLIAM PHIPPS

At Whitehall in London, England on October 7, 1691 the new charter for Massachusetts finally was declared in force. The colony was reconstituted as a province, and now included the old Plymouth colony. The new governor would be appointed by the crown. The charter gave the right of suffrage to any man with land yielding an income of at least two pounds sterling a year, or a personal estate of forty pounds sterling or more. Membership in the Puritan church was no longer a requirement for voting. And most significant of all, the new charter allowed religious freedom. Thus, with a single stroke, Puritan supremacy in New England was put to an end. Although Increase Mather, in England since 1688, did have a hand in the selection of the new royal governor, he had failed the colony in his assignment to preserve their vaunted theocracy.

King William, following Increase Mather's suggestions, appointed Sir William Phipps, a native of Maine, as the royal governor, and William Stoughton as the royal lieutenant governor. Except for the three small settlements of Wells, York, and Kittery, the French and the Indians had captured all of Maine in the year 1690. This bitter defeat killed hundreds and left thousands homeless and destitute. The cause of the French victory can be directly traced to the lethargy of the ruling old guard in Boston. Leaving the defense of Casco almost wholly to the inadequate resources of its terrified inhabitants, they had refused to send relief, with the predictable result of the slaughter of May 1690.

Early in the spring of 1690, before Casco had been attacked, Sir William had led an expedition, with eight vessels and eight hundred men, against Port Royal in Arcadia (now called Nova Scotia). Phipps was completely successful, and his reputation as a commander was made. This achievement prompted the ruling old guard in Boston to send Phipps against Quebec in late summer of 1690, to counter the Casco defeat. His fleet consisted of thirty-two vessels, and twenty-three hundred men. Phipps, however, did not receive the promised land support, and the expedition was a failure, attributable again to the poor planning and apathy of officials in Boston and New York. The cost of the expedition was £140,000, besides the lives of several hundred men.

The impoverished people of New England, at the end of their resources, could see nothing but overwhelming defeat. The returning soldiers could not be paid, and the government resorted to the expedient of issuing paper money, which soon became worthless. With the loss of Maine and the ill-fated Quebec expedition, New England suffered its worst humiliation. In the tinder box of inevitable and angry recriminations, the witch hunt caught fire.

When appointed to the royal governorship, Phipps had been in England for some time, and he and the Rev. Increase Mather returned to Boston together. On Tuesday May 14, 1692, they sailed into Boston harbor on the frigate *Nonesuch*. Sir William Phipps, all set to take up his new duties, brought the new royal charter with which he was to govern New England.

Phipps immediately replaced the eighty-nine-year-old Simon Bradstreet, the acting governor, who had been seriously ill throughout the initiation of the witch hunt. William Stoughton of Dorchester replaced Thomas Danforth, the acting lieutenant governor. William Stoughton, a man of cold affections, arrogant, self-willed, and overbearing, indeed one of God's angrier men, held views on witchcraft even more extreme than those of Cotton Mather.

The chief reason that King William had selected Phipps, a military man, as governor was to retrieve Maine from the French and their Indian allies.[126] With the capture of Maine, the French had obtained a near monopoly on the lucrative fur trade and the rich cod fisheries, to England's loss. But on his arrival in Boston, Phipps discovered the province "miserably harassed with a most horrible witchcraft or possession of Devils." The prisons in Essex and Suffolk counties were crowded with accused witches and wizards. Smarting from the onus of defeat at Quebec two years previously, Phipps understood that his political life depended on decisive military action. Accordingly, he decided to devote his complete attention to retaking Maine and, consequently, he did nothing to interfere with the witch hunt in progress.

Examinations and imprisonments continued unabated. The witchcraft tumult had reached a fever pitch, and public infatuation was intense. The afflicted continued to cry out against those already in prison, claiming that, in order to hold back the prisoners' specters which still tormented them, the prisoners' legs and arms should be clamped in irons. On the advice of Council, Sir William gave the order to put irons on all the imprisoned.

On about May 18, 1692 the conspiracy filed a complaint [No. 19] against Roger Toothaker, charging him with afflicting Elizabeth Hubbard, Anne Putnam, Jr., and Mary Walcott. The name of Elizabeth Hubbard, the niece of conspirator Dr. William Griggs, is significant here. Dr. Toothaker and Dr. Griggs both employed various forms of folk magic as an accepted part of their medical treatments. Dr. Toothaker recently had instructed his daughter on how "to kill one Button, a reputed witch" by supernatural means. She followed his instructions, and Thomas Gage later testified, "The next morning, the witch was dead. Other things I have forgotten, and further say not."

---

126 Phipps failed in this enterprise, and Maine stayed in French hands for another twenty years. From the beginning of King Philip's War in 1675 to the close of Queen Anne's War in 1713, more than 6,000 New England soldiers perished, a tremendous loss for a population of about 100,000.

19. House of John Turner in Salem, built in 1668-69. Tradition says that one of the carpenters was Samuel Wardwell, the real-life counterpart of Nathaniel Hawthorne's fictional Matthew Maule, who, "in a word, was executed for the crime of witchcraft. ... This pestilent wizard had an inveterate habit of haunting a certain mansion, styled the House of the Seven Gables." (Photograph taken in 1906.)

20. Execution of the carpenter, Samuel Wardwell, in Salem on September 22, 1692. In Hawthorne's The House of the Seven Gables, "At midnight, all the dead Pyncheons [who correspond to the romanticist's own family, the Hathornes] are bound to assemble in this parlor. First comes the ancestor himself [the fictional counterpart of magistrate John Hathorne, later made a colonel], in his black cloak, steeple-hat, and trunk-breeches. ... The stout Colonel is dissatisfied! ... Something has strangely vexed the ancestor! ... In a corner, meanwhile, stands the figure of an elderly man, in a leather jerkin and breeches, with a carpenter's rule sticking out of his side pocket; he points his finger to the bearded Colonel and

his descendants, nodding, jeering, mocking, and finally bursting into obstreperous, though inaudible laughter."

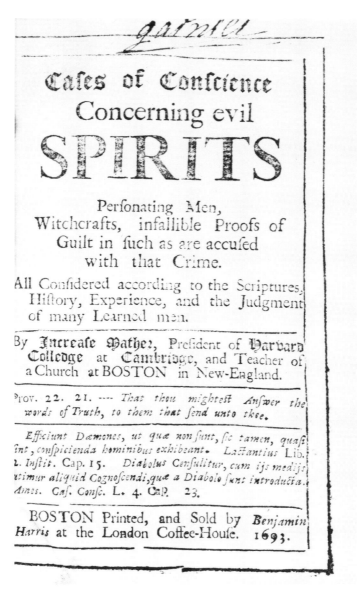

Cases of Conscience
Concerning evil
SPIRITS

Perfonating Men,
Witchcrafts, infallible Proofs of
Guilt in fuch as are accufed
with that Crime.

All Confidered according to the Scriptures,
Hiftory, Experience, and the Judgment
of many Learned men.

By **Increafe Mather**, Prefident of **Harvard College** at **Cambridge**, and Teacher of
a Church at BOSTON in New-England.

Prov. 22. 21. ---- *That thou mighteft Anfwer the
words of Truth, to them that fend unto thee.*

*Efficiunt Dæmones, ut quæ non funt, fic tamen, quafi
fint, confpicienda hominibus exhibeant. Lactantius Lib.
2. Inftit. Cap.* 15. *Diabolus Confulitur, cum ijs medijs
utimur aliquid Cognofcendi,quæ a Diabolo funt introducta.
Ames. Caf. Confc. L. 4. Cap. 23.*

BOSTON Printed, and Sold by *Benjamin
Harris* at the London Coffee-Houfe. 1693.

21. Title page of Cases of Conscience Concerning Evil Spirits by Increase
Mather, first published in Boston in October 1692. (This reprint is dated 1693.)
Increase Mather wrote, "The scripture which says, Thou must not suffer a witch
to live, clearly implies, that some of the world may be known and proved to be
witches. For until they be so, they may and must be suffered to live." The book
was instrumental in bringing an end to the witchcraft trials.

The Wonders of the Invifible World:

Being an Account of the

TRYALS

OF

Several Witches,

Lately Excuted in

NEW-ENGLAND:

And of feveral remarkable Curiofities therein Occurring.

Together with,

I. Obfervations upon the Nature, the Number, and the Operations of the Devils.

II. A fhort Narrative of a late outrage committed by a knot of Witches in *Swede-Land*, very much refembling, and fo far explaining, that under which *New-England* has laboured.

III. Some Councels direfting a due Improvement of the Terrible things lately done by the unufual and amazing Range of *Evil-Spirits* in *New-England*.

IV. A brief Difcourfe upon thofe *Temptations* which are the more ordinary Devices of Satan.

By COTTON MATHER.

Publifhed by the Special Command of his EXCELLENCY the Govencur of the Province of the *Maffachufetts-Bay* in *New-England*.

Printed firft, at *Boftun* in *New-England* ; and Reprinted at *London*, for *John Dunton*, at the *Raven* in the *Poultry*. 1693.

22. Title page of The Wonders of the Invisible World by Cotton Mather, first published in Boston in October 1692. (This is the London reprint, dated 1693.) Cotton Mather wrote this book to justify the Salem witchcraft proceedings of 1692, In it he wrote, "None but the Father, who sees in secret, knows the heart-breaking exercises wherewith I have composed what is now going to be exposed, lest I should in any one thing miss of doing my designed service for his glory."

MORE WONDERS

OF THE

INVISIBLE WORLD:

OR,

THE WONDERS OF THE

INVISIBLE WORLD,

DISPLAYED
IN FIVE PARTS.

PART I.—An Account of the Sufferings of MARGARET RULE, written by the Rev. C. M.

PART II.—Several Letters to the Author, &c. And his REPLY relating to WITCHCRAFT.

PART III.—The differences between the Inhabitants of SALEM-VILLAGE, and Mr. PARRIS, their Minifter, in New-England.

PART IV.—Letters of a Gentleman uninterefted, endeavouring to prove the received opinions about WITCHCRAFT to be Orthodox. With fhort Effays to their Anfwers.

PART V.—A fhort Hiftorical Account of Matters of Faſt in that Affair.

TO WHICH IS ADDED,

A POSTSCRIPT,

Relating to a Book entitled, " The Life of Sir WILLIAM PHIPS."

Colleſted by ROBERT CALEF,
Merchant, of BOSTON, in New-England.

PRINTED IN LONDON IN THE YEAR 1700.

Re-printed in SALEM, MASSACHUSETTS, 1796,
BY WILLIAM CARLTON.

Sold at CUSHING & CARLTON'S Book-Store, at the Bible and Heart, Effex-Street.

Title page of More Wonders of the Invisible World by Robert Calef, published in London in 1700. This book discredited the Salem witchcraft proceedings of 1692. Cotton Mather was furious because "this vile volume" was "written on purpose to damnify my precious opportunities of glorifying my Lord Jesus Christ."

This Bill Bindeth mee William Wardall of Andover in ye County of Essex in New England Weaver, mee, my heirs Executo's administrators, To pay or cause To bepaid, unto my Brother in Law John Wright of ye same Towne County & Country hosbandman, To him, his heirs Executors administrat' or Assigns ye full & just Sum of fourteen pounds in Good & Lawfull silver Mony of New England So bepaid as followeth, (viz) Seven pounds in Mony att or before ye 25 Day of March in ye year of our Lord God Seventeen hundred & Six & ye Remaining Seven pounds to bepaid upon or before ye 25 Day of March in ye year of our Lord God Seventeen hundred & Eight, all which is in Considuration of som certain Lands Sold To mee by my said Brother, To full Content and Satisfaction, & for ye Sure performance of ye above written p'misses I bind my Selfe, my heirs, Executo's Administrato', unto my said Brother John Wright his heirs & Assignss: in ye Penall Sum of Twenty Eight pounds Currant silver Mony, and for ye Confirmation of all which I have hereunto sett my hand & seale This Twentieth day of April Anno Domj Seventeen hundred & Three: 1703

Signed sealed & D'd
in ye presence of us

Andrew Peters

Samuell Peters

William Wardell

Promissory note dated April 20, 1703 by "William Wardwell of Andover in the County of Essex in New England, weaver," son of Samuel and Sarah Wardwell and the writer's great, great, great, great, great grandfather. Samuel Wardwell's eldest son, Thomas, [corresponding to the fictional Matthew Maule's son, Thomas, in Hawthorne's romance], was also a carpenter.

Regni *ANNÆ* Reginæ Decimo.

Province of the Massachusetts=Bay.

AN ACT,

Made and Paffed by the Great and General Court or Affembly of Her Majefty's Province of the Maffachufetts-Bay in New-England, Held at Bofton the 17th Day of October, 1711.

An Act to Reverfe the Attainders of *George Burroughs* and others for Witchcraft.

FOR AS MUCH *as in the Year of our Lord One Thoufand Six Hundred Ninety Two, Several Towns within this Province were Infefted with a horrible Witchcraft or Poffeffion of Devils ; And at a Special Court of Oyer and Terminer holden at* Salem, *in the County of* Effex *in the fame Year One Thoufand Six Hundred Ninety Two,* George Burroughs *of Wells,* John Procter, George Jacob, John Willard, Giles Core, *and his Wife,* Rebecca Nurfe, *and* Sarah Good, *all of Salem aforefaid :* Elizabeth How, *of Ipfwich,* Mary Eaftey, Sarah Wild *and* Abigail Hobbs *all of Topsfield :* Samuel Wardell, Mary Parker, Martha Carrier, Abigail Falkner, Anne Fofter, Rebecca Eames, Mary Poft, *and* Mary Lacey, *all of Andover :* Mary Bradbury *of Salisbury : and* Dorcas Hoar *of Beverly ; Were feverally Indicted, Convicted and Attained of Witchcraft, and fome of them put to Death, Others lying ftill under the like Sentence of the faid Court, and liable to have the fame Executed upon them.*

A   The

First page of An Act to Reverse the Attainders of George Burroughs and others for Witchcraft, made and passed by the General Court at Boston on October 17, 1711. Nathaniel Hawthorne wrote, "Clergymen, judges, statesmen,the wisest, calmest, holiest persons of their day,stood in the inner circle round about the gallows, loudest to applaud the work of blood, latest to confess themselves miserably deceived." This document constitutes official retraction of the witchcraft convictions. (Courtesy of the Danvers Archival Center.)

Commission of Stephen Barker, Jr. in 1743 as an ensign in the "Regiment of
Militia in the County of Essex whereof Richard Saltonstall Esq. is Colonel."
Stephen Barker, Jr. was the nephew of Lieutenant John Barker and William
Barker, and was the writer's great, great, great, great, great grandfather. John
Barker's daughter, Mary; William Barker; and William's son, William Barker Jr.,
were arrested for witchcraft in 1692.

Anna (Wardwell) Robinson (1846-1909), great, great, great, great granddaughter of Samuel and Sarah Wardwell, and the writer's grandmother.

On May 21, 1692 the conspiracy filed a complaint [No. 20] against Sarah Bassett, Sarah Proctor, and Susannah Roots. Sarah Bassett was the wife of Captain William Bassett, Jr., and Sarah Proctor was his niece. Captain Bassett commanded the company of soldiers impressed from Lynn and sent out against the Indians in Maine in the dead of winter, 1688-1689. He was a member of the council of war with Major Benjamin Church at Scarborough, Maine on November 11, 1689. The ruling old guard had singled out Captain Bassett as an officer to be used as a scapegoat for the defeats in Maine. Knowing that they could not succeed by attacking Captain Bassett openly, they instead chose to make witchcraft accusations against his family.

On May 23, 1692 the conspirators filed a complaint [No. 21] against Mary De Rich, Benjamin Proctor, and Sarah Pease. They accused them of "sundry acts of witchcraft by them committed on the bodies of Mary Warren, Abigail Williams, Elizabeth Hubbard, whereby great hurt is done them, therefore craves justice." Mary De Rich was a sister of Captain Bassett. A second sister, Elizabeth, was married to John Proctor. The accused Benjamin Proctor was the son of John by a previous marriage.

Almost as soon as Sir William Phipps arrived, Stoughton persuaded him to set up a court for the trial of the witches. Stoughton advised Phipps not to follow the legal measures required by the new charter, which authorized only the provincial legislature (the General Court) to establish judicial bodies. Instead, Stoughton recommended the establishment of a flagrantly illegal tribunal, by means of a special executive commission. Naively, Phipps followed Stoughton's advice, and on May 25, 1692 instituted a Court of Oyer and Terminer to try the suspected witches.[127] In one stroke, the legal machinery was by-passed, and its concomitant legal safeguards were avoided.[128] Phipps unwittingly had created a kangaroo court, a tool giving

---

127 *Oyer* and *Terminer* are Norman French for "to hear" and "to determine."

128 The illegality of the very existence of the court is discussed in Hutchinson, 2:37, and in Upham, 2: 251-252.

arbitrary power to the Puritan old guard; its use would not go wanting.

On May 27, 1692 the members of the court were appointed. William Stoughton (Harvard, 1650) was named chief justice. The eight justices were Nathaniel Saltonstall (Harvard, 1659), John Richards, Peter Sergeant, Wait Still Winthrop (Harvard class of 1662 but did not graduate), Samuel Sewall (Harvard, 1671), John Hathorne, Jonathan Corwin, and Bartholomew Gedney. The court could be made up of any five of the nine. The justices, all members of the board of assistants in the provisional government, were recently appointed members of the council under the new charter.[129]

Thomas Newton, a young attorney recently arrived from London with a name and a fortune to make, was named king's attorney (or attorney general), i.e., the prosecuting attorney for the court.[130] Stephen Sewall of Salem, the brother of justice Samuel Sewall, was named the clerk of the court.[131] Jonathan Corwin's nephew, George Corwin, only twenty-six years old, was appointed high sheriff of Essex County.[132] The duty of executing the condemned persons and confiscating their property fell upon him.

William Stoughton of Dorchester praised Cotton Mather for "lifting up a standard against the infernal enemy that has been coming in like a flood upon us." Nathaniel Saltonstall of Haverhill, the major in command of the Essex North

---

129 For the complete list of council members, see Hutchinson, 2:11.

130 Thomas Newton was born in England in 1660, was sworn an attorney in London in 1683, and died in Boston in 1721, age 61.

131 Justice Samuel Sewall, born in 1652, and clerk Stephen Sewall, born in 1657, were the sons of Henry Sewall, whose brother was Major Samuel Sewall of Salem.

132 George Corwin served as a captain in Phipps' ill-fated expedition against Quebec in 1690.

Regiment,[133] came from an illustrious family; his grandfather Sir Richard Saltonstall was one of the founders of the colony. John Richards and Peter Sergeant, both wealthy Boston merchants, had lost heavily in the defeats at the hands of the French. Richards held the military rank of major.[134] Wait Still Winthrop also of Boston was the grandson of the first governor of Massachusetts. He was the major general, the highest ranking officer in New England, and was the commander-in-chief of the military during the recent humiliations. Samuel Sewall of Boston was a captain, and in his decisions as a magistrate he had gained a reputation for fairness. Bartholomew Gedney of Salem Town was the owner of a wharf and a shipyard. He was the major in command of the Essex South Regiment.[135] Having lived his life in Salem, he had acquired a long-standing reputation as the leading land speculator in Maine, although his holdings were now worthless under the heel of the French. John Hathorne of Salem Town was the iron-fisted magistrate of the witchcraft examinations, the witch-hunter general. Always at Hathorne's side was Jonathan Corwin of Salem Town.

Four of the nine members of the court, William Stoughton, John Richards, Wait Still Winthrop, and Samuel Sewall, were close friends of Cotton Mather. As representative of the church in Dorchester, just south of Boston, Stoughton had attended Cotton Mather's ordination, and always favored him. John Richards, a member of Increase Mather's church, gave the largest contribution to the salary of Cotton Mather when he became assistant minister in 1680. Cotton Mather ranked Wait Still

---

133 The Essex North Regiment was made up of companies from the towns of Newbury, Rowley, Bradford, Andover, Topsfield, Salisbury, Amesbury, and Haverhill.

134 Richards was a prominent member of the Second (Old North) Church in Boston, of which Increase and Cotton Mather were the ministers.

135 In the regiment there were four companies and a troop of horse (cavalry unit) from Salem, as well as companies from Beverly, Manchester, Marblehead, and Lynn.

Winthrop "among best of my friends." Samuel Sewall admired
Cotton Mather's sermons, which he often went to hear.[136]

Not one justice on the court had any legal training. As chief
justice, Stoughton leaned heavily on his religious training for
guidance. He firmly believed in the use of spectral evidence to
prove witchcraft. A prime example of spectral evidence occurred
during the examination of Rebecca Nurse on March 24, 1692.
Thomas Putnam's wife cried out to Rebecca Nurse, "Did you not
bring the Black Man with you?" Hathorne said to Rebecca Nurse,
"You are at this very present charged with familiar spirits. Now
when you are here present to see such a thing as these [afflicted
persons] testify a Black Man whispering in your ear and birds
about you." Stoughton interpreted this evidence as absolute legal
proof that Rebecca Nurse was in league with the Devil. Cotton
Mather and William Stoughton were in close agreement, yet not
even Cotton Mather was so adamant as Stoughton on the sole use
of spectral evidence. Still, Cotton Mather hedged on the fine
points just enough that his advice would not actually prevent the
conviction of the accused on the basis of spectral evidence alone.
From a practical point of view all the justices knew that spectral
evidence provided the most effective method to obtain witchcraft
convictions.

Before its first meeting, Cotton Mather had pondered what
actions the court should take. He wrote Richards a long letter on
May 31, 1692, summarizing his views and offering firm advice on
the impending trials, at which Richards would sit as a justice.
"Do not lay more stress upon pure specter testimony than it will
bear. I am far from urging the un-English method of torture, but
whatever has a tendency to put the witches into confusion is

---

136 However, Samuel Sewall was not a member of the Second Church (Old
    North) in Boston where the Mathers, father and son, were the ministers,
    but was a member of the Third Church (Old South) in Boston, as were
    fellow justices, Sergeant and Winthrop. The minister of the Old South
    Church was the Rev. Samuel Willard, whose nephew John Willard had
    been arrested on May 17, 1692.

likely to bring them into confession too. Here cross and swift questions have their use."

On Saturday, May 28, 1692 the conspiracy filed a complaint [No. 22] against Elizabeth Cary, wife of sea-captain Nathaniel Cary. They also filed a complaint [No. 23] against sea-captain John Alden, Captain John Floyd, Elizabeth Fosdick, Wilmot Redd, Sarah Rice, William Proctor, Elizabeth Howe, Arthur Abbot, Martha Carrier, Mary Toothaker, and Margaret Toothaker. They were accused of committing "sundry acts of witchcraft on the bodies of Anne Putnam, Jr., Mary Walcott, Mercy Lewis, Abigail Williams and others to the hurt and injury of their bodies, therefore craves justice." Captain John Alden and Captain John Floyd, like Captain Bassett, were being used as scapegoats. All had served gallantly in the defense of Maine.

To take revenge on Alden for the loss of his property in Maine, Gedney appeared as one of the magistrates in his preliminary examination which took place on Tuesday May 31, 1692. Gedney stated, "he had known Alden many years, and had been to sea with him, and always looked upon him to be an honest man, but now he did see cause to alter his judgment." However, the true friends of Alden did not desert him. He was sent to Boston under arrest. After fifteen weeks of confinement, he escaped and was concealed by friends in Duxbury until the delusion was over in the spring of 1693.[137]

Thomas Newton, the new attorney general, spent May 31, 1692, the day of Captain Alden's preliminary examination, at Salem Village. He wrote Isaac Addington, the secretary of the province, in Boston, "I have beheld most strange things, scarcely credible. The afflicted spare no person of whatever quality." His

---

137 On June 12, 1693, after Alden had been cleared of all charges, justice Samuel Sewall made this entry in his diary. "I visit Captain Alden and his wife, and tell them I was sorry for their sorrow by reason of his imprisonment, and was glad of his restoration." Sewall was uneasy throughout the witch hunt, but, leashed to the old guard, he was unable to act freely.

legal training had taught him that witchcraft accusations were supposed to be reserved for the poor and outcast.

On Monday May 30, 1692, the conspiracy filed a complaint [No. 24] against Elizabeth Paine and Elizabeth Fosdick, both of Malden, for afflicting Mercy Lewis and Mary Warren. On June 2, 1692, Peter Tufts of Charlestown filed a complaint [No. 25] against the same two for "acts of witchcraft by them committed on his Negro woman." Curiously, Tufts' daughter-in-law, Mary (Cotton) Tufts, was the first cousin of the Rev. Cotton Mather.

The new court met for the first trial on Thursday June 2, 1692, just nineteen days after the arrival of Sir William from England. After this meeting, justice Saltonstall resigned. The second meeting of the court started on June 30, 1692. Newton resigned after this occasion, and was replaced as attorney general by Anthony Checkley. The third meeting of the court started on August 5, 1692; the fourth meeting, on September 9, 1692, and the fifth meeting, which turned out to be the last, on September 17, 1692.

On Saturday June 4, 1692, the conspiracy filed one complaint [No. 26] against Mary Ireson, and another [No. 27] against Job Tookey. On June 6, 1692, the conspiracy filed a complaint [No. 28] against Ann Dolliver, daughter of the Rev. John Higginson, the elder minister of the Salem church. All the accused were imprisoned.

On Tuesday June 28, 1692, the conspiracy filed a complaint [No. 29] against Mary Bradbury, and on July 1 they filed a complaint [No. 30] against Margaret Hawkes and her slave Candy. The accused were imprisoned. These accusations effectively end the work of the Salem Village conspiracy. Their role would taken up in July by a new group of conspirators in Andover, who proceeded to carry out the Andover witch hunt. As the swan song of the Salem Village conspiracy, the case of Mary Bradbury deserves some attention.

In 1692 Mrs. Mary Bradbury, somewhat infirm in health, was seventy-seven and her husband, Captain Thomas Bradbury, was eighty-two. By position, as well as character, they were at the highest level of society. He had risen to the command of the company of militia in Salisbury, and, in the latter portion of his life, was universally spoken of as Captain Bradbury. She was always addressed by the title *Mrs.*, which in those days was one of honor. Thomas Bradbury had been prominent in the colony for more than fifty years. He had been clerk of the writs for Salisbury, with the functions of a magistrate to execute legal processes. He had been a deputy (an elected member of the lower legislative body of the colony) and a commissioner for the town.

Mary Bradbury is described in the indictment as "wife of Captain Thomas Bradbury, of Salisbury, gentleman." Surely the high government officials sanctioning the witch hunt knew of her position. If not, they were soon informed because Robert Pike came to her defense, and in no small way.

Robert Pike, age seventy-six in 1692, was a deputy at thirty-two, and an associate justice at thirty-four. In 1682 he became a magistrate, an assistant to the governor, and he held that position, by annual elections, up to the year in question, 1692. The leading witch-hunters, John Hathorne and Jonathan Corwin, were also assistants, of the same rank as Robert Pike.

The Rev. James Allin, pastor of the Salisbury church, made an oath before Robert Pike. "Mary Bradbury has lived according to the rules of the gospel among us, full of works of charity and mercy." Her neighbors, 117 strong, comprising most of the heads of family of Salisbury, submitted a paper saying, "Neither did any of us (some of whom have lived in the town with her above fifty years) ever hear or ever know that she had any differences or falling out with any of her neighbors, man, woman, or child."

Can any explanation be found for the motives leading to the arrest of such a respectable woman, living at a distance from Salem Village, beyond the Merrimack River?

One explanation is to be found in the envy of physicians who resented Mary Bradbury's success in treating the sick. At her trial on September 9, 1692, James Carr, forty-two, a brother of Ann Putnam, Sr., testified that Dr. Crosby, in 1672, had said that "he did believe that Mrs. Bradbury was a great deal worse than Goody Martin," a Salisbury woman accused of witchcraft in 1669.[138] Only after James Carr struck at Mrs. Bradbury's familiar which appeared to him in the shape of a cat one night, did Dr. Crosby's "physic work on me." James Carr concluded his testimony, "And I believe in my heart that Mrs. Bradbury, the prisoner at the bar, has often afflicted me by acts of witchcraft."

Ann Putnam, Sr., the wife of Sergeant Thomas Putnam since 1678, was born Ann Carr in Salisbury. Her father, George Carr, was enterprising and prosperous. The ferry across the Merrimack was under his charge; he also engaged in shipbuilding.

In 1677, the wife of Dr. Zerubabel Endicott of Salem died.[139] Because he had many children, Dr. Endicott placed his son Zerubabel with the Carr family to learn about shipbuilding. Young Zerubabel became friendly with George Carr's son, Richard Carr, the brother of Ann.

At Mary Bradbury's witchcraft trial in 1692, Richard testified that, in the year 1679, when he was twenty and Zerubabel Endicott was fifteen, his father, George Carr, had a falling out with Mrs. Bradbury. After the altercation, Richard rode home with his father and Zerubabel Endicott. "By the house of Captain Thomas Bradbury, I saw Mrs. Bradbury go into her gate, turn the corner of, and immediately there darted out of her gate a blue boar. It darted at the legs of my father's horse, which made him

---

138   Susannah Martin was hanged for witchcraft on July 19, 1692.

139   Elizabeth Booth testified that on June 8, 1692 the ghost of Dr. Zerubabel Endicott, dead for 8 years, appeared to her and said that "Elizabeth Proctor killed him because they differed on their judgments about Thomas Veries' wife."

stumble but I saw it no more. And my father said, 'Boys, what do you see?' We both answered, 'A blue boar.' "

Zerubabel Endicott, also at the trial, confirmed the story, adding, "Mr. Carr immediately said, 'Boys, what did you see?' And we both said, 'A blue boar.' Then said he, 'From whence came it?' And we said, 'Out of Mr. Bradbury's gate.' Then said he, 'I am glad you see it as well as I.' "

George Carr had been dead some ten years by the time of the trial, but the clerk of the court, Stephen Sewall, with his usual zeal to make the most of testimony against the accused, added, "And they both further say that Mr. Carr talked with them, as they went home, about what had happened. They all concluded that it was Mrs. Bradbury who so appeared as a blue boar."

George Carr had habitually encouraged the boys and the other children in his household to believe stories such as this one. Young and gullible, they imagined they saw much that was preternatural about Mrs. Bradbury. With these fantasies circulating in the family, other stories quickly spread. Zerubabel's brother Samuel Endicott began to tell fanciful tales. At the 1692 inquest he testified about a voyage to Barbados in which all the storms and various disasters were caused by Mrs. Bradbury. He claimed that on a bright moonshine night, while he was sitting upon the windlass, to which he had been sent forward to look out for land, he heard a rumbling noise. "I saw the appearance of a woman, from her middle upwards, having a white cap and white neck-cloth."[140]

Such fantasies were admitted as evidence against Mrs. Bradbury, while the statements by her minister and the 117 neighbors were thrown aside. In her trial, as in all the others, every friendly voice was silenced. The accused were allowed no counsel or other means of defense. The efforts of Robert Pike,

---

140   The two boys, Zerubabel and Samuel, were sons of Dr. Zerubabel Endicott (1635–1684) and grandsons of Governor John Endicott (1589-1665). Their stepmother Elizabeth (Winthrop) Newman Endicott was the sister of Wait Still Winthrop, one of the justices on the court.

despite his high office as magistrate and an assistant to the governor, were in vain.

A witchcraft persecution may be described as man's inhumanity against woman. Although some of the sufferers were men, most were girls and women, and this includes the afflicted as well as the accused. The conspiracy consisted only of men, who drove the witch hunt with relentless efficiency. The family of Mrs. Ann Putnam was the most troubled by afflictions in 1692. She, her daughter Ann Putnam, Jr., and her servant Mercy Lewis were all severely affected. The sensitivity found in Mrs. Putnam can be traced directly back to the influence of her father, George Carr, who had preyed early on the excitable and malleable natures of his children. Their judgment, reason, and physical health were subjected to the power of his fancies and bizarre beliefs. One of his sons, jilted by a young widow, was thrown into a morbid depression for a year. Another son, also crossed in love, went to an early grave. A daughter, who had married the Rev. Bayley of Salem Village, grew completely distraught over the controversies in the parish; eventually she died. Clearly, the sufferings of her siblings weighed on Ann Putnam, Sr. and must be taken into account of her conduct during the witch hunt.

A man of action, Sir William Phipps understood conventional warfare; he did not understand a war with the Devil. In June and July 1692, Phipps raised an army to confront the imminent threat from the Indians. In August, about three months after his arrival from England, he left Boston to command the army in New Hampshire and Maine. Stoughton, who was both lieutenant governor and chief justice of the court, became deputy governor in Phipps' absence.

In the meantime, the old guard continued expertly to engineer the witch hunt. They had allowed the Salem Village conspiracy to do the dirty work of accusation. By the end of May 1692, the Salem Village conspiracy had seen family members of most of its enemies imprisoned. It then turned to its final task, pressing for convictions.[141]

---

141 In the middle of July 1692, the old guard sanctioned a second conspiracy, this one in Andover, and a new round of accusations took place.

CHAPTER 12

TRIALS OF CRUEL MOCKINGS

Captain Nathaniel Cary, a sea captain whose wife, Elizabeth, was imprisoned for witchcraft, attended many of the trials and wrote this account. "But to speak of their usage of the prisoners, and their inhumanity shown to them at the time of their execution, no sober Christian could bear. They had also *trials of cruel mockings*; which is the more, considering what a people for religion, I mean the profession of it, we have been."

By the end of May the authorities had imprisoned about seventy-five persons. Only some would be brought to trial. While the trials were taking place in the summer of 1692, John Hathorne continued to devote much of his time to conducting preliminary examinations for the newly accused, as he had done since March 1. Between June 1, 1692 and October 15, 1692, about one hundred more accused persons appeared before John Hathorne and his fellow magistrates. Confessions were extracted from many of this new group, and all were committed to prison.

The first meeting of the Court of Oyer and Terminer began in Salem on June 2, 1692. There were seven judges sitting for this session, Lieutenant Governor William Stoughton, Major Nathaniel Saltonstall, Major John Richards, Mr. Peter Sergeant, Major General Wait Still Winthrop, Captain Samuel Sewall, and Major Bartholomew Gedney.

With the highest ranking military officers in the colony sitting as justices, one thinly veiled purpose of the court was to act as a military tribunal, holding a mock court-martial to punish the scapegoats of the military defeats in Maine. During the summer, the wife of Captain John Osgood and the daughter of

202

Lieutenant John Barker were arrested, as well as others who might be blamed for military losses. The reason for their arrests, and for the arrests of Captain John Alden, Captain John Floyd, and several in the family of Captain William Bassett, now becomes plain.

Badly stung by their own military failures, the general staff (excepting Saltonstall) turned to lash out at field commanders and lesser officers. Indeed, under the pretense of witchcraft, they stood ready to see some hang. Out of concern that a stratagem too transparent could expose their own disgrace, they shifted blame still further and directed charges against the women in these men's families. A baser display of deceit and cowardice is hard to imagine.

A more important purpose of the court was to act as a mock ecclesiastical court to set a lesson for any ministers in the colony who might show glimmerings of religious tolerance The reason that the Rev. George Burroughs, the daughter of the Rev. John Higginson, the nephew of the Rev. Samuel Willard, and two daughters, a daughter-in-law, and five grandchildren of the Rev. Francis Dane were arrested, now is made patently clear.

The Rev. Burroughs ministered to all faiths without prejudice during his career in Maine. The Rev. Higginson spoke out against the witchcraft proceedings, disclaiming the very falsehoods championed by his assistant minister, Nicholas Noyes. The Rev. Samuel Willard was the liberal minister of Boston's Third Church (Old South); it became the headquarters for the underground opposition to the witchcraft proceedings.[142] The Rev. Dane, the liberal, elderly, senior minister in Andover, had been in disputes, monetary as well as theological, with the conservative, young, new assistant minister, Thomas Barnard. But Dane neglected to reckon with the fact that Barnard (Harvard,

---

142 The Rev. Willard's approach was to counsel an afflicted girl to help her to the understanding that her afflictions were not caused by witchcraft, and that the accused person was innocent. Cotton Mather's attitude was that the afflictions were caused by witchcraft, and that the accused person was guilty.

1679) was the best friend of Cotton Mather (Harvard, 1678) during their college days.

The third and principal purpose of the court was to close the cracks that were opening in the hitherto rock-hard system of Puritan rule. In defiance of the new charter the old guard would reaffirm, in no uncertain terms, that the narrow and dogmatic codes put into place by their fathers and grandfathers would continue in force. They would proclaim, once and for all, that skeptics and those who promoted laxities in Puritan custom would be harshly dealt with.

Why would a healthy child suddenly come down with an ailment and die? In the light of the scientific revolution of the times, the ordinary person was beginning to search for rational explanations. The old guard rulers and old time clergy were at a loss in dealing with the new ideas which they believed were undermining their position. They felt increasingly threatened. They grabbed at a handy, if unreasonable, answer to the questions people were asking; it was witchcraft.[143] They claimed that the Puritan church alone had the power to rescue its flock from the Devil. They would snuff out witchcraft with prayer, and prosecution.

Bridget Bishop was the only one of the accused brought to trial in the first meeting of the court.[144] On April 19, 1692 she had been

---

143 Most of the official documents, as preserved in the *Salem Witchcraft Papers (SWP)* are one-sided attempts to justify the persecutions on the basis that witchcraft was a real threat. The common people's feeling about witchcraft can be summed up in the words of George Jacobs, Sr., "You tax me for a wizard. You may as well tax me for a buzzard." Modern historians prefer the official line because, as Cotton Mather showed when he composed *The Wonders of the Invisible World*, it makes for better reading.

144 Cotton Mather was ill and could not attend this first trial. "I am languishing under an overthrow of my health. The least excess of travel, or diet, or anything that may decompose me, would at this time threaten perhaps my life itself." Cotton Mather, *Selected Letters*, 35.

arrested, taken to Salem Village, examined, and imprisoned. Her trial starting on June 2 was a test case, and a formidable number of accusers and accusations were brought against the poor woman. She was charged with assorted losses sustained by her neighbors of their pigs and poultry, and with overturning their carts. These things, claimed to have been done by her specter, were now given as evidence against her. The most blatant fabrications were that her specter caused the death of William Stacy's child, the death of Samuel Gray's child, and the illness of Samuel Shattuck's child.

William Stacy testified that he believed "Bridget Bishop was instrumental in his daughter Priscilla's death about two years ago. The child was a thriving child, and suddenly screeched out and continued in an unusual condition for about a fortnight, and so died." The reason he suspected Bridget was that, fourteen years previously, she had paid him three pence for some work but, before he had gone one hundred feet, he looked in his pocket and could not find the money.

The accusation of Samuel Gray, age forty-two, was based on a nightmare many years before.[145] His testimony, as preserved by Cotton Mather, reads, "About 14 years ago, he [Gray] waked on a night and saw plainly a woman between the cradle and the bed. He rose and it vanished, although he found the doors all fast. The child in the cradle gave a great screech. Although it was a thriving child, yet from this time it pined away, and after divers months, died in a sad condition. He did not know Bishop or her name, but when he saw her he knew that it was the apparition of this Bishop which had thus troubled him."[146]

The accusation of Samuel Shattuck is contained in his testimony as preserved by Cotton Mather. "In the year 1680, Bridget Oliver, now called Bishop, often came to his [Shattuck's] house upon such frivolous and foolish errands that they suspected she came indeed with a purpose of mischief. Presently,

---

145 Upon his death bed, Samuel Gray acknowledged sorrow and repentance for his wholly groundless accusations. Calef, 247.

146 Cotton Mather, *Wonders*, 132-137.

his eldest child, which was of as promising health as any child of its age, began to droop exceedingly, and the oftener that Bishop came to the house, the worse that the child grew. About 17 or 18 months after, there came a stranger to Shattuck's house, who said 'This poor child is bewitched.' He [Shattuck] then remembered that Bishop had parted in muttering and menacing terms, a little before the child was taken ill."

The estate of John Gedney, Sr. in Salem had an extensive orchard, contiguous with the orchard of Bridget Bishop.[147] In 1685 John Louder, one of the servants on the estate, had "some little controversy with Bridget Bishop about her fouls that used to come into our orchard." Cotton Mather wrote, "Immediately after, being at home with the doors shut, John Louder saw a black thing jump in at the window, and come and stand before him. The body was that of a monkey, the feet like a cock's, but the face much like a man's. He went out the back door, and spied this Bishop in her orchard, going toward her house. Whereupon, returning to the house, he was immediately accosted by the monster he had seen before. He cried out, 'The whole armor of God be between me and you.' So it sprang back and flew over the apple tree, shaking many apples off the tree." Louder's testimony was accepted by the court as valid evidence. Bridget could not be punished for the nuisance of her strayed chickens, but she could be hanged for letting her specter wing its way over the apple tree.

Bridget lived in an expensive house in the best section of Salem Town. Across the street from her house sat the mansion of the Rev. Nicholas Noyes. A confirmed bachelor, he did not like "her red paragon bodice and the rest of her clothing that she usually did wear." Two workmen testified that in her cellar they found puppets made of hog bristles and rags, and stuck with headless pins. Once again, Bridget could be hanged on such evidence, but not because the Rev. Noyes disapproved of her as a neighbor.

---

147   John Gedney, Sr. died in 1688. His son, Bartholomew Gedney, was one of the justices of the court.

Mary Warren described how Bridget was able to afflict and torture while in prison. "When she was in the jail in Salem, being in chains, though she could not do it, she would bring one that would do it." Susannah Sheldon described Bridget's familiar. "Then there came a streaked snake creeping over her shoulder and crept into her bosom." Bridget's body was searched; a teat was found.[148] The jury pronounced her guilty, and she was sentenced to die. To the end, she did not make the least confession of anything relating to witchcraft. The court adjourned until June 30, 1692.

On June 10, 1692 Bridget Bishop rode in an open horse-drawn cart, forced to stand so that the hundreds of spectators lining the streets could see her. Cotton Mather described what happened. "As this woman was under guard, passing by the great and spacious meeting house of Salem, she gave a look towards the house, and immediately a demon invisibly entering the meeting house, tore down part of it. The people at the noise, running in, found a board, which was strongly fastened with several nails, transported unto another quarter of the house." Cotton Mather genuinely expected his readers to believe that her witchcraft had caused the board to break away and fly into the opposite wall.

At the outskirts of Salem Town, the cart turned from the main road onto a narrow path, jolting up a rocky hill, later named Gallows Hill. The highest point in Salem, it forms a rocky ridge. Scattered with the few oaks and locusts able to take root in its shallow soil, the hill overlooks the town and the sea beyond. The first execution was not to be missed by John Hathorne. He and

---

148 In his letter to justice John Richards on May 31, 1692, Cotton Mather wrote, "I add, why should not witch marks be searched for? It is apparent that these witches have gone so far in their wickedness as to admit most cursed suckages, whereby the Devils have infused a venom into them which exalts the malignity of their spirits as well as of their bodies, and it is likely, that by means of this ferment, they would be found buoyant, if the water ordeal were made of them." (Cotton Mather, *Selected Letters*, 39.) Despite his advice, the water ordeal was not used in Salem.

other justices of the court looked on while Bridget Bishop was hanged. Her body was thrown into a shallow, unmarked grave dug among the rocks close by. Sheriff George Corwin answered the death warrant, "I have taken the body of Bridget Bishop and safely conveyed her to the place provided for her execution, and caused the said Bridget to be hanged by the neck until she was dead, and buried in the place, all of which was within the time required."

The crazed proceedings of this court, a travesty of justice, rapidly became untenable to justice Nathaniel Saltonstall. Unable to prevail against the tide, he resigned from the bench after this first meeting. Returning home to Haverhill, Major Saltonstall spoke out so strongly against the witch hunt that the afflicted girls started crying out against him. Some claimed that they had seen his specter at several witch meetings. Undaunted, Saltonstall continued his courageous opposition.

The injustice of Bridget Bishop's execution also alarmed some ministers, and Cotton Mather quickly saw that they could call his witchcraft war to a halt. At this pivotal moment, he reached for his strongest weapon, the printed document. With the aid of some ministers in his camp, he drew up a statement entitled *The Return of Several Ministers*. The advice in this document was, by design, as equivocal and as dangerous as the three witches' advice to Macbeth in Shakespeare's great play. While it appeared to give the court instructions carefully to weigh the evidence, in reality the document skillfully encouraged the court to do the opposite. The conclusion reads, "Nevertheless, we cannot but humbly recommend unto the government, the speedy and vigorous prosecution of such as have rendered themselves obnoxious, according to the direction given in the laws of God, and the wholesome statutes of the English nation, for the detection of witchcrafts." This strong conclusion overwhelmed any cautionary lines in the body of the report. The document was presented to the Council on June 15, 1692, and the prosecutions continued with renewed vigor.

Deadly earnest, Cotton Mather understood that his success in the witch hunt was critically dependent upon an appearance of respectability and balanced judgment.   His document served neatly to disguise his deception with the cloak of objectivity. Cotton Mather gave the court a justification to proceed as it had done in the trial of Bridget Bishop, about whom he remarked, "There was little occasion to prove the witchcraft, it being evident and notorious to all beholders."   Of the many disguises that deception may wear, few carry more power than the printed statement of an authority.   Through shrewd use of his theological writings, Cotton Mather gained full control of the court.

The court convened again at Salem, June 30, 1692, for its second meeting.   Five women were brought to trial: Sarah Good and Rebecca Nurse, of Salem Village; Susannah Martin of Amesbury; Elizabeth Howe of Ipswich; and Sarah Wildes of Topsfield.   All were found guilty and sentenced to death.   The five were executed on July 19, just nineteen days after the trial had started.

When Rebecca Nurse came to trial, many testimonials about her Christian behavior, her care in educating her children, and her exemplary conduct were entered in court.   The jury brought in the verdict not guilty.   The afflicted, surprised and unhappy at this unexpected outcome, immediately put up a hideous outcry.   In response, one of the judges expressed himself dissatisfied; another judge said that Rebecca should be indicted again.   The chief judge, William Stoughton, saying that he did not want to impose upon the jury, immediately brought up a technicality which was later shown to be false.   He asked the jury to go out again and reconsider the verdict.   This time the jury found her guilty.

Rebecca Nurse was a long standing member of the church in Salem Town.   The Rev. Nicholas Noyes, the younger of the two ministers of the church, claimed that her witchcraft represented an insidious attack by the Devil against the congregation.   On Sunday July 3, 1693, he had Rebecca Nurse taken from her prison cell and brought to the meetinghouse. There, at the afternoon church service, he excommunicated her in front of the entire congregation.

Meanwhile, influential friends of Rebecca Nurse appealed to the governor, Sir William Phipps, who reprieved her from the death sentence. But the reprieve was not a pardon; it was only a temporary postponement of her execution. She remained in prison. When the afflicted learned of this, they renewed their outcries; a Salem gentleman prevailed upon the governor's council, and the reprieve was recalled. Rebecca, age seventy, was executed with the other four.

Cotton Mather reported the following interchange in his account of Susannah Martin's trial. "There were produced the evidences of many persons bewitched.

"*Magistrate*: 'How comes your appearance to hurt these?'

"*Martin*: 'How do I know? He that appeared in the shape of Samuel, a glorified saint, may appear in anyone's shape.'

"It was then also noted that if the afflicted went to approach her, they were flung down to the ground. And when she was asked, the reason for it, she said, 'I cannot tell. It may be that the Devil bears me more malice than another.' "

With her reference to the prophet Samuel, Susannah Martin repudiated spectral evidence on biblical grounds. From this testimony, it appears that Susannah's main crime was to challenge the clergy at their own game.[149] Unable to refute

---

149 The biblical king Saul consulted a female soothsayer, the witch of Endor, and she agreed to summon the spirit of his predecessor, Samuel. "And the woman said unto Saul, I saw gods [i.e. demons] ascending out of the earth. And he said unto her, What form is he of? And she said, An old man cometh up, and he is covered with a mantle. And Saul perceived that it was Samuel." (1 Sam. 28.) Then Saul supposedly heard the voice of Samuel through the medium of the witch. Theologians have debated whether Saul heard Samuel himself or merely the Devil impersonating him. The latter view was prevalent in 1692. Thus Cotton Mather wrote in *The Return of Several Ministers* (June 15, 1692), "It is an undoubted

Susannah Martin's theological argument, Cotton Mather in his account turned to the "evidence" of her specter striking down the afflicted in front of the court. Apparently, what he wrote in *The Return of Several Ministers* did not to apply to her, a further evidence of his deception through equivocation. Dismissing Susannah Martin's fine defense, Cotton Mather concluded his account of her trial with character assassination. "This woman was one of the most impudent, scurrilous, wicked creatures of this world; and she did now throughout her whole trial, discover herself to be such an one. Yet when she was asked, what she had to say for herself? Her chief plea was, *That she had led a most virtuous and holy life.*"[150]

At the trial of Sarah Good, one of the afflicted girls fell into a fit.[151] She accused Sarah of stabbing her in the breast with a knife, claiming that Sarah had broken the knife in the act. Sarah was searched, and a piece of a knife blade was found on her person. However a courageous spectator stepped forward and told the court of an incident that had happened the previous day, involving a young man. When called before the court, he produced a knife with the end of its blade missing. The court looked at the piece found on Sarah Good, and saw that it was the missing part. Upon inquiry the young man said that he had broken the end off his knife the day before, and had thrown away the fragment. He added that the afflicted girl making the accusation was with him at the time. The court dismissed the young man and instructed the afflicted girl not to tell lies. Significantly, however, she was allowed to continue to give evidence against other prisoners.[152]

---

and notorious thing that a demon may, by God's permission, appear even to ill purposes in the shape of an innocent, yea, and a virtuous man." Indeed, Susannah Martin's defense was that the afflicted saw the specter, not of her, but the Devil impersonating her.

150 Cotton Mather, *Wonders*, 138-140, 148.
151 Calef, 249-250.
152 A similar incident occurred at a witchcraft trial in England. There the afflicted children would shriek out upon the least touch from a supposed

Sarah Good's spirit was not easy to break. She knew she was innocent, and her persecutors roused her indignation. At her execution, the Rev. Nicholas Noyes urged her to confess, telling her, "You are a witch, and you know you are a witch." Replied Sarah Good, "You are a liar. I am no more a witch than you are a wizard, and if you take away my life, God will give you blood to drink."[153]   Tradition has it that the Rev. Noyes, who was exceedingly fat, eventually died of an internal hemorrhage, bleeding profusely at the mouth.[154]

At the third meeting of the court, August 5, 1692, six more were tried, four men and two women: the Rev. George Burroughs, the minister at Wells, Maine; John Proctor and his wife, Elizabeth Proctor, of Salem Farms; John Willard of Salem Village; George Jacobs, Sr. of Salem; and Martha Carrier of Andover. All were found guilty and condemned to death. Because Elizabeth Proctor was pregnant, she was reprieved from death until the birth of her child. She remained in prison. The other five were executed on August 19.

Cotton Mather described Burroughs as "one who had the promise of being a King in Satan's kingdom, now going to be erected." He described Martha Carrier as "this rampant hag whom the Devil promised should be Queen of Hell."

---

witch, but not when touched by any other person. Lest there be any fraud, an experiment was performed by some local gentlemen. The eyes of one of the girls were covered by an apron, and a witch was brought in. But instead of the witch someone else touched the girl, who thereupon shrieked out just as before. The gentlemen declared to the court that they believed the whole thing was an imposture. However, the witch was still found guilty, and the English court was fully satisfied with the verdict. (Hutchinson, 2:41.)

153 Calef, 250.

154 Preserved in fictional form in Nathaniel Hawthorne's *The House of the Seven Gables*.

Burroughs pleaded not guilty.[155] The afflicted girls were the principal witnesses against him. The girls not only accused him of the usual witchcraft, but went further and pronounced him a king in Satan's empire. Confessions of accused witches were entered in court for use as additional evidence. "Margaret Jacobs being one that confessed her own guilt, and testified against her grandfather Jacobs, Mr. Burroughs and John Willard, the day before execution came to Mr. Burroughs, acknowledging she had belied them, and begged Mr. Burroughs's forgiveness; who not only forgave her, but also prayed with and for her."[156]

Testimony was given that Burroughs, despite his small stature, performed feats beyond the strength of a giant. Several soldiers were summoned from Maine to testify about these so-called feats.[157] They confirmed he had taken a gun seven feet long and held it out. They also confirmed that he had lifted a barrel of molasses out of a canoe, and carried it to the shore. One of the soldiers did not appear for his summons, but was persuaded to give testimony later.

Burroughs' first two wives had died. The afflicted girls testified that he had treated both harshly, and had made each swear that she would never reveal any of his secrets. The girls also testified that each of the wives privately had complained to neighbors that her house sometimes was infested with frightful apparitions of evil spirits.

---

155 The trial of George Burroughs is reported by Cotton Mather under the title "The Trial of G. B. at a Court of Oyer and Terminer held in Salem in 1692" in his book *The Wonders of the Invisible World.* His account begins, "The government requiring some account of his trial, it becomes me with all obedience to submit unto the order."

156 Calef, 258.

157 Two were Captain William Wormall and James Greenslade. Greenslade was intimidated because his mother, Ann Pudeator, had been imprisoned for witchcraft on June 2, 1692 and her trial was coming up. Failure to appear for the summons incurred a penalty of £100 to be levied on his goods and chattels (*SWP*, 159).

Also appearing as witnesses against Burroughs were members of the Ruck family, his in-laws from his second marriage. His brother-in-law Thomas Ruck testified that once he, Burroughs, and Burroughs' wife Sarah (Thomas Ruck's sister) went out to pick wild strawberries. The three traveled into the woods for two or three miles, Ruck and his sister on horseback, Burroughs on foot. After picking the strawberries, they headed home, with the two on horseback riding slowly so that Burroughs could keep up with them. Suddenly Burroughs stepped off the road and into the bushes. Ruck and his sister Sarah halted their horses and hallooed for him. No answer. In dismay they rode homewards without him, at a quickened pace. When nearly home, to their astonishment, they came upon Burroughs, on foot with his basket of strawberries. Burroughs chided his wife, Sarah, for what she had said about him to her brother while the two were riding home. When they asked how he knew what had been said, he replied, "I know your thoughts." Ruck told him that the Devil himself did not go so far. Burroughs replied, "My god makes known your thoughts unto me."

Who was his god? Cotton Mather had the answer. "The Court began to think that only by the assistance of the Black Man, Burroughs might put upon his invisibility, and in that fascinating mist, gratify his own jealous humor, to hear what they said about him."[158] Included among the judges on the court was Samuel Sewall, Burroughs' Harvard classmate.

While John Proctor and his wife were imprisoned, Sheriff George Corwin came to their house and seized all the movables and cattle that he could find. The sheriff sold some of the cattle at half price and killed others, shipping the meat to the West Indies. Having taken all the provisions in the house, he had the audacity to leave the Proctor children struggling on their own, with

---

158 Calef, 330, states, "His [Cotton Mather's] telling that the court began to think that Burroughs stepped aside to put on invisibility, is a rendering them so mean philosophers, and such weak Christians, as to be fit to be imposed upon by any silly pretender."

nothing to eat. He drained beer out of a barrel and carried away the barrel. He even emptied a pot of broth and took away the pot. Nothing was ever returned to the family.

Proctor earnestly asked his minister, the Rev. Nicholas Noyes, to pray with him and for him. Noyes refused because Proctor would not admit that he was a witch. As the execution neared, Proctor pleaded for a little extension of time, saying that he was not fit to die, but it was denied.

Similarly, when old George Jacobs, Sr. was condemned to death, Sheriff George Corwin and officers came to his house and seized all that he had. Still not satisfied, the sheriff took his wife's wedding ring; only after great difficulty was she finally able to get it back. To feed her children, she was forced to buy back from the sheriff the very provisions that he had taken from her. Unable to manage, she was sustained by the charity of her neighbors.

On the day after his execution, Jacobs' granddaughter, Margaret Jacobs, wrote to her father in hiding. "Being close confined here in a loathsome dungeon, the Lord look down in mercy on me, not knowing how soon I shall be put to death, by means of the afflicted persons, my grandfather having suffered already, and all his estate seized for the king. The reason for my confinement is this: I having through the magistrates' threatenings, and my own vile and wretched heart, confessed several things contrary to my conscience and knowledge."[159]

In the trials of the previous session of the court (June 30, 1692), an afflicted girl had cried out publicly upon the Rev. Samuel Willard, the minister of the Third Church (Old South) in Boston. "She was sent out of court, and it was told about that she was mistaken in the person."[160] Three of the justices, Samuel Sewall, Peter Sergeant and Wait Still Winthrop, were members of the Rev. Willard's congregation, and for them even to suggest that

---

159 Calef, 259.
160 Calef, 253.

their minister was an agent of Satan would be disastrous to their prestige. Under this umbrella, the Rev. Willard worked to dispel the delusion.

As we have noted, the Rev. Samuel Willard and the Rev. Joshua Moody effected the escape of Philip English and his wife. The Rev. Willard's son, John Willard, instrumental in the escape of the wife of Captain Nathaniel Cary on July 30, 1692, was "bound over upon suspicion of conveying off Mrs. Elizabeth Cary from their Majesties' jail in Cambridge." The imprisoned John Proctor wrote a letter dated July 23, 1692 to five ministers known to harbor some doubts about the delusion; they were Samuel Willard, together with James Allen, Joshua Moody, John Baily, and Increase Mather.[161]

Thomas Brattle, in his letter of October 8, 1692 opposing the witch trials, stated, "In particular, I cannot but think very honorably of the endeavors of a reverend person [the Rev. Samuel Willard] in Boston, whose good affection to his country in general, and spiritual relation to three of the judges [Sewall, Sergeant, and Winthrop] in particular, has made him very industrious in this matter. Had his proposals been followed when these troubles were in their birth, they never would have grown. He has met with little but unkindness, abuse, and reproach from many men, but I trust that, in after times, his wisdom and service will find a more universal acknowledgment; and, if not, his reward is with the Lord."

Yet at the present session August 5, 1692, John Willard, the nephew of the Rev. Samuel Willard, was sentenced to death. The Rev. Willard's work failed to save his kinsman, but by inspiring Brattle and others it helped finally put a stop to the witch hunt.[162]

---

161 Allen, Moody, and Baily were of the First Church (Old Church) in Boston, whereas Increase Mather was of the Second Church (Old North).

162 In February 1701, the Rev. Samuel Willard was made vice-president of Harvard, and in September the president, Increase Mather, was dismissed and Willard was made temporary president.

On Thursday morning, August 19, 1692, Lecture Day, the condemned, the Rev. George Burroughs, John Proctor, John Willard, George Jacobs, Sr., and Martha Carrier, were carried in a cart through the streets of Salem to execution. As Burroughs went to the place of death, he moved his lips in prayer, not a petition for himself alone, but embracing all, his fellow sufferers and the frantic multitude. As he stood upon the ladder, he made a speech stating his innocence with such solemn conviction that the crowd was deeply moved. His prayer, which he concluded by repeating the Lord's Prayer, was truly remarkable, spoken with compassion, spirit and grace. So affected were the people that many were left in tears. For a moment, it seemed that the crowd would force the sheriff to stop the execution. Ever alert, the afflicted girls instantly proclaimed that the Black Man had stood and dictated the prayer to him. While the executioner prevented Burroughs from speaking further, Cotton Mather, mounted upon a horse, seized the moment to address the people. To avoid a stain on the reputation of the Puritan clergy, he told the crowd that Burroughs was not a properly ordained minister. To convince them that a man of Burroughs' education and background could be guilty, Cotton Mather cited scripture, shouting, "For Satan himself is transformed into an Angel of Light."[163] The executions went on.

When Burroughs was cut down, he was dragged by the halter to a grave, only about two feet deep, scraped into the shallow soil between two rocky outcrops. Burroughs had been wearing the good quality clothing customary for a minister. The sheriff pulled the shirt and trousers from Burroughs' body, replacing them with the old pair of trousers of one of the others executed. His body was then thrown into the grave with the bodies of Willard and Carrier. One of his hands and his chin, and a foot of one of the other bodies, were left uncovered. In the afternoon, the Rev. Nicholas Noyes gave the Lecture Day service in the church.

On that day, August 19, 1692, when his Harvard chum Burroughs was hanged, judge Samuel Sewall made this entry in

---

163 2 Cor. 11:14.

his diary, "This day George Burroughs, John Willard, John Proctor, Martha Carrier and George Jacobs were executed at Salem, a very great number of spectators being present. Mr. Cotton Mather was there, Mr. Symmes, Hale, Noyes, Cheever, &c.[164] All of them [the victims] said they were innocent, Carrier and all. Mr. Mather says they all died by a righteous sentence. Mr. Burroughs by his speech, prayer, protestation of his innocence, did much move unthinking persons, which occasions their speaking hardly concerning his being executed." In the margin Sewall later added, "Doleful Witchcraft."

On Thursday September 1, 1692, several justices took time off from their "doleful" duties to attend a wedding. Justice John Richards married Anne Winthrop before William Stoughton, the Chief Justice. Attending were her brother, justice Wait Still Winthrop, as well as justices Jonathan Corwin, Bartholomew Gedney, and John Hathorne.

Except for William Stoughton, Peter Sergeant, and Samuel Sewall, all the justices of the Court of Oyer and Terminer belonged to the same extended family.[165] The most important

---

164 This group was made up of Harvard graduates: Sewall, class of 1671; Burroughs, 1670; Cotton Mather, 1678; Zachariah Symmes (minister at Bradford), 1657; John Hale (minister at Beverly), 1657; Nicholas Noyes (assistant minister at Salem Town), 1667; Samuel Cheever (minister at Marblehead), 1659.

165 John Winthrop, Sr. (1587–1649), was the first governor of Massachusetts. His son John Winthrop, Jr. (1606–1676) was the first governor of Connecticut. He had seven children, among them were Elizabeth, Margaret, Anne, John, and Wait Still. Elizabeth Winthrop, married the Rev. Antipas Newman of Wenham in 1658, and after his death in 1672, she married Dr. Zerubabel Endicott (1635-1684). Margaret Winthrop married, in 1665, John Corwin (1638–1683), the brother of justice Jonathan Corwin. Their son Sheriff George Corwin married Lydia Gedney, daughter of justice Bartholomew Gedney. Anne Winthrop married justice John Richards of Boston in 1692. Wait Still Winthrop, born in 1642, was a soldier in the Indian wars, major general, and a justice on the court.

fact embedded in the genealogy of the old guard families is the extent of intermarriage. In their choice for marriage partners, they largely restricted themselves to their own class.

The fourth meeting of the Court of Oyer and Terminer was held on Friday September 9, 1692. Six women were tried and sentenced to death: Martha Corey of Salem Village, Mary Easty of Topsfield, Alice Parker of Salem, Ann Pudeator of Salem, Dorcas Hoar of Beverly, and Mary Bradbury of Salisbury.

Mary Easty, one of the three Towne sisters (the other two were Rebecca Nurse and Sarah Cloyce), entered several petitions into the court. In June, when there was still hope of saving Rebecca's life, she and Sarah Cloyce had pleaded for more justice at the trials. Since Puritan law allowed no counsel for the accused, the petition asked, "Would you, who are our judges, please counsel to us, and direct us wherein we may stand in need." It asked that the testimony of ministers, friends, and their children be admitted, and that the testimony of confessing witches not be used without additional legal evidence. The petition had not the slightest effect. The court would countenance nothing that might risk the thrust of the entire prosecution.

Ann Pudeator had challenged her accusers. She had asked that the testimony sworn against her by Sarah Churchill, Mary Warren, and John Best be stricken from the record as "altogether false and untrue," and that "my life not be taken away by such false evidence." Although the judges were told that Best had formerly suffered public whipping as a proven liar, Ann's defense, too, was fruitless.

On Saturday September 17, 1692, the fifth meeting of the court was held. In three or four hours, eight women and one man were tried and sentenced to death. The women were: Margaret Scott of

---

Justice John Hathorne's brother Eleazer Hathorne (1637-1680) married, in 1663, justice Jonathan Corwin's sister, Abigail. After being widowed, Abigail married James Russell of Charlestown, a powerful member of the old guard.

Rowley, Wilmot Redd of Marblehead, Mary Parker of Andover, Abigail Faulkner of Andover, Rebecca Eames of Boxford, Mary Lacey of Andover, Ann Foster of Andover, and Abigail Hobbs of Topsfield. The man was Samuel Wardwell of Andover.

On September 19, 1692 Giles Corey was pressed to death.

During the last two court meetings, a total of fourteen women and one man was convicted. One of the women, Mary Bradbury, escaped. Six others were continued in prison: Dorcas Hoar, Abigail Faulkner, Rebecca Eames, Mary Lacey, Ann Foster, and Abigail Hobbs. Abigail Faulkner, being pregnant, was spared execution until the birth of her child. Ann Foster, elderly and exhausted, died in Boston prison in December.

The remaining seven women and the man were hanged on Thursday morning, September 22, 1692, a chill and rainy day. They were Martha Corey, Mary Easty, Alice Parker, Ann Pudeator, Margaret Scott, Wilmot Redd, Mary Parker, and Samuel Wardwell. On Gallows Hill, the rain obscured what would have been their final view of the open sea.

Giles Corey was the only person ever pressed to death in the history of New England. The law stated that before a person could be tried, he must plead either guilty or not guilty. Seeing that the court had convicted everyone brought to trial, Giles Corey decided to stand mute. When asked whether he was guilty or not guilty, this obstinate man simply declined to speak. In their collective rage, the justices used an archaic law, "peine forte et dure," against him: his body could be pressed until he made a plea. Corey, stalwart, chose to undergo whatever death they would put him to, but he would say nothing. With astonishing stoicism, he refused to speak, right up to the end. As he was dying, his tongue was pressed out of his mouth. Sheriff George Corwin used his cane to force it in again.

Giles Corey, an obscure husbandman who demonstrated amazing fortitude, soon became a hero, the subject of a popular ballad:

Giles Corey was a wizard strong,
A stubborn wretch was he,
And fit was he to hang on high
Upon the locust tree.

So when before the magistrates
For trial he did come,
He would no true confession make
But was completely dumb.

"Giles Corey," said the magistrate,
"What have thou here to plead
To these who now accuse thy soul
Of crimes and horrid deed?"

Giles Corey —he said not a word,
No single word spoke he.
"Giles Corey," said the magistrate,
"We'll press it out of thee."

They got them then a heavy beam,
They laid it on his breast.
They loaded it with heavy stones,
And hard upon him pressed.

"More weight," now said this wretched man,
"More weight," again he cried,
And he did no confession make
But wickedly he died.

Dame Corey lived but three days more,
But three days more lived she,
For she was hanged at Gallows Hill
Upon the locust tree.

The tradition was long standing in Salem that at stated periods the ghost of Giles Corey walked abroad, a precursor of some calamity threatening the community.

In his diary justice Samuel Sewall recorded, "Monday, September 19, 1692. About noon, at Salem, Giles Corey was pressed to death for standing mute." On the next day, he made the entry, "Sept. 20. Now I hear from Salem that about 18 years ago, he was suspected to have stamped and pressed a man to death, but was cleared. Twas not remembered till Ann Putnam, Jr. was told of it by said Corey's specter, the Sabbath-day night before the execution."

Cotton Mather preserved the original letter received by Samuel Sewall. Written by Sergeant Thomas Putnam, it reads, "The last night, my daughter Ann was grievously tormented by witches, threatening that she should be pressed to death before Giles Corey. A man in a winding sheet[166] told her that Giles Corey had murdered him by pressing him to death. The apparition said that Giles Corey was carried to court for this, and the jury had found the murder, and that her father knew the man, and the thing was done before she was born. Now, Sir, this is not a little strange to us, that nobody should remember these things, all the while that Giles Corey was in prison, and so often before the court. For all people now remember very well that about seventeen years ago, Giles Corey kept a man in his house, which man died suddenly. A jury was impaneled, among whom was Dr. Zerubabel Endicott, who found the man bruised to death, and having clodders of blood about his heart. The jury, whereof several are yet alive, brought in the man murdered, but as if some enchantment had hindered the prosecution, the court proceeded not against Giles Corey, though it cost him a great deal of money to get off."

This letter reveals something about Sergeant Thomas Putnam's thinking. In 1675 Giles Corey had killed Jacob

---

166 The ghost of Jacob Goodale, clothed in the white sheet used to lay out his dead body.

Goodale, and Putnam, then twenty-two years old, saw Corey bribe his way free. Now, in 1692, largely through the efforts of Thomas Putnam, the court had Giles Corey but was uninterested in prosecuting him for his real crimes. Instead the court was accepting the flimsiest type of spectral evidence, taking only a few minutes to sentence an accused person to death.[167] Even to Thomas Putnam, the operation of the court had become a mockery, a fraud.

During the summer the court seemed to adopt a policy of not bringing to trial any accused person who confessed to witchcraft. Certainly this became the critical factor in obtaining so many confessions. Several reasons have been put forward to explain this course. Cotton Mather needed confessions to establish the reality of his invisible world of witches; the civil authorities needed accusations made by confessing witches to implicate other targeted people. Still, it was generally believed that when the authorities had collected enough people in jail, they would execute them all.

After her conviction, Mary Easty made one last petition, not for herself, but for the others accused, people she knew to be as innocent as herself. She asked that, before any more were condemned, the court re-examine some of the confessing witches whom she knew had committed perjury.

In his efforts to make Dorcas Hoar confess, her minister, the Rev. John Hale, reached back into his memory to dredge up her sins. The worst seemed to be that some quarter of a century ago, Dorcas had borrowed a book on palmistry. At the time, the Rev. Hale's little daughter Rebecca had seen the book "with many streaks and pictures in it." Convicted on September 9, 1692, her execution imminent, Dorcas gave in to the pressure and became a

---

167 Typical of the evidence was the deposition of the erstwhile bare-footed Benjamin Gould, age 25, "On the 6th of April 1692, [the specters of] Giles Corey and his wife came to my bed side and looked upon me, and then went away. Immediately I had two pinches upon my side, and I had such a pain in my feet that I could not wear my shoes for two or three days."

last-minute confessor. The Rev. Hale helped her initiate a petition that asked "that there may be granted her one month's time or more to prepare for death and eternity." As a result she was reprieved, being given, according to the petition, "a little time of life to realize and perfect her repentance for the salvation of her soul." Dorcas grasped that last-minute repentance might save her life, as well as her soul. In his diary Samuel Sewall recorded, "Sept. 21. A petition is sent on behalf of Dorcas Hoar, who now confesses. Accordingly an order is sent to the sheriff to forbear her execution, not withstanding her being in the warrant to die tomorrow. This is the first condemned person who has confessed."

Paradoxically, execution had been reserved not for those who pleaded guilty, but for those who professed innocence. Samuel Wardwell initially had pleaded guilty by making a confession. But a few days later he denied his confession: "Samuel Wardwell admitted to the grand inquest that the above written confession was taken from his mouth, and that he said it. But he said, *I belied myself.* He also said, *It is all one. I know I shall die for it whether I admit it or not.*" He was promptly convicted. Starkey wrote, "Samuel Wardwell of Andover stood his trial, heard his sentence, and suffered it without once going back to his former story, his confession, What was it that guided Wardwell now? Was it the Devil, or was it perhaps an angel of God, and if the latter, who were the sinners, who the murderers?"[168]

On the day of execution, Thursday, Lecture Day, September 22, 1692, the eight, Martha Corey, Mary Easty, Alice Parker, Ann Pudeator, Margaret Scott, Wilmot Redd, Mary Parker, and Samuel Wardwell, like the others before them, were loaded onto a cart. The local taverns were filled with people awaiting the executions, and a huge throng lined the streets despite the rain. Some had traveled from far; more had come from nearby towns. Many children stood with their parents. No one was discouraged from attending, for an execution was regarded as a deterrent to

168   Starkey, *Devil*, 202.

sin. When the cart reached the outskirts of the town, it turned aside from the main road and began to ascend Gallows Hill. With its dark slope and the even line of its summit, the hill resembled a green rampart, its rocky soil covered by scraggly underbrush.

The cart became stuck going uphill, mired in a muddy rut. The horses strained under the whip, trying to free it. The afflicted girls, following immediately behind in another cart, chorused, "The Devil hinders the cart! The Devil hinders the cart!" With their spectral sight, they saw the Black Man struggling against the horses, vainly attempting to pull back the cart, to stop them from taking his eight witches to the hanging tree. But the path was less steep than it appeared, and the horses soon managed to pull the cart to the top of Gallows Hill. There, spreading its branches towards heaven like a lone sentinel stood the great locust tree.

Martha Corey, wife of Giles Corey, protesting her innocence upon the ladder, concluded her life with a prayer. Martha had been imprisoned for over six months. On September 14 the Rev. Parris and a delegation from the Salem Village church visited her in prison, notifying her of her excommunication. Parris entered in the parish book only the observation that she was "very obdurate, justifying herself and condemning all that had done anything to her just discovery and condemnation." He did not mention his own words, except to say that they had been few, "for her imperiousness would not suffer much."

Mary Easty, sister of Rebecca Nurse, made her last parting from her devoted husband, children, and friends. Her calm and gentle farewell, distinctly heard, drew tears from many.

Wilmot Redd, the wife of a fisherman, had been accused of generally harmless sorceries, such as curdling milk and spoiling butter. Reputedly she could cause milk to curdle as soon as it left the cow. She had said, "I know nothing of it," at her trial. In the minds of later generations, she is remembered in the children's doggerel:

Old Mammy Redd
Of Marblehead
Sweet milk could turn
To mold in churn.

At his execution, Samuel Wardwell, a carpenter, addressed the people with the truth, saying that he was innocent, as were the others who were convicted. As he spoke, the executioner stood beside him, casually smoking a pipe of Virginia tobacco. The smoke blew into Wardwell's face, choking him and interrupting his speech. Watching from the front row, the afflicted girls saw, in their invisible world, the Devil. To stop Wardwell from speaking, the Devil was directing the hot vapors of hellfire into Wardwell's face to choke him. "The Devil hinders Wardwell with smoke! The Devil hinders Wardwell with smoke!" chanted the girls.

Afterwards, the Rev. Nicholas Noyes pointed to the locust tree, with its broad branches holding their heavy burden. Turning to the crowd, he cried, "What a sad thing it is to see eight firebrands of hell hanging there." And sadder still when, in truth, all eight were innocent. The Rev. Noyes, a corpulent man who enjoyed eating, partook of a leisurely noon meal with friends. Refreshed, then he delivered his Lecture Day sermon at the meetinghouse.

That evening, Thursday September 22, 1692, justices William Stoughton, John Hathorne, and Samuel Sewall met with Cotton Mather. Here was the hard core of the old guard. Their meeting place was Samuel Sewall's house in Boston. It was raining so hard that William Stoughton stayed overnight, leaving early in the morning. Throughout the trials, Cotton Mather's great respect for William Stoughton never wavered. Calling him "a worthy person who has generally expressed his good will to my endeavors" Cotton Mather found in Stoughton a Puritan even more fanatic than himself.[169] Samuel Sewall recorded their meeting in his diary. Because he left the pages of his diary mostly

---

169 Cotton Mather, *Magnalia*, 2: 489.

empty throughout the witch hunt, any other private meetings of this small group can only be inferred.

Also present was Stephen Sewall, Samuel Sewall's brother. Stephen was the clerk of the court. The day before he had received a letter from Cotton Mather requesting the trial records.[170] Samuel Sewall brought with him the transcripts of the Court of Oyer and Terminer, dampened from the rain. He handed them over to Cotton Mather. Before going to bed that night, Samuel Sewall read 1 John 1, "God is light, and in him there is no darkness at all. If we say we have no sin, we deceive ourselves, and the truth is not in us."

Cotton Mather wanted the records to use in his upcoming book on the trials of the witches. The book, *The Wonders of the Invisible World*, was rushed through press, the first (Boston) edition appearing in October 1692. It gives an account of five of the trials at Salem, compares the doings of the witches in New England with those in other parts of the world, and adds an elaborate dissertation on witchcraft in general.[171] A sensational account, it sold briskly, not only in New England but also in England. In this, his most popular publication, he assures his readers that, with allusion to the parable of the witch of Endor, it is his own soul speaking through the medium of the book. "With such a spirit of love, is this book now before us written. It is not written with an evil spirit."

Did Cotton Mather ever return the trial records to the Essex County Courthouse? Charles W. Upham, who in 1831 published his "Lectures on Witchcraft," wrote: "The journal of the Special Court of Oyer and Terminer is nowhere to be found. It cannot be supposed to be lost by fire or other accident, because the records of the regular court, up to the very time when the Special Court came

---

170 Cotton Mather, *Selected Letters*, 44.

171 The trials included were those of George Burroughs ("one who had the promise of being a king in Satan's Kingdom"), Bridget Bishop, Susannah Martin, Elizabeth Howe, and Martha Carrier (who "the Devil promised should be queen of Hell).

into operation, and from the time when it expired, are preserved in order. A portion of the papers connected with the trials have come down in a miscellaneous, scattered, and dilapidated state." All the extant legal records are now printed in the three volumes of *The Salem Witchcraft Papers*. What happened at the sessions of the Court of Oyer and Terminer must be determined from these volumes and Mather's book.

Concerning the preservation of other documents, Upham wrote: "The effect produced on the public mind, when it became convinced that the proceedings had been wrong, and innocent blood shed, was a universal disposition to bury the recollection of the whole transaction in silence, and, if possible, in oblivion. This led to a suppression and destruction of the ordinary materials of history. Papers were abstracted from the files, documents in private hands were committed to the flames, and a chasm left in the records of churches and public bodies. The records of the parish of Salem Village, although exceedingly well kept before and after 1692 by Thomas Putnam, are in another hand for that year, very brief, and make no reference whatever to the witchcraft transactions. This general desire to obliterate the memory of the calamity has nearly extinguished tradition. While writing the 'Lectures on Witchcraft,' I was occupying a part of the estate of Bridget Bishop, if not actually living in her house. Little, however did I suspect, while delivering these lectures in the Lyceum Hall, that we were assembled in her orchard, the scene of the preternatural and diabolical feats charged upon her by the testimony of Louder and others. Her estate was one of the most valuable in the old town. It is truly remarkable that the locality of the residence of a person of her position should have become wholly obliterated from memory in a community of such intelligence. Tradition was stifled by horror and shame. The only recourse was in oblivion; and all, sufferers and actors alike, found shelter under it."[172]

---

172 Upham, 2:462-464.

CHAPTER 13

THE SPECTERS CEASED TO ROAM

In his poem, "The Witch of Wenham," John Greenleaf Whittier (1807-1892) describes the end of the witch hunt in May 1693, when Sir William Phipps ordered the release of all of the imprisoned.

> For spell and charm had power no more,
> *The specters ceased to roam,*
> And scattered households knelt again
> Around the hearths of home.
>
> The smith filed off the chains he forged,
> The jail-bolts backward fell;
> And youth and hoary age came forth
> Like souls escaped from hell.

How Sir William Phipps managed to put a stop to the delusion is the subject of this chapter.

During August and September 1692 William Stoughton, in his capacities as both acting governor and chief justice, continued pressing the witchcraft proceedings while Governor Sir William Phipps was away leading the army in Maine. King William had directed Phipps to rebuild the fort at Pemaquid in order to hold the Indians in check and to reassert the English claim to the lost province of Maine. Phipps applied himself vigorously to the task. Upon his arrival in Pemaquid, he set part of his force to work on the fort, while the rest started off to harass the enemy. Unlike the

229

witchcraft battle against specters and other invisible forces of night, Phipps' battle was quite real.

During Phipps' absence, Stoughton, as acting governor, ordered the estates and goods of the executed seized and disposed of. He did this with neither the knowledge nor the consent of Governor Phipps. After Dorcas Hoar was condemned, her estate was seized; only some of it would later be regained by her family. After Philip English and his wife fled to New York, Sheriff George Corwin seized their estate to the value of about fifteen hundred pounds sterling. It was lost to them, except for about three hundred pounds sterling which was afterwards restored.

On October 7, 1692 Edward Bishop, Jr. and his wife made their escape from prison; in anger Sheriff George Corwin immediately seized their goods and cattle. Had it not been for their second son, who borrowed money to bribe Corwin, their property would have been lost entirely.

Leading citizens such as Philip English and his wife, Captain John Alden, and the wife of Captain Cary, had been charged and imprisoned. Moreover several people of still higher rank were named by the afflicted or by confessing witches. Dudley Bradstreet, justice of the peace in Andover, was cried out upon, and so was his brother John Bradstreet. Sons of Simon Bradstreet, the respected former governor, both brothers fled to New Hampshire for safety.[173] Hysterical girls, not belonging to the sanctioned circles, were crying out upon more and more people in the upper levels of society. An afflicted girl in Boston cried out upon John Allyn, the secretary of the Connecticut colony.

Many men of high station, unaffected by the witch hunt, had chosen to stay silent. Now, faced with the possibility of having their wives and mothers accused, they began to see the witch hunt as a very near threat. A general fear swept through the upper echelon of society. Their reaction against the escalating

---

173 New Hampshire was safe because the province was not under control of Massachusetts. Maine, on the other hand, was, and would remain so until the nineteenth century.

accusations grew sufficiently strong that they started, at last, to express openly their bitter opposition to the whole proceedings.

Meanwhile Phipps, leading the forces in Maine, found his men critically low on provisions. On September 29, 1692 he returned home to Boston to restock supplies. Major Benjamin Church, the acting commander, was forced to borrow bread to feed the troops. Soon they engaged the Indian forces, and Phipps missed a "smart fight with the enemy in Kennebec River."[174] However serious the war in Maine, Phipps was appalled to discover a far more acute situation at home, deteriorating by the day. Suspicion, resentment, and dread dominated the colony. But numerous officials were expressing aloud their alarm; sustained resistance to the witch hunt finally had set in.

Nineteen persons had been hanged, one pressed to death, and eight more were under sentence of death. Of these twenty-eight, more than a third were members of churches. Most had unblemished reputations, yet the court had found not one innocent. The prison at Salem was so full of people awaiting trial that some prisoners had to be placed elsewhere. The prisons in Boston, Cambridge, and Ipswich were overflowing. In all there were more than one hundred fifty in prison, and another two hundred accused but not yet imprisoned. Phipps was confronted with the necessity of identifying and challenging the motivating forces that lay at the root of these grim statistics.

Phipps saw easily enough what was wrong and he faced his duty. He would need to recruit sufficient allies to defeat the purposes of Stoughton and the rest of the old-guard Puritan leaders. It was hardly an enviable task but it had to be done. First he exerted his authority as royal governor by directing a letter to the English crown giving his position. This letter, dated at Boston, October 12, 1692, states, "When I came home I found many persons in a strange ferment of dissatisfaction which was increased by some hot spirits that blew up the flame. I have now forbidden the committing of any more, and those that have been

---

174 Church, 214.

committed I would shelter from any proceedings against them. I have also put a stop to the printing of any discourses that may increase the needless disputes of people on this occasion, and I have grieved to see that some have so far taken the counsel of passion as to desire the precipitancy of these matters. As soon as I came home from the fighting, I put a stop to the proceedings of the Court [of Oyer and Terminer]."

In his letter Phipps was circumspect, as it was not wise to broadcast the names of those responsible at this juncture. Phipps knew it was essential that he first obtain support from some of the judges and clergy. As concerned people started to unite behind him, they further encouraged him to take the necessary measures. He knew that he could count on the support of leading merchants, Thomas Brattle being the most prominent.

The most effective voices raised against the Salem witch hunt were those of two Boston merchants, Thomas Brattle and Robert Calef. Both were opposed to Cotton Mather and the entire witchcraft proceedings. Born in Boston in 1658, Thomas Brattle (Harvard, 1676) won such distinction as a mathematician, and notably as an astronomer, as to be made a member of the British Royal Society. His career was that of a cultivated Boston merchant, and from 1693 to his death in 1713 he was treasurer of Harvard College.[175]

Thomas Brattle had written a letter, dated October 8, 1692, addressed to a minister whose name has been lost. It was a private letter, not intended for publication, although he may have intended its circulation in manuscript form. The letter states, "The chief judge [William Stoughton] is very zealous in these proceedings. Wisdom and counsel are withheld from his honor as to this matter. Yet there are men of understanding, judgment, and

---

175 The *Boston News-Letter* said of Brattle, "In the church he was known for his charity to all of the reformed religion, but more especially his great veneration for the Church of England, although his general communion was with non-conformists." As an eminent opponent of the Puritan theocracy, he did not escape the epithets "apostate" and "infidel."

piety, inferior to few, if any, that do utterly condemn the proceedings." He explicitly mentions former governor Simon Bradstreet, the Rev. Increase Mather, the Rev. Samuel Willard, and Major Nathaniel Saltonstall. He then writes, "Except for Mr. Hale, Mr. Noyes, and Mr. Parris, the reverend elders are very much dissatisfied. Several of the former justices are much dissatisfied; also several of the present justices, and in particular some of the Boston justices, were resolved rather to throw up their commissions than be active in [prosecuting on the basis of] the accusations of these afflicted children."

Of the personal life Robert Calef (1648-1719) little is known beyond his serving his townsmen in capacities as an overseer of the poor and as a selectman. His place in history rests in his book, *More Wonders of the Invisible World*, first published in London in a small quarto volume in 1700. It was a firsthand report of the Salem witchcraft episode. He placed in the book accounts written by people directly involved, including Captain Nathaniel Cary, Captain John Alden, Rebecca Nurse, John Proctor, Margaret Jacobs, and Mary Easty.

Ironically, even justice Jonathan Corwin, a member of the old guard, found himself with cause to stop the witch hunt.[176] Mrs. Margaret Thatcher, his very rich mother-in-law, was cried out upon, not once but many times. In his letter of October 8, 1692 Thomas Brattle states, "Many things I wonder at. I do admire that some particular persons, and particularly Mrs. Thatcher of Boston, should be much complained of by the afflicted persons, and yet the justices should never issue out warrants to apprehend them, whereas for the same account they issue out warrants for

---

176 His house, still standing in Salem, is known as the Witch House. It is on the corner of Essex (formerly Main) and North streets, and was erected in 1642 by the magistrate's father, Captain George Corwin. It is said that some of the accused were brought before magistrate Corwin and other magistrates for their preliminary examinations in the eastern front lower room of this house, although they were tried and condemned in the meetinghouse which stood at the corner of Essex and Washington streets.

imprisoning many others. Although Mrs. Thatcher be mother-in-law to Mr. Corwin, who is one of the justices and judges, yet if justice do oblige them to apprehend others, I cannot see how Mrs. Thatcher can escape, when it is well known how much she is, and has been, complained of." But Shakespeare already had answered Brattle's question:

> Through tattered clothes small vices do appear;
> Robes and furred gowns hide all. Plate sin with gold,
> And the strong lance of justice hurtless breaks;
> Arm it in rags, a pygmy's straw does pierce it.[177]

These accusations of high-level people were a key factor in stopping the witch hunt. A letter from Boston notes, "The witchcraft at Salem went on vigorously until at last members of Council and Justices were accused."[178] There is even evidence that the governor's wife, Lady Mary Phipps, had been accused.[179]

As Brattle's letter indicates, the methods of the court had disturbed many in addition to Nathaniel Saltonstall. But lacking Saltonstall's courage, they had remained silent. Some of the judges on the court now admitted to Phipps that "their former proceedings were too violent and not grounded on a right foundation."

The use of spectral evidence was a flashpoint of controversy in the witch trials. Except for fanatics like William Stoughton, nearly everyone, including prominent clerics, were skeptical of it. Phipps was especially unhappy about its use. Inquiring into the matter, he was informed by Stoughton and the other judges that they did not entirely rely on spectral evidence. They assured him that they also used human testimony. Just what was human testimony? Phipps saw that it consisted of little more than vicious slander and unsupported verbal attacks. These lame

---

177 Shakespeare, *King Lear*, act 4, sc. 6.
178 United Kingdom, *Calendar of State Papers, Colonial, 1693–1696*, 63.
179 Calef, 362. Hutchinson, 2:45.

explanations confirmed to Phipps that a complete lack of justice prevailed in the Court of Oyer and Terminer.

The case of the wife of the Rev. John Hale, the minister of Beverly, helped to discredit the use of spectral evidence. An afflicted girl of Wenham had cried out upon Mrs. Hale.[180] The girl claimed that the specter of Mrs. Hale afflicted her.[181] Until that point, the Rev. Hale had been a defender of the use of spectral evidence. Now spectral testimony was being thrown at his wife. The afflicted girl was not a member of the circle; she was only one of a number of girls and young women caught up in the general hysteria.

Since Hale was a minister who actively supported the conspiracy, he knew that they would never file a legal complaint against his wife. However, Hale was embarrassed that his wife had been accused; it never had occurred to him that such a thing could happen. It was all the more troubling because people were asking for explanations, even members of his own congregation.

Although he had strongly advocated the use of spectral evidence in the prosecutions, Hale knew that many of his fellow clergymen were uneasy about its use. He could solve his problem

---

180 Mrs. Hale was born Sarah Noyes, and was the first cousin of the Rev. Nicholas Noyes.

181 The girl was Mary Herrick, who first told her story to her minister, the Rev. Joseph Gerrish (Harvard, 1669). Gerrish was not a supporter of the witch hunt. On November 14, 1692, he took the girl to the Rev. John Hale (Harvard, 1657) of Beverly, and she made the following statement in front of them both. "An account received from the mouth of Mary Herrick, aged about 17 years, having been afflicted by the Devil about two months. She saith that she had oft been afflicted and that the shape of Mrs. Hale had been represented to her. On the 5th of November she appeared again with the ghost of Goody Easty, and that Mrs. Hale did sorely afflict her by pinching, pricking, and choking her. Easty said she came to tell her she had been put to death wrongfully and was innocent of witchcraft, and she came to vindicate her cause, and bid her to reveal this to Mr. Hale and Gerrish." (*New England Historical and Genealogical Register* 27:55.)

by a mere reversal of reasoning. Abruptly, he changed his mind. He told his congregation that his wife was innocent, and that the specter seen by the afflicted girl was the Devil taking the shape of his innocent wife. In so doing, he affirmed that the Devil could afflict in the shape of an innocent person. In short, his simple explanation for the whole embarrassing situation was that spectral evidence was unreliable. Did that mean that the one hundred fifty people in jail, all imprisoned on spectral evidence, were also innocent? To Hale, the question was so peripheral as to be irrelevant; pragmatism and expedience automatically took precedence.

A select group of clerics led by the Rev. Increase Mather had started to re-examine thoroughly the legal and moral bases of the proceedings. On October 3, 1692 Increase Mather presented his *Cases of Conscience Concerning Evil Spirits Personating Men, Witchcrafts, infallible Proofs of Guilt in such as are accused with that Crime. All considered according to the Scriptures, History, Experience, and the Judgment of many Learned men* before a conference of ministers in Cambridge. His forceful language suggested a new urgency. He pointed out the dangers of "over-hasty suspecting or too precipitant judging." He stated as well, "It is better that ten suspected witches should escape than one innocent person should be condemned." Increase Mather, to his credit, had listened to Thomas Brattle and came out strongly against the use of spectral evidence.[182] Concurring with the defense offered by the now dead Susannah Martin, Increase Mather decisively wrote, "The Devil by the instigation of the witch at Endor appeared in the likeness of the prophet Samuel."

---

182 In *Cases of Conscience* Increase Mather wrote, "it is possible for the Devil to impose on the imaginations of the persons bewitched, and cause them to believe that an innocent person torments them, when the Devil himself does it. Satan seems to be what he is not, and makes others to seem to be what they are not. The Devil represents evil men as good, and good men as evil."

The preface of Increase Mather's text was signed by fourteen ministers.[183] Significantly, his son, Cotton Mather, was not among them. Instead Cotton Mather had produced his own book *The Wonders of the Invisible World,* a contrivance to justify the witchcraft trials and the spectral evidence used to convict the "witches."

Father and son, in this month of October 1692, had each come out with a publication about the witch hunt. Claiming in public that there were no essential differences between their views, they acted as one in defending themselves against their common enemies.[184] But, in fact, their views, as expressed in their printed documents, were widely divergent. Increase Mather, the president of Harvard College, had fallen under the influence of Thomas

---

183 The Rev. James Allen and the Rev. John Baily of the First Church of Boston (Old Church), the Rev. Samuel Willard of the Third Church of Boston (Old South Church), the Rev. Charles Morton of Charlestown, the Rev. Nehemiah Walter of Roxbury, the Rev. William Hubbard of Ipswich, the Rev. John Wise of Ipswich Village, the Rev. Samuel Phillips of Rowley, the Rev. Michael Wigglesworth of Malden, the Rev. Samuel Whiting, Sr. of Lynn, the Rev. Jabez Fox of Woburn, the Rev. Joseph Gerrish of Wenham, the Rev. Samuel Angier of West Watertown, and the Rev. Joseph Capen of Topsfield.

184 In a postscript to his *Cases of Conscience,* Increase Mather, in reference to William Stoughton and the other justices, wrote, "Nor is there designed any reflection on those worthy persons who have been concerned in the late proceedings in Salem. They are wise and good men. Pity and prayers rather than censure are their due, on which account I am glad there is published by my son a *Brevate of the Trials* [i.e., *The Wonders of the Invisible World*]. I was not myself present at any of the trials, excepting one, viz. that of George Burroughs; had I been one of the judges, I would not have acquitted him." The execution of Burroughs, a Puritan minister, had split the clergy. After the death of Burroughs, the court continued to pile up evidence against him to justify its action. Did Increase Mather concur with the execution of Burroughs from conviction or from expediency? In this instance, it appears that Increase Mather placed politics before principle.

Brattle, who was the representative of the wealthy Boston merchants and who soon would be made treasurer of Harvard College. Cotton Mather remained solidly in the old ways of Puritanism, now in disfavor with the majority. What private rift, if any, father and son might have experienced in their enigmatic relationship is unknown, but it is tempting to think that tensions ran high over what was, at base, an issue of life and death for those awaiting trial.

Increase Mather, again to his everlasting credit, then took the critical step of discrediting the veracity of the confessions. Brattle, in his letter of October 8, 1692, had already described the intolerable conditions under which some of these confessions were extracted. He wrote that the accused "denied their guilt, and maintained the innocence for above eighteen hours, after most violent, distracting, and dragooning methods had been used with them, to make them confess. They thought that their very lives would have gone out of their bodies, and wished that they might have been cast in the lowest dungeon, rather than be tortured with such repeated buzzings and unreasonable urgings."

About fifty of the imprisoned had confessed to be witches. Many of them were from Andover. In October 1692, Increase Mather visited the Salem prison to talk with the prisoners about the conditions under which the confessions were obtained. His investigation revealed that respectable women, subjected to undue pressure, had been forced into false confessions. Soon afterwards, these women had wanted to retract their words. However, they were warned, "Samuel Wardwell had renounced his confession, and quickly after was condemned and executed." If they renounced their confessions, they would "go after Wardwell."[185] Because of these threats, they had decided to stick to their confessions, even though they were false.

Indeed no one who did confess and stuck to the confession in the September trials was executed. Calef writes, "And though the confessing witches were many; yet not one of them that confessed

---

185   Recantation of six Andover women. (Hutchinson, 2:31-32.)

their own guilt, and abode by their confession were put to death."[186] Although this was true in September, the intent of the judges was that it not remain true at future trials.[187]

Thanks to the work of Thomas Brattle, Increase Mather, and others, Sir William Phipps now had the ethical and moral ammunition he required to bring the witch hunt to an end. Despite these findings, Chief Justice William Stoughton and his cohorts insisted on holding new trials without any change in procedure. At the adjournment of the last meeting, the Court of Oyer and Terminer had been scheduled to meet again in Salem on Tuesday November 1, 1692.

The old guard was well-aware that the unquestioned support of the clergy was fast eroding. In addition, they now faced the active opposition of an alarmed governor and powerful merchants. In response, the old guard found it expedient to withdraw support from their client conspiracies, in Salem Village and in Andover. Still, residual accusations continued through the rest of October 1692, and even into November. The focal point was the town of Gloucester, where some of the afflicted girls of Salem Village had been sent to act as seers. As a result four women were sent to prison. Because Salem prison was so crowded, it could take only two; the other two were sent to Ipswich prison.

In November 1692, the same girls were sent again to Gloucester, this time at the request of Lieutenant James Stephens. "In their way, passing over Ipswich bridge, they met with an old woman, and instantly fell into their fits. But by this time the validity of such accusations being much questioned, they found not the encouragement they had done elsewhere, and soon withdrew."[188] The work of the Salem Village conspiracy and their afflicted girls had ended.

---

186 Calef, 271.
187 Stoughton, in the Superior Court trials held in January 1693, wrote death warrants for eight convicted women, most of them confessing witches.
188 Calef, 269-270.

The afflicted girls in Andover, the counterparts of the circle in Salem Village, had cried out upon a "worthy gentleman of Boston." In response, this worthy sent "a writ to arrest those accusers in a thousand pound action for defamation."[189] Confronted by this aggressive legal maneuver and sensing that they had lost general support, the Andover conspiracy also withdrew and desisted from any further accusations. Their work, too, had come to an end.

Rumors expressing doubt about the Court of Oyer and Terminer had run rife ever since the mass executions on September 22, 1692. On October 15 in Cambridge, justice Samuel Sewall visited Thomas Danforth to discuss the witchcraft proceedings. Danforth conceded that the court would not be able to continue unless there was some way to deal with the growing dissent among the ministry and the people.

On Saturday, October 29, 1692, a council meeting took place. The members of the old guard were dismayed at the prospect of the dissolution of the Court of Oyer and Terminer. To the governor, they expressed their desire that the court should meet the following Tuesday, as scheduled, to try more witches. They claimed that that there would be "some inconvenience" if it did not convene. Despite constant pressure from the old guard Puritans to continue the crusade, Phipps' answer was unequivocal. "It must fall," he said. And with these three words, Phipps ended the dreaded Court of Oyer and Terminer.

Faced with defeat, the old guard remained unyielding, refusing to admit that those whom they had misled for so many years were no longer ready blindly to follow their direction. Unwilling to capitulate, they made a last ditch stand. They enacted yet another law "against conjurations, witchcraft, and dealing with evil and wicked spirits," assigning the "pains of death" to any that shall "entertain, employ, feed, or reward any evil or wicked spirit." However, the people were not fooled. Concerning this new law, Calef observed, "It has not yet been

---

189 Calef, 269.

explained what is intended thereby, or what it is to feed, reward, or employ Devils, etc., yet some of the legislators have given this instead of an explanation."[190]

The Court of Oyer and Terminer was dissolved; the prisoners were now safe from its mock trials.   Sir William Phipps next turned his attention to the prisoners themselves.   The miserable conditions in the prisons jeopardized their lives.   At least fifty of them were suffering severely from sickness and the bitter cold. Phipps allowed their families and friends to bail them out.   For bail they had to post recognizance bonds which would be forfeited if the prisoners did not appear for their later trails.   He instructed the judges to find means to relieve others to prevent them from dying in prison.

A new court was to be formed, and here Phipps' careful preparation came into play.   With the opinion of prominent clergy for once on his side, Phipps made the old guard agree that the new court would proceed very differently.   He reminded them that the Rev. Increase Mather and other leading ministers believed that spectral evidence was "not sufficient proof."   He demanded their assurance that spectral evidence would not be used.

On November 25, 1692, the old guard in Council passed an act constituting a Superior Court of Judicature; the first meeting of the new court was set for January 3, 1693.   The Council elected justices for the court on Tuesday December 6, 1692, a dark, wintry day.   With fifteen men present, William Stoughton was elected unanimously, Thomas Danforth received twelve votes, Major Richards seven, Major General Winthrop seven, and Captain Samuel Sewall seven.   These five were chosen as the justices, with

---

190   The new law was passed by the General Court in Boston on December 14, 1692. The extensive confiscations of property made during the previous months were illegal under existing law. One purpose of this new law was to legalize these confiscations so as to prevent legal retributions. The new law was finally disallowed by the crown's privy council in England on August 22, 1695. (*SWP*, 885-886. Burr, 381. Calef, 332.)

Stoughton as chief justice. As anticipated, the old guard filled every position. All of the five, except Thomas Danforth, were from the old Court of Oyer and Terminer. John Hathorne was not elected to the new court; he received only three votes, one of which was from Samuel Sewall. Major Bartholomew Gedney, Jonathan Corwin, and Peter Sergeant were also omitted from the new court.

As noted earlier, Cotton Mather had seen to it that Stoughton replaced Danforth as lieutenant governor in May 1692, Stoughton being the more aggressive man. By that stroke Cotton Mather had assured the outcomes he sought from the trials during the summer. Danforth now sat on the new court; the old guard needed all their top players on stage to convict as many of the prisoners as possible.

The first meeting of the Superior Court of Judicature was held at Salem, starting on the set date, January 3, 1693. All five justices, Stoughton, Danforth, Richards, Winthrop, and Sewall, were sitting on the bench. This was ten months after the witch hunt had begun. There were two fundamental differences between this court and the dissolved Court of Oyer and Terminer.

First, spectral testimony was not allowed as evidence. Essentially this left only slander and the confessions as possible evidence against the accused. Learning of this, the accused who previously had confessed immediately began retracting their statements. The court, however, tended to ignore these retractions; whenever possible they used the former confessions as evidence of witchcraft.

Second, the juries were chosen from virtually the entire male population, and not merely from the small minority of freemen (male church members), as previously. The new charter had extended the franchise to all male citizens who owned even a modest amount of property. Predictably, the influence of the clergy on the juries of this new court was far less than in the dissolved court. In fact, because non-church members could vote and shape the course of government, the power of the Puritan theocracy had been broken forever.

Despite these two new factors, the old guard of high officials clung stubbornly to their old habits. William Stoughton and the other judges never relaxed their efforts to obtain convictions. Fifty-six prisoners were brought to the court. The two conspiracies, in Salem Village and in Andover, played their parts. Obediently the afflicted girls gave their evidence at the grand jury inquests. Bold as brass, Elizabeth Hubbard claimed that she was "tortured, afflicted, consumed, pined, wasted and tormented." Mary Walcott stood ready to assist in convicting the accused of "certain detestable arts called witchcraft and sorceries." Mary Warren testified that the accused "wickedly, maliciously and feloniously have used, practiced, and exercised witchcraft in the town of Salem." Ann Putnam, Jr. diligently tried to secure a death sentence "by the laws made and provided" for "Candy, a Negro servant [slave]" as well as others of the accused.

The juries did not hesitate to demonstrate their newly achieved independence; the old guard suffered a string of defeats in the many verdicts of innocence brought in by the juries. Of the fifty-six prisoners, the grand jury cleared thirty and indicted twenty-six, who were bound over for trial. Of these twenty-six only three, Elizabeth Johnson, Jr., Mary Post, and Sarah Wardwell (the wife of the executed Samuel Wardwell), were found guilty in trial by jury.

Chief Justice Stoughton signed death warrants for the speedy execution of the three convicted, and also for the others who had been convicted at the former Court of Oyer and Terminer, but had not been executed. "The warrant for their execution was sent, and the graves digged for the said three, and for about five more that had been condemned at Salem formerly."[191]

191 The previously convicted still in jail were Elizabeth Proctor, Abigail Faulkner, Dorcas Hoar, Rebecca Eames, Mary Lacey, and Abigail Hobbs. The convicted Ann Foster had died in prison in December 1692. Both Elizabeth Proctor and Abigail Faulkner were pregnant. But Elizabeth Proctor, in giving birth to a baby girl on January 27, 1693, found herself included among those to be executed. Abigail Faulkner was not included;

But Governor Sir William Phipps, not about to be duped again, was ready to make his counter strike and save the lives of these eight women. When the attorney general, Anthony Checkley,[192] informed Phipps that the three convicted were as innocent as the fifty-three who had been cleared, Phipps immediately dispatched a reprieve to Salem for all eight executions.[193] He explained that he had first to obtain advice from the crown, knowing full well that advice from England would take months to arrive, not only because of the ocean voyage, but also because of the snail's pace of English bureaucracy.

The second session of the new court was held at Charlestown on January 31, 1693. The justices present were Stoughton, Danforth, Winthrop, and Sewall; Richards did not appear. The grand jury cleared some of the prisoners and indicted others. As the court was sitting, word came in that Phipps had sent the reprieve to Salem. Chief Justice Stoughton was "enraged and filled with passionate anger."[194] "We were in a way to have cleared the land of these. Who it is that obstructs the course of justice, I know not. The Lord be merciful to the country," he cried.[195] In his fury, he left the bench, and did not return to that session. Stoughton at long last had met his match. Once and for all, Phipps had gained the upper hand; the ability of the old guard to continue the witch hunt had collapsed.[196]

One of the prisoners bound over for trial at that session was Lydia Dustin. A woman of nearly seventy, a widow for twenty-

---

she did not give birth to her baby boy until March 1693. (*A Further Account*, 216.)

192 Anthony Checkley had been assigned the position of king's attorney (or attorney general) on July 26, 1692. His predecessor, Thomas Newton, appeared as secretary of the province of New Hampshire on August 15, 1692.

193 Sir William Phipps' letter dated at Boston, February 21, 1693.

194 Sir William Phipps' letter dated at Boston, February 21, 1693.

195 Calef, 333.

196 The old guard, however, still constituted a strong political force in other matters.

one years, she had been chained in prison for nine months. Rumors had spread that if there were ever a witch in the world, she was one; she had been shamefully slandered in this way for some twenty or thirty years. Spectators came from Boston and neighboring towns to see her trial. The conspiracy supplied a multitude of witnesses to testify against her. Their testimony, a rerun of the same old charade, consisted entirely of extraneous incidents, accidents and illnesses that had happened years ago. But spectral evidence was not allowed, and the jury soon brought her in as innocent. Her daughter and granddaughter, as well as all the others tried at that session, were also found not guilty by the jury.

After Lydia Dustin was cleared, justice Danforth ranted at her, "Woman! Woman! Repent! There are shrewd things come in against you!" Acting as chief justice, Danforth played his final card. Lydia Dustin, her daughter, and granddaughter were penniless; Danforth demanded exorbitant fees for their release, knowing that they could not pay. With relish, he ordered them back to prison on short rations. Lydia Dustin, her strength fading, died within six weeks in the dismal cold cell.

In a letter to the crown, dated at Boston, February 21, 1693, Governor Phipps took care to lay the blame explicitly on Stoughton and the old guard.[197] He wrote, "By advice of the Lieut. Governor and Council, I gave a commission of Oyer and Terminer to try the suspected witches. The first in the Commission was the Lieut. Governor, and I depended upon the court for a right method of proceeding. Some were accused of whose innocence I was well assured, and many considerable persons of unblameable life and conversation were cried out upon as witches and wizards. The Deputy Governor notwithstanding persisted vigorously in the same method, to the great dissatisfaction and disturbance of the people, until I put an end to the court and stopped the

---

197 He sent this letter without having received a reply to his letter of October 12, 1692. The February 21, 1693 letter was endorsed in England, "Received May 24, 1693, about witches."

proceedings." *Lieutenant governor* refers to Stoughton while Phipps was in Boston, and *deputy governor* refers to Stoughton while Phipps was at the front.

The Superior Court sat again on April 25, 1693, this time in Boston, for the county of Suffolk. The judges present were Stoughton, Danforth, Richards, and Sewall; Winthrop did not attend. Captain John Alden was summoned, but since no one appeared against him, he was cleared by proclamation. The prisoners not acquitted by the grand jury, were either continued in prison, or tried by jury and found not guilty.

The final sitting of the Superior Court to hear witchcraft cases was May 9, 1693, at Ipswich, for the county of Essex. No one was found guilty.

In every case tried by the Superior Court, the acquittals were the decisions of the juries, not the judges. Despite their conceit about their superior intellect, the judges were eager to play dumb when it came to identifying and acknowledging their own errors. In covering up their complicity in the witch hunt, the old guard preferred to feign ignorance rather than admit guilt.

The royal advice which Phipps requested from England in his first letter, dated at Boston, October 12, 1692, was indeed slow in coming. The matter was brought up in England in council on January 26, 1693 and the Earl of Nottingham was directed to prepare an answering letter for the royal signature. But the letter was not signed until April 15, 1693, and reached America still later. When it did arrive, with Queen Mary's signature, it had little to offer. "We do hereby require you to give all necessary directions that in all proceedings against persons accused for witchcraft or being possessed by the Devil the greatest moderation and all due circumspection be used, so far as the same may be without impediment to the ordinary course of justice within Our said Province. And so We bid you very heartily farewell."[198] Such vagueness meant nothing.

---

198 *Historical Collections of the Essex Institute*, 9 (2d ser. 1), Part 2, 89-90. Burr, 328.

Obviously frustrated with the court's foot-dragging in clearing the remaining prisoners awaiting trial, Sir William Phipps decided to act on his own authority. In May 1693, he issued a general release for every one. But the condemned women reprieved in January were still under sentence of death. Before he was called back to England,[199] Sir William Phipps granted a pardon to each of these women, "for which they gave about thirty shillings each to the king's attorney."[200] One was Sarah Wardwell.

---

199 On November 17, 1694 Sir William Phipps left Boston for England, where he died on February 18, 1695. The affairs of Massachusetts passed to William Stoughton, the lieutenant governor and former chief justice of the witchcraft trials.

200 Calef, 336.

CHAPTER 14

A GREAT DELUSION OF SATAN

"I desire to be humbled before God. It was *a great delusion of Satan* that deceived me in that sad time. I did it not out of anger, malice, or ill-will." This public apology was offered in 1706 by Ann Putnam, Jr. when she was twenty-six. Ann was the only one of the afflicted girls to make such a confession. Seven years before, her parents had died within fifteen days of each other, possibly one or both by their own hand.[201] Then only nineteen, Ann accepted the responsibility of raising her nine orphaned siblings, who ranged in age from seven months to eighteen years.[202] Never marrying, she devoted her life to them, dying herself in 1716 at the young age of thirty-seven, as her mother had done.

The confession of Ann Putnam, Jr. signified an honorable attempt to express her remorse and at the same time free herself from her parents' web of deceit. Ann was as much a casualty of the witchcraft proceedings as those who were accused. That the afflicted suffered is of central importance. It was not the witches

---

201 Thomas Putnam died at age forty-six on May 24, 1699. His wife, Ann Putnam, Sr. died, at age thirty-seven, on June 8, 1699.

202 The twelve children of Thomas and Ann Putnam were Ann, Jr., born October 18, 1679, Thomas, born 1681, Elizabeth, born 1683, Ebenezer, born 1685, Deliverance, born 1687, Sarah, born 1689, died at age six weeks, Timothy, born April 1691, Abigail, born October 27, 1692, Sarah, born 1693, died at age eight months, Seth, born 1695, Experience and Susannah, twins born 1698.

who hurt them; rather, it was their own parents and guardians. At the deepest level, the girls were afflicted by the manipulations of those they most trusted. To a greater degree than any group, the girls were victims of deceit. Because their elders were the offenders, the afflicted girls had no place to turn for counsel or help. When the tragic play-act was finished, each was left with cruel markings on her spirit which, whether subtle or obvious, were unlikely to heal.

Yet Ann Putnam, Jr. was not the only girl to become a responsible adult. Elizabeth Booth married at age eighteen during the witch hunt. In 1695, Mary Walcott, almost twenty, married Isaac Farrer of Woburn and raised six children. After the Salem tragedy was over Mercy Lewis went to Greenland (not the ice-bound domain of Erik the Red, but a small hamlet with the same name in New Hampshire), where her aunt, Mary (Lewis) Lewis was living. In 1695, at the home of Abraham Lewis, Mercy had an illegitimate child. James Darling, husband of her aunt Hannah, was her bondsman, and her aunt Mary and Charles Allen, Jr., age twenty-four, testified for her. Allen later married her and they moved to Boston. In 1696, Elizabeth Booth's sister, Alice, who had participated as an afflicted girl, married, at age eighteen, Ebenezer Marsh, age twenty-five. In 1709, at the age of thirty-seven, Sarah Churchill married a weaver in Berwick, Maine. In 1710 Elizabeth (Betty) Parris, age twenty-seven, married Benjamin Barnes in Concord. The writer has not yet found records for Abigail Williams, Elizabeth Hubbard, Susannah Sheldon, and Mary Warren. That the girls found the strength to grow beyond their damaging early experiences and become contributing members of their communities was their remarkable achievement.

We never can grasp completely the anguish and terrors experienced by the accused. Trapped and tormented, they, like the afflicted, had nowhere to turn. Their own government leaders were their enemies, responsible for their suffering. They were scorned by neighbors, friends, and occasionally their family. If they were to believe their ministers, these people could not turn even to God, because, as witches, they were deserving only of punishment. Many church members were excommunicated, spurned by the very congregations founded to provide them solace and refuge. Those twenty who were executed stood by their declarations of innocence to the end. It is not an overstatement to say that many of these women and men deliberately chose to die rather than to sign a false confession. They lost their lives because they committed the error of truth.

In the Salem tragedy much has been said about the twenty who were executed. However, eight more should be added to this list, bringing the total number of deaths in the Salem witchcraft delusion to twenty-eight. These additional people all died in prison. Sarah Good's nursing infant died in May 1692; Sarah Osborne, on May 10, 1692. Roger Toothaker, a "doctor of physic," was murdered in prison on June 16, 1692. Elizabeth Scargen's child died after four months confinement; Ann Foster, sentenced to death, died in December 1692. Lydia Dustin, found innocent by trial by jury, was not released, and died on March 10, 1693 in Cambridge prison, where Rebecca Chamberlain and John Durrant also died.

Also to the honored list should be added the slaves who suffered not only from bondage, but from witchcraft accusations as well. They were Tituba, Mary Black, Candy, Mrs. Thatcher's woman slave, and the Rev. Dane's man slave. Mary Watkins "was continued for some time in prison, and at length was sold to Virginia."[203]

A witch hunt on a grand scale, a massive firestorm, the Salem tragedy was out of place in time. It cannot be dismissed simply as mindless mass hysteria. The age of rationality already had reached America's shores. The Salem episode can be explained only as a delusion, born of deceit. It can be labeled the last of the religious witch hunts. Furthermore, it marks the first of the series of political and criminal witch hunts that have plagued society ever since.

---

203 Calef, 335.

Innocent citizens, either as individuals or as members of extended families, suffered from legally authorized murderous attacks. The afflicted girls were encouraged to engage in hysterical outbursts to deliver patently false testimony. People were invited into the courtroom to give the most brazen slander against the accused.

In his book published in 1768, Hutchinson came to this conclusion about the Salem witchcraft tragedy. "A little attention must force conviction that the whole was a scheme of fraud and imposture."[204] Who were the people responsible for this deception?

Because of his morbid fascination with the diabolical and his cravings for power, Cotton Mather contributed greatly to the fueling of the flames of witchcraft in 1692. Instead of fighting a military war with the French and the Indians, Cotton Mather preferred the safer position of crusader in an imaginary war with the Devil. He saw the affair as one in which the powers of darkness preyed on the unregenerate condition of mankind. He pressed the fantasy that New England was threatened by a coven of witches. He believed that ferreting out these agents of Satan championed the cause of God.

With the human tendency to find individual scapegoats for the errors of the past, historians have delighted in placing the blame for the persecution in the hands of Cotton Mather. But culpability does not lie with Cotton Mather alone.

The sordid business was carried out at two levels. At the tactical level, ten men in Salem Village formed themselves into a conspiracy. The names of the Rev. Samuel Parris and Thomas Putnam are most conspicuous in this group. Later a similar conspiracy was formed in Andover. The power of these conspiracies resided in higher authority.

---

204 Hutchinson 2:47. Thomas Hutchinson (1711–1780) became the royal governor of colonial Massachusetts in 1769. He had access to original records, many of which are no longer extant.

At the strategic level, the old-guard Puritans granted the authority under which the conspiracies operated. The beginning of 1692 saw the old guard running an outlaw government in New England. These men were the councilors, magistrates, judges, and high military officers. Only the old guard had sufficient authority to sanction the atrocities of the witch hunt.

The old guard harbored a deep-seated fear and hatred of the new royal charter which, among other things, promised democracy and freedom of religion in the colony. It was for precisely these rights that the ordinary people longed and patiently waited. When accused of witchcraft, William Barker (the brother of Lieutenant John Barker) was speaking for the common person when he said "that all people should live bravely; that all persons should be equal; that there should be no day of resurrection or of judgment, and neither punishment nor shame for sin."

The old guard eagerly accepted the outmoded doctrines preached by Cotton Mather and subtly encouraged superstition and prejudice. They were willing to pervert the legal system into a judicial massacre. They urged forward the witchcraft persecutions in a desperate attempt to retain the power of their old Puritan theocracy. Ultimate responsibility for the Salem disaster of 1692, therefore, must be laid on them.

The most prominent names in the old guard were those of William Stoughton and John Hathorne. Hathorne, in carrying out most of the preliminary examinations, was especially abusive. Later, the transcripts of these examinations were used as evidence in the grand jury inquests and in the trials. Stoughton, as chief justice in the witchcraft trials, was the chief culprit, callous and ruthless. None of the other magistrates or judges was more fanatical than these two.

Cotton Mather was the link between the conspiracies and the old guard. By calculated action and by deliberate neglect, he used his position to offer tacit if not outright encouragement to both groups. He was blinded to a bitter truth. The real threat was never Satan, but rather the glimmers of enlightened thinking among plain citizens.

The most effective voices raised by citizens against the Salem witch hunt were those of Robert Calef and Thomas Brattle. As earlier seen, Brattle stated his findings in his letter of October 8, 1692. He attacked the proceedings so incisively that his letter was an important factor in ending the witchcraft trials.

When Governor Phipps, in May 1693, ordered the release of all the suspected witches who were then in jail, Cotton Mather refused to accept the ruling as final. He continued his campaign to warn New England of the dangers it faced from the forces of Satan. His fanaticism was so extreme that he could well have succeeded in reviving the witch hunt. However, he was countered by material that Robert Calef had painstakingly compiled.[205]

By 1698 Cotton Mather had become seriously alarmed. In his diary he wrote that "there is a sort of Sadducee [Calef] in this town, a man [some words in the manuscript have been carefully obliterated at this point] ... whom no reason will divert from his malicious purposes. This man, out of enmity to me for my publicly asserting such truths about the existence and influence of the Invisible World, has often abused me with venomous reproaches, and most palpable injuries." Because of pressure from the Mathers, no printer in New England would publish Calef's manuscript. Calef, undeterred, sent it to England, where it was printed in 1700. The book, entitled *More Wonders of the Invisible World*, provided an antidote to the poison of Cotton Mather's *The Wonders of the Invisible World*. In spite of their efforts, Cotton Mather and his father, Increase Mather, were unable to suppress its sale throughout New England. The cold, hard logic of the book spoke for itself.

On December 28, 1700 Cotton Mather wrote, "Calef's book sets the people in a mighty ferment." As president of Harvard College, Increase Mather "ordered the wicked book to be burned in the

---

205 "In his [Calef's] account of the facts which can be evidenced by records, and other original writings, he appears to have been a fair relater." (Hutchinson 2:41).

college yard."[206]   His efforts were to no avail. The Mathers' fight was almost over.   In 1701, Increase Mather was fired from Harvard College, and Samuel Willard, whose nephew had been executed in 1692, became the temporary president.

Robert Calef had the courage to expose Cotton Mather. John Greenleaf Whittier (1807-1892), in his poem "Calef in Boston, 1692" compares Cotton Mather's deceit with the unseen wires used to manipulate puppets in a puppet show. In the poem Calef, the tradesman, tells Cotton Mather, the preacher:

> God is good and God is light,
>   In this faith I rest secure;
> Evil can but serve the right,
>   Over all shall love endure.

> Of your spectral puppet play
>   I have traced the cunning wires;
> Come what will, I needs must say,
>   God is true, and ye are liars.

Whittier concludes his poem with the stanza:

> But the Lord hath blest the seed
>   Which that tradesman scattered then,
> And the preacher's spectral creed
>   Chills no more the blood of men.

The publication of Calef's book destroyed, once and for all, the concept of the invisible world of the Devil and witches which had plagued western society for centuries. Calef's book put an end to the conventional witch hunt. Future witch hunts would have to find new devices of deceit.

---

206 Burr, 293.

The old guard, acting in collusion and consumed by avarice, envy, and pride, had no respect for the dignity and value of human life. Their sermons, court records, and publications were cunningly designed so as to hide the truth, and justify their actions to a gullible public and to posterity. To keep the witch hunt burning, they became masterful at spreading distrust and fear.

They easily deceived their own governor. When Sir William Phipps arrived in New England as royal governor in May 1692, the old guard tricked him into delegating the responsibilities of the witch hunt to them. He gratefully trusted them because he felt compelled to turn his attention to a still larger danger, the war with the French and the Indians. It was while he was away at the front during the summer, that the old guard carried out their greatest atrocities. Upon his return in the fall, he quickly realized that he had been mistaken in his trust, and he began to take steps to stop the witchcraft proceedings. Keen on retaining their usurped power, the old guard put up a stiff defense, but Phipps finally prevailed. The whole tragic episode came to a conclusion in the spring of 1693.

In 1697, four years after the end of the witch hunt, one of the judges, Samuel Sewall, handed a note to the Rev. Samuel Willard, minister of the Third Church (South Church) in Boston during a public fast. Sewall stood alone in church while the note was read aloud. "Samuel Sewall, sensible that, as to the guilt contracted upon the opening of the late Commission of Oyer and Terminer, he is more concerned than any he knows of, desires to take the blame and shame of it, asking pardon of men."[207]

Chief Justice Stoughton, informed of Sewall's act, offered a typically arrogant rejoinder. "When he [Stoughton] sat in judgment he had the fear of God before his eyes, and gave his opinion according to the best of his understanding. Although it

---

207 Samuel Sewall, *Diary*, entry of January 14, 1697.

may appear afterwards that he had been in an error, yet he saw no necessity of a public acknowledgment of it."[208]

Except for Samuel Sewall, none of the members of the old guard ever acknowledged remorse or shame for the events that they had sponsored.　Not only did they escape immediate judgment for their crimes, but they succeeded in clinging to the position and authority that they had won.　Despite the revulsion of the general populace against what had happened, these men held on to their superstitions, insisting that they had done right. They repressed any motion, even the slightest, towards redress and restitution.

Their chief, William Stoughton, retained power until his death in 1701. Even afterwards, the old guard Puritans conspired to frustrate and discourage every effort made on behalf of those imprisoned in 1692 and their families.　Finally, when the rising tide of retribution became too great for them to resist, compensation was arranged through channels skillfully contrived to deny their responsibility in engineering the first of the modern political witch hunts.

The old guard and the Salem Village and Andover conspiracies betrayed not only their children and communities, but also their faith.　Those thought to stand closest to God had proved false.　Cotton Mather, so fond of preaching about damnation and hellfire, had made himself, by his own inflammatory acts, a prime candidate for both.

With the outstanding exception of Samuel Sewall, the old guard expressed not the smallest sign of regret.　Certainly neither the Putnams, Samuel Parris, nor the other conspirators were likely to speak out.　And the ministers either kept a convenient silence or tried to deflect their responsibility by appealing to abstruse theological arguments.　It was left to the common people to step forward.　And this they did.　In a highly unusual act, twelve members of the witchcraft juries were moved to sign and circulate

---

208　Hutchinson 2:46

a declaration of regret.[209] These ordinary citizens commanded the wisdom and moral integrity which their Puritan leaders so sadly lacked.

> We do signify to all in general, and to the surviving sufferers in special, our deep sense of, and sorrow for, our errors in acting on such evidence to the condemning of any person; and do declare, that we justly fear that we were sadly deluded and mistaken; for which we are much disquieted and distressed in our minds. We do heartily ask forgiveness of you all, whom we have justly offended; and do declare, according to our present minds, we would none of us do such things again, on such grounds, for the whole world.

---

209 Calef, 339-341. It was signed by Thomas Fisk, Foreman, William Fisk, John Bacheler, Thomas Fisk, Jr., John Dane, Joseph Evelith, Thomas Pearly, Sr., John Peabody, Thomas Perkins, Samuel Sayer, Andrew Elliot, and Henry Herrick, Sr.

CHAPTER 15

THE LIVES OF THE WITCHES AND WIZARDS

INTRODUCTION

In order to indicate family and social structures, this chapter groups the seventy-four accused witches and wizards in the Salem Village witch hunt into ten categories. The groupings are intended to be general, not hard and fast. Following a short description of each group as a whole, the individuals are treated separately. Each entry starts with the complete name of the accused, the town of domicile, and the date when the legal complaint was filed. The basic reference is Boyer and Nissenbaum, eds., *The Salem Witchcraft Papers*, abbreviated as *SWP*. In the charts, the names of the accused are shown in boldface.

GANG OF FOUR AND ASSOCIATED VICTIMS

The arrest on March 1, 1692 of Tituba, Sarah Good and Sarah Osborne set the witch hunt in motion. Tituba, the Caribbean Indian slave, was used as a witness for the prosecution against the other two, as well as against some of the others accused later. Upham explains, "It is quite evident that the part played by the Indian woman was pre-arranged. She had, from the first, been concerned with the circle of girls in their necromantic operations; and her statements show the materials out of which their ridiculous and monstrous stories were constructed. She said that there were four who 'hurt the children.' Upon being pressed by the magistrates to tell who they were, she named Osborne and Good, but 'did not know who the others were.' Two others were marked; but it was not thought best to bring them out until these three examinations had first been made to tell upon the public mind."[210]   The other two were Martha Corey and Rebecca Nurse. These four marked witches are called the gang of four.

Sarah Good was a poor woman, a beggarwoman. She lacked respectability, and because of slander and innuendo she was stereotyped as a witch. The first of the gang of four, she was on the periphery of an extended family that was going to be hit hard in the Andover witch hunt. The imprisonment of her four-year old daughter, Dorcas Good, was an act of pure malice on the part of the conspiracy.

Sarah Osborne was a rich woman, considered a thief by Captain John Putnam, Sr. In defiance of the will of her dead husband, Robert Prince, she refused to part with the inheritance that rightfully belonged to her two sons. Her new husband, Alexander Osborne, allegedly treated his two stepsons, the Prince boys, with cruelty and made them sign a deed renouncing land belonging to their patrimony. The dead husband's sister was married to Captain John Putnam, Sr., and he "craved justice" for his two nephews. As one of the conspiracy, he saw to it that Sarah Osborne was the second member of the gang of four. Sarah Osborne died in prison on May 10, 1692, and Sarah Good was executed that summer.

At the outset the conspiracy did not know how far the authorities would let them proceed in the witch hunt. As a result they decided to pick off a few choice enemies right away. Giles Corey had always been an irritant to the Putnam family. Now he was old, and had much valuable land. His wife, Martha Corey, was chosen as the third member of the gang of four. When the Putnams saw how easy it was to bring her to "justice," they soon instituted charges against her husband. Wife and husband were both executed in September, one with a trial and the other without.

---

210   Upham, 2: 27-28.

Ann Putnam, Sr. had a personal grudge against Rebecca Nurse, the final member of the gang of four. "Jealousies and prejudices may have been engendered by the prosperity and growing influence of the Nurse family."[211]   Rebecca Nurse's husband, Francis Nurse, was a strong political rival of the Putnams. The Nurses were allied to the Porters and supported them in the anti-Parris campaign. "When the excitement occasioned by the extraordinary doings in Mr. Parris' family began to display itself, and the afflicted children were brought into notice, the members of the Nurse family, with the exception, for a time, of Thomas Preston, discountenanced the whole thing. They absented themselves from meeting, on account of the disturbances and disorders the girls were allowed to make during the services of worship."[212]

Rebecca Nurse's two sisters, Sarah Cloyce and Mary Easty, were also to be accused. Because their maiden name was Towne, the three are referred to as the Towne sisters. Sarah Cloyce's husband, Peter Cloyce, was elected as a selectman of Salem in 1692, which did not sit well with the Putnams. The third sister's husband, Isaac Easty, was a member of the Topsfield men who had fought with the Putnams over property rights. Two of the three Towne sisters were hanged, Rebecca in July and Mary in September.

Like Tituba, the slave Mary Black was accused with the intent that she become a witness for the prosecution. However she had the fortitude not to yield to the threats.

Sarah (Solart) Poole Good
Salem Village   *February 29, 1692*

Sarah Solart was born 1653 in Wenham, daughter of Elizabeth (mnu) and John Solart. Sarah's father was a well-to-do Wenham innkeeper. His death by drowning in 1672 was ruled a suicide. He left an estate of five hundred pounds sterling and

---

211   Upham, 2: 56.
212   Upham, 2: 57.

seventy-seven acres of land, a very sizable estate for the time. About 1673, Sarah's widowed mother, Elizabeth Solart, married widower Ezekiel Woodward of Ipswich. He attempted to deprive his step-daughter Sarah and her six siblings of their rightful share of their father's estate. In 1682 these children petitioned the General Court for redress, saying in particular that Sarah's portion was far less than the share to which she was entitled. Meanwhile Sarah had married Daniel Poole, a penniless indentured servant, who soon died, leaving her with a mountain of debt. She married again; her new husband was William Good variously described as weaver and laborer. In 1686, one of Poole's creditors filed suit against Sarah and William Good.[213] Because the Goods were unable to pay the judgment of nine pounds sterling, the court seized and sold land that Sarah had finally inherited from her father's estate. Shortly thereafter, the Goods in dire need sold off more land. Homeless and utterly destitute, they appeared in Salem Village, begging for food and shelter from the householders. "For want of clothes" she never attended church services in Salem Village.

In 1692 Sarah Good, thirty-eight, was the mother of several children including Dorcas Good and a recently born infant. Her husband, an itinerant worker, was usually unemployed. Their lifestyle of begging was an outrage to the Puritan Covenant of Work. Sarah's mutterings when citizens refused her food or lodging were often taken as curses.

On February 29, 1692 the conspiracy filed a complaint [No. 1] against Sarah Good, Sarah Osborne, and Tituba. The three woman were arrested on March 1, and Sarah Good was the first to be examined.

Sarah Good refused to confess, but she did name Sarah Osborne as a witch. In his version of Sarah Good's testimony, Ezekiel Cheever wrote, "Her husband had said that he was afraid that she either was a witch or would be one very quickly. When

---

213 "Mr. John Cromwell vs. William Good and Sarah, his wife, for debt. Sworn before John Hathorne, assistant, March 26, 1686." *Records of Quarterly Courts of Essex County*, vol. 9.

the worshipful Mr. Hathorne asked him his reason why he said so of her, whether he had ever seen anything by her, he answered, 'No, not in this nature, but it was her bad carriage to me.' And indeed said he, 'I may say with tears, that she is an enemy to all good.' " In his version Joseph Putnam wrote, "William Good saith that she is an enemy to all good," but he added, "She saith she is clear of being a witch."

Sarah was transported to Ipswich prison. "Samuel Braybrook said that carrying Sarah Good to Ipswich, the said Sarah leapt off her horse three times which was between 12 and 3 of the clock. She continued railing against the magistrates and she endeavored to kill herself."

On March 5, 1692 the testimony against Sarah continued. "William Good saith that the night before his said wife was examined he saw a wart or teat a little below her right shoulder which he never saw before, and asked Goodwife Ingersoll whether she did not see it when she searched her."

On March 7 Sarah Good, Sarah Osborne, and Tituba were sent to Boston prison and put in chains. On March 9 John Arnold, the prison keeper, wrote out the account, "Chains for Sarah Good & Sarah Osborne, 14s." On March 23 Sarah's daughter, Dorcas Good, four years old, was accused and imprisoned. On April 21, Sarah's infant died at Boston prison.

On June 2, 1692 Sarah underwent two physical examinations, one in the morning and one in the afternoon. On June 30 the Court of Oyer and Terminer condemned her to death. Chief Justice William Stoughton signed her death warrant, and on July 19, 1692 she was hanged at Salem.

Family of Sarah Good

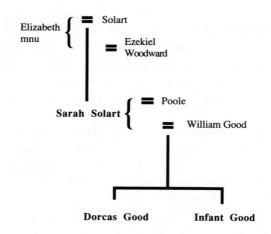

The above chart shows Sarah Good under her maiden name, Sarah Solart. It shows her two husbands, as well as the two husbands of her mother, Elizabeth. The chart also shows Sarah's two children who were imprisoned.

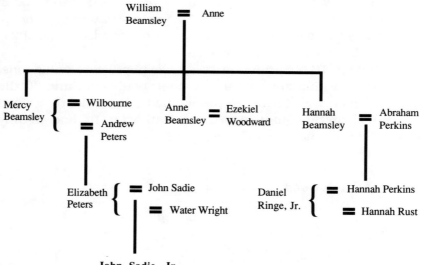

From the above chart, Ezekiel Woodward's first wife was Anne Beamsley (1633-c. 1671). Anne Beamsley had two sisters whose families would become involved in the witchcraft accusations. One of the sisters was Mercy Beamsley (1637-1726), whose second marriage was to Andrew Peters. Their daughter Elizabeth Peters married John Sadie, by whom she had a son, John Sadie, Jr. Upon the death of John Sadie, the widow Elizabeth (Peters) Sadie married Walter Wright of Andover. John Sadie, Jr., thirteen, now the step-son of Walter Wright, was imprisoned for witchcraft on September 9, 1692. The other sister, Hannah Beamsley (1643-1732), married Abraham Perkins. Their daughter Hannah Perkins married Daniel Ringe, Jr. Upon the death of his wife, Daniel Ringe, Jr. married Hannah Rust.[214]

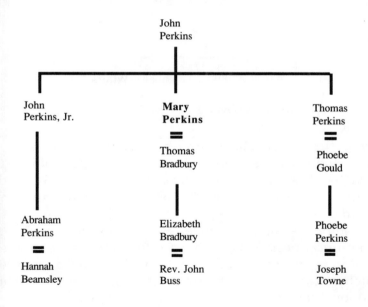

---

214 Elizabeth and Walter Wright are the six-times-great grandparents of the writer. Daniel Ringe, Jr. was a step-son of Uzal Wardwell. Uzal Wardwell was the first cousin of Samuel Wardwell, hanged for witchcraft on September 22, 1692. Hannah Rust was a niece of Uzal Wardwell. (Otten, *Wardwell*, 2.24-2.26.)

From the above chart, Abraham Perkins, who had married Hannah Beamsley, was the son of John Perkins, Jr. John Perkins, Jr. had a sister Mary Perkins and a brother Thomas Perkins. The sister married Thomas Bradbury, and became Mary Bradbury. Seventy-seven in 1692 and living in Salisbury, Mary Bradbury was imprisoned for witchcraft on May 28. However, her family was eventually able to smuggle her out of prison and hid her until the following spring. The brother Thomas Perkins married Phoebe Gould.

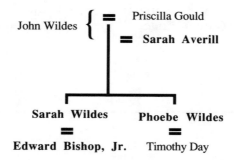

From the above chart, Phoebe's sister, Priscilla Gould, married John Wildes. After Priscilla's death, John Wildes married Sarah Averill. Sarah (Averill) Wildes was hanged for witchcraft in Salem on July 19, 1692. Executed with her was Sarah Good.

The story has come full circle. Sarah Good and Sarah Wildes were not unconnected people hanged for witchcraft on the same day, but were members of an extended family that was singled out for witchcraft accusations in 1692. Also arrested for witchcraft were John Wildes' two married daughters Sarah Bishop and Phoebe Day and his son-in-law Edward Bishop, Jr.

Sarah (Warren) Prince Osborne

Salem Village   *February 29, 1692*

Sarah Warren was born about 1643, the daughter of Margaret (mnu) and John Warren of Watertown. In 1662 she married Robert Prince of Salem Village. His one-hundred-fifty-acre farm was next to that of John Putnam, Sr., who was married to Robert Prince's sister, Rebecca. Robert Prince fully identified himself with the Putnam family. When he died in 1675, he left his land in trust to his wife, with the condition that it be given to their two sons, six-year-old James Prince and two-year-old Joseph Prince, when they came of age. As executors he named his in-laws and neighbors, the patriarch Thomas Putnam and John Putnam, Sr. Soon after her bereavement, the widow Sarah Prince purchased for fifteen pounds sterling the indenture of Alexander Osborne, a young Irish immigrant, and around 1677 the two were married. They tried to gain full control of the Prince lands, in defiance of Robert Prince's will. A protracted dispute ensued, and was still unresolved in 1692.

In 1692 Sarah, about fifty, was ill and often bedridden. John Putnam, Sr. did not like the fact that Sarah and her husband were trying to disinherit her sons, who were also his nephews. James Prince was now of age, and was entitled to his share of his deceased father's estate. Sarah Osborne and her second husband were threatening established patterns of land tenure and inheritance.

On February 29, 1692 Sarah Osborne was named on the same complaint [No. 1] as Sarah Good and Tituba. On March 1 the three were arrested and taken for examination. Sarah Osborne's examination took place after that of Sarah Good. Sarah Osborne refused to confess and was imprisoned.

On May 10, 1692 Sarah Osborne died in Boston prison.

In 1696, James Prince and Joseph Prince were confirmed in the possession of some of their patrimony, but the rest lay under a legal cloud for twenty-four more years. Finally in 1720, the Princes met the Osborne heirs in court. The testimony exposed the latent hostility in Salem Village toward Sarah Osborne's attempts to disinherit her own sons.

Tituba

Salem Village   *February 29, 1692*

Tituba and her husband, John Indian, were slaves in the parsonage of the Rev. Samuel Parris in Salem Village. He had purchased them in Barbados. John worked part-time in the tavern of Nathaniel Ingersoll.

In the winter of 1691-1692, Tituba taught the art of black magic to a small group of pre-teen and teenage girls in Salem Village. These girls were to become the first of the afflicted. Unknowingly, she was used as an instrument to help ignite the witchcraft delusion.

On February 29, 1692 Tituba was named on the same complaint [No. 1] as Sarah Good and Sarah Osborne. On March 1 the three were arrested and taken for examination. Tituba's examination occurred after those of Sarah Good and Sarah Osborne. Tituba confessed to everything and was imprisoned. She was examined for several days thereafter.

Jonathan and Elizabeth Corwin's ten children were born between 1678 and 1690. Six died within a few months of birth, and one died at nine years. Only three were alive in 1692. In the examination of Tituba on March 1 conducted by magistrates John Hathorne and Jonathan Corwin, Hathorne asked Tituba, "Did you hurt Mr. Corwin's child?" She answered, "Goody Good and Goody Osborne told that they did hurt Mr. Corwin's child, and would have me hurt him too, but I did not."

Hathorne asked, "What has Osborne got to go with her?" "She has two of them. One of them has wings, two legs, and a head like a woman," replied Tituba. Intrigued, Hathorne asked, "What is the other thing that Goody Osborne has?" Tituba answered, "A thing all over hairy, all the face hairy, and a long nose, with two legs. It is about two or three foot high, and goes upright like a man & last night it stood by the fire in Mr. Parris' hall." Hathorne then asked, "Who was [it] that appeared like a wolf to

[Elizabeth] Hubbard as she was going from Proctor's?" Gravely. Tituba said, "It was Sarah Good and I saw her send the wolf to her."

Hathorne was obsessed with graphic details. When he asked, "How did you go? What did you ride upon?" Tituba wisely answered, "I ride upon a stick or pole, and Good and Osborne behind me. We ride taking hold of one another. Don't know how we go, for I saw no trees or path, but was presently there." Delighted, Hathorne inquired, "Have you seen Good and Osborne ride upon a pole?" Again, Tituba gave the right answer. "Yes, and [they] have held fast by me. Last night they tell me I must kill somebody with the knife. They would have had me kill Thomas Putnam's child [Ann Putnam, Jr.] last night."[215] The examination is surprising, not only for its content but also because the questions were even more ridiculous than the answers. This examination was the prototype; throughout the witch hunt Hathorne discharged his fury chiefly at those who returned sensible answers to his absurd leading questions.

On May 23, 1692 at Salem, Elizabeth Hubbard, Ann Putnam, Jr., and the Rev. Samuel Parris gave testimony against Tituba. The testimony was attested by Thomas Putnam and Ezekiel Cheever.

A May 31, 1692 letter from Thomas Newton, attorney general, to Isaac Addington, secretary of the province reads, "We pray that Tituba, the Indian, and Mrs. Thatcher's maid, may be transferred as evidence, but desire they may not come amongst the [other] prisoners but rather by themselves." This showed that the authorities were keeping the accused slaves away from the rest of the prisoners. On June 1 Tituba was made to give testimony in Salem.

Tituba remained in prison until May 9, 1693. On this date the grand jury for the Superior Court of Judicature at Ipswich dismissed the charge against her, which was "covenant with the Devil the latter end of the year 1691." The Rev. Samuel Parris

---

215 *SWP*, 746-753.

would not pay the prison fees required for her release, so she was sold to a slave trader in Virginia.

Infant Good
Salem Village   *February 29, 1692*

Dorcas Good
Salem Village   *March 23, 1692*

Dorcas Good was born about 1688 in Salem Village, daughter of Sarah (Solart) Poole and William Good. They had another child, known only as infant Good, born in late 1691 or early 1692.

When her mother, Sarah Good, was imprisoned for witchcraft on March 1, 1692 Dorcas was only four years old, still a small girl. Sarah took her infant to prison with her, where it soon expired.

On March 23, 1692 the conspiracy filed a complaint [No. 4] against Dorcas Good. The afflicted girls claimed that her specter bit and pinched them, tortured them most grievously, and urged them to write in the Devil's book. On March 24, 1692 Samuel Brabrook, marshal's deputy, arrested Dorcas. The abstract of Tituba's confession against herself and Sarah Good says, "Dorcas Good's charge against her mother Sarah Good. That she had three birds, one black, one yellow. These birds hurt the children and afflicted persons." Dorcas was imprisoned, with hands and feet chained.

After her mother's hanging on July 19, 1692, Dorcas remained in prison. On December 10, 1692 Samuel Ray of Salem posted a recognizance bond of fifty pounds sterling as bail for Dorcas' release until trial. There is no extant account of any trial.

In 1710 her father, William Good, wrote, "Dorcas, a child of 4 or 5 years old, was in prison 7 or 8 months, and, being chained in the dungeon, was so hardly used and terrified that she has ever since been very chargeable, having little or no reason to govern herself."

Martha (mnu) Rich Corey

Salem Village   *March 19, 1692*

Giles Corey

Salem Village   *April 18, 1692*

Giles Corey was born about 1612 in England. He married Margaret (mnu) by whom he had four daughters. After her death he married, in 1664, Mary Britt, who died in 1684. Finally he married, about 1685, the widow Martha (mnu) Rich. Martha had been born in the late 1620s in England.

In 1692 Giles Corey, about eighty, was a large landholder with some one hundred acres of valuable land. He had joined the Salem church in 1691. Somewhat eccentric, he was a stubborn man of singular force. His wife Martha Corey, about sixty-five, was a woman of eminent piety and was often called a "professor of religion." She had joined the Salem church in 1690. Because the distance to Salem Town was a long one for a woman her age, she became a tireless attendant at the Salem Village church. In the early days of March 1692 the afflicted girls started crying out upon her, implying that she was a witch. On March 12, 1692 Edward Putnam and Ezekiel Cheever visited her at home to discuss these accusations. On March 14 Martha visited the house of Thomas Putnam to see his daughter Ann, who had charged her of witchcraft. As soon as Martha entered, Ann Putnam, Jr. fell into "grievous fits" and told Martha that "she did it." Soon Mercy Lewis joined in, and the two put on a display to show how badly they were bewitched. For Martha, the visit was a dismal failure.

On March 19, 1692 the conspiracy filed a complaint [No. 2] against Martha Corey. On March 21 she was arrested and examined. She refused to confess and was imprisoned at Salem. On April 11 at the examination of Elizabeth Proctor and Sarah Cloyce, Benjamin Gould, twenty-five, accused Martha's husband, Giles Corey. On April 18 the conspiracy filed a complaint against Giles Corey [No. 8]. The next day, Giles Corey was arrested, examined, and imprisoned.

On June 2, 1692 at the first sitting of the Court of Oyer and Terminer, Ann Putnam, Sr. and Joseph Fuller testified against

Martha Corey, accusing her of killing Samuel Fuller by witchcraft. On June 30 before the grand jury, Elizabeth Booth testified about a vision which she had on June 8. In the vision, Martha Corey had killed George Nedom and Thomas Gould, Sr. by witchcraft. On September 5 a jury was impaneled to search the bodies of Giles Corey and his wife. On September 7 several witnesses were summoned to court to testify against Giles Corey. John De Rich was forced to testify against him and a large number of other persons. John De Rich complied out of fear, as his mother, Mary (Bassett) De Rich and other members of their extended family were imprisoned.

When Giles Corey was indicted he chose to stand mute. That is, he refused to plead either guilty or not guilty. Under law, a man who refused to plead could not be tried. The court turned to an old torture known as *peine forte et dure*, an ancient English procedure designed to force recalcitrant prisoners either to enter a plea (so their trials might proceed) or to die. The victim was made to lie upon the ground with gradually increased weight (rocks) piled upon him. Giles Corey died in this way on Monday September 19, 1692. The day before his death, the Rev. Nicholas Noyes excommunicated him from the Salem church.

On September 9, 1692 the Court of Oyer and Terminer condemned Giles' wife, Martha Corey, to death. On Sunday September 11, she was taken from prison to the Salem church where the Rev. Nicholas Noyes excommunicated her. On September 22, 1692, three days after her husband was pressed to death, Martha Corey was hanged at Salem.

In 1710 John Moulton, husband of Giles Corey's daughter Elizabeth, wrote, "Giles Corey and Martha, his wife, were accused for supposed witchcraft and imprisoned. They were removed from one prison to another, as from Salem to Ipswich, and from Ipswich to Boston, and from Boston to Salem again, and so remained in close imprisonment about four months. We were at the whole charge of their maintenance, which was very chargeable, and so much the more being so far a distance from us, as also by reason of so many removes. After our father's death the sheriff threatened to seize our father's estate and for fear thereof, we complied with him and paid him £11.06.0 in money by all which we have been greatly damnified and impoverished by being exposed to sell creatures and other things for little more than half their worth of them, to get the money to pay as aforesaid and to maintain our father and mother in prison."

Rebecca (Towne) Nurse
Salem Village   *March 23, 1692*

Sarah (Towne) Bridges Cloyce
Salem Village   *April 4, 1692*

Mary (Towne) Easty
Topsfield   *April 21, 1692*

The three sisters, Rebecca, Mary, and Sarah, were the daughters of Joanna (Blessing) and William Towne. Many members of the extended family network of the Towne sisters were accused and imprisoned in 1692. Rebecca and Mary themselves would be hanged.

Rebecca Towne was born 1622 in England. About 1644 she married Francis Nurse. In 1678, Francis purchased on credit a rich three-hundred-acre farm near the Ipswich River in Salem Village. (The house still stands in Danvers.) All eight of the Nurse children, with their spouses, settled on this farm. The debt was paid off on time, and the Nurse families prospered. In late 1691, Francis was elected a member of the Village Committee, which managed the affairs of Salem Village. He was in the anti-Parris group. Also he was a supporter of the Topsfield men in their land dispute with the Putnams. These facts were cause enough for the conspiracy to accuse his wife, Rebecca (Towne) Nurse.

Mary Towne was born 1634 in England. She married, about 1655, Isaac Easty of Topsfield. He was one of the Topsfield Men in the land dispute with the Putnams. This fact led to Mary (Towne) Easty's accusation by the conspiracy in 1692.

Sarah Towne was born about 1641 in Salem. In 1660 she married Edmund Bridges, Jr. of Topsfield, by whom she had five children. After his death she married, about 1681, the widower

Peter Cloyce of Salem Village. His first wife, Hannah Littlefield of Wells, Maine had died in 1680, and he had six children by that marriage. Peter was a member of the Salem Village church, to which Sarah was admitted as a member in 1690. Peter Cloyce was a member of the anti-Parris group He had served as one of Salem's representatives to the General Court in 1689, as had his good friend Daniel Andrew. In 1692 both men were elected selectmen of Salem. His anti-Parris sympathies and his election as a selectman were ample reason for the conspiracy to accuse his wife, Sarah (Towne) Cloyce.

In 1692 Rebecca Nurse, seventy, was nearly totally deaf and often bed-ridden, living with her family in Salem Village. Her sister Mary Easty, fifty-seven, lived with her husband, Isaac Easty, on a large and valuable farm in Topsfield, where they had raised seven children. The other sister, Sarah Cloyce, about fifty-one, lived in Salem Village with her husband, Peter Cloyce, by whom she had three children.

In March 1692 the afflicted girls began alluding to Rebecca Nurse in their fits. On about March 18, 1692 her brother-in-law Peter Cloyce and her friends Israel Porter, his wife, Elizabeth (Hathorne) Porter (who was the sister of Magistrate John Hathorne), and Daniel Andrew visited her to quell the rumors of witchcraft springing up against her. On March 23, 1692 the conspiracy filed a complaint [No. 3] against Rebecca Nurse. She was arrested on March 24. At her examination she refused to confess. She was accused not only by the pre-teen and teenage afflicted girls but also by the grown woman, Ann Putnam, Sr. "Samuel Parris read what he had in characters taken from Ann Putnam, Sr. in her fits." Edward Putnam and Henry Kenny, and Mrs. Bathsheba Pope as well, accused Rebecca Nurse of witchcraft. She was imprisoned at Salem.

On April 4, 1692 the conspiracy filed a complaint [No. 6] against Sarah Cloyce and Elizabeth Proctor. On April 11 the two women were arrested. The examinations were held in Salem Town before Thomas Danforth (the deputy governor), Isaac Addington (the secretary of the province), John Hathorne, Major Samuel Appleton, James Russell, Captain Samuel Sewall, and

Jonathan Corwin.   All of the last five were assistants to the governor; that is, they were members of the upper legislative chamber.[216] Sarah Cloyce refused to confess, and in response to testimony by John Indian said, "Oh! You are a grievous liar." She was imprisoned at Salem, then Boston.

On April 21, 1692 the conspiracy filed a complaint [No. 9] against Mary Easty. She was arrested on April 22. At her examination, Mary refused to confess, "I am clear of this sin of witchcraft." She maintained her innocence with such candor and conviction that Hathorne asked the afflicted girls, "Are you certain this is the woman?" She was imprisoned in Salem. However on May 18 Mary Easty was released. This freedom did not last long. On May 20 the conspiracy filed another complaint against Mary Easty, and she was arrested again.   After examination at Beadles' Tavern in Salem, Mary Easty was sent to Boston prison.

On about May 14, 1692 a petition for Rebecca Nurse was signed by thirty-nine of her friends and neighbors including Daniel Andrew and his wife, Sarah (Porter) Andrew; John Putnam, Sr. and his wife, Rebecca (Prince) Putnam; Jonathan Putnam and his wife, Lydia (Potter) Putnam; Benjamin Putnam and his wife, Hannah Putnam; Sarah Putnam; and Joseph Putnam. Un-dated testimony by John Putnam, Sr. and his wife refuted the charge that Rebecca Nurse had killed their son-in-law John Fuller and their daughter Rebecca Shepard.

On June 1, 1692 at Boston prison Mary Easty, along with Edward Bishop, Jr. and his wife Sarah Bishop, testified against Mary Warren, an afflicted girl temporarily imprisoned. On June 2 two physical examinations, one in the morning and one in the afternoon, were made of Rebecca Nurse's body.

On June 3 at the grand jury inquest Ann Putnam, Sr. accused Rebecca Nurse of killing Benjamin Houlton, John Fuller, and Rebecca Shepard. She also charged that Rebecca Nurse, together

---

216 The period between the complaint and the examinations permitted these top government officials to gather in Salem. This was the first time the examinations were held in Salem Town, instead of Salem Village.

with Sarah Cloyce and Sarah (Wildes) Bishop, "had killed young John Putnam's child, because young John Putnam had said that it was no wonder that they were witches for their mother [Joanna (Blessing) Towne] was so before them, and because they could not avenge themselves on him, they did kill his child." John Putnam, Jr. and his wife Hannah (Cutler) Putnam, confirming the story of Anne Putnam, Sr., testified, "Our child which died about the middle of April 1692 was as well and as thriving a child as most was, till about eight weeks ago. But I the said John Putnam had reported something which I had heard concerning the mother of Rebecca Nurse, Mary Easty, and Sarah Cloyce. Our poor young child was taken with strange and violent fits. As fast as possible we got a doctor to it, but all he did give it could do no good. It departed this life by a cruel and violent death being enough to pierce a stony heart."

On June 28, 1692 Rebecca Nurse petitioned the court for another physical examination, saying, "One of the women [who did the previous examination], the most ancient, skillful, prudent person of them all, did express herself to be of a contrary opinion from the rest." Rebecca requested that other women, such as Mrs. John Higginson (the wife of the Salem minister), Mrs. Buckstone and Mrs. Woodbery (mid-wives), and Mrs. Porter, with others, re-examine her.

Rebecca Nurse's daughter, Sarah Nurse, submitted the testimony, "On June 29, 1692, I saw Goodwife Bibber [an afflicted woman] pull pins out of her close and hold them between her fingers, and clasp her hands round her knees, and then she cried out and said Goody Nurse pricked her."

On June 30, 1692, Ann Putnam, Sr. testified against Sarah Cloyce at the grand jury inquest. An undated declaration by John Arnold, prison keeper at Boston, and Mary, his wife, regarding the behavior of Sarah Cloyce and her sister Mary Easty in prison states, "We do affirm that we saw no ill carriage or behavior in them, but that their deportment was very sober and civil." In mid-June Mary Easty and Sarah Cloyce were transferred from the Boston prison to the Ipswich prison. An account of Robert Lord, blacksmith of Ipswich from about July 31 reads, "For making four pairs of iron fetters and two pairs of handcuffs and putting them on to the legs and hands of Goodwife Cloyce, Easty, Brumidge, and Green. £1.12.0."

On June 29 the jury of the Court of Oyer and Terminer found Rebecca Nurse not guilty. Chief justice William Stoughton instructed the jury to return to the jury room and reconsider their verdict. The jury came back with a verdict of guilty. The Court of Oyer and Terminer sentenced Rebecca to death. On Sunday July 3, she was taken from prison to the Salem church, where the Rev. Nicholas Noyes excommunicated her. On July 19 Rebecca Nurse was hanged at Salem.

In a September 5, 1692 statement, Thomas Fosse, prison keeper at Ipswich, and Elizabeth, his wife, gave this account of Mary Easty. "She behaved herself while she remained in Ipswich prison and we saw no ill carriage or behavior." On about September 6 the surviving Towne sisters, Sarah Cloyce and Mary Easty, made this petition to the court. "That seeing we are neither able to plead our own cause, nor is counsel allowed to those in our condition, that you who are our judges would please to be of counsel to us, to direct us wherein we may stand in need. Those who have had the longest and best knowledge of us, being persons of good report, may be allowed to testify upon oath what they know concerning each of us. That the testimony of witches, or such as are afflicted, may not be improved to condemn us, without other legal evidence concurring."

On September 6, 1692 witnesses were summoned from Topsfield to testify against Mary Easty and Sarah Cloyce. Among them were their sister-in-law, the widow Mary (Browning) Towne, and her children, William, thirty-four, Rebecca, about twenty-three, Samuel, nineteen, and Elizabeth, about eighteen. On September 7 the widow Towne sent her regrets to the court, "I humbly beg that your honors will not impute anything concerning our not coming as contempt of authority. We would come, but we are in a strange condition. Most of us can scarcely get out of our beds, we are so weak, and not able to ride at all. As for my daughter, Rebecca, she has strange fits and sometimes she is knocked down of a sudden."

On September 8, 1692 a second summons for the widow Towne and her daughter Rebecca stated, "We command you, all excuses set apart to be and appear at the Court of Oyer and Terminer holden at Salem tomorrow morning at eight of the clock precisely, there to testify the truth against Mary Easty. Hereof, fail not at your utmost peril." Ephraim Wildes, constable of Topsfield, answered, "I have warned the widow Towne and her daughter to appear at the court." No Towne testimony is extant.

On September 9, 1692 the Court of Oyer and Terminer condemned Mary Easty to death. On about September 13 Mary petitioned the governor, the judges, and the reverend ministers, "Knowing my own innocence and seeing plainly the wiles and subtlety of my accusers, I petition not for my own life, for I know I must die and my appointed time is set, but that, if it be possible, no more innocent blood may be shed. I would humbly beg of you that your honors examine these afflicted persons strictly and keep them apart some time, and likewise to try some of these confessing witches, I being confident there is several of them has belied themselves. I cannot, I dare not belie my own soul." On September 22, 1692 Mary Easty was hanged at Salem.

On January 3, 1693 at the Superior Court of Judicature at Salem, the grand jury dismissed the charge against Sarah Cloyce. Peter Cloyce paid his wife's prison fees. Eventually they left Salem Village and settled in Marlborough. Afterwards they moved to neighboring Sudbury. In 1703 Sarah Cloyce died, aged about sixty-two, and in 1708 Peter Cloyce died at sixty-eight.

In 1694, William Towne (a brother of the three sisters) married Margaret (Wilkins) Willard, the widow of John Willard, who had been hanged for witchcraft on August 19, 1692. In 1697 Rebecca's husband, Francis Nurse, died at Salem Village, aged seventy-seven years. In 1710, Rebecca's son Samuel Nurse gave this account of his mother. "We were at the whole charge of providing for her during her imprisonment in Salem and Boston for the space of almost four months. We spent much time and made many journeys to Boston and Salem and other places in order to have vindicated her innocence. Although we produced plentiful testimony that my honored mother had led a blameless life from her youth up, yet she was condemned and executed."

In 1710 Isaac Easty stated, "My wife was near upon 5 months imprisoned, all which time I provided maintenance for her at my own cost and charge, went constantly twice a week to provide for her what she needed. For 3 weeks of this 5 months she was in prison at Boston and I was constrained to be at the charge of transporting her to and fro." In 1711 Isaac died at Topsfield.

Mary Black
Salem Village   *April 21, 1692*

In 1692 Mary, a Negro slave, was owned by Lieutenant Nathaniel Putnam, but was working in the home of his son, John Putnam, Jr.

On April 21, 1692 the conspiracy filed a complaint [No. 21] against Mary Black. At her April 22 examination in Salem Village, Mary denied the charges and confessed nothing. She was required to "take out a pin and pin it again." Three of the afflicted girls declared they had been pricked, one in the foot, one in the stomach, and one in the arm "till the blood came." She was imprisoned at Salem.

On January 19, 1693 at the Superior Court of Judicature at Salem, Mary Black was "cleared by proclamation."

THE PROCTORS

The Proctors were a successful family who challenged the Putnams, Jonathan Walcott, and Nathaniel Ingersoll in every sphere of Salem Village politics. John Proctor's tavern was in direct competition with Ingersoll's. On the basis of complaints filed by the conspiracy, nine members of the Proctor family and related Bassett and Hood families were imprisoned between April 4 and May 28, 1692. Of these nine, John Proctor was hanged, and Elizabeth, his wife, was sentenced to death. On September 5, 1692 Jane Lilly, another member of this extended family was imprisoned. The following chart illustrates this extended family and the members imprisoned.

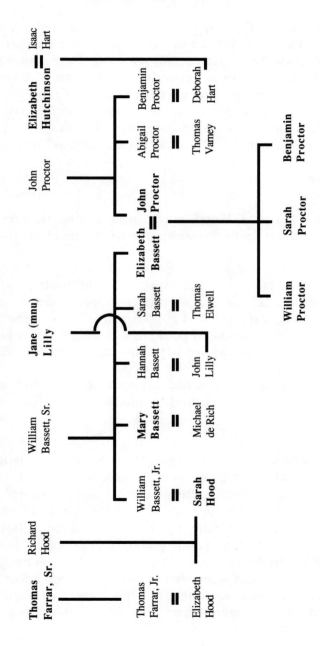

Elizabeth (Bassett) Proctor[217]
Salem   *April 4, 1692*

John Proctor
Salem   *April 11, 1692*

Sarah Proctor
Salem   *May 21, 1692*

Benjamin Proctor
Salem   *May 23, 1692*

William Proctor
Salem   *May 28, 1692*

John Proctor was born about 1632 in England, son of Martha (Harper) and John Proctor. The family emigrated to New England and settled in Ipswich. Since we do not refer to the father again by name, we will always designate the son as John Proctor. John Proctor about 1655 married Martha (mnu). Their son Benjamin Proctor, born in 1659 in Ipswich, was the only surviving child of this marriage.

After Martha's death John Proctor married, in 1662, Elizabeth Thorndike, daughter of John Thorndike, an original founder of Ipswich. In 1666 John Proctor leased the seven-hundred-acre estate "Groton," which lay in Salem Farms, the section of Salem township just south of Salem Village. In 1672 he inherited one-third of his father's estate in Ipswich. His brothers, Benjamin Proctor and Joseph Proctor, also inherited one-third shares.[218] Their sister, Abigail, was married to Thomas Varney of Ipswich.[219] John Proctor's second wife,

---

217 Otten, *Wardwell*, 1.74-1.75.

218 The brother Benjamin Proctor was married to Deborah, the daughter of Elizabeth (Hutchinson) Hart, against whom the conspiracy filed a complaint [No. 17] on May 14, 1692.

219 Thomas Varney's sister was the widow Rachel (Varney) Vinson of Gloucester, who was accused of witchcraft in September 1692.

Elizabeth, died in 1672, shortly after the birth of her seventh child, not counting two who had died in infancy.[220]

In 1674, John Proctor married his third wife, Elizabeth Bassett. At the time of the marriage there were already six children in the Proctor household from John's two previous marriages. He was some twenty years older than his new wife. She was born about 1651, the daughter of Elizabeth (mnu) and William Bassett of Lynn. John Proctor and Elizabeth (Bassett) Proctor had five children of their own. One was son William Proctor born in 1675; another was daughter Sarah Proctor born in 1677.

Elizabeth (Bassett) Proctor's grandmother was Ann (Holland) Bassett Burt. Because Ann Burt, a midwife, had acquired a local reputation for ministering to the sick, she had been presented on charges of witchcraft in 1669. "Widow Burt practiced healing. Like certain other women who had this skill, she was vulnerable to accusations of witchcraft from disappointed patients or suspicious neighbors. One of the witnesses against her, Phillip Read, practiced medicine himself and was known as a doctor. Ann Burt died in 1673."[221] Another testifying in the Burt case was Bethia (Pearson) Carter, who was accused in 1692, as was her daughter Bethia Carter, Jr. A "taint" within a family consistently provided an excuse for charges of witchcraft in 1692.

In 1692 John Proctor, about sixty, was a licensed tavern keeper in Salem Farms. Living with him was his wife Elizabeth, about forty-one, and many children. These included their own children William Proctor, seventeen, and Sarah Proctor, fifteen, and John Proctor's eldest son, Benjamin Proctor, who was thirty-three and a bachelor.

John Proctor had received his first license to operate a tavern in 1668, and the regular renewal of Proctor's license was a gauge

---

220 John and Elizabeth's eldest child was Elizabeth Proctor, who in 1681 married Thomas Very. His sister Elizabeth Very was the second wife of John Nurse, eldest son of Rebecca Nurse. This relationship connects the Nurse and Proctor families, both sufferers in the witchcraft delusion.

221 Hall, *Witch-Hunting*, 185.

of his status. Tavern-keeping was a lucrative business and only a select few were granted licenses. His inn was located on the Ipswich Road in Salem, about a mile south of the Salem Village line. His wife and some of the older children operated the business, while he and his eldest son, Benjamin Proctor, managed the extensive Proctor properties. A servant in the Proctor home, Mary Warren, became one of the afflicted.

On March 25, 1692 Samuel Sibley encountered John Proctor.[222] It was the day after the examination of Rebecca Nurse. Proctor said, "I am going to fetch home my jade [referring to his servant girl Mary Warren]. I left her there [in Salem Village] last night." When Sibley asked why he talked so, Proctor replied, "If they were let alone so, we should all be Devils and witches quickly. They should rather be had to the whipping post. But I will fetch home my jade and thrash the Devil out of her." According to Sibley, Proctor continued in the same vein, crying, "Hang them! Hang them [referring to the afflicted girls]!" Proctor also added, "When Mary was first taken with fits, I kept her close to the [spinning] wheel and threatened to thrash her, and then she had no more fits till the next day [when] I was gone forth. Then she must have her fits again, forsooth."

On March 29, 1692 Samuel Barton, twenty-eight, was at the house of Thomas Putnam to help the afflicted girls, and heard the adults talking. "I heard them tell Mercy Lewis that she cried out on Goody Proctor. Mercy Lewis said that she did not cry out on Goody Proctor. Thomas Putnam and his wife and others said that she cried out on Goody Proctor." John Houghton, twenty-three, testified, "I was present at the same time, and I heard Thomas Putnam, and his wife, say that Mercy Lewis saw or named Elizabeth Proctor in her fit, and we heard Mercy Lewis affirm

---

222 Samuel Sibley, age about thirty-four, was the husband of Mary Sibley, age thirty-two. She was the one who had instructed John Indian on how to make the witch cake and who confessed her error to the Rev. Parris on the same day, March 25, 1692. Samuel Sibley's sister, Mary (Sibley) Walcott, who had died in 1683, was the mother of afflicted girl Mary Walcott.

that she never said that ever she saw her." Three months later Mercy Lewis gave this sworn testimony. "On March 26, 1692, I saw the apparition of Elizabeth Proctor and she did most grievously torture me. Mercy Lewis owned this her testimony to be the truth on her oath before the Jury of Inquest, this 30 of June 1692." Mercy Lewis' memory improved with time.

On April 4, 1692 the conspiracy filed a complaint [No. 6] against Sarah Cloyce and Elizabeth Proctor. On the same day, the afflicted girl Abigail Williams cried out upon John Proctor, but no formal document was filed. On April 6 Abigail Williams again cried out upon John Proctor, but no formal complaint was filed this time, either. On April 11 Elizabeth Proctor and Sarah Cloyce were arrested. They were examined in Salem before a panel of distinguished judges. Sarah Cloyce was examined first, and then Elizabeth Proctor. Elizabeth refused to confess. In answer to an afflicted girl, she replied, "There is another judgment, dear child." Both accused women were committed to prison.

During the examination of Elizabeth Proctor "John Proctor, being then personally present, was charged by Abigail Williams and Ann Putnam, Jr., with several acts of witchcraft by him committed on the person of Mrs. Bathsheba Pope, the wife of Mr. Joseph Pope, and others. Likewise Mercy Lewis and Mary Walcott charged said Proctor." Benjamin Gould then testified against John Proctor. John Proctor was arrested on the spot and was imprisoned with his wife.

In May 1692 a petition of twenty men and women of Ipswich testified to the Christian life led by Elizabeth and John Proctor, who "were ever ready to help such as stood in need of their help." In April a petition of thirty-one men of Ipswich testified as to the fine characters of John and Elizabeth Proctor.

On May 20, 1692 Elizabeth Booth, an afflicted girl, testified against John and Elizabeth Proctor, and their daughter Sarah Proctor. On May 21 the conspiracy filed a complaint [No. 20] against Sarah Proctor, her aunt Sarah (Hood) Bassett,[223] and

---

223 Sarah (Hood) Bassett was the wife of William Bassett, Elizabeth (Bassett) Proctor's brother.

Susannah Roots. On May 23 the three were examined and imprisoned.

On May 23, 1692 the conspiracy filed a complaint [No. 21] against Benjamin Proctor, his step-aunt Mary (Bassett) De Rich, and Sarah (mnu) Pease.[224] They were arrested and imprisoned that day. On May 28 the conspiracy filed a complaint [No. 23] against William Proctor and nine others. On May 31 he was arrested and taken to Lieutenant Nathaniel Ingersoll's house in Salem Village for examination He was physically tortured to make him confess.

On June 2, 1692 Elizabeth Proctor underwent physical examinations, one in the morning and one in the afternoon. In the grand jury inquest on June 30, several afflicted girls testified against Elizabeth Proctor and her husband, John. Stephen Bittford, about twenty-three, accused Elizabeth Proctor of afflicting him at the beginning of April. The veracity of the afflicted girls was questioned by several present. Daniel Elliott testified, "I being at the house of Lieut. Ingersoll on the 28 of March in the year 1692, there being present one of the afflicted persons who cried out and said there's Goody Proctor. William Rayment, Jr., being there present told the girl he believed she lied for he saw nothing. Then Goody Ingersoll told the girl she told a lie for there was nothing. Then the girl said that she did it for sport; they must have some sport."

On June 30, 1692 Elizabeth Booth (an afflicted girl in the outer circle) testified that the Proctors had killed Robert Stone, Sr., Robert Stone, Jr., and "father-in-law Shafling" on June 8. Statements of other afflicted girls were attested by the Rev. Samuel Parris, Nathaniel Ingersoll, Thomas Putnam, and John Putnam, Jr. Joseph Pope testified that on April 11 he had heard John Proctor say, "If Mr. Parris would let me have his Indian (i.e. John Indian), I would soon drive the Devil out of him."

On July 23, 1692 John Proctor sent the following petition from Salem prison to the distinguished ministers the Revs.

---

224 The accused Benjamin Proctor was John Proctor's son, not his brother. Mary (Bassett) De Rich was Elizabeth (Bassett) Proctor's sister

Increase Mather, James Allen, Joshua Moody, Samuel Willard, and John Baily. "The innocence of our case with the enmity of our accusers and our judges, and jury, whom nothing but our innocent blood will serve their turn, having condemned us already before our trials, being so much incensed and engaged against by the Devil, makes us bold to beg and implore your favorable assistance of this our humble petition to his Excellency. That if it be possible our innocent blood may be spared, which undoubtedly otherwise will be shed, if the Lord does not mercifully step in."

The petition continues, "Here are five persons who have lately confessed themselves to be witches, and do accuse some of us, of being along with them at a sacrament, since we were committed into close prison, which we know to be lies. Two of the five are young men [Martha Carrier's two sons] who would not confess anything till they tied them neck and heels, till the blood was ready to come out of their noses, and this was the occasion of making them confess. My son William Proctor, when he was examined, because he would not confess that he was guilty, when he was innocent, they tied him neck and heels till the blood gushed out at his nose, and would have kept him so 24 hours, if one more merciful than the rest, had not taken pity on him, and caused him to be unbound. These actions are very like the Popish cruelties."

The petition concludes, "They have already undone us in our estates, and that will not serve their turns without our innocent bloods. If it cannot be granted that we can have our trials at Boston, we humbly beg that you would endeavor to have these magistrates changed, and others in their rooms; begging also and beseeching you would be pleased to be here, if not all, some of you, at our trials, hoping thereby you may be the means of saving the shedding our innocent bloods."

On August 5, 1692 the Court of Oyer and Terminer condemned John Proctor and his wife, Elizabeth (Bassett) Proctor, to death. She was temporarily reprieved until after the birth of her child. On August 19 John Proctor was hanged at Salem.

On September 8, 1692 at the grand jury inquest, Elizabeth Hubbard testified against William Proctor, "He did afflict me on May 31 at the time of his examination and also Mary Warren." In the examination of William Proctor on September 17, 1692, all of the afflicted girls accused him, as did Mary Pickworth.

On January 7, 1693 at the Superior Court of Judicature at Salem, the grand jury dismissed the case of William Proctor. Chief Justice Stoughton signed death warrants for the speedy execution of the three convicted by the Superior Court in January, and also for the prisoners who had been convicted at the former Court of Oyer and Terminer but not yet executed. One of these formerly convicted prisoners was Elizabeth Proctor; according to Stoughton's warrant she was to be executed right after childbirth, which was imminent. On January 27, 1693 Elizabeth's child, Abigail Proctor, was born. Elizabeth was saved when Governor Sir William Phipps dispatched a reprieve to Salem for all the executions. Finally, in May 1693 Elizabeth was freed in the general release of all remaining witchcraft prisoners upon payment of prison fees.

In 1694 in Lynn, Benjamin Proctor married widow Mary (Buckley) Whittredge, who had been imprisoned for witchcraft in 1692. About 1696 Sarah Proctor married a man named Munion.

In 1696 widow Elizabeth Proctor wrote, "In 1692, my husband and myself were so far proceeded against that we were condemned. But in that sad time of darkness before my said husband was executed, it is evident somebody had contrived a will and brought it to him to sign, wherein his whole estate is disposed of, not having regard to a contract in writing made with me before marriage with him. Since my husband's death, the said will is proved and approved by the Judge of Probate and by that kind of disposal the whole estate is disposed of, and those that claim my husband's estate will not suffer me to have one penny of the estate, neither upon the account of my husband's contract with me before marriage, nor yet upon the account of the dower which, as I humbly conceive, does belong or ought to belong to me by law, for they say that I am dead in the law." In the same year, 1696, Elizabeth married Daniel Richards.

In 1712 Benjamin Proctor wrote, "I was imprisoned for several months in the time they called witchcraft, and was by that a great sufferer. I was the eldest son of my father and worked hard with my father till I was about thirty years of age, and helped bring up all my father's children, by all his wives, one after another. After my father's death I was at great cost and trouble in the disposition of my father's affairs as to the relieving of his family, some of them helpless, with answering debts, charges, legacies, etc."

Elizabeth (Hutchinson) Hart

Reading   *May 14, 1692*

Elizabeth Hutchinson was born about 1628 in England, daughter of Ann (Browne) and Thomas Hutchinson.[225] Elizabeth Hutchinson married, about 1650, Isaac Hart of Reading. They had six children, including Deborah, who in 1673 married Benjamin Proctor of Salem, the brother of John Proctor.

In 1692 Elizabeth Hart was in her mid-sixties. She and her husband lived in Reading. Her brother Captain Francis Hutchinson in Reading, and her half-brother John Hawkes in Lynn, were both men of influence.

On May 14, 1692 the conspiracy filed a complaint [No. 17] against Elizabeth Hart and seven others. On May 15 she was arrested, examined, and imprisoned. A major reason for her accusation was her connection to the Proctor family through her daughter Deborah.

On October 19, 1692 Elizabeth's son, Thomas Hart, presented a petition to the General Court at Boston for the release of his

---

225 After the death of Thomas Hutchinson, his widow Ann married, about 1630, Adam Hawkes of Lynn. After Ann's death, Adam, age sixty-five, married, in 1670, Sarah Hooper, age nineteen. After Adam's death in 1672, Sarah married Samuel Wardwell. On September 1, 1692, Sarah (Hooper) Hawkes Wardwell, age forty-one, her daughter by Adam, Sarah Hawkes, age twenty-one, and her daughter by Samuel, Mercy Wardwell, age nineteen, were imprisoned for witchcraft.

mother on bail. It stated, "Mother was taken into custody in the latter end of May last, and ever since committed a prisoner in Boston jail. She being ancient and not able to undergo the hardship that is inflicted from lying in misery, and death rather to be chosen than a life in her circumstances, my father being ancient and decrepit was wholly unable to attend in this matter." It is not known whether the petition was granted.

In the Superior Court of Judicature at Salem, January 1693, the grand jury dismissed the case of Elizabeth Hart.

In 1710 Isaac Hart died, and later the same year Elizabeth Hart died, both at Reading.

Thomas Farrar, Sr.
Lynn   *May 14, 1692*

Thomas Farrar was born about 1617 in England. He married Elizabeth (mnu), who died 1680 in Lynn. Thomas was an early settler of Lynn. Their children included his only son, Thomas Farrar, Jr. As a widower he married, in 1682, Elizabeth Hood, daughter of Richard Hood of Lynn.

In 1692 Thomas was in his mid-seventies, living in Lynn. His son, Thomas, Jr., was a selectman of Lynn, and in the May election of 1692, was chosen one of the town's representatives to the General Court.

On May 14, 1692 the conspiracy filed a complaint [No. 17] against Thomas Farrar, Sr. and seven others. He was arrested, examined at Lieutenant Nathaniel Ingersoll's tavern, and then imprisoned. A major reason for his accusation was his connection to the Proctor family through his daughter-in-law Elizabeth (Hood) Farrar. Her sister Sarah was married to William Bassett, Jr., the brother of Elizabeth (Bassett) Proctor.

Ann Putnam, Jr. testified, "On the 8th of May 1692, there appeared to me the apparition of an old gray-headed man with a great nose, which tortured me." Mercy Lewis testified that "old Farrar of Lynn" urged her to set her hand to the book.

In January 1693 the Grand Jury for the Superior Court of Judicature at Salem dismissed the case of Thomas Farrar, Sr. In 1694 he died at Lynn.

Sarah (Hood) Bassett
Lynn   *May 21, 1692*

Sarah Hood was born 1657 in Lynn, daughter of Mary (Newhall) and Richard Hood of Lynn. She married William Bassett, Jr.,[226] also of Lynn, whose grandmother Ann (Holland) Bassett Burt had been presented for trial on charges of witchcraft in 1670.

In 1692 Sarah, thirty-five, resided in Lynn with her husband and six children. On May 21, 1692 the conspiracy filed a complaint [No. 20] against Sarah Bassett, along with her niece Sarah Proctor and one other. On May 23 the three were examined and imprisoned.

On January 3, 1693 the grand jury at the Superior Court of Judicature at Salem dismissed the charge against Sarah Bassett.

Mary (Bassett) De Rich
Salem Village   *May 23, 1692*

Mary Bassett was born 1657 in Lynn, daughter of William Bassett of Lynn. She married, about 1676, Michael De Rich of Salem Farms, a husbandman.[227] Their eldest child, John De Rich, was born about 1677.

In 1692 Mary, thirty-five, lived in Salem Farms with her husband and children. On May 23, 1692 Elizabeth Booth, an afflicted girl in the outer circle, testified, "Sarah Proctor and Mary De Rich appeared to this deponent in the night and called her jade, and afflicted and pinched this deponent most grievously." On the same day, the conspiracy filed a complaint [No. 21] against Mary De Rich, along with her step-nephew

---

226 William Bassett, Jr. was the brother of Sarah (Bassett) Proctor.
227 The specific kinship between Michael De Rich and the first husband of Martha (mnu) Rich Corey is not known.

Benjamin Proctor and one other. The three were arrested, examined, and imprisoned. A major reason for the accusation of Mary De Rich was her connection to the Proctor family through her sister Elizabeth (Bassett) Proctor.

Mary's son John De Rich, then about sixteen, was intimidated but was never a member of the afflicted group of Salem Village. He may have been imprisoned after his mother. He was used to testify against various people including his kinsmen. At the Court of Oyer and Terminer on August 3 and 4, 1692 John De Rich testified against George Jacobs, Sr.; Giles Corey and his wife, Martha (Rich) Corey; John Proctor and his wife, Elizabeth (Bassett) Proctor; Philip English and his wife, Mary English; Sarah Pease; Deliverance Hobbs; Abigail Hobbs; and "a woman who lives at Boston at the upper end of the town whose name is Mary. She goes in black clothes, has but one eye, with a crooked neck, and she saith there is none in Boston like her." He also testified against Sarah Proctor. On September 7, 1692, John De Rich testified again against Giles Corey and Sarah Pease, and against Margaret Jacobs.

There is no record of Mary De Rich's trial at the Superior Court of Judicature at Salem in January 1693. In 1712 she wrote, "Mary Rich of Lynn, widow, in the year 1692 was imprisoned and lost her bed and pot and other household stuff in about half year."

THE TOPSFIELD MEN

Animosities ran high from a long and violent land controversy. "The passions awakened by the angry contest between the Village and 'Topsfield men,' and which the collisions of a half-century had all along exasperated and hardened, may have been concentrated against the Nurses. Isaac Easty, whose wife was a sister of Rebecca Nurse, and the Townes who were her brothers, were the leaders of the Topsfield men. So far as the family sided with Topsfield in that controversy, it naturally exposed them to the ill-will of the people of the Village. An analysis will show to what extent hostile motives were supplied from this quarter. The families of Wildes, Howe, Hobbs, Towne,

Easty, and others who were cried out upon by the afflicted children, occupied lands claimed by parties adverse to the Village."[228]

Abigail Hobbs
Topsfield   *April 18, 1692*

William Hobbs
Topsfield   *April 21, 1692*

Deliverance (mnu) Hobbs
Topsfield   *April 21, 1692*

William Hobbs was one of the earliest settlers of Topsfield. As a Topsfield Man, he and his family were natural targets for the Salem Village accusers. In 1692 he was about fifty and his wife, Deliverance Hobbs, was in her mid-forties. Their children included Abigail Hobbs, born about 1670 in Topsfield. Abigail, about twenty-two, was living with her parents in Topsfield, although some years earlier she had lived in Casco, Maine as a servant. In testimony against her, Abigail was described as one who liked to lie out at nights in the woods alone, who had a "wicked carriage" and was disobedient to her parents, and was blasphemous.

On April 18, 1692 the conspiracy filed a complaint [No. 8] against Abigail. On April 19 she was arrested and taken to Lieutenant Nathaniel Ingersoll's inn in Salem Village for examination.[229] Abigail was eager and cooperative, and made a confession. She named Sarah Wildes of Topsfield and the imprisoned Sarah Good as witches. Abigail was herself imprisoned at Salem. On April 20 she was examined in prison. She named as witches Judith White, who was "a Jersey maid that lived at Casco, but now lives at Boston," as well as the imprisoned Sarah Good and Sarah Osborne. On April 21, 1692 the conspiracy filed a complaint [No. 9] against William Hobbs, his wife

---

228 Upham, 2:56.
229 *SWP*, 239-240.

Deliverance Hobbs, and seven others, including Sarah Wildes. On April 22 Ephraim Wildes, constable of Topsfield and the son of Sarah Wildes, following orders, arrested William Hobbs and his wife, Deliverance, and took them to Salem Village.

At her examination in Salem Village, Deliverance was at first reluctant to confess, but eventually did so. In her confession she named Sarah Wildes as a witch. William's examination was held after his wife's, and he refused to confess. "I can deny it to my dying day." When questioned as to why he had not attended religious services, he said, "Because I was not well. I had a distemper that none knows." He would not say that his wife and daughter were witches. Husband and wife were imprisoned at Salem.

On May 3, 1692 Abigail's mother was examined in prison, with Abigail present. Deliverance named the Rev. George Burroughs and others already in prison. Abigail named Giles Corey and "the Gentlewoman of Boston," who was possibly Mrs. Thatcher. At a second examination in Salem prison, at which her daughter was again present, Deliverance Hobbs named the same ones as before. The examinations of May 3 were arranged to implicate the Rev. Burroughs, who was still en route to Salem for his preliminary examination. On May 12 Abigail also named the Rev. George Burroughs.

On June 1, 1692 in court, Deliverance Hobbs and her daughter testified against the Rev. Burroughs. On June 1 in court, Abigail testified against Bridget Bishop, the Rev. George Burroughs, Sarah Good, Giles Corey, and the now dead Sarah Osborne. Abigail and her mother were used frequently by the accusers to supplement the afflicted group. In court on June 2 Ann Putnam, Sr. testified that William Hobbs had helped John Willard kill eight persons by witchcraft. On the following day, Susannah Sheldon gave similar testimony. On June 29 in court, Abigail testified against John Proctor. On July 4 Abigail and her mother were used as part of the afflicted group at the examination of Candy. Unlike the afflicted girls, Deliverance Hobbs and her daughter Abigail were always returned to prison as witches.

On September 9, 1692 Abigail signed and reaffirmed her confession of April 19. On September 10 she was indicted for afflicting Mercy Lewis and also for making a covenant with the Evil Spirit, the Devil, "in the year of our Lord 1688, in Casco Bay in the Province of Maine in New England."

On September 17, 1692 the Court of Oyer and Terminer condemned Abigail Hobbs to death. She was one of the four women condemned on that day who had confessed.[230] These four confessors were given temporary reprieves from death, and held in prison. On December 17, 1692 John Nichols and Joseph Towne (the brother of the three sisters, Rebecca Nurse, Mary Easty, and Sarah Cloyce) posted a recognizance bond of twelve hundred pounds sterling for William Hobbs' release on bail.

William Hobbs was in Salem prison during three weeks in January 1693, but there is no record of a trial for either him or his wife, Deliverance, at the January session of the Superior Court in Salem. At the end of the session Chief Justice Stoughton signed death warrants for the speedy execution of the three convicted at that session, and also for the others in prison who had been convicted at the former Court of Oyer and Terminer, but had not been executed. One was Abigail Hobbs. However, within a few days Governor Sir William Phipps reprieved the convicted. On about April 17, 1693 Deliverance Hobbs and her daughter Abigail were released from Salem prison, according to the account of William Dounton, the jail keeper.[231]

Sarah (Averill) Wildes
Topsfield   *April 21, 1692*

Sarah Averill was born about 1627 in England, daughter of Abigail (Hynton) and William Averill, later of Ipswich. In 1649,

---

230 The other three condemned on September 17, 1692 who confessed were Rebecca Eames, Ann Foster, and Mary Lacey, Sr. On the same day five others were condemned: four were women who had not confessed, and the fifth was Samuel Wardwell, who had retracted his confession.

231 *SWP*, 91-92, 172, 179, 239-240, 423, 429, 838-839, 958.

when Sarah was about twenty-two, she was brought before the Ipswich Quarterly Court on the charge, "Sarah Averill of Ipswich to be whipped for fornication. Thomas Wordell named Party." She was presented in court for the minor offense of wearing a silk scarf in May 1663.[232]

In November 1663, Sarah Averill married widower John Wildes of Topsfield. By his first wife, Priscilla Gould (who died in 1663), he had five daughters, including Sarah Wildes who married Edward Bishop, Jr. of Salem Village, and Phoebe Wildes who married Timothy Day of Gloucester.[233]

After the marriage of John Wildes to Sarah, his former wife's siblings, John Gould and Mary (Gould) Reddington, started to slander Sarah which led to witchcraft allegations by 1676.[234]

John Wildes was an early settler of Topsfield. He owned extensive land, and had held many town offices as well as being active in church affairs. In 1659 and again in 1686, John was on the committee to run the controversial boundary line between Salem and Topsfield. His family became a target for the Salem Village accusers.

In 1692 Sarah, about sixty-five, lived with her husband, a carpenter in Topsfield. Their son, Ephraim Wildes, was serving as constable there. Sarah was a member of the Topsfield church.

On April 21, 1692 the conspiracy filed a complaint [No. 9] against Sarah Wildes, her stepdaughter Sarah Bishop, her step son-in-law Edward Bishop, Jr., and six others, including William Hobbs and his wife, Deliverance. On April 22 George Herrick, marshal of Essex County, ordered Sarah's son, constable

---

232 Otten, *Witch Hunt*, 269.

233 Priscilla (Gould) Wildes' aunt was Priscilla (Gould) Putnam, the mother of patriarch Thomas Putnam, Nathaniel Putnam, and John Putnam, Sr.

234 Priscilla (Gould) Wildes had siblings Phoebe, Mary, and John. Phoebe Gould married Deacon Thomas Perkins, and their daughter Phoebe Perkins married Joseph Towne, the brother of Rebecca (Towne) Nurse. Mary Gould married John Reddington, and her aunt by marriage, Margaret Reddington, testified against Mary (Towne) Easty in the September 1692 trial. (McMillen, 29, 89-92.)

Ephraim Wildes, to arrest William and Deliverance Hobbs and all the others of Topsfield accused on the same complaint, except his mother. Herrick himself arrested her. At her examination in Salem Village, Sarah Wildes refused to confess and she was conveyed to Salem prison by marshal George Herrick.

On June 30, 1692, at the grand jury inquest, testimony concerning gossip spread by Mary (Gould) Reddington was given by Elizabeth Symonds, about fifty, John Gould, about fifty-six, and Zacheus Perkins. John and Joseph Andrew, brothers of Boxford, testified about their mishaps at haying one day in 1674 for which "they still do think that Goody Wildes who now stands charged with high suspicion of several acts of witchcraft had a hand." They said that "we could no ways bind our load with our cart rope, but it would hang loose on our load."

In an undated document John Wildes "testifies that he did hear that Mary, the wife of John Reddington, did raise a report that my wife had bewitched her and I went to the said John Reddington & told him I would arrest him for his wife's defaming of my wife. But the said Reddington desired me not to do it, for it would but waste his estate & that his wife would a done with it in time. And that he knew nothing she had against my wife."

In an undated document constable Ephraim Wildes informed the court, "I have had serious thoughts many times since, whether my seizing of Deliverance Hobbs thus caused her to accuse my mother, thereby in some measure to be revenged of me. The woman did show a very hard spirit when I seized her. Almost I could see revenge in her face she looked so molishly on me. As for my mother, I never saw any harm by her upon any in word nor action. She has always instructed me in the Christian religion and the ways of God ever since I was able to take instructions."

On July 2, 1692 the Rev. John Hale of Beverly testified to incidents of fifteen or sixteen years ago when "Goody Reddington" stated she was bewitched by Sarah (Averill) Wildes. Mary Reddington also said that Sarah Wildes had bewitched her two step-sons, i.e., John Wildes, Jr., died 1677, and Jonathan Wildes, died 1676, both nephews of Reddington.

On July 12, 1692 the Court of Oyer and Terminer condemned Sarah Wildes to death, and Chief Justice William Stoughton signed her death warrant. On July 19, 1692 she was hanged at Salem. In August Edward Bishop, Jr. and his wife, Sarah (Wildes) Bishop, escaped from the Boston prison and went into hiding. In September Phoebe (Wildes) Day of Gloucester was accused and imprisoned.

In 1694 widower John Wildes married Mary Jacobs, widow of George Jacobs, Sr., of Salem, who was hanged August 19, 1692. In 1705 John Wildes died at Topsfield, nearly one hundred. In 1710 his son Ephraim Wildes gave the account, "My mother was carried to Salem prison some time in April. We were at the cost of it there a considerable while. And afterwards she was removed to Boston prison for about two months. And then from Boston she was removed back to Ipswich prison. And after a while she was removed to Salem. And [at all places] we were at all the cost both of caring and providing for her maintenance. Either father or myself went once a week to see how she did, and some times twice a week, which was a great cost and damage in our estate."[235]

Edward Bishop, Jr.
Salem Village   *April 21, 1692*

Sarah (Wildes) Bishop
Salem Village   *April 21, 1692*

Edward Bishop, Jr. was born 1648 in Salem, son of Hannah (mnu) and Edward Bishop, an early settler of Beverly and a founding member of its church. Edward Bishop, Jr. married, about 1672, Sarah Wildes, born about 1651, daughter of Priscilla (Gould) and John Wildes of Topsfield. After Priscilla's death, John Wildes married Sarah Averill in 1663.

Sarah (Wildes) Bishop and Edward Bishop, Jr. had twelve children, five of whom were baptized by the Rev. John Hale of the Beverly church. Edward ran an unlicensed inn and was accused of selling strong beer, cider, and rum illegally. In July and

---

235 *SWP*, 337, 429, 1007.

November of 1685, he was presented at the Salem Quarterly Court for "selling drink contrary to law and for his children and servants profaning the Sabbath and abusing swine."

In 1692 Edward, forty-four, and Sarah, about forty-one, resided in Salem Village near the Beverly line. The Bishop's place was on the Ipswich Road, which was the major northward route from Boston. The Ipswich Road crossed three rivers which flowed into Salem Harbor; at these points there were wharves for shipping goods to and from Salem. The Salem Village people who lived along Ipswich Road generally allied themselves with Salem Town and were members of the anti-Parris group. Exceptions were Christian and John Trask, nearby neighbors of the Bishops. The Trasks were related to the Putnam family.

On April 21, 1692 the conspiracy filed a complaint [No. 9] against Edward Bishop, Jr.; his wife, Sarah Bishop; his wife's step-mother, Sarah (Averill) Wildes; and six others. After examination they were all imprisoned at Salem.

On May 20, 1692 the Rev. John Hale gave a deposition against "Goody Bishop" (Sarah (Wildes) Bishop). Hale's statement related in part to the problems with the Bishops' neighbors, Christian and John Trask. However this deposition was mistakenly placed with the records of Bridget Bishop of Salem. This was the reason that two of the afflicted girls, Susannah Sheldon and Sarah Churchill, applied Hale's charges erroneously to Bridget Bishop.[236]

On about June 1, 1692 Sarah Bishop and her husband, Edward Bishop, Jr., along with Mary (Towne) Easty, testified in prison against Mary Warren, an afflicted girl also imprisoned. On July 19, 1692 Sarah Bishop's step-mother, Sarah (Averill) Wildes, was hanged at Salem.

In August 1692, Edward Bishop, Jr. and his wife Sarah Bishop escaped from prison and fled to New York, where they remained until the following spring. In September 1692 Sarah Bishop's sister, Phoebe (Wildes) Day of Gloucester, was accused and imprisoned.

---

236 Greene, "Salem Witches I," 1157.

In 1710 Edward Bishop, Jr., now living in Rehoboth, Massachusetts, wrote "in my absence the Sheriff went to my house and took away so much of my household goods as afterwards I paid ten pounds for to have it again: six cows, swine, six and forty sheep."[237]

In his contemporary account Calef wrote, "October 7. Edward Bishop, [Jr.] and his wife having made their escape out of prison, this day Mr. Corwin, the sheriff, came and seized his goods and chattels, and had it not been for his second son (who borrowed ten pound and gave it him) they had been wholly lost."

Phoebe (Wildes) Day
Gloucester   *late September 1692*

Phoebe Wildes was born about 1653, daughter of Priscilla (Gould) and John Wildes of Topsfield. After her mother's death her father married, in 1663, Sarah Averill. Phoebe grew up in Topsfield, where her father and her uncle John Gould "one of the greatest land holders in the Topsfield area," were among the group of Topsfield men disliked by the Salem Village accusers. In 1679, Phoebe Wildes married Timothy Day in Gloucester.

In 1692 Phoebe, then about thirty-nine, resided with her husband and their six children in Gloucester, on their homestead on the westerly side of the Annisquam River. On April 21, 1692 her sister, Sarah (Wildes) Bishop; her brother-in-law, Edward Bishop, Jr.; and her step-mother, Sarah (Averill) Wildes, were accused [Complaint No. 9] and the next day they were imprisoned. On July 19 her step-mother was hanged at Salem.

In late September or early October 1692, Phoebe (Wildes) Day was accused, arrested, examined, and imprisoned at Ipswich. In mid-December Phoebe was one of the ten prisoners who signed a petition from that prison.[238] There is no extant record of Phoebe Day at the sessions of the Superior Court of Judicature at Salem in January, nor at Ipswich in May.

---

237 *SWP*, 429, 979.
238 *SWP*, 880-881.

Nehemiah Abbot, Jr.

Topsfield   *April 21, 1692*

Nehemiah Abbot, Jr. was born about 1665 in Topsfield, and grew up to be the only living child of Mary (Howe) and Nehemiah Abbot, Sr. of Topsfield. In 1690 he married Remember Fiske, Jr., daughter of Remember and John Fiske. (In 1689, the Widow Remember Fiske, Sr. had married William Goodhue. She was his third wife. In 1666 his only son, William Goodhue, Jr., had married Hannah Dane, daughter of the Rev. Francis Dane of Andover. The Rev. Dane was an uncle of Nehemiah Abbot, Sr. The Dane family saw more of its members imprisoned for witchcraft in 1692 than did any other family.)

In 1692 Nehemiah Abbot, Jr., a weaver, was in his late twenties, and resided in Topsfield with his wife, Remember. On April 21, 1692 the conspiracy filed a complaint [No. 9] against him and eight others. On April 22 he was arrested and taken to Salem Village for examination. After Nehemiah's first interrogation, at which he refused to confess, he was sent out until several others had been examined. When he was brought in again, there were many spectators present. Some blocked the windows and the accusers did not have a clear view of him. He was ordered outside so that the accusers could see him in the light. The afflicted did not recognize him to be the same person as the apparition or specter which they had seen. He was a rough faced man and his features were shaded by his own hair. Because the afflicted girls could not identify him, Nehemiah was released. He was the only person known to have been released after examination. Hathorne later used the release of Nehemiah in the Willard case to illustrate the supposed fairness of the investigations.[239]

---

239 *SWP*, 824.

Arthur Abbot
Topsfield   *May 28, 1692*

Arthur Abbot was born about 1639 in Salem or Ipswich, son of Arthur Abbot of Marblehead.[240] The father was originally of Totness near Ivy Bridge, Devonshire, England, and was an early settler of Salem, Massachusetts, but then moved on to Ipswich, and finally settled at Marblehead, where he died between 1671 and 1679. The son Arthur Abbot married, in 1669 in Ipswich, Elizabeth White (c. 1648-1738).

In 1692 Arthur, a farmer, was about fifty-three, and lived "between Ipswich, Topsfield, and Wenham," close to Major Samuel Appleton's farms. In 1675 his wife Elizabeth had been "presented to the court for excess in apparel," and had been fined for "wearing silk." However, the accusation against Arthur in 1692 resulted from his association with the Topsfield Men.

On May 28, 1692 the conspiracy filed a complaint [No. 23] against Arthur Abbot and ten others. On May 31 he was arrested and imprisoned in Ipswich.

On October 15, 1692, "finding himself very weak and ill," Arthur sent for Daniel Epps and Captain Thomas Wade, justices of the peace at Ipswich, "in order to the making of his will, leaving something that might be to the view of the world." He refers to "the evidence that he had given in the honored Court of Oyer and Terminer held at Salem a little before." Arthur was perhaps one of the "three or four men" prisoners referred to in the petition of ten women prisoners at Ipswich prison.[241]

Elizabeth (Jackson) Howe
Topsfield   *May 28, 1692*

Elizabeth Jackson was born about 1637 in England, the daughter of Joanne and William Jackson, an original settler of Rowley. In 1658 in Rowley, she married James Howe, Jr., born

---

240 There was no known kinship of Arthur Abbot with the Abbots of Rowley and Andover, nor the other Abbot family in Topsfield.
241 *Essex Antiquarian*, Sept. 1897. *SWP*, 665-666, 880-881.

about 1633, the son of Elizabeth (Dane) and James Howe who lived near the border of Ipswich and Topsfield. Elizabeth (Dane) Howe was the sister of the Rev. Francis Dane of Andover, making James Howe, Jr. the Rev. Dane's nephew.

Elizabeth was one of four children. Upon William Jackson's death in 1688, his large estate had gone to his only son, John Jackson, to be held in trust for his grandson John Jackson, Jr. If anything were to happen to the two Johns, the estate would be divided between the three Jackson sisters. Both of Elizabeth's sisters were widowed by the year 1691.

In 1682 Elizabeth Howe and her husband had a quarrel with Samuel Perley of Topsfield. Elizabeth applied for membership in the Ipswich church, but this was denied, blocked by Samuel Perley and Isaac Foster of Ipswich. Isaac Foster was the brother-in-law of Mary (Jackson) Foster (Elizabeth's sister) and Elizabeth (Dane) Foster (James Howe, Jr.'s first cousin). Isaac Foster was also the uncle of Ephraim Foster of Andover, who brought charges of witchcraft against John Jackson, Sr. and John Jackson, Jr.[242]

In 1692 Elizabeth Howe, about fifty-three, lived with her blind husband, James Howe, Jr., and their children, in Topsfield close to the Ipswich boundary. James had been without sight for about seven years, and Elizabeth had assumed the burden of managing the farm. The accusation against Elizabeth in 1692 was not only the result of her husband's association with the Topsfield men so disliked by the conspiracy, but also the result of her membership in the targeted families of the Jacksons and Howes. A contributing factor was the envy stirred up by the legacy left by William Jackson.

On May 28, 1692 the conspiracy filed a complaint [No. 23] against Elizabeth Howe and ten others. They cited "sundry acts of witchcraft by them and every one of them committed on the bodies of Mary Walcott, Abigail Williams, Mercy Lewis, Ann

---

242 Otten, *Witch Hunt*, 158; Robinson and Otten, A4.24-A4.27, A4.34-A4.37.

Putnam, Jr., and others to the hurt and injury of their bodies, therefore craves justice."

On May 31, 1692 Elizabeth Howe was arrested by Ephraim Wildes, constable of Topsfield, and taken to Salem Village. At her examination Elizabeth refused to confess, saying, "If it was the last moment I was to live, God knows I am innocent of anything in this nature." Asked, "Is this the first time that ever you were accused?" she answered "Yes, Sir." To the question, "Do not you know that one at Ipswich has accused you?" she replied, "This is the first time that ever I heard of it." She was imprisoned.

On June 1, 1692 Samuel Perley, fifty-two, and his wife, Ruth, forty-six, testified that they had a disagreement with James Howe, Jr. and his wife in 1682. Soon after the altercation, "our daughter [ten-year-old Hannah Perley] told us that it was James Howe, [Jr.]'s wife that afflicted her night and day, sometimes complaining of being pricked with pins and sometimes falling down into dreadful fits. We went to several doctors and they told us that she was under an evil hand. Our daughter told us that when she came near fire or water this witch pulls me in, and was often sorely burned. Our daughter continuing about two or three years constantly affirming to the last that this Goody Howe, that is now seized, was the cause of her sorrows, and so pined away to skin and bone, and ended her sorrowful life."

On June 3, 1692 the two ministers of Rowley, the Rev. Samuel Phillips and the Rev. Edward Payson refuted the testimonies of the Pearlys. The Rev. Phillips said, "When we were in the house the child had one of her fits but made no mention of Goodwife Howe. When the fit was over, Goodwife Howe went to the child and asked her whether she had ever done her any hurt. And she answered, 'No, never, and if I did complain of you in my fits I know not that I did so.' I can further affirm under oath that young Samuel Pearly, brother to the afflicted girl, said to his sister, 'Say Goodwife Howe is a witch! Say she is a witch!' and the child spoke not a word that way, but I looked up to where the youth stood and rebuked him for his boldness to stir up his sister to accuse Goodwife Howe. I added no wonder that the child in her fits did mention Goodwife Howe, when her nearest relations were so frequent in expressing their suspicions in the child's hearing when she was out of her fits, saying that Goodwife Howe was an instrument of mischief to the child."

At the end of June 1692, Elizabeth Howe's case came up before the second sitting of the Court of Oyer and Terminer at Salem. Depositions supporting Elizabeth's character and Christian behavior were given by many of her neighbors. Her husband's father, James Howe, Sr., about ninety-four, stated that Elizabeth was "very dutiful, careful, loving, obedient and kind, tenderly leading her husband about by the hand in his want of eyesight." However the court preferred to listen to Elizabeth's brother-in-law John Howe of Topsfield. He said that when he had asked her if she were a witch, she had become angry. Later, his sow "gave one squeak and fell down dead," and he said, "I suspected no other person than my sister Elizabeth Howe." Deacon Isaac Cummings of Ipswich, his wife, and son Isaac, Jr. testified about the distemper of their horse, eight years previously, after James Howe, Jr. attempted to borrow it.

On July 2, 1692 Elizabeth was condemned by the Court of Oyer and Terminer. On July 12 Chief Justice William Stoughton signed her death warrant, and on July 19, 1692 Elizabeth (Jackson) Howe was hanged at Salem.

On July 28, 1692 Mary (Tyler) Post Bridges of Andover (second wife of John Bridges, Elizabeth's brother-in-law) was accused and imprisoned. On August 2 Mary Post of Rowley and Andover (Mary Bridges' daughter) was accused and imprisoned. On August 25 Elizabeth's niece, Sarah Bridges, along with the latter's three step-sisters, were accused and imprisoned. On August 26, 1692 Elizabeth's brother John Jackson, Sr. and his son John Jackson, Jr. of Rowley were accused and imprisoned.

In 1704, James Howe, Jr. died at Topsfield. In 1710 Mary and Abigail Howe gave the account, "We only survive in this family. We know that our honored father went twice a week the whole time of our mother's imprisonment to carry her maintenance which was procured with much difficulty, and one of us went with him because he could not go alone for want of sight."[243]

STEREOTYPED WITCHES

"Witches are generally portrayed in the literature as disagreeable women, at best aggressive and abrasive, at worst ill-tempered, quarrelsome, and spiteful. They are almost always described as deviants—disorderly women who failed to, or refused to abide by the behavioral norms of their society. Drawn primarily from descriptions left to us by witches' accusers, this portrait conforms to the popular stereotype of the witch."[244]

In 1692 the conspirators used all kinds of deceit in their attempts to convince the populace that certain women fitted the stereotype of witch. These efforts were made to give credibility to the witch hunt. They chose those women whom they regarded as being particularly vulnerable to their false accusations. Favorite targets were women who had been smeared by witchcraft allegations before. Widows were often picked because, without their husbands to protect them in a male-dominated society, it was difficult for them to ward off vicious libels and slander. If the widow was left with even moderate wealth, the forces of envy were so great that any kind of attack might be made against her.

Typical of this group, Rachel Clinton, Bridget Bishop, and Susannah Martin had been slurred by malicious neighbors prior to 1692. Because a seemingly iron-clad case was constructed in 1692 against John Willard, he is the one man included here.

Rachel Clinton, a divorced woman, had been accused of witchcraft in 1687.[245] She was accused and imprisoned close to the beginning of the Salem Village witch hunt.

Bridget Bishop had first been accused in 1680, less than a year after the death of her husband Thomas Oliver who left her a wealthy woman. For her 1692 trial, the court dragged up all the

---

243 *SWP*, 377-378, 434, 438-442, 997.
244 Karlsen, 118.
245 *Suffolk Files*, 2660. Karlsen, 110.

testimony from her previous indictment and used it against her once again. This material referred to her by her married name at the time, Bridget Oliver. After remarrying, she became Bridget Bishop. So that the previous testimony would seem immediately relevant in 1692, the court carefully referred to her as Bridget Bishop alias Oliver.

In 1669 Susannah Martin had been slandered by witchcraft allegations. Stories circulated at the time that her son Richard Martin was not human at all, but was one of her familiars.[246] A widow in 1692, she was described by Cotton Mather as "one of the most impudent, scurrilous creatures of the world."[247]

Dorcas Hoar had the reputation of being an assertive person. Incensed at the prospect of a panel investigating the sudden death of her husband in 1691, "she broke out in a very great passion, wringing her hands and stamping her feet, and said, 'You wicked wretches! What? Do you think I murdered him?' "[248] As a recent widow, she was a ready target in 1692.

Both Wilmot Redd and Alice Parker were the wives of fishermen. It proved easy to find many slanderous stories to support the cases against them in 1692.

Rachel (Haffield) Clinton

Ipswich   *March 29, 1692*

Rachel Haffield was born about 1629 in England, daughter of Richard Haffield and his second wife, Martha Mansfield. The family then came to America, settling in Ipswich. Richard Haffield died at Ipswich in 1639, leaving his widow wealthy. The widow had care of their three daughters and of his two daughters by an earlier marriage. Many years of litigation ensued over control of the estate. Finally the widow Martha Haffield died in 1668, "judged insane." Rachel Haffield had married, in 1665 in Ipswich, Lawrence Clinton, a man fifteen years her junior. After

---

246 *Essex Court Records*, 4:129, 133.
247 Cotton Mather, *Wonders*, 148.
248 *SWP*, 394.

many appeals to the court, Rachel finally divorced him in 1681, on grounds of adultery.[249]

In 1692 Rachel Clinton, about sixty-three, was living alone in poverty in Ipswich. This was in contrast to her early years of relative wealth. She had been accused of witchcraft in 1687, and neighborhood hostility surfaced in connection with the Salem outbreak. Seizing upon the situation, some in Ipswich took the opportunity to get rid of their long-standing "town charge."

On March 29, 1692 a complaint was filed in Ipswich against Rachel Clinton. She was arrested the next day and taken to Ipswich court. Various people testified against her including Mary Fuller, Sr., forty-one, and James Fuller, Jr., eighteen. The Fuller testimony related to the supposed death of Betty Fuller, who actually had recovered. The Fullers had also testified against Rachel some years earlier. Rachel was imprisoned at Ipswich and fettered.[250]

Rachel Clinton was held in prison from April 11, 1692 until March 23, 1693 when her fees were paid and she was released. In 1695, Rachel Clinton, about sixty-six, died at Ipswich.

Bridget (Playfer) Wasselbe Oliver Bishop
Salem   *April 18, 1692*

Bridget Playfer was born about 1640 in England. She first married, about 1660 in England, Samuel Wasselbe, who died in 1664. Two years later she married widower Thomas Oliver in Salem and he died in June 1679. The next year, 1680, as widow Bridget Oliver, she was charged with witchcraft, but was found innocent. She married a third time, about 1684, widower Edward Bishop.

There has been much confusion in the literature over the identity of this last husband of Bridget, as there were four men by

---

249 Demos, 19-35.

250 *SWP*, 950. (*The Salem Witchcraft Papers* erroneously list Rachel twice: in volume 1 as Rachel Clenton, and in volume 2 as Rachel Hatfield.)

the name of Edward Bishop in the Salem area.[251]   Three of the four were of the Bishop family of Beverly, namely Edward Bishop I (born 1618 and died after 1693), an original settler of Beverly, his son Edward Bishop, Jr., who with his wife, Sarah (Wildes) Bishop, resided in Salem Village and operated a tavern, and their son Edward Bishop III. The remaining Edward Bishop, a sawyer of Salem with no known relationship with the Bishop family of Beverly, was the husband of Bridget. (Many books erroneously state that Bridget Bishop lived in Salem Village and operated an illegal tavern, and that her husband was the son of Edward Bishop I and, at the same time, the father of Edward Bishop, Jr.)

In 1692 Bridget Bishop, then around fifty-two, lived with her husband, Edward Bishop the sawyer, in the Oliver house in Salem. On April 18, 1692 the conspiracy filed a complaint [No. 8] against Bridget Bishop and three others, including Giles Corey. On April 19 she was arrested and taken to Salem Village for examination. Bridget refused to confess. She was imprisoned.[252]

On May 31, 1692 Thomas Newton, attorney general, in a letter to Isaac Addington, the secretary of the province, wrote concerning "the records in the Court of Assistants, 1679, against Bridget Oliver, left in Mr. Webb's hands by the order of the Council." His intent was to obtain Bridget's earlier trial records to use against her in her forthcoming trial. On June 2 two physical examinations, one in the morning and one in the afternoon, were made of Bridget Bishop. On June 1 and 2 in the grand jury inquest, all the testimony against her, except for the antics of the afflicted girls present, was about events that had happened many years past.

On June 4, 1692 the Court of Oyer and Terminer in Salem found her guilty. Witchcraft was no longer a capital offense.

---

251 Greene, "Salem Witches I."

252 On May 20 a deposition by the Rev. John Hale against "Goody Bishop" (i.e., Sarah (Wildes) Bishop of Salem Village) was erroneously placed in the file of Bridget Bishop. This clerical error misled some of the afflicted girls in their testimony. Hale specifically talked about "the wife of Edward Bishop, Jr." and her conflict with Christian Trask.

However on June 8 the General Court at Boston revived the death penalty for those found guilty of witchcraft. Chief Justice William Stoughton then signed a death warrant for Bridget. On June 10, 1692 she was hanged at Salem.

In 1711 Nehemiah Jewett wrote to Samuel Sewall, "I thought to return you the names of several persons that were condemned and executed that not any person or relations appeared in the behalf of for the taking of the attainder or for other expenses."[253] Bridget Bishop alias Oliver was one of the six women mentioned.

Susannah (North) Martin
Amesbury   *April 30, 1692*

Susannah North was born about 1625 in England, the daughter of Ursula and Richard North, later of the towns of Salisbury and Amesbury in Massachusetts. She married, in 1646 in Salisbury, widower George Martin, a blacksmith. George Martin had been an early settler of Salisbury and then one of the first settlers of Amesbury when it was set apart from Salisbury. Old records of the two towns show that George Martin had been very active in land dealings. There are thirty deeds and mortgages in which he was a principal.[254]

One day in 1660 William Brown of Salisbury, then about thirty-eight, came home from Hampton and found that "his wife would not own him but said they were divorced. And from that time, [she has] been incapable of any rational action, though strong and healthy of body. [He] procured Doctors Fuller and Crosby. They did both say that her distemper was supernatural and no sickness of body, but that some evil person had bewitched her." Susannah Martin was chosen as the scapegoat. (Twelve years later, it was the same Dr. Crosby who told James Carr, the brother of Ann Putnam, Sr., that "Mrs. [Mary] Bradbury was a great deal worse [in acts of witchcraft] than Goody Martin.")

---

253 *SWP*, 108, 1012.
254 Greene, "Salem Witches III," 1158.

In 1669 William Sargent accused Susannah Martin of being a witch. Right away George Martin countered with a suit against William Sargent for slander. Although many of the legal records are missing, it can be inferred that George Martin prevailed.[255] Martin died in 1686 at Amesbury, leaving Susannah a widow with seven adult children.

In 1692 Susannah was around sixty-seven, a widow of some six years. She was described as a short, active woman, slightly plump, and of remarkable personal neatness. However, Susannah was highly intelligent and occasionally breached the traditions imposed on women by the male-dominated Puritan society. She "spoke her mind freely, and with strength of expression. From this cause, perhaps, she had shocked the prejudices and violated the conventional scrupulosities then prevalent, to such a degree as to incur much comment, if not scandal."[256]

On April 30, 1692 the conspiracy filed a complaint [No. 10] against Susannah Martin and five others. On May 2 she was arrested and taken to Salem Village. At her examination Susannah refused to confess, "I dare not tell a lie if it would save my life." John Indian fell into a violent fit, and said it was caused by that woman. "She bites! She bites!" The magistrate asked, "Have you no compassion for these inflicted?" Susannah answered, "No, I have none." Susannah was ordered to Boston prison.

On June 7, 1692 John Allen, about forty-five, of Salisbury, stated in court that some years previously, some of his cattle, bewitched by Susannah North, plunged into the Merrimack River and drowned. On June 27 William Brown, then about seventy, testified in court that his wife's "distemper" had been caused by Susannah Martin. The afflicted girls also testified against her, their statements attested by Thomas Putnam, Edward Putnam, Nathaniel Ingersoll, and the Rev. Samuel Parris. Thomas

---

255 Karlsen, 91.
256 Upham, 2:140.

Putnam testified that he saw several bites and pinches on the girls made by Susannah Martin.

Sarah Atkinson, about forty-eight, of Newbury, testified that about eighteen years ago in the spring, Susannah had come to her house at Newbury from Amesbury. It had been an extraordinarily dirty season, not fit for any person to travel. When she entered the house, Sarah asked her, "Did you come from Amesbury on foot?" Susannah answered, "I did." Sarah then said, "Come to the fire and dry yourself." Susannah replied, "I am as dry as you are." Sarah observed that the soles of Susannah's shoes were not wet. Sarah was startled that Susannah could arrive so dry and told her, "I should have been wet up to my knees if I had come so far on foot." Susannah replied, "I scorn to have a draggled tail." The implication of Sarah's testimony was that Susannah, arriving so wonderfully dry, had not walked but, being a witch, had flown on a pole. More likely, Susannah had carefully picked her way around the puddles as she walked.

On June 30, 1692 the Court of Oyer and Terminer condemned Susannah Martin to death, and on July 19 she was hanged at Salem. The return of George Corwin, sheriff of Essex County, states, "I have caused the within mentioned persons to be executed according to the tenor of the warrant."

Dorcas (Galley) Hoar
Beverly   *April 30, 1692*

Dorcas Galley was born in the mid-1630s. She had married, by 1658, William Hoar of Beverly, who died in 1691. His death was sudden, and a jury was impaneled to determine the cause. In 1692 Dorcas was a grandmother in her late fifties. She resided in Beverly. Even her small inheritance made her subject to envy.

On April 30, 1692 the conspiracy filed a complaint [No. 10] against Dorcas Hoar and five others, including Sarah Morrell, also of Beverly. On May 2 George Herrick, marshal of Essex, arrested Dorcas Hoar and Sarah Morrell, but said that Philip English was not to be found.

At her examination in Salem Village on May 2, Dorcas was asked, "What do you say about killing your husband?" Before the widow could answer, Susannah Sheldon charged Dorcas with coming into the courtroom with two cats. The magistrate asked, "What black cats were those you had?" Dorcas answered, "I had none." To destroy the veracity of Dorcas' answer, Susannah said, "I see the Black Man whispering into your ear." Mary Walcott and Elizabeth Hubbard said they saw the same thing. Dorcas rejoined, "Oh! You are liars, and God will stop the mouths of liars." The magistrate, still wanting to clear up the mystery of the cats, asked, "What do you say to those cats that sucked your breast? What are they?" Again Dorcas answered, "I had no cats." Not accepting her answer, he said, "You do not call them cats. What are they that suck you?" The examination went on in this manner, until Dorcas said, "Why should I confess that [which] I do not know?" The magistrate observed, "This is unusual impudence to threaten before authority." Dorcas was committed to the prison in Boston.

After the ignition of the Andover phase of the witch hunt in July 1692, there were many confessions made by the newly accused. These confessions were largely due to the preparatory work of the assistant minister of Andover, the Rev. Thomas Barnard, an old college chum of Cotton Mather. The Rev. John Hale of Beverly, fifty-six, was upset because he had not elicited even one confession. Dorcas Hoar was his chance. He had known her for many years.

On September 6, 1692, the Rev. Hale gave testimony to strike fear into the heart of the prisoner Dorcas Hoar. First there was sin. He said that many years ago, there "were stories told concerning her being a fortuneteller." Then came repentance. He said, "About twenty-two years ago, Dorcas manifested to me great repentance for the sins of her former life." Then came sin again. He said, "But fourteen years ago I discovered an evil practice between a servant of mine and some of Hoar's children in conveying goods out of my house to Hoar's." His eleven-year-old daughter Rebecca knew about the stealing but had not told him. She later explained that she was afraid that, if she had told him,

"Hoar would raise the Devil to kill me, or bewitch me." Rebecca eventually died, and at the time it was considered a natural death. Now in 1692 in court, Hale remembered, "After my daughter's death a friend told me that my daughter said to her that she went in fear of her life by the Hoars, till quieted by the Scripture." The implication was clear; Dorcas must now once again confess and repent her sins.

On September 9, 1692 the Court of Oyer and Terminer condemned Dorcas Hoar to death. On September 21 the Rev. John Hale, together with the Rev. Nicholas Noyes, the Rev. Daniel Epes, and the Rev. John Emerson, Jr., petitioned 'His excellency, Sir William Phipps, Governor, or in his absence the Honorable William Stoughton, Lieutenant Governor." They stated that Dorcas Hoar had confessed herself guilty of the heinous crime of witchcraft and, "being in a great distress of conscience, craves a little longer time of life to realize and perfect her repentance for the salvation of her soul." The petition succeeded. Magistrate Bartholomew Gedney signed the document, "Having heard & taken the confession of Dorcas Hoar do consent that her execution be respited until further ordered." Judge Samuel Sewall wrote, "An order is sent to the sheriff to forbear her execution, notwithstanding her being in the warrant to die tomorrow. This is the first condemned person who has confessed." Dorcas Hoar escaped the mass execution on September 22, 1692.

In January 1693 Chief Justice William Stoughton signed death warrants for Dorcas Hoar and the others in prison who had been condemned by the Court of Oyer and Terminer but had not yet been executed. Apparently he felt that she had been given enough time to perfect her repentance. However, within a few days Governor Sir William Phipps reprieved all those under the death order. That spring Dorcas Hoar was released from prison. While she was in prison, the sheriff had seized her two cows, her ox, her mare, her bed, curtains, bedding, and other household goods.[257]

---

257 *SWP*, 389-391, 550, 873, 996.

John Willard

Salem Village   *May 10, 1692*

John Willard was born about 1662 in Massachusetts. He married, in 1685, Margaret Wilkins, born 1668, the daughter of Hannah (Nichols) and Thomas Wilkins of Salem Village. Thomas Wilkins was a son of Bray Wilkins. Bray Wilkins (1610–1702) had, among other children, Henry Wilkins and Benjamin Wilkins.

John Willard had previously lived in Lancaster, but settled in Salem Village after his marriage to Margaret Wilkins. Some animosity towards John had since developed among other members of the Wilkins family, for nine of them would later testify against him.

In 1692 John, about thirty and black haired, was a farmer with a comfortable estate. He and Margaret had three children. On May 10, 1692 Benjamin Wilkins and Thomas Fuller, Jr. filed a complaint [No. 14] against John Willard. They accused him of afflicting Bray Wilkins and Daniel Wilkins, born in 1675, the son of Henry Wilkins. A warrant for arrest was issued for appearance on May 11 at Beadle's Tavern in Salem. On May 12 John Putnam, Jr., constable of Salem, reported, "I went to the house of the usual abode of John Willard and made search for him, and in several other houses and places, but could not find him. His relations and friends then gave me account that to their best knowledge he was fled." On May 15 another warrant for arrest was issued to the marshal of Essex, the constables of Salem, and marshals and constables within the colony. On May 17 George Herrick, marshal of Essex County, wrote to the magistrates John Hathorne and Jonathan Corwin, "I found all the five persons which we were in pursuit of, and constable John Putnam, Jr. came in with John Willard having seized him at Nashaway [Lancaster]."

Herrick took his account of Daniel Wilkins' death from Benjamin Wilkins. "On 14th day of May, Daniel Wilkins was taken speechless and never spoke until the 16th day. We sent to the French doctor but he sent word again that it was not a natural cause but absolutely witchcraft to his judgment. That same day two of the afflicted persons came to visit Daniel Wilkins. Mercy Lewis and Mary Walcott both did see the [specters of] John Willard and Goodwife Buckley upon Daniel Wilkins, and said they would kill him, and in three hours Daniel departed this life in the most doleful and solemn condition." This account was sent by Ezekiel Cheever and attested by Herrick, constable Joseph Neale, constable John Putnam, Jr., constable Jonathan Putnam, Nathaniel Putnam, John Putnam, Sr., Jonathan Walcott, Thomas Flint, Edward Putnam, John Buxton, and Thomas Putnam. The notation, "Mr. Parris is gone to Salem" explains why his signature is absent. The jury of inquest returned the verdict, "To the best of our judgments, he died an unnatural death by some cruel hands of witchcraft or diabolical act." The twelve-man jury was made up of almost the same men as had attested Herrick's report.

On May 18, 1692 in his examination, John Willard was accused of murdering Daniel Wilkins, bewitching Bray Wilkins, and abusing his own wife. Willard said, "There are a great many lies told. I would desire my wife might be called." The magistrate said, "Confess and give glory to God. Take counsel while it is offered." He answered, "I desire to take good counsel, but if it was the last time I was to speak, I am innocent." He would not confess.

When Susannah Sheldon, one of the afflicted girls, tried to come near Willard, she "fell down immediately." Magistrate John Hathorne asked, "What is the reason she cannot come near you?" Willard answered, "They cannot come near any that are accused." Hathorne then said, "Why do you say so, they could come near Nehemiah Abbot, the children could talk with him." Hathorne, in referring to Abbot, was trying to present the fairness of the proceedings, as Nehemiah Abbot, Jr., was the only person known to have been released after examination.

On June 2, 1692 at the first sitting of the Court of Oyer and Terminer at Salem, John Willard and John Proctor were given physical examinations which yielded the report, "We do not find anything to further suspect them." At the jury of inquest, Ann Putnam, Sr. stated that the apparition of John Willard had told her that he had killed thirteen people including her baby, Sarah Putnam, six weeks old. On June 3 depositions were entered against John Willard. In addition to the usual negative statements from the Putnams, the afflicted girls, and the Rev. Samuel Parris, there were depositions made against him by many of his own in-laws such as Margaret (Wilkins) Knight, twenty, Samuel Wilkins, nineteen, Rebecca Wilkins, nineteen, Henry Wilkins, forty-one, Benjamin Wilkins, thirty-six, John Wilkins, twenty-six, and Bray Wilkins, eighty-one. On a list of evidences against John Willard appear the names of the afflicted girls, "Nathaniel Putnam etc. upon murder," and Ann Putnam, Sr. The names of Sarah Churchill and Margaret Jacobs are given with the comment, "that Willard dissuaded from confession."

At the grand jury inquest for the Court of Oyer and Terminer at Salem, Elizabeth Hubbard, Rebecca Wilkins, the Rev. Samuel Parris, Nathaniel Ingersoll, Edward Putnam, Thomas Putnam, and others testified against John Willard. At the August 5 session, the court sentenced him to death. On about August 8, "for a little time," Margaret (Wilkins) Willard obtained a reprieve for her husband. On August 19, 1692 John Willard, about thirty, was hanged at Salem.

In 1694 his widow, Margaret (Wilkins) Willard, married William Towne of Topsfield. William Towne's three aunts, Rebecca (Towne) Nurse, Sarah (Towne) Bridges Cloyce, and Mary (Towne) Easty, had been imprisoned, and Rebecca and Mary had been hanged in 1692. In December 1694 Margaret's brother, Thomas Wilkins, Jr., twenty-one, married Elizabeth Towne, who was the sister of William Towne.

In 1710 Margaret (Wilkins) Willard Towne recorded, "John Willard suffered death in that hour of the power of darkness as if he had been guilty of one of the greatest crimes that ever any of the sons of Adam have been left of God to fall into. The fearful odium cast on him by imputing to him and causing him to suffer death for such a piece of wickedness as I have not the least reason in the world to think he was guilty of, I say besides that reproach and the grief and sorrow I was exposed to by that means, I do account that our damage as to our outward estate to have been very considerable. My husband being seized and imprisoned, all our husband's concerns were laid by for that summer. We had not opportunity to plant or sow whereas we were wont to raise our own bread corn."[258]

Ann (mnu) Greenslade Pudeator
Salem   May 12, 1692

Ann was born about 1632. She first married, about 1651 in Casco, Maine, Thomas Greenslade. The Greenslades resided in Casco. He was badly wounded by the Indians in their destruction of Casco in 1676 and soon died. Ann remarried in Salem around 1678. Her new husband was widower Jacob Pudeator, who died in 1682 in Salem. Her marriage to Jacob Pudeator was a good one. Upon his death he gave Ann his whole estate apart from legacies of five pounds sterling to each of her five Greenslade children. Her older sons had returned to Maine. Her daughter Ruth had married Josiah Bridges, a blacksmith of Boxford.

In 1692 twice-widowed Ann Pudeator was in her early sixties. She lived in Salem on the north line of the common. On May 12, 1692 the conspiracy filed a complaint [No. 15] against the two widows, Ann Pudeator and Alice Parker of Salem, for "sundry acts of witchcraft." They were committed to prison. On June 1, for the first session of the Court of Oyer and Terminer, Sarah Churchill gave testimony against Ann Pudeator, Bridget Bishop, and George Jacobs, Sr.

On July 2, 1692 Ann Pudeator was examined at Beadle's Tavern in Salem before the magistrates. She refused to confess. Sarah Churchill testified that Ann had brought her the Devil's book to sign when Sarah was at the home of George Jacobs, Sr. Lieutenant Jeremiah Neal stated, "She [Ann Pudeator] has been an ill-carriaged woman, and since my wife has been sick of the small pox, this woman has come to my house pretending kindness. She asked whether she might use our mortar. My wife

---

258   Greene, "Bray Wilkins," 1160. *SWP*, 681, 772, 821, 823-826, 836, 839, 874, 1008-1009.

and I consented to it, but I afterwards repented of it, for my wife was the worse. My wife grew worse until she died."

On July 26 Ann's son, James Greenslade, was summoned from Casco, Maine to give evidence against the Rev. George Burroughs at the Court of Oyer and Terminer on August 2. Failure to appear would incur a penalty of one hundred pounds sterling to be levied on his goods and chattels. There is no record of his testimony.

On September 7, 1692 at the jury of inquest, Mary Warren accused Ann of killing Jeremiah Neal's wife, her husband Pudeator and his first wife, and John Best, Sr.'s wife. John Best, Sr., forty-eight, accused Ann of afflicting his wife and causing her death, and this was corroborated by John Best, Jr. Samuel Pickworth stated that, as he was going along Salem Street one evening about six weeks ago, he saw a woman "near Captain Higginson's Corner, which I supposed to be Ann Pudeator. She passed by me as swift as if a bird flew by me and entered the Pudeator house." On September 9, the Court of Oyer and Terminer condemned Ann to death.

On about September 12, Ann petitioned the Court of Oyer and Terminer for a reconsideration of her case. "The evidence of John Best, Sr. and John Best, Jr. and Samuel Pickworth were all of them altogether false and untrue. And besides the above-said, John Best has been formerly whipped, and likewise is recorded for a liar."

On September 15, in an effort to save his mother, eldest son, Thomas Greenslade, gave testimony against the Rev. George Burroughs who had been hanged on August 19. This is an example of the authorities augmenting a file after a case had been closed. On September 22, 1692, Ann Greenslade Pudeator was hanged at Salem.[259]

---

259 *SWP*, 159-160, 474, 702.

Alice (mnu) Parker
Salem   *May 12, 1692*

In 1692 Alice was the wife of John Parker, a fisherman and mariner of Salem. On May 12, 1692 the conspiracy filed a complaint [No. 15] against Alice Parker and Ann Pudeator for afflicting Mary Warren. Both were arrested. In Alice Parker's examination, "Mary Warren affirmed that her father had promised to mow the grass for her if he had time. He not doing so, she came to the house, and told him he had better he had done it. Presently after that her sister fell ill, and shortly after that her mother was taken ill, and died." The Rev. Nicholas Noyes testified against Alice as did Margaret Jacobs who had been imprisoned on May 10. Alice did not confess.

On June 2, 1692 at the first sitting of the Court of Oyer and Terminer, Alice was subjected to two physical examinations, one in the morning and one in the afternoon. John Westgate and Samuel Shattuck testified against Alice regarding events which took place in 1685. On about June 27, Widow Martha Dutch and Samuel Perley were among those who gave evidence against Alice.

On September 7, 1692 at the Court of Oyer and Terminer at Salem, Martha Dutch, John Bullock, Abigail Hobbs (imprisoned), and the afflicted girls testified against Alice. Mary Warren said that "she bewitched my mother and was a cause of her death, and also that she bewitched my sister Elizabeth that is both death and dumb." The prior testimonies of John Westgate and Samuel Shattuck were entered into the record at that time. On September 9 the Court of Oyer and Terminer condemned her to death. On September 22, 1692, Alice Parker was hanged at Salem. She maintained her innocence to the end.

In 1711 Nehemiah Jewett wrote to Samuel Sewall, "I thought good to return you the names of several persons that were condemned & executed that not any person or relations appeared in the behalf of for the taking off the attainder or for other expenses." Included among the six names was that of Alice Parker.[260]

Wilmot (mnu) Redd

Marblehead   *May 28, 1692*

Wilmot (mnu) was born about 1638. She married Samuel Redd about 1657 in Salem. In 1692 Wilmot was in her mid-fifties. She lived with her husband, a fisherman, "upon the hill by the meeting house" in Marblehead.

On May 26, 1692 George Herrick, marshal, attested, "Being at Salem Village with constable Joseph Neale, the persons under written was afflicted much and complained against, viz., Mary Walcott, Mercy Lewis, Ann Putnam upon Goodwife Redd of Marblehead."

On May 28, 1692 the conspiracy filed a complaint [No. 23] against Wilmot Redd and ten others. On May 31 James Smith, constable of Marblehead, arrested her and took her to Salem Village. The written record of her examination reads, "Being often urged what she thought these persons [the afflicted] ailed of, she would reply, 'I cannot tell.' Then being asked if she did not think they were bewitched, she answered, 'I cannot tell.' And being urged for her opinion in the case, all she would say was, 'My opinion is they are in a sad condition.' " She was imprisoned.

At the Court of Oyer and Terminer on September 14, 1692 Charity Pitman, twenty-nine, the wife of John Pitnam and the daughter of Ambrose Gale, one of Marblehead's most outstanding citizens, stated, "About 5 years ago Mrs. Symmes lost some linen which she suspected [her servant] Martha Lawrence, the girl which then lived with Wilmot Redd, had taken up." Mrs. Symmes and Charity made a visit to Samuel Redd's house. An argument ensued, and Mrs. Symmes threatened to take the servant before magistrate John Hathorne. "Wilmot Redd wished that Mrs.

---

260 *SWP*, 106, 440, 632, 634, 635, 1012. The testimonies of John Westgate, Samuel Shattuck, and John Bullock are erroneously placed under the "Case of Mary (Ayer) Parker" in *SWP*.

Symmes might never mingere, nor cacare, if she did not go. A short time after, Mrs. Symmes was taken with the distemper of the dry balk, and so continued many months during her stay in the Town, and was not cured whilst she tarried in the Country."[261] On September 17 the Court of Oyer and Terminer condemned Wilmot Redd, and on September 22, 1692 she was hanged at Salem.

HIGH-PLACED ENEMIES

As spring wore on, the accusations reached out beyond the orbit of Salem Village to strike at powerful and prosperous figures such as Boston's John Alden, whom the afflicted girls knew only by reputation. With these high-level accusations, the deeper motives underlying the witchcraft outbreak become clear.

Mary (Hollingsworth) English
Salem   *April 21, 1692*

Philip English
Salem   *April 30, 1692*

Philip English was born in 1651, on the English Isle of Jersey, the son of John L'Anglois. He married, in 1675 in Salem, Mary Hollingsworth. She was born about 1652 in Salem, the only child of William Hollingsworth. Her father was a wealthy merchant of Salem. After Mary's mother died, he took as his second wife Elizabeth Powell, eldest child of Elder Michael Powell; they were married in Boston on August 23, 1659. On William Hollingsworth's death his only child, Mary, inherited his large estate.

In 1692 Philip English was Salem's richest merchant and largest shipowner. He owned fourteen buildings, a wharf, and twenty-one sailing vessels. He was forty-one and his wife Mary was about forty. They lived with their children in a splendid

---

261 *SWP*, 117, 183, 714, 717, 871. *Mingere* is polite Court Latin for "urinate"; *cacare*, for "defecate."

townhouse with a magnificent view of the harbor. That year Philip was serving his first term as a selectman of Salem.

On April 21, 1692 the conspiracy filed a complaint [No. 9] against Mary English and eight others. On April 22 Mary was arrested, examined, and imprisoned at Salem. On April 30 the conspiracy filed a complaint [No. 10] against Philip English and five others. A warrant for arrest for appearance on May 2 was made out for Philip English, but on that date George Herrick, marshal of Essex, reported "Mr. Philip English not being to be found." On May 6 a second warrant was made out for his arrest. On May 30 Jacob Manning, marshal's deputy, arrested Philip English and committed him to the marshal of Essex. On May 31 he was examined at Salem. Susannah Sheldon testified against Philip English, accusing him of drowning Joseph Rabson in the sea.

On June 1, 1692 at Boston prison Mary English testified about Mary Warren, an afflicted girl briefly imprisoned, "I heard Mary Warren say that the magistrates might as well examine Keyser's daughter, that had been distracted many years, and take notice of what she said as well as any of the afflicted persons."

After Philip English had been imprisoned, George Corwin, sheriff of Essex County, seized his Salem properties, their value estimated at fifteen hundred pounds sterling. This theft was carried out even though English had posted a bond of four thousand pounds sterling with surety at Boston. On August 2 William Beale of Marblehead, who had engaged in lawsuits with Philip English over boundary lines, testified against him.

In August 1692, Mary and Philip escaped from the Boston prison and fled to New York, where they stayed until the following year. On January 12, 1693 at the Superior Court of Judicature at Salem, the grand jury dismissed the case against Philip English.

In 1694 his wife, Mary, died in Salem. In the same year Philip English instigated a lawsuit against George Corwin for the illegal seizure of his property in 1692, but lost the case. In 1697 George Corwin, about thirty-one, died at Salem. Philip English had an outstanding suit against Corwin for debt. Although English could not legally enter the Corwin premises, he said that he would seize Corwin's body in satisfaction of that debt as soon as the body was removed from the premises. As a result the body had to be temporarily interred on the Corwin land until the debt was settled. In 1698 Philip English married Sarah (Haskell) Ingersoll, widow of Samuel Ingersoll of Salem.

In 1710 Philip English wrote, "Imprisoned together with my wife in Salem prison and then carried to Boston prison, and there lay nine weeks from whence we made our escape. The goods taken from my warehouses, home, sailing vessels: £1,183.02. Expenses whilst on my flight for my life, I cannot give a particular account of. I never received any other satisfaction for them than £60 paid me by the administrators of George Corwin, late sheriff, deceased." Finally, in 1718, Philip English was paid only two hundred pounds sterling.[262]

The Rev. George Burroughs
Wells, Maine   *April 30, 1692*

George Burroughs was born about 1651 in Virginia, son of Rebecca (mnu) and Nathaniel Burroughs. He graduated from Harvard in 1670. He married first, around 1673 in Roxbury, Hannah (mnu). He was admitted into the Roxbury church in 1674. He then became minister at Casco (now Portland), Maine. After the Indian raids of 1676, the Burroughs family left Maine and settled at Salisbury, Massachusetts. In 1681 he accepted a calling to Salem Village as minister. His wife, Hannah, died in September 1681 in Salem Village. He married for a second time, about 1682, widow Sarah (Ruck) Hathorne. She was born August 12, 1656, the daughter of Hannah (Spooner) and John Ruck of Salem. Sarah had previously been married to William Hathorne, Jr. of Salem who died in 1678.

As minister at Salem Village, George Burroughs suffered more than the usual bickering between parish and pastor. Early in 1683, since his salary was not being paid, Burroughs stopped

---

262 *SWP*, 105, 151, 320, 429, 693, 803, 805, 998-991, 1044.

meeting with his congregation. In this period of relative peace with the Indians, the settlement at Casco was being reorganized, and he accepted an offer to resume his ministerial duties there. He came back to Salem Village for a few weeks in early May 1683 to discuss the earlier problems and settle debts, and then returned to his ministry at Casco, Maine. Because of renewed Indian attacks, the frontier in Maine was finally forced back to Wells. It was here that Burroughs continued his work as minister. On the death of Sarah, George Burroughs married a third time, about 1691 in Wells, Mary (mnu).

In 1692 Burroughs, in his early forties, resided in Wells with his third wife, Mary, their infant daughter, and his seven children by his previous two marriages. On April 20, 1692 the specter of a minister appeared to Ann Putnam, Jr. She had been only three years old when Burroughs had departed Salem Village. However she easily identified the specter as his. Benjamin Hutchinson stated in a deposition that Abigail Williams had also seen Burroughs' apparition on the same day. On April 21 Thomas Putnam, in a letter to magistrates Hathorne and Corwin, wrote, "We thought it our duty to inform your Honors of what we conceive you have not heard, which are high and dreadful, of a wheel within a wheel, at which our ears do tingle."

On April 30, 1692 the conspiracy filed a complaint [No. 10] against the Rev. George Burroughs and five others. Although he was minister in Wells, they could arrest him because the province of Maine was under the jurisdiction of Massachusetts. The warrant for his arrest was transmitted to Major Elisha Hutchinson at Portsmouth, New Hampshire, who directed it to John Partridge, Field Marshal of the provinces of New Hampshire and Maine. On May 3, 1692 the imprisoned Deliverance Hobbs, about forty-five, was examined at Salem prison, and she named the Rev. George Burroughs. On May 4 Burroughs was arrested and transported by field marshal Partridge to Salem. On May 9, 1692 he was examined in a private room, none of the bewitched being present, by magistrates William Stoughton, Samuel Sewall, Jonathan Corwin, and John Hathorne. He was asked whether he took Communion, whether his children had been baptized, about his "haunted house" at Casco, and about the treatment of his late wife, Sarah (Ruck) Hathorne Burroughs.

The examination then adjourned to a public room where "many (if not all of the bewitched) were grievously tortured." The written testimonies of Deliverance Hobbs, Abigail Hobbs, Eleazer Keyser, Captain Simon Willard, Captain John Brown, and John Wheldon had been taken in advance. Burroughs was imprisoned at Boston. Much of the testimony concerned his unusual strength alleged to be a supernatural attribute given by the Devil.

On August 5, 1692 George Burroughs was tried by the Court of Oyer and Terminer at Salem. Four members of the Ruck family testified against him. James Greenslade of Casco, the son of Ann (mnu) Greenslade Pudeator (imprisoned on May 12) was also called to testify against him. On August 5 the Rev. George Burroughs was condemned and on August 10, 1692, he was hanged at Salem.

In 1693 his widow, Mary (mnu) Burroughs, married Michael Horner in Boston. In 1700, again a widow, Mary married Christopher Hall, Jr. in Cambridge. In 1710 the eldest son of George and Sarah, Charles Burroughs, wrote, "We were left a parcel of small children of us, helpless, & a mother-in-law [i.e., step-mother] with one small child of her own to take care of, whereby she was not so capable to take care of us. Our father's small estate was most of it lost & expended and we scattered."[263]

By his first wife Hannah, the Rev. Burroughs had daughter Rebecca, baptized in Roxbury February 1674, George, who died young, Hannah, born in Salisbury on April 2, 1680, and Elizabeth, born in Salem Village in 1681. Rebecca married a man named Fowle, Hannah married Jabez Fox, and Elizabeth married Peter Thomas.

By his second wife Sarah, the Rev. Burroughs had Charles, George, Jeremiah, and Josiah. In June 1693 the Salem Probate Court appointed John Ruck of Salem, the grandfather of these four boys, as their guardian. George settled in Ipswich. By his

---

263 *SWP*, 171, 176, 982-983.

third wife, Mary, the Rev. Burroughs had Mary, who married after 1712 in Attleborough.

Captain John Alden
Boston   *May 28, 1692*

John Alden was born about 1623 in Plymouth, son of Priscilla (Mullens) and John Alden, Sr.   In 1692 John Alden, about sixty-nine, was a respected sea-captain and merchant of Boston, and a member of the Third Church (Old South) in Boston of which the Rev. Samuel Willard was the minister.

On March 23, 1692, Captain John Alden set sail in his sloop *Mary* to Canada to redeem captives taken by the Indians. On May 28, 1692, after his return, the conspiracy filed a complaint [No. 23] against him and ten others.   They were accused of "committing sundry acts of witchcraft on the bodies of Ann Putnam, Jr., Mary Walcott, Mercy Lewis, Abigail Williams and others to the hurt and injury of their bodies, therefore craves justice."

Alden later wrote an account of his examination for publication in Calef's book.[264] He wrote it in the third person, but at some of the more emotional places he switched to the first person. "John Alden of Boston on the 28th day of May 1692 was sent for by the magistrates of Salem upon the accusation of a company of poor distracted or possessed creatures, or witches; and being sent by Mr. Stoughton, arrived there on the 31st of May, and appeared at Salem Village before Mr. Gedney, Mr. Hathorne, and Mr. Corwin. Those wenches being present, who played their juggling tricks, falling down, crying out, and staring in people's faces; the magistrates demanded of them several times, who it was of all the people in the room that hurt them? One of these accusers [afflicted girls] pointed several times at one Captain Hill, there present, but spake nothing. The same accuser had a man standing at her back to hold her up. He stooped down to her ear, then she cried out, Alden, Alden afflicted her.   One of the

---

264   Calef, 242-246.

magistrates asked her if she had ever seen Alden. She answered no. He asked her how she knew it was Alden? She said, the man told her so.

"Then all were ordered to go down into the street, where a ring was made, and the same accuser cried out, 'There stands Alden, a bold fellow with his hat on before the judges. He sells powder and shot to the Indians and French, and lies with the Indian squaws, and has Indian papooses.' Then was Alden committed to the marshal's custody, and his sword taken from him. After some hours Alden was sent for to the meetinghouse in the Village before the magistrates, who required Alden to stand upon a chair, to the open view of all the people.

"The accusers [afflicted girls] cried out that Alden did pinch them, then, when he stood upon the chair, in sight of all the people, a good way distant from them. Alden asked them why they should think that he should come to that Village to afflict those persons that he never knew or saw before? They [the magistrates] bid Alden look upon the accusers, which he did, and then they fell down. Alden asked Mr. Gedney, what reason there could be given, why Alden's looking upon *him* he did not strike *him* down as well? But no reason was given that I [Alden] heard. Alden told Mr. Gedney that he could assure him that there was a lying spirit in them, for I [Alden] can assure you that there is not a word of truth in all these say of me [Alden]."

On June 1, 1692, "to Boston, Alden was carried by a constable, no bail would be taken, but he was delivered to the prison keeper, where he remained 15 weeks, and then observing the manner of the trials, and evidence then taken, was at length prevailed with to make his escape."

On August 3, 1692 at a jury of inquest, Mary Warren testified against John Alden, George Burroughs, the Coreys, and Ann Pudeator. On December 30, 1692 John Alden together with Nathaniel Williams and Samuel Checkley posted a recognizance bond of two hundred pounds sterling for his appearance at the next Superior Court of Judicature. On April 25, 1693 the Superior Court of Judicature at Boston ruled, "John Alden of Boston, Mariner, who stood recognized for his appearance at this court upon suspicion of witchcraft being called, appeared and was discharged by proclamation."[265]

Captain John Floyd

Malden   *May 28, 1692*

John Floyd lived in Romney Marsh (now Chelsea, Massachusetts), where he owned much land.   He had distinguished himself for service as a captain in the Indian war. By his wife, Sarah, he had seven children born between 1662 and 1675, the first five recorded in Lynn, the last two in Malden.   In 1692 he was in his mid-fifties. On May 28, 1692 the conspiracy filed a complaint [No. 23] against Captain John Floyd and ten others.   He was imprisoned.   On August 11, 1692, at the examination of Abigail (Dane) Faulkner of Andover, "Faulkner had a cloth in her hand, that when she squeezed in her hand, the afflicted fell into grievous fits, as was observed. The afflicted said Daniel Eames & Capt. Floyd was upon that cloth when it was upon the table."[266]

Elizabeth (Walker) Cary

Charlestown   *May 28, 1692*

In 1692 Elizabeth was in her early forties. She resided in Charlestown with her husband Captain Nathaniel Cary, forty-seven, a wealthy ship-owner and ship-captain.

On May 28, 1692 the conspiracy filed a complaint [No. 23] against Elizabeth Cary and ten others. Her husband wrote an account of her imprisonment for publication in Calef's book.[267] "I having heard some days, that my wife was accused of witchcraft, being much disturbed at it, by advice, we went to Salem Village to see if the afflicted did know her. We arrived there 24 May, it happened to be a day appointed for examination. Accordingly soon after our arrival, Mr. Hathorne and Mr.

---

265 *SWP*, 173, 938.
266 *SWP*, 83, 327.
267 Calef, 236-242.

Corwin, etc., went to the meeting house, which was the place appointed for that work. The minister began with prayer. Having taken care to get a convenient place, I observed, that the afflicted were two girls of about ten years old, and about two or three other, of about eighteen. One of the girls talked most, and could discern more than the rest. The prisoners were called in one by one, and as they came in were cried out of, etc. The prisoner was placed about 7 or 8 foot from the justices, and the accusers between the justices and them. The prisoner was ordered to stand right before the justices, with an officer appointed to hold each hand, least they should therewith afflict them, and the prisoner's eyes must be constantly on the justices. For if they looked on the afflicted, they would either fall into their fits, or cry out of being hurt by them. After examination of the prisoners, who it was afflicted these girls, etc., they were put upon saying the Lord's Prayer, as a trial of their guilt. After the afflicted seemed to be out of their fits, they would look steadfastly on some one person, and frequently not speak And then the justices said they were struck dumb. And after a little time would speak again. Then the justices said to the accusers, 'Which of you will go and touch the prisoner at the bar?' Then the most courageous would adventure, but before they had made three steps would ordinarily fall down as in a fit. The justices ordered that they should be taken up and carried to the prisoner, that she might touch them. And as soon as they were touched by the accused, the justices would say, they are well, before I could discern any alteration; by which I observed that the justices understood the manner of it. Thus far I was only as a spectator, my wife also was there part of the time, but no notice taken of her by the afflicted, except once or twice they came to her and asked her name.

"But I having an opportunity to discourse Mr. Hale (with whom I had former acquaintance) I took his advice, what I had best to do, and desired of him that I might have an opportunity to speak with her that accused my wife; which he promised should be, I acquainting him that I reposed my trust in him. Accordingly, he came to me after the examination was over, and told me, I had now an opportunity to speak with the said accuser, viz. Abigail Williams, a girl of 11 or 12 years old; but that we could not be in private at Mr. Parris's house, as he had promised me. We went therefore into the Alehouse [Ingersoll's Tavern], where an Indian man [John Indian] attended us, who it seems was one of the afflicted. To him we gave some cider. He showed several scars, that seemed as if they had been long there, and showed them as done by witchcraft, and acquainted us that his wife, who was also a slave, was imprisoned for witchcraft. Now instead of one accuser, they all came in, who began to tumble down like swine, and then three women were called in to attend them. We in the room were all at a stand, to see who they would cry out of; but in a short time they cried out, Cary. And immediately after a warrant was sent from the justices to bring my wife before them, who were sitting in a chamber near by, waiting for this."

"Being brought before the justices, her chief accusers were two girls. My wife declared to the justices that she never had any knowledge of them before that day. She was forced to stand with her arms stretched out. I did request that I might hold one of her hands, but it was denied me. Then she desired me to wipe the tears from her eyes, and the sweat from her face, which I did. Then she desired she might lean herself on me, saying she should faint.

"Justice Hathorne replied, she had strength enough to torment those persons, and she should have strength enough to stand. I speaking something against their cruel proceedings, they commanded me to be silent, or else I should be turned out of the room. The Indian before mentioned, was also brought in, to be one of her accusers. Being come in, he now (when before the justices) fell down and tumbled about like a hog, but said nothing. The justices asked the girls, who afflicted the Indian? They answered she (meaning my wife) and now lay upon him. The justices ordered her to touch him, in order to his cure. But her head must be turned another way, least instead of curing, she should make him worse by her looking on him, her hand being guided to take hold his. But the Indian took hold on her hand, and pulled her down on the floor in a barbarous manner. Then his hand was taken off, and her hand put on his, and the cure was quickly wrought. Then her mittimus was writ. She was committed to Boston prison. But I obtained a Habeas Corpus to remove her to Cambridge prison, which is in our County of Middlesex. Having been there one night, the next morning the jailer put irons on her legs (having received such a command), the weight of them was about eight pounds. These irons and her other afflictions, soon brought her into convulsion fits, so that I thought she would have died that night. I sent to entreat that the irons might be taken off, but all entreaties were in vain, so that, in this condition, she must continue.

"The trials at Salem coming on, I went thither to see how things were there managed. And finding that the specter evidence was there received, together with idle, if not malicious stories, against people lives, I did easily perceive which way the rest would go; for the same evidence that served for one, would serve for all the rest. I acquainted her with her danger, and that, if she were carried to Salem to be tried, I feared she would never return. I did my utmost that she might have her trial in our own County, I with several others petitioning the Judge for it, and were put in hopes of it. But I soon saw so much, that I understood thereby it was not intended, which put me upon consulting the means of her escape, which through the goodness of God was effected. And she got to Rhode Island, but soon found herself not safe when there, by reason of the pursuit after her. From thence she went to New York, along with some others that had escaped their cruel hands, where we found his Excellency Benjamin Fletcher, Esq., Governor, who was very courteous to us. After this some of my goods were seized in a friend's hands, with whom I had left them, and myself imprisoned by the sheriff, and kept in custody half a day and then dismissed."

Captain Cary's account concludes, "But to speak of their usage of the prisoners, and their inhumanity shown to them at the time of their execution, no sober Christian could bear. They had also trials of cruel mockings, which is the more, considering what a people for religion, I mean the profession of it, we have been. Those that suffered being many of them church members, and most of them unspotted in their conversation, till their adversary, the Devil, took up this method for accusing them. Per Nathaniel Cary."

On June 1, 1692 Mary Warren testified that Bridget Bishop, "being in chains, said, though she [Bridget] could not do it, she would bring one that would do it, which she [Mary Warren] now knows to be Mr. Cary." In an undated document, Ann Putnam, Sr. testified against Rebecca Nurse, Sarah Cloyce, Bridget Bishop, and Elizabeth Cary, with regards to the death of "her sister Baker's children of Boston, and that Goody Nurse and Mistress Cary of Charlestown and an old deaf woman at Boston had murdered them."[268]

Ann (Higginson) Dolliver
Gloucester   *June 5, 1692*

Born about 1663 in Salem, Ann Higginson was the daughter of Sarah (Whitefield) and the Rev. John Higginson. In 1682 she married William Dolliver of Gloucester. In 1692 Ann was about twenty-nine years old. At the time of her arrest, she was living with her father in Salem. Her brother, John Higginson, Jr., was the justice of the peace in Salem, and active in the witchcraft prosecutions. The Rev. John Higginson was "worthy of the title Nestor of the New England Clergy."[269] He was seventy-six years old, and had been a preacher for fifty-five years. For thirty-three years he had been pastor of the Salem church of which his father had been the first minister. The assistant minister of the Salem church was the Rev. Nicholas Noyes, a bachelor and a zealous leader of the witchcraft proceedings. Although the Rev. Higginson had offered prayers at some of the examinations, he soon opposed the proceedings. Because of his high standing in the community, the Salem Village accusers were unable to attack him directly, and so went after his daughter. The Andover conspiracy would later use the same tactic against their senior minister, the Rev. Francis Dane.

---

268 *SWP*, 103, 600-1.
269 Upham, 2:194.

On about June 5, 1692 the conspiracy filed a complaint [No. 28] against Ann Dolliver for afflicting Susannah Sheldon and Mary Warren.   On June 6 Peter Osgood, constable of Salem, arrested her, and she was examined and imprisoned.   "How, for instance, do we classify the witch Ann Dolliver?   The daughter of prominent Salem minister John Higginson, who was well above most of his neighbors in wealth and social status, she was also the deserted wife of William Dolliver, and lived out her life without the support of a husband, dependent first on her father and then on the town for maintenance."[270]

On November 5, 1692, Ann's sister-in-law, Rebecca (Dolliver) Dike, and Rebecca's aunt, Esther (Dutch) Elwell, were accused and imprisoned.   Constable Osgood's mother, Mary (Clement) Osgood of Andover, was imprisoned on September 8, 1692.

Mary (Perkins) Bradbury
Salisbury   *June 28, 1692*

Mary Perkins was born in 1615 in England, the daughter of Judith (Gater) and John Perkins, later of Ipswich, Massachusetts. Around 1636 she married Thomas Bradbury. In 1640 they were among the first settlers of Salisbury, Massachusetts. Because of a disagreement with Mary Bradbury in 1679, George Carr of Salisbury spread vicious rumors that she was a witch.   His daughter was Ann (Carr) Putnam, Sr., the wife of Thomas Putnam, the leading accuser of Salem Village in 1692.

"To flesh out the connection between women's work in a developing economy and the propensity of witches to thwart domestic processes, consider the witches (at least nineteen) who were castigated for their unusual success in domestic pursuits. These were women who turned their food and textile production, brewing and other domestic work into profitable business enterprises. Mary Bradbury's butter business in Salisbury was so successful that she was able to supply outgoing ships; she was accused of witchcraft after two firkins of butter went bad on a

---

270 Karlsen, 78.

ship several days out to sea, confirming rumors the crew had heard that she was a witch."[271]

In 1692, Mary Bradbury, seventy-seven, and her husband, eighty-two, enjoyed high civic and social status. On May 26, 1692 George Herrick, marshal of Essex County, attested at Salem Village that Mary Walcott and Ann Putnam, Jr. "complained against Capt. Bradbury's wife of Salisbury." Because of the prestigious position of the Bradburys and because of the efforts made by Robert Pike of Salisbury, an assistant to the governor, no complaint was made against Mary at that time. At the examination of Job Tookey of Beverly on June 4, Mary Warren "cried out upon one Buss." He was Bradbury's son-in-law, the Rev. John Buss, of Durham, New Hampshire.

On about June 28, 1692 the conspiracy filed a complaint [No. 29] against Mary Bradbury. She was arrested the next day, examined, and imprisoned. On July 22 a petition on behalf of Mary Bradbury was signed by one hundred fifteen friends and neighbors from Salisbury. On July 22, after physical torture, Richard Carrier, eighteen, and his brother, Andrew, fifteen, were forced to confess. Richard said that Mrs. Bradbury had afflicted Timothy Swan of Andover. When asked, "What was the occasion Mrs. Bradbury would have to afflict Timothy Swan?" he answered, "Because her husband and Timothy Swan fell out about a scythe, I think." Asked, "Did they not fall out about thatching of a barn?" he responded, "No, not as I know of." On July 26 Ann Putnam, Jr. and Mary Walcott visited Andover, and later testified that on this date they saw Mrs. Bradbury or her "Appearance" afflict Timothy Swan. On July 28 Captain Bradbury presented a deposition in favor of his "loving and faithful wife, wonderful laborious, diligent, and industrious in her place and employment."

On September 5, 1692 Timothy Swan of Andover and Richard and James Carr of Salisbury were summoned to appear as witnesses against Mary Bradbury at the Court of Oyer and Terminer in Salem. On September 7, Robert Pike took

---

271   Karlsen, 145-146.

depositions in favor of Mary Bradbury from the Rev. James Allin and from John Pike.

On September 9, 1692 Samuel Endicott, thirty-one, testified that "about eleven years since, being bound upon a voyage to sea, just before we sailed, Mrs. Bradbury came to Boston with some firkins of butter of which Captain Smith bought two, one of them proved half-way butter, and after we had been at sea three weeks, our men were not able to eat it, it stank so and run with maggots, which made the men very much disturbed about it and would often say that they heard Mrs. Bradbury was a witch."

Ann Putnam, Jr. stated that, "her Uncle John Carr appeared in a winding sheet and cried for revenge." However her uncle William Carr tried to discredit her assertion. He was the only Carr who took Mary Bradbury's side. William Carr, forty-one, was the son-in-law of Robert Pike. His deposition stated that his brother John "died peacefully and quietly, never manifesting the least trouble in the world about anybody, nor did not say anything [about] Mrs. Bradbury nor anybody else doing him hurt."[272]

On September 9, 1692 Mary Bradbury was condemned by the Court of Oyer and Terminer and sentenced to death. However she was smuggled out of prison and hidden by her family until the following spring.

In 1695 Captain Thomas Bradbury, eighty-four, died in Salisbury, and in 1700, his wife Mrs. Mary (Perkins) Bradbury, eighty-five, died at Salisbury.

THE JACOBS

The Jacobs family was an important target for the Salem Village conspiracy. Daniel Andrew, the fourth richest man in Salem Village and a selectman of Salem, was a member of this family by marriage. His accusation represented a major victory for the conspiracy.

---

272 *SWP*, 117, 121, 125, 126, 198, 762, 956. John Carr had died a natural death in 1689 when his niece Ann Putnam, Jr. was 9 years of age.

George Jacobs, Sr.
Salem   *May 10, 1692*

In 1692 George Jacobs, Sr. was "aged," in his mid-to-late seventies. He walked with the aid of two canes. He had resided in Salem for some thirty-three years and had acquired a large amount of land. George and his second wife, Mary, lived in a substantial home. Living with them were his granddaughter Margaret Jacobs, sixteen, and a servant girl Sarah Churchill, twenty. Sarah Churchill was an important member of the outer circle of the afflicted girls.

On May 10, 1692 the conspiracy filed a complaint [No. 13] against George Jacobs, Sr. and his granddaughter Margaret Jacobs. They were arrested the same day. In his examination George Jacobs, Sr. laughed when he was told that the circle of afflicted girls accused him. He said, "I am as innocent as the child born tonight. I have lived thirty-three years here in Salem. If you can prove that I am guilty, I will lie under it, Sarah." The magistrate said, "Look there, she accuses you to your face." Jacobs answered, "You tax me for a wizard, you may as well tax me for a buzzard. I have done no harm." Sarah Churchill then said, "I know that you have lived a wicked life." When asked "Why do you not pray in your family?" he replied "I cannot read." When asked to repeat the Lord's Prayer, he missed in several parts of it." He was imprisoned.

At another examination on May 11, the bewitched fell into "most grievous fits and screechings" when George Jacobs, Sr. came into the room. George still refused to confess. In Salem prison, he was given a physical examination by marshal George Herrick, prison keeper William Dounton, and constable Joseph Neale.

On May 14, 1692 George Jacobs, Jr., his wife Rebecca (Andrew) Frost Jacobs, and her brother Daniel Andrew were accused. The two men fled, but Rebecca was imprisoned on May 17.

Sarah Churchill had been imprisoned at Salem shortly after the accusations were made against her master. On June 1 she confessed that Ann Pudeator, Bridget Bishop, and "old George Jacobs" had made her a witch, he "having called her bitch-witch & ill names & then afflicted her."[273]

On August 4, 1692 summons were issued to Joseph Flint, John Water, Sr., Corporal John Foster, and John De Rich to give testimony against George Jacobs, Sr. in addition to the usual testimony provided by the afflicted girls and the Salem Village conspirators. On August 5, 1692 the Court of Oyer and Terminer condemned to George Jacobs, Sr. to death.

Some time during the period August 5-18, Jacobs' granddaughter Margaret recanted her confession, in which she had falsely accused him as well as the Rev. George Burroughs. On August 12 in prison, George Jacobs, Sr. changed his will of January 29, 1692 and made his wife, Mary, sole executrix in place of his son George Jacobs, Jr. and son-in-law Daniel Andrew. In a codicil, he granted a legacy of ten pounds sterling to his granddaughter Margaret Jacobs.[274]

On August 19, 1692 George Jacobs, Sr. was hanged at Salem. Sheriff George Corwin immediately seized Jacobs' movable property, including five cows at £3 per cow, eight loads of English hay taken from the barn worth £14.00.0, a parcel of apples that made twenty-five barrels of cider worth £14.16.0, sixty bushels of Indian corn worth £7.10.0, one mare worth £2.00.0, two good feather beds & furniture, rugs, blankets, etc. worth £10.00.0, two brass kettles worth £6.00.0, £0.12.0 in cash, a large gold thumb ring worth £1.00.0, five swine worth £3.16.0, and a quantity of pewter worth £3.00.0. The total came to £67.13.0. In addition, there was an "abundance of small things, meat in the house, fowls, chairs, and other things, took clear away," worth £12.0.0.[275]

In 1693 his widow, Mary Jacobs, married widower John Wildes at Topsfield. She was his third wife. His second wife,

---

273   *SWP*, 211, 701.
274   Greene, "Salem Witches II."
275   *SWP*, 997-998.

Sarah (Averill) Wildes had been hanged for witchcraft at Salem on July 19, 1692, and two of his daughters had been imprisoned.

Margaret Jacobs
Salem Village   *May 10, 1692*

Margaret Jacobs was born in 1675 at Salem Village, the eldest child of Rebecca (Andrew) Frost and George Jacobs, Jr.

In 1692 Margaret, sixteen, was living in the Salem home of her grandfather George Jacobs, Sr.   Sarah Churchill was a servant in the house.

On May 10, 1692 the conspiracy filed a complaint [No. 13] against George Jacobs, Sr. and his granddaughter Margaret Jacobs.   They were arrested the same day.   Margaret was examined after her grandfather, but there is no record of her examination.   According to testimony of Joseph Flint, she confessed.   She was imprisoned.   On May 12 Margaret testified against Alice Parker.   On May 13 Margaret testified against Abigail Somes.[276]

On May 14, 1692 a complaint was made against Margaret's mother and father and her uncle Daniel Andrew.   The two men fled but on May 17 her mother, Rebecca Jacobs, was imprisoned. On August 5 her grandfather George Jacobs, Sr. and the Rev. George Burroughs were condemned by the Court of Oyer and Terminer.   Some time during the period August 5-18, Margaret recanted her confession saying that in it she had falsely accused her grandfather and the Rev. Burroughs.   On August 19 George Jacobs, Sr. and the Rev. George Burroughs were hanged at Salem. The next day, on August 20, 1692 Margaret wrote a letter to her father who was in hiding, "Dear father, let me beg your prayers to the Lord on my behalf, and send us a joyful and happy meeting in heaven."   Samuel Wardwell, forty-nine, was the only other person to recant his confession; he did so on September 13 and was hanged on September 22, 1692.

---

276 *SWP*, 484, 623, 736.

On September 5, 1692 John De Rich, about 16 (whose mother and many other family members were imprisoned) testified against Margaret Jacobs, among others. Because Margaret was very ill, her trial was postponed. In Calef's words, "At the time appointed for her trial, she had an imposthume in her head, which was her escape [from trial]." In early December 1692, a recognizance bond was posted for her.

On January 3, 1693 at the Superior Court of Judicature at Salem, in a trial by jury, she was found not guilty. Her mother also was found not guilty.

In 1699, Margaret Jacobs married John Foster. Although she belonged to the parish of the Rev. Nicholas Noyes, her recollection of his agency in the witchcraft proceedings made it impossible for her to think of being married by him. The Rev. Joseph Greene, the minister who replaced Samuel Parris at Salem Village, was known to sympathize with those who had suffered, and the couple went there to be united.

Daniel Andrew
Salem Village   *May 14, 1692*

Daniel Andrew was born about 1644 in Watertown, son of Rebecca and Thomas Andrew. His widowed mother in 1648 married widower Nicholas Wyeth; again widowed she married Thomas Fox becoming his fourth wife. Daniel Andrew moved in 1669, at twenty-five, to Salem Town. Within a few years he bought two house lots. On one of them there was an apothecary's shop where he dispensed liquor along with medicines. In 1671 he taught school in his home. As he had served an apprenticeship in masonry with his stepfather, he was able soon to settle into the trade of bricklayer in the construction of fine houses. In 1675 he worked on the enlargement of the town house of Jonathan Corwin, son of Salem's most eminent merchant. Two years later, he obtained the contract for the new Salem meetinghouse.

Daniel Andrew married, about 1676 in Salem, Sarah Porter, youngest daughter of John Porter. Her father had recently died, and she inherited a half interest in a large tract of land in Salem

Village close to the Wenham line. After their marriage, Daniel and Sarah moved there. Daniel's Porter brothers-in-law (Israel, Joseph, and Benjamin Porter), and his sister, Rebecca, and her husband George Jacobs, Jr. were his neighbors. A year after his marriage he purchased the remaining half interest in this village farm for cash from another brother-in-law, Thomas Gardner. Daniel Andrew became a dominant presence in Salem Village. Over the years he increased his estate through his construction business. In February 1692 he purchased a wharf situated where the Frost Fish Brook widened into the navigable Frost Fish River. From this dock, produce could be transported from Salem Village to Salem and other seaports. Even though he had been living in Salem Village for many years, it is clear that his loyalties and ambitions, and even his ordinary employment, remained firmly linked to the town. In 1685 and 1691 he was a selectman of Salem Town, and in 1692 he was again elected to this important post.

In 1692 Daniel was about forty-eight. His sister Rebecca was the wife of George Jacobs, Jr. On March 19, Daniel Andrew together with Israel Porter, his wife Elizabeth (Hathorne) Porter, and Peter Cloyce visited Rebecca Nurse regarding the rumors of her being accused of witchcraft. In the first part of May 1692, Sarah and Daniel, with thirty-seven other citizens, signed a petition in favor of Rebecca Nurse.

On May 14, 1692 the conspiracy filed a complaint [No. 17] against Daniel Andrew and seven others, including George Jacobs, Jr. and his wife, Rebecca (Andrew) Frost Jacobs. She was Daniel Andrew's sister. They were all accused "for high suspicion of sundry acts of witchcraft by them done or lately committed on the body of Ann Putnam, Jr., Mercy Lewis, Mary Walcott and Abigail Williams & others whereby much hurt is done to their bodies, therefore craves justice." A warrant was issued for arrest for appearance on May 17. However Daniel Andrew and George Jacobs, Jr. had already fled. On May 17, 1692 Jonathan Putnam, constable in Salem, reported, "Have made diligent search at the home of Daniel Andrew and at the house of George Jacobs for them, but cannot find them." Another warrant for their arrest was forthcoming, "To the marshal general or lawful deputy of constables in Boston or elsewhere," signed by magistrates Hathorne and Corwin.

Elizabeth Booth testified against Daniel Andrew on May 18, 1692, and Susannah Sheldon on May 20. Both of these girls were members of the outer circle. Daniel Andrew and George Jacobs, Jr. remained in hiding until 1693 when the delusion was over.[277]

George Jacobs, Jr.
Salem Village *May 14, 1692*

Rebecca (Andrew) Frost Jacobs
Salem Village *May 14, 1692*

George Jacobs, Jr. was born about 1642, son of George Jacobs, Sr. of Salem. George Jacobs, Jr. married, in 1675 in Salem, Rebecca (Andrew) Frost, born 1646, daughter of Rebecca and Thomas Andrew. Rebecca had first married John Frost in 1666 in Cambridge. John Frost was born about 1634 and died in 1672.

In 1692 George Jacobs, Jr., about fifty, and his wife Rebecca, forty-six, the sister of Daniel Andrew, lived in Salem Village. Four of their children, between the ages of three and fifteen, lived with them. Their daughter Margaret Jacobs, sixteen, was living with her grandfather George Jacobs, Sr. in Salem. Rebecca Jacobs had been emotionally unstable for a number of years, in part due to the death of a two-year-old daughter by accidental drowning, for which Rebecca blamed herself. On May 10 George Jacobs, Sr. and granddaughter Margaret Jacobs were accused and then imprisoned.

On May 14, 1692 the conspiracy filed a complaint [No. 17] against George Jacobs, Jr. and his wife, Rebecca (Andrew) Frost Jacobs and six others, including Rebecca's brother Daniel Andrew. On May 17 constable Jonathan Putnam arrested Rebecca Jacobs, Sarah Buckley, and Mary Whittredge. They were secured in the watch house, and then imprisoned. Daniel Andrew and George Jacobs, Jr. fled and remained in hiding until the following year. After Rebecca's arrest, the house was stripped of

---

277 *SWP*, 487, 493, 494, 592, 593, 693, 803.

its contents and left open and deserted, and the children were scattered and taken in by other people.

On August 5, 1692 George Jacobs, Sr. was condemned by the Court of Oyer and Terminer. Some time between August 5 and August 18, Margaret Jacobs recanted her confession and was placed in the dungeon. Her grandfather was hanged on August 19, and on the next day Margaret wrote to her father, George Jacobs, Jr., in hiding with Daniel Andrew, that "My mother, poor woman, is very crazy, and remembers her kind love to you, and to uncle [Daniel Andrew]."

On September 10, 1692 at the jury of inquest for the Court of Oyer and Terminer at Salem, Elizabeth Hubbard testified, "On the beginning of May 1692, I was afflicted by Rebecca Jacobs, but on the 18th May 1692, being the day of her examination, I saw Rebecca Jacobs or her appearance most grievously afflict Mary Walcott, Abigail Williams, and Ann Putnam [Jr.]. I believe in my heart that Rebecca Jacobs is a witch."

On about September 14, 1692 Rebecca Fox (Rebecca Jacobs' mother) sent a petition to Chief Justice William Stoughton, "Rebecca Jacobs has long lain in prison for witchcraft, and she at some times has uttered hard words of herself as though she had killed her child. Rebecca Jacobs is a woman broken & distracted in her mind, & that she has been so at times above these 12 years." The mother requested that "there may not be stress laid on the confession of a distracted woman to the prejudice of her life."

In November 1692, Rebecca Fox sent a petition to Governor Phipps and his Council, "Rebecca Jacobs has a long time, even many months now, lain in prison for witchcraft, and is well known to be a person crazed, distracted & broken in mind, and that she has been so these twelve years and upwards. Some have died already in prison, and others have been dangerously sick, and how soon others, and among them my poor child, by the difficulties of this confinement may be sick and die, God only knows."

In January 1693, at the Superior Court of Judicature at Salem, Rebecca Jacobs was found not guilty in a trial by jury. Margaret Jacobs' trial followed that of her mother, and she was also found not guilty. Unable to pay her prison fees, Rebecca was not released until April. Her total time in prison was nearly eleven months.

Calef wrote, "George Jacobs, son to old Jacobs, being accused, he fled. Then the officers came to his house. His wife was a woman crazy in her senses, and had been so several years. She it seems also had been accused. There were in the house with her only four small children, and one of them sucked her eldest daughter, being in prison. The officer persuaded her out of the house, to go along with him, telling her she should speedily return. The children ran a great way after her, crying. When she came to where the afflicted were, being asked, they said they did not know her. At length, one said, 'Don't you know Jacobs, the old witch?' And then they cried out against her, and fell down in their fits. She was sent to prison, and lay there ten months. The neighbors of pity took care of the children to preserve them from perishing." In 1710 George Jacobs, Jr. wrote, "When my father was executed and I was forced to fly out of the country to my great damage and distress of my family, my wife imprisoned 11 months and my daughter 7 months, it cost them £12 to the officers besides other charges."[278] George Jacobs, Jr. had died by 1718.

EXPANSION TO THE SOUTHWEST

The Salem Village witch hunt spread southwest to the towns of Reading, Woburn, and Malden.

Lydia (mnu) Dustin
Reading   *April 30, 1692*

Sarah Dustin
Reading   *May 7, 1692*

Mary (Dustin) Colson
Reading   *September 5, 1692*

---

278 Calef, 267. *SWP*, 821.998.

Elizabeth Colson

Reading   *May 14, 1692*

Lydia was born about 1626 in England. She married, about 1644 in Reading, Massachusetts, Josiah Dustin who died in 1671. Her children included Mary, who was born in 1650, and Sarah, who was born in 1653. Mary married Adam Colson in 1668, and their daughter Elizabeth Colson was born in 1676 in Reading.

In 1692 Lydia Dustin, in her mid-sixties and a widow for twenty-one years, resided in Reading with her daughter Sarah Dustin, thirty-nine, her widowed daughter, Mary Colson, forty-two, and Mary's daughter, Elizabeth Colson, fifteen.

On April 30, 1692 the conspiracy filed a complaint [No. 10] against Lydia Dustin. On May 2 she was arrested, examined and imprisoned. On May 8 the conspiracy filed a complaint [No. 11] against her unmarried daughter, Sarah Dustin. On May 9 John Parker, constable of Reading, arrested Sarah and took her to the tavern of Lieutenant Nathaniel Ingersoll in Salem Village for examination. She was imprisoned. On May 14 the conspiracy filed a complaint [No. 17] against Lydia Dustin's granddaughter, Elizabeth Colson. On May 16 John Parker, constable of Reading, reported, "I have made diligent search for Elizabeth Colson and find she is fled and by the best information she is at Boston in order to be shipped off, and by way of escape to be transported to some other country." On May 17 a second warrant was issued for her arrest, but she still was not captured. On September 5, 1692, in order to flush out Elizabeth, a complaint was filed against Elizabeth's mother, Mary (Dustin) Colson, who was then arrested and imprisoned. On September 10 a third warrant was issued for Elizabeth Colson's arrest. William Arnold of Reading revealed the "she is now concealed in Boston." On September 14 Elizabeth Colson was finally captured, and she was imprisoned in Cambridge. Thus, by mid-September 1692, the mother, her two daughters, and her granddaughter were in prison.

On January 28, 1693 the four were taken from Salem prison and returned to Cambridge prison. On January 31 they were taken out of Cambridge prison and sent to Charlestown prison.

On February 1, 1693 Lydia Dustin and her daughter Sarah Dustin were tried by jury at the sitting of the Superior Court of Judicature at Charlestown for Middlesex County. The verdict for both was not guilty. There is no record of the trial of either Elizabeth Colson or Mary Colson. According to Calef, the "daughter and granddaughter were also acquitted."

An eyewitness gave this account of Lydia's trial. "The most remarkable was an old woman named Dustin, of whom it was said, *If any in the world were a witch, she was one, and had been so accounted 30 years.* I had the curiosity to see her tried; she was a decrepit woman of about 80 years of age, and did not use many words in her own defense. She was accused by about 30 witnesses; but the matter alleged against her was such as needed little apology, on her part not one passionate word, or immoral action, or evil, was then objected against her for 20 years past, only strange accidents falling out, after some Christian admonition given by her, as saying, *God would not proper them, if they wronged the widow.* Upon the whole, there was not proved against her anything worthy of reproof, or just admonition, much less so heinous a charge."[279]

Calef reports, "After she was cleared, judge Danforth admonished her in these words, *Woman, woman, repent; there are shrewd things come in against you.*" Not being able to pay the exorbitant prison fees, Lydia, her two daughters, and her granddaughter were returned to prison. On February 11 Lydia Dustin, her daughter Sarah Dustin, and her granddaughter were moved to Cambridge prison from the Charlestown prison. On March 2 Elizabeth Colson was released. On March 10 Lydia Dustin died in Cambridge prison. On March 23, 1693 Sarah Dustin was released.[280] There is no record for Mary Colson.

---

279 *A Further Account*, 216-217.

280 *SWP*, 936-937, 957-958. Calef, 333-334. (Calef mistakenly wrote Sarah Dustin's name when he meant Lydia Dustin. Speaking of Lydia, he wrote, "The specter evidence was not made use of in these trials, so the jury soon brought her in not guilty. Her daughter and granddaughter, and the rest that

Bethia (Pearson) Carter
Woburn   *May 8, 1692*

Bethia Carter, Jr.
Woburn   *May 8, 1692*

Bethia Pearson was born in 1645 in Lynn, daughter of Maudlin (mnu) and John Pearson of Reading. About 1668 she married Joseph Carter, Jr. They had seven children. Their eldest child, Bethia Carter, Jr. was born in 1671 in Woburn. Joseph Carter, Jr. died in early 1692. In 1669 at the witchcraft trial of Ann (Holland) Bassett Burt, Bethia (Pearson) Carter testified and mentioned her sister, Sarah (Pearson) Townsend, who had been a maid at the widow Burt's house.[281]

In 1692 Bethia, forty-six, recently widowed, resided in Woburn with six or seven of her children, including the eldest, Bethia Carter, Jr., twenty-one. On May 8, 1692 the conspiracy filed a complaint [No. 12] against Bethia (Pearson) Carter, Bethia Carter, Jr., and Ann Farrar Sears, all of Woburn. On May 9 Ephraim Bock, constable of Woburn, arrested widow Bethia Carter and Ann Sears and took them to the tavern of Lieutenant Nathaniel Ingersoll in Salem Village. They were then imprisoned. Young Bethia Carter, Jr. had fled. On May 14 the conspiracy included her in another complaint.[282] There is no further record of Bethia Carter, Jr. She remained in hiding until the following year.

On December 8, 1692 Captain John Pearson posted a recognizance bond of two hundred pounds sterling to bail out his sister Bethia Carter, Sr. and also George Lilly, Jr. "For appearance at Middlesex Court" is written on the reverse side of the bond. In February 1693 the Superior Court of Judicature for

---

were then tried, were also acquitted. She was remanded to prison for her fees, and there in a short time expired.")

281 Hall, *Witch-Hunting*, 185-186.
282 *SWP*, 487, 729.

Middlesex County was held at Charlestown. However there is no record extant for Bethia Carter, Sr.

Ann (mnu) Farrar Sears
Woburn   *May 8, 1692*

Ann was born about 1621 in England. There, about 1642, she married Jacob Farrar, who was slain by Indians at Lancaster, Massachusetts, in 1675. (There is no apparent kinship with the Thomas Farrar family of Lynn.) She married again in 1680, John Sears of Woburn, who had been twice a widower.

In 1692 Ann, in her early seventies, resided in Woburn with her husband. On May 8, 1692 the conspiracy named Ann Sears on the same complaint [No. 12] as that of widow Bethia Carter, Sr. and daughter. On May 9 Ann Sears and Bethia Carter, Sr. were both arrested by constable Ephraim Bock and imprisoned.

On December 3, 1692 a recognizance bond of two hundred pounds sterling was posted by Jonathan Prescott of Concord and John Horton of Lancaster, presumed to be her sons-in-law, to bail out Ann for her appearance at the next court in Middlesex County. There is no record of Ann Sears' case.

Sarah (mnu) Davis Rice
Reading   *May 28, 1692*

Sarah was born about 1631. About 1650 she married George Davis of Lynn and Reading, and after his death married, about 1670, Nicholas Rice of Reading.

In 1692 Sarah was around sixty and resided in Reading with her second husband. On May 26 George Herrick, marshal of Essex County, attested at Salem Village that Ann Putnam, Jr., Mary Walcott, and Mrs. Mary (Swayne) Marshall were "afflicted much and complained against Goodwife Rice of Reading."

On May 28, 1692 the conspiracy filed a complaint [No. 23] against Sarah Rice. On May 31 John Parker, constable of Reading, arrested her and took her to the tavern of Lieutenant Nathaniel Ingersoll in Salem Village. There is no extant record of her examination. She was ordered to Boston prison along with Captain John Alden.[283]

On October 19, 1692 Nicholas Rice petitioned the General Court on behalf of his wife, "who was taken into custody the first day of June last and ever since lain in Boston jail for witchcraft, though in all this time nothing has been made appear for which she deserved imprisonment or death. She lived with me above twenty years as a good faithful dutiful wife. It is deplorable that in old age the poor decrepit woman should lie under confinement so long in a stenching jail when her circumstances rather require a nurse to attend her." There is no further record extant.

Elizabeth (mnu) Betts Fosdick

Malden   *May 28, 1692*

Elizabeth was born about 1660. About 1680 she married widower John Betts of Charlestown, who died May 22, 1684. About 1685 she married widower John Fosdick of Malden, a carpenter.

In 1692, Elizabeth Fosdick, in her early thirties, resided in Malden with her husband. On May 26 at Salem Village George Herrick, marshal of Essex, stated that Mercy Lewis, Ann Putnam, Jr., and Mary Walcott were afflicted "much and complained against Goody Fosdick, the same woman tells them that she afflicts Mr. Tufts' Negro." Three other women, Mary Bradbury, Sarah Rice, and Wilmot Redd, were also cried out upon.

On May 28, 1692 the conspiracy filed a complaint [No. 23] against Elizabeth Fosdick. On May 30 the conspiracy filed another complaint [No. 24] against her and Elizabeth Paine. On June 2 Peter Tufts of Charlestown filed still another complaint [No. 25] against both of them, claiming that they afflicted his Negro woman slave. Tufts' daughter-in-law, Mary (Cotton) Tufts, was a first cousin of the Rev. Cotton Mather. Elizabeth Paine was

---

283 *SWP*, 117, 54.

arrested on June 2, but Elizabeth Fosdick was not arrested until the following day.[284] Both were imprisoned.

There remains no record of Elizabeth Fosdick's trial from the session of the Superior Court of Judicature for the County of Middlesex held on January 31, 1693 at Charlestown. In 1716 she died at Malden.

Elizabeth (Carrington) Paine
Malden *May 30, 1692*

Elizabeth Carrington was born about 1636. About 1657 she married Stephen Paine, a husbandman of Malden. In 1692 Elizabeth Paine was in her mid-fifties, living with her husband in Malden.

On May 30, 1692 the conspiracy filed a complaint [No. 24] against her and Elizabeth Fosdick. On June 2 Peter Tufts of Charlestown filed another complaint [No. 25] against them for afflicting his Negro woman slave. Elizabeth Paine was arrested on June 2, but Elizabeth Fosdick was not arrested until the following day. Both were imprisoned.

There is no record of Elizabeth Paine's trial from the session of the Superior Court of Judicature for Middlesex County held on January 31, 1693 at Charlestown. It is believed that Stephen Paine died in 1693, and Elizabeth then married David Carwithen. In 1711 Elizabeth Carwithen died at Malden.

Mary (Leach) Ireson
Lynn *June 4, 1692*

Mary Leach, born about 1655, married, in 1680 in Lynn, Benjamin Ireson (also spelled Iyerson), born in 1645, the son of Edward Ireson of Lynn. In 1692, Mary, about thirty-seven, lived in Lynn with her husband.

On Saturday June 4, 1692 the conspiracy filed a complaint [No. 26] against her. On June 6 Henry Collins, constable of Lynn, arrested her and took her to Thomas Beadle's tavern in Salem.

---

284 *SWP*, 117, 183, 339, 340.

There is no extant record of her examination. She was imprisoned. A deposition against both Mary Toothaker and Mary Ireson states that "Mary Warren told us that Dr. Toothaker's wife brought the book to her, and a basin and a winding sheet and grave clothes, and said that she must set her hand to the book or else she would kill her, and still she urged to touch the book or else be wrapped in that sheet. Mary Iyerson, wife to Benjamin Iyerson at Lynn, in the same manner has tormented almost to death and brought the book to her."[285]

EXPANSION TO THE NORTHWEST

The Salem Village witch hunt spread to Billerica and Andover, towns northwest of Salem Village. These arrests were the precursors of the Andover witch hunt.

Dr. Roger Toothaker
Billerica   *May 18, 1692*

Mary (Allen) Toothaker
Billerica   *May 28, 1692*

Margaret Toothaker
Billerica   *May 28, 1692*

Roger Toothaker was born about 1634 in England, son of Margaret and Roger Toothaker. He became a physician and settled in Billerica, Massachusetts. In 1665 he married Mary Allen. She was born about 1645 in Andover, daughter of Faith (Ingalls) and Andrew Allen. The children of Roger and Mary included Martha, born 1668, Allen, born 1670, and Margaret, born 1683.

---

285 *SWP*, 765. The name Jerson Toothaker which appears there is in error. The reverse side of the original document reads, "Mary Warren ag't Iyerson [and] Toothaker." The WPA transcriber mistook the "Iy" as a "J," making Iyerson into Jerson. Thus the transcription came out as "Mary Warren ag't Jerson Toothaker." There was never any such person as Jerson Toothaker.

In 1692 Roger, about fifty-eight, resided in Billerica with his wife Mary, about forty-seven, two sons, and daughter Margaret, nine. Daughter Martha was married to Joseph Emerson in Haverhill, and son Allen Toothaker resided in Andover.

On about May 18, 1692 the conspiracy filed a complaint [No. 19] against Dr. Roger Toothaker. They charged him with afflicting, among others, Elizabeth Hubbard, servant of Dr. Griggs of Salem Village. He was arrested and sent to Boston prison. On May 28 the conspiracy filed a complaint [No. 23] against his wife, Mary Toothaker, his young daughter Margaret Toothaker and his sister-in-law Martha (Allen) Carrier of Andover. They were arrested and taken to Salem Village for examination, and then imprisoned at Salem.

Thomas Gage, about thirty-six, and Elias Pickworth, about thirty-four, gave depositions about the illnesses of two children that spring. The two men claimed that Dr. Toothaker had said, "I have already seen both the children, and my opinion is they are under an evil hand. My daughter, Martha Emerson, killed a witch. She had learned something from me. She got some of the afflicted person's urine and put it into an earthen pot. She covered the pot very tightly, and put it into a hot oven and closed up the oven. The next morning the witch was dead."

On June 16, 1692 Dr. Roger Toothaker died in the Boston prison. The coroner's warrant required "twenty-four able and sufficient men appear before me at the prison forthwith." In the return of the coroner's jury, Benjamin Walker, foreman, stated, "We have viewed the body and obtained the best information we can from the persons near and present at his death and do find he came to his end by a natural death on this 16 of June 1692." The impaneling of a coroner's jury indicates that Dr. Toothaker died under suspicious circumstances.

On July 23, 1692 Mary's daughter Martha (Toothaker) Emerson was accused, arrested, and imprisoned. On July 30 Mary Toothaker, now a widow, made a confession before the magistrates at Salem. She related her terror of the Indians, a well-grounded fear as Billerica was still subject to periodic raids. Mary confessed to having made a covenant with the Devil in the past May for protection from the Indians. On August 1, the Indians raided Billerica and at least six persons were slain. The Indians returned a few days later and burned down the deserted Toothaker farm.

On August 5, 1692 Mary's sister Martha (Allen) Carrier was condemned by the Court of Oyer and Terminer, and on August 10 she was hanged at Salem. On February 1, 1693 at the Superior Court of Judicature at Charlestown for Middlesex County, Mary Toothaker was found not guilty in a trial by jury.

In 1695 the "Indian enemy" raided Billerica. They killed widow Mary (Allen) Toothaker and carried off her twelve-year old daughter Margaret. After suffering a long imprisonment for witchcraft when she was nine, Margaret Toothaker, "never to be heard of again," was now in the hands of "the children of the Devil."[286]

Martha (Allen) Carrier
Andover   *May 28, 1692*

Martha Allen was born about 1654 in Andover, daughter of Faith (Ingalls) and Andrew Allen, an original proprietor of Andover. In 1674 she married Thomas Carrier of Billerica, who was at least twenty years her senior. Their children included Richard Carrier, born 1674, Andrew Carrier, born 1677, Thomas Carrier, Jr., born 1682, and Sarah Carrier, born 1684, all in Billerica.

In 1692 Martha, about thirty-eight, resided in the south part of Andover with her husband, Thomas, and their five children. When first married, the Carriers had lived in Billerica, where Martha's sister, Mary (Allen) Toothaker, and her family still lived. Around 1686, the Carrier family moved to Andover. In the fall of 1690, the small-pox epidemic which had begun in Boston in late 1689 reached Andover, killing over a dozen people there. Included in this number were seven members of the Allen family.

---

286 *SWP*, 772, 874, 932-933, 949. Robinson and Otten, 2.4-2.6.

The Carriers were accused of bring small-pox to Andover, and were banned from entering public places.

On May 18, 1692 Dr. Roger Toothaker of Billerica was accused, examined, and imprisoned at Boston. On May 28 the conspiracy filed a complaint [No. 23] against Martha Carrier. She was the first person from Andover accused in 1692. On May 31 she was arrested and taken to Lieutenant Nathaniel Ingersoll's tavern in Salem Village for examination. Martha refused to confess. Hathorne asked, "Can you look upon these [the afflicted girls] and not knock them down?" Martha replied, "They will dissemble if I look upon them." She also said, "It is a shameful thing that you should mind these folks that are out of their wits." Another time, she said, "You lie, I am wronged." The written record states, "The tortures of the afflicted was so great that there was no enduring of it, so that she was ordered away & to be bound hand & foot with all expedition." Martha was imprisoned at Salem.

On July 1, 1692 Elizabeth Hubbard and Mary Walcott of the afflicted circle testified against Martha. John Rogers testified that seven years ago, after a dispute with Martha, some of his cattle died. The Rev. Samuel Parris and John Putnam also testified against her. On July 21 Mary Lacey, Jr., eighteen, of Andover, who was imprisoned, stated, "Goody Carrier told me the Devil said to her she should be Queen in Hell." Mary Lacey, Sr., also imprisoned, confirmed her daughter's statement saying, "Carrier told me also that she should be Queen of Hell." Samuel Preston, Jr. testified as to the loss of cattle, two years previously, which Martha had predicted.[287]

On July 22 Martha's sons Richard Carrier, eighteen, and Andrew Carrier, fifteen, were imprisoned. Because they would not name their mother, magistrate John Hathorne ordered them to be physically tortured. Each was tied neck and heels for extended periods, blood coming profusely from their noses. The official document reads, "Richard and Andrew were carried out to another chamber, and there feet and hands bound a little while.

---

287 His brother, Thomas Preston of Salem Village, was married to Rebecca Nurse, daughter of Rebecca (Towne) and Francis Nurse.

After, Richard was brought in again. Q. Richard, though you have been very obstinate, yet tell us how long ago it is since you were taken in this snare? A. A year last May and no more. Unto many questions propounded, he answered affirmatively as followeth." The result was a "confession" induced by Hathorne's leading questions. "Andrew Carrier brought in. Unto many questions asked, he returned the following answers. The Devil is a black man. He was to serve the Devil five years and the Devil was to give him house and land in Andover. Memorandum. This Andrew in his examination stammered and stuttered exceedingly in speaking which some of his neighbors present said he was not wont to do."[288]

On August 5, 1692 Martha Carrier was condemned by the Court of Oyer and Terminer. On August 10 Martha's children Thomas Carrier, Jr., ten, and Sarah Carrier, seven, were imprisoned. Both were tricked by magistrate Hathorne into naming their mother. The abuse of Martha Carrier's four children by the court was a tactic by which they hoped to make her confess; she never did. On August 19, 1692 Martha Carrier was hanged at Salem.

The Rev. Cotton Mather would later write of Martha Carrier, "This rampant hag was the person of whom the confessions of the witches, and of her own children among the rest, agreed that the Devil had promised her that she should be Queen of Hell." The confessions were those of Mary Lacey and her daughter Mary Lacy, Jr. who, terrified, admitted everything put to them; of Martha's sons Richard and Andrew Carrier, who had been tortured; and of Martha's two small children Thomas, Jr. and Sarah Carrier who were too young to fend off Hathorne's abusive questions.

---

288 *SWP*, 523, 525, 527, 530, 598, 599.

EXPANSION TO THE EAST

The accusations spread to Beverly, Ipswich, Gloucester, and Salisbury, towns east of Salem Village. Because Sarah Buckley and her daughter Mary Whittredge were originally from Ipswich and Gloucester, they are included in this group.

Sarah Morrell
Beverly   *April 30, 1692*

Sarah Morrell was born about 1678, daughter of Mary (Butler) and Peter Morrell of Beverly. In 1692 Sarah was about fourteen years old and resided with her parents in Beverly.

On April 30, 1692 the conspiracy filed a complaint [No. 10] against Sarah Morrell and five others, including Dorcas Hoar. On May 2 George Herrick, marshal of Essex, arrested Sarah Morrell and Dorcas Hoar, and they were committed to Boston prison.[289]

In January 1693 Sarah Morrell was cleared by the Superior Court of Judicature at Salem. In 1698 she married John Elinwood at Beverly. In 1710 her mother gave this account, "Our daughter, Sarah Morrell, was falsely accused and imprisoned for the sin of witchcraft in the month of May 1692, and remained in prison till January following. Our daughter was tried and cleared by law, which imprisonment was much more to our damage than I can think or know or can speak."

Sarah (Smith) Buckley
Salem Village   *May 14, 1692*

Mary (Buckley) Whittredge
Salem Village   *May 14, 1692*

Sarah Smith was born about 1636 in England. She married, about 1656, William Buckley, a shoemaker. Their children included Mary Buckley, born about 1664, who married Sylvester Whittredge in 1684. He died a few years later, prior to 1692.

---

289 *SWP*, 550, 873. The name Morrell appears as Morey in *SWP*.

In 1692 Sarah Buckley was in her mid-fifties and a church member. Her husband, William Buckley, originally of Ipswich, then Marblehead, had come upon hard times and the couple, now quite poor, were residing in Salem Village. Their daughter, Mary Whittredge, recently widowed, had returned home to live with her parents. On May 2, 1692, at her preliminary examination, widow Dorcas Hoar of Beverly disclaimed knowing Sarah Buckley, though William Buckley stated that Hoar "had been at the house often."

On May 14, 1692 the conspiracy filed a complaint [No. 17] against Sarah Buckley and her daughter Mary Whittredge. On May 17 Jonathan Putnam, constable of Salem, arrested them. On May 18 at her examination, Sarah refused to confess. Together with John Willard, Sarah was accused of the death of Daniel Wilkins. She was imprisoned with her daughter.[290]

On June 20, 1692, the Rev. William Hubbard of Ipswich gave a deposition as to his long knowledge of Sarah, "I have known Sarah ever since she was brought out of England which is above fifty year ago and in all that time I never knew or heard of any evil in her carriage or conversation unbecoming a Christian." On September 15, 1692 at the grand jury inquest, Benjamin Hutchinson accused Sarah and her daughter Mary of afflicting his wife.

On January 2, 1693, the Rev. John Higginson of Salem and the Rev. Samuel Cheever of Marblehead gave a deposition as to Sarah's "pious conversation." At the Superior Court of Judicature in Salem in January, Sarah Buckley and Mary Whittredge were each found not guilty in trial by jury. They were discharged after paying fees.

"Their goods and chattels had all been seized by the officers, as was the usual practice at the time of their arrest. In humble circumstances before, it took their last shilling to meet the charges of their imprisonment. The poor old woman, with her aged husband, suffered much, there is reason to fear, from absolute want during all the rest of their days. The Rev. Joseph

---

290 *SWP*, 390, 487, 849.

Green has this entry in his diary: 'January 2, 1702. Old William Buckley died this evening. He died with the cold, I fear, for want of comforts and good tending. Lord forgive! He was about eighty years old. He was very poor; but, I hope, had not his portion in this life.' "[291] In 1710 William Buckley, Jr. wrote, "My honored mother Sarah Buckley, and my sister Mary Whittredge were both in prison from May until January following, during which time we were at the whole charge of their maintenance, and, when they were cleared & came out of prison, we were forced to pay for each of them £5 to the officers."[292]

Susannah (mnu) Roots
Beverly   *May 21, 1692*

Susannah was born about 1620 in England. She married, about 1639 in Salem, Josiah Roots. He was born in 1612 in England, and he died in 1683 in Beverly.

In 1692 Susannah was seventy-two and a widow of nine years. On May 21, 1692 the conspiracy filed a complaint [No. 20] against Susannah Roots. On May 23 she was arrested. Andrew Elliott stated, "Leonard Austen of Beverly thought she was a bad woman, who would not say prayers with Austen and his wife when they lived at the Roots home." Elliott also stated that when he had lived at the Roots house, his chamber was below that of Susannah, and "she would rise in the night and talk aloud as if there were 5 or 6 persons with her."

John Lovett, Sr. had married Susannah's daughter Bethia. In June 1692 their son, John Lovett, Jr., about twenty-five, visited his grandmother in prison.[293] No further records are extant.

---

291 Upham, 199.
292 *SWP*, 982.
293 *SWP*, 401-402, 722.

Mehitabel (Brabrook) Downing
Ipswich   *May 15, 1692*

Joanna (mnu) Brabrook Penny
Gloucester   *September 13, 1692*

Joanna was born about 1620 in England. She married, about 1649, widower Richard Brabrook of Ipswich, who died in 1681. She married a second time in 1682, becoming the third wife of Thomas Penny of Gloucester, who died in August of 1692.

Mehitabel Brabrook was born about 1652 in Ipswich, the daughter of Richard Brabrook. Her birth may have been the result of an extramarital relationship of her father. His second wife, Joanna, raised Mehitabel.

On an August afternoon in 1668, Mehitabel Brabrook, then the sixteen-year-old servant of Elizabeth and Jacob Perkins of Ipswich, was alone in the house and was smoking a pipe. Going outside, she climbed to the top of the oven, which projected from the back of the house, "to look if there were any hogs in the corn," and knocked out her pipe on the thatch at the eaves. The house caught fire. The efforts of the neighbors to save it were futile and it burned to the ground. Mehitabel, convicted of extreme carelessness "if not willfully burning the house," was severely whipped and ordered to pay forty pounds sterling to her master.[294] In 1669, Mehitabel Brabrook married John Downing of Ipswich.

In 1692, Mehitabel Downing, about forty, lived in Ipswich with her husband and children. On about May 15, 1692 the conspiracy filed a complaint [No. 18] against her. She was arrested and imprisoned for witchcraft. Few records are extant.

On June 1, 1692, Mary Warren, an afflicted girl who at that time was imprisoned at Salem, testified, "When I was in prison in Salem a fortnight ago, Mr. George Burroughs, Goody Nurse, Goody

---

294 Otten, *Witch Hunt*, 104. Karlsen, 96. (Jacob Perkins was the brother of Mary (Perkins) Bradbury condemned for witchcraft on September 9, 1692.)

Proctor, Goody Darling [Downing?] and others [specters] unknown came to this deponent."[295]

In September 1692 Joanna Penny, just widowed, was in her early seventies. On September 13, 1692 Zebulon Hill of Salem filed a complaint against her for afflicting his daughter Mary Hill. (This complaint, belonging to the second phase, or Andover witch hunt, is not listed in the table in Chapter 7, which includes only complaints for the first phase, or Salem Village witch hunt.) Zebulon Hill was formerly of Gloucester but had moved to Salem by 1662. His nephew Ebenezer Babson of Gloucester was also an accuser in 1692. On September 20 Zebulon Hill posted a bond for one hundred pounds sterling for execution of his complaint and warrant for arrest. On September 21 John Chote, constable of Ipswich, arrested Joanna and took her to Salem for examination.

On about December 12, 1692, Joanna Penny, Mehitabel Downing, and Rachel (Haffield) Clinton were among the ten signers of a petition from Ipswich prison. In 1693 Joanna Penny and Mehitabel Downing were released.

Abigail Somes
Gloucester   *May 13, 1692*

Abigail Somes was born in 1655 in Gloucester, daughter of Elizabeth (Kendall) and Morris Somes.

In 1692 Abigail, thirty-seven, was living at the home of Samuel Gaskill in Salem. She had been bed-ridden for about a year, recuperating from disfiguring small-pox. On about May 13, 1692 the conspiracy filed a complaint [No. 16] against Abigail Somes. She was arrested and taken to Thomas Beadle's tavern in Salem. She would not confess at her examination. The scribe wrote, "Mary Warren affirmed that Somes was the instrumental means of the death of Southwick. Upon which Somes, casting her eye on Warren, pitched her into a dreadful fit, and [Somes' specter] bit her so dreadfully that the like was never seen on any of the afflicted. Further Warren affirms that Somes ran two pins

---

295 *SWP*, 173.

into her side this day, which, being plucked out, the blood ran out after them. Warren further affirms she told her that when she did go abroad at any time it was in the night." Abigail Somes was imprisoned.[296]

On January 6, 1693 at the grand jury inquest of the Superior Court of Judicature at Salem, Mary Warren stated that Abigail had afflicted her, that Abigail "had been bedridden a twelvemonth or thereabouts & that she had never been out in the daytime in that time, but had been very often abroad in the night." The grand jury dismissed the case.

Sarah (mnu) Pease
Salem   *May 23, 1692*

In 1692, Sarah resided in Salem with her husband, Robert Pease, Jr., a weaver. On May 23, 1692 the conspiracy filed a complaint [No. 21] against Sarah Pease.[297]   Peter Osgood, constable in Salem, arrested her, and she was imprisoned.

Job Tookey
Beverly   *June 4, 1692*

Job Tookey was born about 1665 in England, eldest son of an English minister. In 1692 he was about twenty-seven and well-educated. He worked as a laborer and "waterman" [seahand]. He apparently antagonized people by his manner and preoccupation with status. On June 3, 1692 the conspiracy filed a complaint [No. 27] against Job Tookey. He was arrested, and at his examination on June 4 the circle of afflicted girls accused him. The scribe wrote, "Job Tookey told Mary Warren and Ann Putnam, Jr. and Susannah Sheldon that he had learning and could raise the Devil when he pleased. Susannah Sheldon says that he told her he was not only a wizard but a murderer too." In an examination on June 7, "Mary Warren in a trance said that Gamaliel Hawkins was dead in Barbados, and Job Tookey did stick a great pin into

---

him. Being out of her trance she said that [the specter of] Tookey
had murdered Trask's child, and that he had run a great pin into a
puppet's heart which killed Hawkins. Warren said she saw a
young child [Trask's] under the table crying out for vengeance
upon Tookey." At a trial by jury on January 5, 1693 at the
Superior Court of Judicature at Salem, he was found not guilty.[298]

Margaret (mnu) Hawkes
Salem   *July 1, 1692*

Candy
Salem   *July 1, 1692*

In 1692 Mrs. Margaret (mnu) Hawkes, formerly of Barbados,
resided as a widow in Salem with her black woman slave, Candy.
Margaret had possibly been married to Thomas Hawkes of Salem.
On July 1, 1692 the conspiracy filed a complaint [No. 30] against
Margaret Hawkes and Candy.[299] The two women were arrested
and imprisoned. On July 4 Candy was examined at Salem, and
magistrate John Hathorne attests that, "she brought in two
cloths, one with two knots tied in it. The other one being seen by
Mary Warren, Deliverance Hobbs, and Abigail Hobbs, they were
greatly affrighted and fell into violent fits. A bit of one of the rags
being set on fire, the afflicted all said that they were burned, and
cried out dreadfully. The rags being put into water, two of the
before named persons were in dreadful fits almost choked, and
the other [Abigail Hobbs] was violently running down to the river,
but was stopped." Was Abigail trying to find open air after
months in darkness and chains? On September 17 Abigail Hobbs
both an "afflicter" and an "afflicted," was sentenced to death by
the Court of Oyer and Terminer.

On January 6, 1693 at a trial by jury at the Superior Court of
Judicature at Salem, Candy was found not guilty and was
discharged upon payment of fees. There are no further extant

---

298   *SWP*, 759, 762, 909-910.
299   *SWP*, 385.

records for Margaret, but it is assumed she was released by May 1693.

UNKNOWNS IMPRISONED

So little information remains about the arrests of these individuals for witchcraft that their stories are all but lost. How many more fall into this category is unknown.

Samuel Passanauton
Unknown

In 1692 John Arnold, prison keeper at Boston drew up the account, "The keeping of Samuel Passanauton, an Indian, 8 weeks and 4 days, from the 28th of April, at 2 shillings and 6 pence a week. £1.1.5"[300]

Rebecca (mnu) Chamberlain
Billerica

John Durrant
Billerica

"Rebecca, the wife of William Chamberlain, and John Durrant, both of Billerica, died in prison in Cambridge, where they were incarcerated for witchcraft."[301] In 1692 John Durrant, about forty-four, formerly of Reading, lived in Billerica with his wife, Susannah (Dutton) Durrant. Susannah was the step-daughter of Ruth (mnu) Hooper Dutton. Ruth was the also the step-mother of Sarah (Hooper) Hawkes Wardwell. It is not known when John Durrant was accused and arrested; he died on October 27, 1692 in Cambridge prison.

---

300 *SWP*, 954.
301 Samuel Adams Drake, *Middlesex County*, 1:261.

Thomas Dyer
Unknown

In 1692 Thomas Fossey, prison keeper of Ipswich drew up an account, "for dieting of several prisoners committed by order of authority, Thomas Dyer from the 27th of April until the 8th of July. £1.03.0."[302]

Mary Cox
[Malden]

The May 29, 1692 account of John Arnold, Boston prison keeper, reads, "1 pair of irons for Mary Cox. £0.7.0."[303]

Soon after taking office in Boston in May 1692, Governor Phipps was told that the spectral figures of some of the imprisoned still afflicted the girls. He then ordered chains made for all of the prisoners incarcerated. The irons were supposed to prevent the specter from leaving a witch's body. Some jailers, out of pity, permitted their prisoners to remove their shackles. The afflicted girls, who thought these witches were still in chains, did not resume their crying out upon them.

Mrs. Thatcher's Slave
Boston

In 1692 a woman slave in the household of Margaret Thatcher, widow of the Rev. Thomas Thatcher of Boston and mother-in-law of magistrate Jonathan Corwin, was imprisoned. On May 31, Thomas Newton, attorney general, wrote to Isaac Addington, secretary of the province of Massachusetts, "I have herewith sent you the names of the persons that are desired to be transmitted hither by habeas corpus. I fear we shall not this week try all that we have sent for, by reason the trials will be tedious. We pray that Tituba, the Indian, & Mrs. Thatcher's maid may be

302 *SWP*, 955.
303 *SWP*, 953.

transferred as evidences, but desire they may not come amongst the [other] prisoners, but rather by themselves."[304]

Elizabeth (mnu) Scargen
[Beverly]

Scargen Child
[Beverly]

At the second examination of Job Tookey of Beverly, on June 7, Mary Warren said that "she saw also the apparitions of Scargen & her child."[305] The account of William Dounton, prison keeper at Salem, reads, "Elizabeth Scargen, 6 months diet and for her child, 4 months diet £4."[306] The child had died after four months imprisonment.

Edward Wooland
Unknown

"Salem, 1692. The County of Essex is debtor to William Douton, jail keeper in Salem. To: Ewd Wooland. £3.00.00."[307]

---

304 *SWP*, 867.

305 *SWP*, 762.

306 *SWP*, 958.

307 *SWP*, 958-959. The notation £3.00.00 means three pounds sterling, no shillings, and no pence.

BIBLIOGRAPHY

Note: The abbreviation *SWP* is used for Paul Boyer and Stephen Nissenbaum, eds., *The Salem Witchcraft Papers* (see below).

"A Further Account of the Trials of the New England Witches, sent in a letter from thence, to a Gentleman in London." Contemporary letter by an unknown writer printed in the 1862 edition of Cotton Mather, *The Wonders of the Invisible World*, 214-217.

Ady, Thomas. *A Candle in the Dark*. London, 1656.

Alderman, Clifford. *The Devil's Shadow: The Story of Witchcraft in Massachusetts*. New York, 1967.

Arrington, Benjamin F. *Municipal History of Essex County in Massachusetts*. 4 vols. New York, 1922.

Austin, George Lowell. *The History of Massachusetts from the Landing of the Pilgrims to the Present Time*. Boston, 1876.

Babson, John J. *History of The Town of Gloucester*. Gloucester, MA, 1860.

Bailey, Sarah Loring. *Historical Sketches of Andover, Massachusetts*. Boston, 1880.

Bailyn, Bernard. *The New England Merchants in the Seventeenth Century*. Cambridge, MA, 1979.

Boas, Ralph, and Louise Boas. *Cotton Mather, Keeper of the Puritan Conscience*. New York, 1928.

Bonfanti, Leo. *The Witchcraft Hysteria of 1692*. 2 vols. Wakefield, MA, 1977.

Booth, Sally Smith. *The Witches of Early America*. New York, 1975.

Bourne, Edward E. *The History of Wells and Kennebunk*. Portland, ME, 1875. Reprint. Bowie, MD, 1988.

Bouton, Nathaniel, ed., "Provincial Papers, 1623-1686," Vol. 1, *Documents and Records Relating to the Province of New Hampshire*. Concord, NH, 1867.

Boyer, Paul, and Stephen Nissenbaum, eds. *The Salem Witchcraft Papers: Verbatim Transcripts of the Legal Documents of the Salem Witchcraft Outbreak of 1692*. 3 vols, New York, 1977.

Boyer, Paul, and Stephen Nissenbaum, eds., *Salem Village Witchcraft: A Documentary Record of Local Conflict in Colonial New England*. Belmont, CA, 1972.

Boyer, Paul, and Stephen Nissenbaum. *Salem Possessed: The Social Origins of Witchcraft*. Cambridge, MA, 1974.

Bradford, William. *Of Plymouth Plantation, 1620-1647*. Edited by Samuel Eliot Morison. New York, 1952.

Brattle, Thomas. "Letter of October 8, 1692." Reprinted in Burr, ed. *Narratives of the Witchcraft Cases*, 169-90.

Bremmer, Francis J. *The Puritan Experiment.* New York, 1970.

Brown, David C. "The Case of Giles Corey." *Historical Collections of the Essex Institute,* 122 (July, 1986).

Brown, David C. *A Guide to the Salem Witchcraft Hysteria of 1692.* Washington Crossing, PA, 1984.

Burr, George Lincoln , ed. *Narratives of the Witchcraft Cases, 1648-1706.* New York, 1914. Reprint. New York, 1968.   [Contains narrative accounts of the events of 1692 by eye-witnesses and contemporaries, including Thomas Brattle, Robert Calef, John Hale, Deodat Lawson, Cotton Mather, and Increase Mather.]

Calef, Robert. *More Wonders of the Invisible World, or the Wonders of the Invisible World Displayed in Five Parts.* London, 1700. Reprinted (slightly abbrevated) in Burr, ed., *Narratives of the Witchcraft Cases,* 296-393. Reprint. Salem, MA, 1861.

Chamberlain, N. H. *Samuel Sewall and The World He Lived In.* New York,1897.

Chase, George Wingate. *History of Haverhill, Massachusetts.* Haverhill, MA, 1861.

Cheever, George F. "Phillip English." *Historical Collections of the Essex Institute,* 1-3 (1859–1861).

Church, Thomas. *The History of Philip's War, Commonly Called the Great Indian War, of 1675 and 1676. Also of the French and Indian Wars at the Eastward in 1689, 1690, 1692, 1696, and 1704.* Exeter, NH, 1829. Reprint. Bowie, MD, 1989.

Clark, Charles E. *The Eastern Frontier, 1610-1763.* New York, 1970.

Connecticut Historical Society. *Records of the Particular Court of Connecticut, 1639-1663.* Hartford, 1928.

Cotta, John. *The Tryall of Witchcraft.* London, 1616.

Danvers Historical Society. "A Book of Record of the Several Publique Transactions of the Inhabitants of Salem Village vulgarly called the Farmes." *Historical Collections,* 14 (1926), 65-99.

Danvers Historical Society. "Salem Village Parish Records." *Historical Collections,* 14 (1926).

Davis, Walter Goodwin. *The Ancestry of Amos Towne.* Portland, ME, 1959.

Davis, Walter Goodwin. *The Ancestry of Dudley Wildes.* Portland, ME, 1959.

Demos, John P. *Entertaining Satan.* New York. 1982.

Demos, John P. "John Godfrey and His Neighbors: Witchcraft and the Social Web in Colonial Massachusetts" *William and Mary Quarterly,* 33 (April 1976), 242-265.

Demos, John P. "Underlying Themes in the Witchcraft of Seventeenth-Century New England." *American Historical Review,* 75 (1970), 1311-1326.

Dow, George Francis. *History of Topsfield, Massachusetts.* Boston, 1940.

Drake, Frederick C. "Witchcraft in the American Colonies, 1647-62." *American Quarterly.* 20 (1968), 694-725.

Drake, Samuel Adams. *History of Middlesex County,* Vol. 1, Boston, 1885.

Drake, Samuel Adams. *History of Middlesex County.* Boston, 1886.

Drake, Samuel Adams. *The Border Wars of New England.* New York, 1897.

Drake, Samuel Adams. *The Pine Tree Coast.* Boston, 1891. Reprint. Bowie, MD, 1988.

Drake, Samuel G. *Annals of Witchcraft in New England.* Boston, 1869. Reprint. New York, 1972.

Drake, Samuel G. *The Witchcraft Delusion in New England: Its Rise, Progress, and Termination.* 3 vols. New York, 1866. Reprint. New York, 1970.

Easton, John. *A Relacion of the Indyan Warre, Roadies Island,* 1675. Reprinted in Lincoln, Charles H. ed. *Narratives of the Indian Wars. 1675–1699.*

Eliot, Charles W. *New England History.* New York, 1857.

Erikson, Kai T. *Wayward Puritans: A Study in the Sociology of Deviance.* New York, 1966.

Essex County, Massachusetts. *Probate Records 1635-1681.* 3 vols. Salem, 1916-1920.

Felt, Joseph B. *The Annals of Salem.* Salem, 1827.

Fiske, John. *Witchcraft in Salem Village,* Boston, 1902.

Forbes, Thomas Rogers. *The Midwife and the Witch.* New York, 1966.

Foster, Stephen. *Their Solitary Way: The Puritan Social Ethic in the First Century of Settlement in New England.* New Haven, 1971.

Fowler, Samuel P. "Biographical Sketch and Diary of the Rev. Joseph Green of Salem Village." *Historical Collections of the Essex Institute,* 8 (1866), 91-96, 165-175; 10 (1869), 73-104; 36 (1900), 323-330.

Fowler, Samuel P. *Account of the Life and Character of the Rev. Samuel Parris.* Salem, 1857.

Fox, Sanford J., Jr. *Science and Justice: The Massachusetts Witchcraft Trials.* Baltimore, 1968.

Gifford, George. *A Dialogue Concerning Witches and Witchcraftes.* London, 1593.

Gildrie, Richard P. *Salem, Massachusetts, 1626-1683.* Charlottesville, 1975.

Glanvill, Joseph. *Saducismus Triumphatus.* London, 1681.

Goodell, Abner Cheney, Jr. *Further Notes on the History of Witchcraft in Massachusetts.* Cambridge, 1884.

Green, Samuel A. *Groton in the Witchcraft Times.* Groton, MA, 1883.

Greene, David L. "Bray Wilkins of Salem Village, Massachusetts, and His Children." *The American Genealogist,* 60 (1984).

Greene, David L. "Salem Witches I: Bridget Bishop." *The American Genealogist.* 57 (1981).

Greene, David L. "Salem Witches II: George Jacobs." *The American Genealogist.* 58 (1982).

Greene, David L. "Salem Witches III: Susannah Martin." *The American Genealogist.* 58 (1982); 59 (1983).

Greene, David L. "The Third Wife of the Rev. George Burroughs." *The American Genealogist.* 56 (1980).

Greven, Philip J. *Four Generations: Population, Land and Family in Colonial Andover, Massachusetts.* Ithaca, NY, 1970.

Hale, John. *A Modest Enquiry into the Nature of Witchcraft.* Boston, 1702. Reprinted in Burr, ed., *Narratives of the Witchcraft Cases,* 399–432.

Hall, David D. *Witch-Hunting.* Boston, 1991.

Hall, David D. *Worlds of Wonder: Days of Judgment.* New York, 1989.

Hall, Michael G. *The Last American Puritan, The Life of Increase Mather, 1639–1723.* Middletown, CT, 1988.

Hansen, Chadwick. *Witchcraft at Salem.* New York, 1969.

Hoadly, C. J. *Records of the Colony or Jurisdiction of New Haven from May 1653 to the Union.* Hartford, 1858.

Hopkins, Matthew. *The Discovery of Witches.* 1647. Reprint. London, 1928.

Hoyt, David Webster. *Old Families of Salisbury and Amesbury, Massachusetts.* Providence, RI, 1897.

Hubbard, William. *A General History of New England from the Discovery to 1680.* Reprint. Boston, 1848.

Hutchinson, Thomas. *The History of the Colony and Province of Massachusetts-Bay.* London, 1768. Reprint. 3 vols. Cambridge, MA, 1936.

Jackson, Shirley. *Witchcraft in Salem Village.* New York, 1956.

Karlsen, Carol F. *The Devil in the Shape of A Woman.* New York, 1987.

Kences, James E. "Some Unexplored Relationships of Essex County Witchcraft to the Indian Wars of 1675 and 1689." *Historical Collections of the Essex Institute,* 120 (July, 1984), 179-212.

Kittredge, George. *Witchcraft in Old and New England.* Cambridge, MA, 1929. Reprint. New York, 1956.

Konig, David Thomas. *Law and Society in Puritan Massachusetts: Essex County, 1629-1692.* Chapel Hill, NC, 1979.

Lawson, Deodat. *A Brief and True Narrative of Some Remarkable Passages Relating to Sundry Persons Afflicted by Witchcraft, at Salem Village Which Happened from the Nineteenth of March to the Fifth of April, 1692.* Boston, 1692. Reprinted in Burr, ed., *Narratives of the Witchcraft Cases,* 152-164.

Lawson, Deodat. *Christ's Fidelity the Only Shield against Satan's Malignity.* 2d ed. London, 1704.

Levin, David. "Salem Witchcraft in Recent Fiction and Drama." *New England Quarterly,* 28 (1955), 537-546.

Levin, David. *What Happened in Salem?* New York, 1960.

Lewis, Alonzo, and James R. Newhall. *History of Lynn, Essex County, Massachusetts.* Boston, 1865. Reprint. Bowie, MD, 1989.

Lincoln, Charles H. ed. *Narratives of the Indian Wars, 1675–1699.* New York, 1913.

Lockridge, Kenneth A. *A New England Town: The First Hundred Years.* New York, 1970.

Loggins, Vernon. *The Hawthornes.* New York, 1951.

Macfarlane, Alan D. J. *Witchcraft in Tudor and Stuart England.* London, 1970.

Mappen, Marc. *Witches and Historians: Interpretations of Salem.* New York, 1980

Marder, Daniel. *Exiles at Home: A Story of Literature in Nineteenth Century America.* Lanham, MD, 1984.

Massachusetts Historical Society. "Mather-Calef Papers on Witchcraft." 1695. *Proceedings,* 47 (1914), 240-268.

Massachusetts Historical Society. "Recantation of Confessors of Witchcraft." *Massachusetts Historical Society Collections,* 2d ser., 3, 221-225.

Massachusetts Historical Society. "Reply of the Dutch and French Ministers of the Province of New York." 1692. *Proceedings,* 2d ser. 1 (1884), 384-85.

Mather, Cotton. *A Brand Plucked out of the Burning.* 1693. Reprinted in Burr, ed., *Narratives of the Witchcraft Cases,* 259-287.

Mather, Cotton. "A Discourse on Witchcraft." Boston, 1689. Reprinted in Levin, *What Happened in Salem?*, 96-106.

Mather, Cotton. "Diary of Cotton Mather, 1681-1708." *Massachusetts Historical Society Collections*, 7th ser., 7-8, (1911-12). Also published New York, 1957.

Mather, Cotton. "Letter of May 31, 1692 to John Richards." Reprinted in Levin, *What Happened in Salem?*, 106-110. Also reprinted in Cotton Mather, *Selected Letters*, 35-40.

Mather, Cotton. *Magnalia Christi Americana, or the Ecclesiastical History of New England, in Seven Books.* London, 1702. Reprinted in 2 vols. Hartford, 1855.

Mather, Cotton. *Memorable Providences Relating to Witchcrafts and Possessions.* Boston, 1689. Reprinted in Burr, ed., *Narratives of the Witchcraft Cases*, 93-143.

Mather, Cotton. *Pillars of Salt.* Boston, 1699.

Mather, Cotton. *Selected Letters of Cotton Mather.* Kenneth Silverman, ed., Baton Rouge, 1971.

Mather, Cotton. *The Return of Several Ministers.* Boston, 1692. Reprinted in Levin, *What Happened in Salem?*, 110-111.

Mather, Cotton. *The Wonders of the Invisible World.* Boston, 1692. Reprint (facsimile of the 1862 edition). Amherst, WI, 1980. Also reprinted in Burr, ed.*Narratives of the Witchcraft Cases*, 209-251.

Mather, Increase. *A Brief History of the War with the Indians in New England.* Boston, 1676. Reprint. Bowie, MD, 1989.

Mather, Increase. *A Disquisition Concerning Angelical Apparitions.* Boston, 1696.

Mather, Increase. *An Essay for the Recording of Illustrious Providences.* Boston, 1684. Reprint with title *Remarkable Providences.* London, 1890.

Mather, Increase. *Angelographia.* Boston, 1696.

Mather, Increase. *Cases of Conscience Concerning Evil Spirits Personating Men.* Boston, 1692. Reprinted in the 1862 edition of Cotton Mather, *The Wonders of the Invisible World*, 225-284.

Mather, Increase. *Kometographia.* Boston, 1683.

Maule, Thomas. *The Truth Held Forth and Maintained.* Boston, 1695.

McMillen, Persis W., *Currents of Malice: Mary Towne Esty and Her Family in Salem Witchcraft.* Portsmouth, N.H., 1990.

McWilliams, Carey. *Witch Hunt: The Revival of Heresy.* Boston, 1950.

Miller, Arthur. *The Crucible.* New York, 1959.

Miller, Perry. *The New England Mind: From Colony to Province.* Boston, 1953.

Miller, Perry. *The New England Mind: The Seventeenth Century.* New York, 1939.

Mofford, Juliet Haines. *And Firm Thine Ancient Vow: The History of the North Parish Church of North Andover, 1645-1974.* North Andover, MA, 1975.

Moody, Robert Earle, and Richard Clive Simmons. *The Glorious Revolution in Massachusetts, Selected Documents, 1689–1692.* Boston, 1988.

Moore, George H. *Final Notes on Witchcraft in Massachusetts, A Summary Vindication of the Laws and Liberties.* New York, 1885.

Morgan, Edmund. *The Puritan Family.* New York,1944.

Murdock, Kenneth B. *Increase Mather, The Foremost American Puritan.* Cambridge, MA, 1925.

Murdock, Kenneth B., *Cotton Mather Selections.* New York, 1973.

Nevins, Winfield S., *Witchcraft in Salem Village in 1692.* Salem, 1916.

Noble, John, ed. *Records of the Court of Assistants of the Colony of the Massachusetts Bay*, 1630-1692. 3 vols. Boston, 1901-1928.

Noble, John. "Some Documentary Fragments Touching the Witchcraft Episode of 1692," *Publications of the Colonial Society of Massachusetts, Transactions 1904-1906*. 10:12-26.

Noble, John. "Some Documentary Fragments Touching the Witchcraft Episode of 1692." *Publications of the Colonial Society of Massachusetts*, 10 (1904), 12-26.

Notestein, Wallace. *A History of Witchcraft in England from 1558 to 1718*. New York, 1909.

Noyes, Sybil, Charles Thorton Libby, and Walter Goodwin Davis. *Genealogical Dictionary of Maine and New Hampshire*. Baltimore, 1972.

Oberholzer, Emil, Jr. *Delinquent Saints: Disciplinary Action in the Early Congregational Churches of Massachusetts*. New York, 1956.

Otten, Marjorie Wardwell. *Samuel Wardwell of Andover and a Line of his Descendants*, (typescript). 1989.

Otten, Marjorie Wardwell. *The Witch Hunt of 1692*, (typescript). 1990.

Paine, Robert. *The Ships and Sailors of Old Salem*. Boston, 1927.

Perkins, William. *Discourse on the Damned Art of Witchcraft*. London, 1608.

Perley, Sidney. *The History of Boxford, Essex County, Massachusetts*. Boxford, MA, 1880.

Perley, Sidney. *The History of Salem, Massachusetts*, 3 vols. Salem, MA, 1924, 1926, 1928.

Phillips, James Duncan. *Salem in the Seventeenth Century*. Boston, 1933.

Phipps, Sir William. "Letter dated at Boston, October 12, 1692," and "Letter dated at Boston, February 21, 1693." Reprinted in Burr, ed., *Narratives of the Witchcraft Cases*, 196-202.

Powell, Sumner Chilton. *Puritan Village: The Formation of a New England Town*. Middletown, CT, 1964.

Public Broadcasting System. "Three Sovereigns for Sarah," [Television drama, 3 hours.]

Quarterly Courts of Essex County, Massachusetts. *Records and Files,1636–1683*. 8 vols, Salem, MA, 1911-21.

Quincy, Josiah. *The History of Harvard University*. Cambridge, MA,1840.

Robbins, Rossell H. *The Encyclopedia of Witchcraft and Demonology*. New York, 1959.

Robinson, Enders A. *Salem Witchcraft and the Heritage of Nathaniel Hathorne*, (typescript). 1988.

Robinson, Enders A. *Wardwell and Barker Families of Andover in the Seventeenth Century*, (typescript). 1986.

Robinson, Enders A., and Marjorie Wardwell Otten. *Salem Witchcraft Genealogy*, (typescript). 1987.

Robotti, Frances Diane. *Chronicles of Old Salem*. New York, 1948.

Salem Club. *Sketches about Salem*. Salem, MA, 1930.

Savage, James. *A Genealogical Dictionary of the First Settlers of New England*. Boston, 1860. Reprint. Baltimore, 1990.

Scot, Reginald. *The Discoverie of Witchcraft*. London, 1584. Reprint. New York, 1972.

Scottow, Joshua. *Narrative of the Planting.* Boston, 1694.

Sewall, Rufus King. *Ancient Dominions of Maine,* Bath, ME, 1859.

Sewall, Samuel. *The Diary of Samuel Sewall.* M. Halsey Thomas ed. New York, 1973.

Sewall, Samuel. *The Diary of Samuel Sewall.* Vol. 1. New York, 1973.

Shurtleff, Nathaniel, ed., *Records of the Governor and Company of the Massachusetts Bay in New England, 1626-1686.* 5 vols. Boston, 1853-54.

Sibley, John Langdon. *Biographical Sketches of the Graduates of Harvard University.* 2 vols. Cambridge, MA, 1863.

Sibley, John Langdon. *Biographical Sketches of the Graduates of Harvard University. Cambridge,* 1863.

Silverman, Kenneth. *The Times and Life of Cotton Mather.* New York, 1984.

Sprenger, Jacob, and Heinrich Institoris. *Malleus Maleficarum.* Introduction by Montague Summers. New York, 1928.

Starkey, Marion. *The Devil in Massachusetts.* New York, 1949.

Starkey, Marion. *The Visionary Girls.* Boston, 1960.

Swan, Marshall W. S. "The Bedevilment at Cape Ann (1692)." *Historical Collections of the Essex Institute.* 117 (1981), 153-177.

Tapley, Harriet S. "William Walcott of Salem Village and Some of his Descendants." *Historical Collections of the Danvers Historical Society.* 12 (1924), 89-104.

Taylor, John M. *The Witchcraft Delusion in Colonial Connecticut.* New York, 1908.

Teall, John L. "Witchcraft and Calvinism in Elizabethan England." *Journal of the History of Ideas.* 23 (1962), 21-36.

Topsfield Historical Society. "Witchcraft Records Relating to Topsfield." *Historical Collections,* 13 (1908), 39-142.

Trevor-Roper, H. R. *The European Witch-Craze of the Sixteenth and Seventeenth Centuries.* New York, 1956.

Turell, "Detection of Witchcraft." 1728. Reprinted in *Massachusetts Historical Society Collections,* 2d ser., 10 (1833), 6-22.

Ulrich, Laurel Thatcher. *Good Wives: Image and Reality in the Lives of Women in Northern New England, 1650-1750.* New York, 1982.

Upham, Charles W. *Salem Witchcraft.* 2 vols. Boston, 1867.

Vaughan, Alden T., and Edward W. Clark, *Puritans Among the Indians.* Cambridge, MA, 1981.

Weisman, Richard. *Witchcraft, Magic, and Religion in 17th-Century Massachusetts.* Amherst, MA, 1984.

Wendell, Barrett. *Cotton Mather.* New York, 1980.

Wertenbaker, Thomas J. *The Puritan Oligarchy.* New York, 1947.

Whining, John. "Letter of John Whiting to Increase Mather." 1682, Massachusetts Historical Society Collections, 4th ser., 8 (1868), 466-469.

Whitmore, William H., ed., *The Colonial Laws of Massachusetts.* Boston, 1889.

Willard, Samuel. "A briefe account of a strange and unusuall Providence of God befallen to Elizabeth Knap of Groton." Letter, 1679. Reprinted in Samuel Green, *Groton in the Witchcraft Times.* 6-22.

Willard, Samuel. *Christian's Exercise against Satan's Temptation.* Boston, 1701.

Willard, Samuel. *Some Miscellany Observations on Our Present Debates respecting Witchcraft, in a Dialogue between S[alem] and B[oston].* Philadelphia, 1692. [An unpublished attack on the proceedings of the Court of Oyer and Terminer generally attributed to the Rev. Samuel Willard.]

Williams, Selma R., and Pamela Williams. *Riding the Nightmare: Women and Witchcraft.* 1978.

Williamson, William. *History of the State of Maine.* Hallowell, ME, 1832.

Willis, William. *History of Portland.* Portland, ME, 1865.

Woodward, W. Elliot. *Records of Salem Witchcraft, Copied from the Original Documents.* 2 vols. Roxbury, MA, 1864.

PLACES OF INTEREST IN SALEM

Burying Point (grave of John Hathorne and others of the witchcraft trials), Charter Street

Essex Institute Museum, 132 Essex St.

First Church, 316 Essex Street

Fort Pickering, Winter Island

Gallows Hill Park, Witch Hill Road

House of the Seven Gables. 54 Turner Street

John Ward House (built 1684), Brown Street

Old Town Hall, 32 Derby Square

Peabody Museum of Salem, East India Square

Pioneer Village (a repoduction of Salem in 1630), Forest River Park

Salem Maritime Historic Site, Custom House, Derby Street

Salem Witch Museum, 19 1/2 Washington Square N.

Witch Dungeon Museum, 16 Lynde Street

Witch House (the home of magistrate Jonathan Corwin), Essex Street

Name Index

SUBJECT INDEX

previous married name, 60
Principia Matematica, 50
pro-Parris, 82-84
Protestant, 25-26, 91
Providence, 42, 180
Puritan, 19
Queen of Hell, 212, 353-354
Reading, 5, 93, 171, 288-289, 343-344,
    346-347, 362
Rehoboth, 299
Restoration, 22-23, 50
Return of Several Ministers, 208, 211
righteous few, 21
rock-hard system of Puritan rule, 204
Romney Marsh, 38, 328
Rowley, 132, 220, 301, 303-304
Roxbury, 78-79, 87, 323, 325
sabbat, 8, 157, 166
Saco, 92, 95, 97, 124-125
Sadducee, 51, 253
Salem Farms, 124, 141, 162, 212, 281-
    282, 290
Salem Witchcraft Papers, 15, 104, 228,
    259
Salisbury, 67, 78, 80, 90, 197-198, 219,
    266, 309-310, 323, 325, 333-335, 355
Samuel, a glorified saint, 210
scapegoats, 195, 202, 251
selectmen, 63, 175, 187, 274
shape, 7-11, 46, 152, 170, 198, 210, 236,
    242
Shawsheen, 7
slave, 89, 107, 112, 115, 134, 137, 140,
    171, 196, 243, 250, 259, 261, 270,
    279, 329, 348-349, 361, 363
sorcery, 1, 6, 9, 152
specter, 10
spectral evidence, 13-14, 16, 119, 159,
    181, 194, 210, 223, 234-237, 241,
    245
sponsors, 128-129
stereotyped witches, 305
Sudbury, 278
Superior Court of Judicature, 241-242,
    269, 278-279, 287, 289-291, 299,
    322, 327, 339, 342, 345, 347, 349,
    352, 355-356, 360-361

Topsfield men, 62, 136, 261, 273, 291,
    299, 301-302
Topsfield, 57-58, 61-62, 136, 162, 166,
    168, 170-173, 209, 219-220, 261,
    273-274, 277-279, 291-297, 299-
    302, 304, 316, 337
torture, 134, 164, 166, 194, 207, 272,
    284, 334
trial by jury, 15, 243, 250, 339, 342,
    352, 356, 361
unknowns imprisioned, 362
visible saint, 19
Wampanoag, 41
Wells, 27, 33, 37, 95-100, 120, 178-179,
    188, 212, 274, 323-324
Wenham, 58, 61, 145, 229, 235, 261,
    301, 340
winding sheet, 10, 180, 222, 335, 350
Witch of Wenham, 229
witch of Endor, 227
witches' marks, 10
witches' sabbath, 157
wizard, 9, 164, 179, 212, 221, 336, 360
Woburn, 182, 249, 343, 346-347
Wonders of the Invisible World, 227,
    233, 237, 253
York, 24, 26-27, 37-38, 95, 99-100, 132,
    134, 177, 179, 188-189, 230, 298,
    322, 331